The Cromarty Library Circle

Also by Shona MacLean writing as S. G. MacLean

THE ALEXANDER SEATON SERIES

The Redemption of Alexander Seaton
A Game of Sorrows
Crucible of Secrets
The Devil's Recruit

THE CAPTAIN DAMIAN SEEKER SERIES

The Seeker
The Black Friar
Destroying Angel
The Bear Pit
The House of Lamentations
The Winter List

STANDALONE

The Bookseller of Inverness

SHONA
MACLEAN

The Cromarty Library Circle

QUERCUS

First published in Great Britain in 2026 by Quercus
Part of John Murray Group

1

A CIP catalogue record for this book is available from the British Library

HB ISBN 978 1 52944 549 7
TPB ISBN 978 1 52944 550 3
EBOOK ISBN 978 1 52944 551 0

Typeset in Bembo by CC Book Production

Printed and bound in Great Britain by Clays Ltd, Elcograf S.p.A.

MIX
Paper | Supporting responsible forestry
FSC® C104740

Papers used by Quercus are from well-managed forests and other responsible sources.

Quercus
Carmelite House
50 Victoria Embankment
London EC4Y 0DZ

John Murray Group
Part of Hodder & Stoughton Limited
An Hachette UK company

The authorised representative in the EEA is Hachette Ireland,
8 Castlecourt Centre, Dublin 15, D15 XTP3, Ireland (email: info@hbgi.ie)

To Jane Wood

CROM
The MAJOR'S HOUSE
The Commercial HOTEL
Hossack HOUSE
THE LINKS
Fordyce HOUSE
BANK STREET
Rope WORKS
The BANK
Clock MAKER'S
Clockmakers
The GAELIC CHAPEL
The COURTHOUSE
1

ARTY
N
W
E
S
The Gilfeather HOUSE
The Gardeners' LODGE
Miss Juniper's COTTAGE
VENNEL
The MANSE
The CHURCH
OLD BURIAL GROUND
Rose LODGE
CROMARTY HOUSE
SOAP

ADVISORY NOTE ON LANGUAGE IN THE BOOK

Due to this novel's setting in an 1830s Scottish town heavily involved in Transatlantic slave plantations, some of the terminology used by characters, while historically accurate and demonstrating the social and racial hierarchies of the time, are now offensive and may cause upset to some readers. For instance, where we would now talk of an enslaved person or enslaved people to describe those born or sold into chattel slavery, the terminology at the time was simply 'slave'. Similarly, the terms 'negro' to describe a black person or 'mulatto', used in the period to refer to a person of colour who had one black and one white parent, are now recognised as outdated and offensive due to their derogatory connotations. Any such language which appears in this book is used intentionally for historical authenticity and is in no way the author's endorsement of the views or prejudices of that era.

CHARACTER LIST

Cromarty Manse

The Reverend Alasdair Mackay, minister of Cromarty
Rachel Mackay, his second wife, former pupil of Miss Juniper and former governess to the Hossacks

Cromarty House

Sir William Mackenzie
Charlotte, Lady Mackenzie, his wife, former pupil of Miss Juniper
Morag Mackenzie, housekeeper

Harbour House

Major Charles Munro, friend of Sir William

Miss Juniper's Cottage, Little Vennel

Miss Juniper, governess
Mairead Buchan, pupil
Alicia Middleton, pupil

Commercial Hotel

Mrs Janet Cameron, hotelkeeper, whose late husband worked on Sir William's Caribbean plantations
Ludovic Cameron, her son and bank clerk
Hester, a young servant, formerly enslaved, brought back from Demerara by Sir William

Rose Lodge

Miss Elspeth Rose
Miss Anna Rose

The Gilfeather House

Mr Alexander Gilfeather, bank manager
Mrs Margaret Gilfeather

Fordyce House

Mr Isaac Fordyce, antiquarian

The Schoolhouse

John Learmonth, schoolteacher

The Clockmaker's

James Craig, clockmaker, former Jacobin
Stanislas Jeszewski, a Polish refugee, his apprentice

Hossach House

Willie Hossack, owner of Cromarty Ropeworks
Mrs Marjorie Hossack
Farquhar Hossack, their son, medical student

The Manse of Resolis

The Reverend Dr Micah Fraser, minister of Resolis

PART ONE

Autumn/Winter 1831

ONE

Saturday, 1 October

Cromarty

Hester

The grocer's boy emerged from the back shop bearing the sugar loaf with all the importance of an athlete carrying the caber. Hester smiled as he heaved it towards her.

'You're sure you'll manage?' Mr Taylor said. 'I can easily send it down in the barrow.'

'I will manage.' She shouldered the two-foot long, fourteen-pound cone in its bright blue paper wrapping, and the boy hastened to open the door for her, making the little bell above tinkle. Stepping back out onto the street, she paused a moment as two children ran past, waving dandelions at one another and laughing as the wind sent the feathery white seeds dancing in the air.

The wind. It could not make up its mind which direction to blow from and had her apron flapping about her like a great white bird. Down on the links, golf balls went astray and gentlemen hacked helplessly through marram grass at the shore's edge, while the ribbons of spectating ladies' bonnets undid themselves. Hester's cap, though, stayed firmly on her head. To Hester, who had known the winds of the Caribbean, this was nothing.

She crossed the street and began to make her way back down to the hotel where much work awaited her. Mrs Cameron would have the palette knife ready, and the sugar nippers and mortar and pestle, for her to attack the loaf with. The gentlemen would want sugar for their coffee. Later, there would be other tasks – clarifying, candying, blowing, feathering, crackling and caramelising – all learned from Mrs Cameron, for Hester had arrived in Cromarty almost twelve years ago, quite untaught. Plant. Tend. Harvest. Crush. The workings of a sugar plantation she had understood. Sugar was boiled there too, on the plantation, but not in small copper pans like those that shone so prettily from their hooks in the hotel kitchen, cleaned by the scullery maid with lemon skins dipped in salt and silver sand. The maid grumbled that the copper pans were a lot of work. Hester rubbed at the pale scars on her own arms and told her she had no idea.

The wind was blowing up Bank Street too, right from the harbour. The town was a triangle, pointed out into the sea. The wind would get you every way. Ahead of her, out in the bay, ships and boats bobbed and swayed. All was activity and a constant toing and froing from the hempworks and the fish-curing stations to the pier. Bundle upon bundle of Inverness sacking; endless yards of rope, for which there were many uses; numberless barrels of salt herring to be transported over the ocean to feed the people who grew and packed the cotton into the Inverness sacking and those who planted and harvested the sugar that she carried now on her shoulder. Circling above, rising on the wind, the seagulls called and shrieked hysterically. Hester thought they were maybe complaining about the herring. Soon, the anchor would be weighed and the sails unfurled and the loaded ship would set out upon its Atlantic journey, and so the world would turn.

Somewhere behind her, away down Church Street, the bell of the courthouse clock chimed the hour. Up ahead, Hester saw Ludo dart from the door of the bank and then Mr Gilfeather, punctual as ever, emerge and lock the door behind them. The bank manager held onto his hat as he made his way homewards for, she supposed, an early dinner. The meeting of the circulating library was to begin in the hotel coffee room in exactly one hour. He would need to hurry. Hester shifted the sugar loaf onto her other shoulder as the wind made the clock bell chime again – a thin, accidental note. They would all need to hurry.

Charlotte

Charlotte Mackenzie looked out over the lawns of Cromarty House. William was there, striding towards the tradesmen's tunnel that led out onto the main road.

'It's quicker,' he'd told her when she'd queried it, as if a man in his position had anything to be in a hurry about, and off across the lawns he'd gone, making for the tunnel, like a tradesman. But not so much like a tradesman really. Charlotte knew how a tradesman walked. She had seen how her father had walked, back and forth, behind his draper's counter. An imperious walk, he'd had, when checking on his apprentices, or presenting himself to view on the High Street of Inverness, but the grander the customer who'd set foot in his shop, the more obsequious that walk had become. On those occasions when some titled person had stepped across the door, Charlotte's mother had been wont to remark to her that it was a great thing, was it not, how far her father had come in the world?

Charlotte watched her husband. Sir William Mackenzie was no tradesman, after all; he could do what he liked. The second son of a minor laird, he had followed the pattern set out for his kind: a commission in the army, a time in India, an honourable discharge and then to the Caribbean, to see to the family investments before coming home to lease some small estate and acquire a suitable wife. The following of this path had brought him back here to Cromarty, and to Charlotte.

She turned away from the window. She'd left her embroidery lying on the table by the sofa. Miss Juniper had always said that Charlotte was wasted on embroidery, or that it was wasted on Charlotte. She wished she could remember, that she had understood, then, that a person, a life, could be wasted. She walked past the table and took up the book that her friend Rachel had left with her. As if she had been waiting for that moment, Morag Mackenzie, William's childhood nurse, their housekeeper, came into the room. Morag's black eyes darted to the volume in Charlotte's hand.

'*Adam Blair*,' she said, as though pronouncing a judgement of the kirk session. 'I would not have thought that suitable reading material for Sir William's wife.'

'And I would not have thought the contents of Mr Lockhart's book to be something within your ken, Miss Mackenzie,' retorted Charlotte. She stepped past the woman and, taking with her the story of the widowed minister and his lover, destroyed by desire the pair of them, she retreated up the east stairs to her bedroom.

Rachel

Rachel moved aside a chair in order to set the minister's place at the end of the dining table. The chair was one of eight – painted satinwood, she had learned – with panels showing cupids and flowers, and with cane seats. They were hardly proper things, she thought, to be found in a manse, but it was not her place to say so. They had been here more than twenty years, since a young Reverend Alasdair Mackay had brought home his bride, alongside the furnishings gifted to her by her wealthy family.

Rachel's eye was taken by a cobweb, spanning from the corner of the mantelpiece to the wall behind. She huffed a sigh and lifted the corner of her apron to dust it away. The mirror above the mantelpiece showed her the habitual escape had been made by a strand of her hair from its pins beneath her cap. Behind her, also reflected in the mirror, were the creamy cheeks and rose-kissed lips of Gwendolen Mackay, in their habitual, knowing smile. Leave me alone, thought Rachel, though she did not dare to say it out loud.

The sound of the door opening almost made her jump. It was him. No longer the young minister and bridegroom, but a man well into the middle of life, a man who had grown into his authority. He hadn't changed so very much, she thought, from the figure she had heard for most of her life declaiming from the pulpit of the parish church, or walking around the classroom of their school, inspecting their writing and testing them on their catechism. He had perhaps broadened a little from the leanness of youth, but only a little. His strong features, still tanned from the long summer just past, were lined, certainly. The hair, kept longer than was nowadays the fashion, was grey at temples and sideburns.

Rachel became aware of her heart beating, but she didn't turn around. In the mirror she saw him see her, and begin to come towards her, never glancing behind to where Gwendolen was. Still Rachel didn't turn around. It was like the first time. When he came upon her like this it was like the first time, and the tension almost stopped her breath. He lifted a hand and touched her neck, long, tanned fingers pushing back the hair that had come loose, then he lowered his mouth and kissed her softly. Once, twice. His hand was on her waist and Rachel turned around and gave herself completely into his embrace.

After a while he stepped back, smiling down at her. 'So, this is where you've been hiding, is it?'

She laughed and began to tidy her hair. 'Not hiding, Alasdair, but setting the table for our dinner later.'

He frowned. 'Could Mrs Cramond not do that? You're not a servant in this house, Rachel, nor any other, any more.'

'I know that. But if we are to have Sir William and Charlotte tonight, it must be done right.'

It hung in the air, unsaid, never said, but always there, 'as she would have done it'.

'No one is judging you, Rachel.'

'Are they not? A governess, a fatherless girl from amongst their own number, that married their minister, and his first wife a daughter of the gentry! Seven years, and I doubt they will ever forgive me. '

He pulled her to him again. 'What they will never forgive you, my dear, is that you are young and you are bonny.' Then he laughed, 'And that you married their minister.'

John Learmonth

The schoolmaster's hair blew about him as he locked the door of the schoolroom. The spirits of the children were always high when the wind was up; they could hardly sit to their lessons, and as soon as they were released they were chasing each other through the streets faster than the leaves swirling about the schoolyard. It was a day to grab hold of the world and set one's foot upon it and John could almost have run with them into their half-day's freedom but, mindful of the eyes of the matrons of the town and of the ears of the elders to whom they were married, he contented himself with a restrained stride as he made his way to his lodging on the Paye. A quarter-hour would see to a change of clothes and a raid on Mrs Baxter's kitchen, then off he would be, sketchbook in hand and cold supper in his bag, to Kirkmichael. John Learmonth felt a rush of happiness flare inside him, that for a moment made him forget that he had already run as far as he could. He had even begun to whistle, but at the top of the vennel his tune was brought to an abrupt halt by a near-collision with the trim form, at least twenty years out of date, of Mr Isaac Fordyce. Mr Fordyce, of a naturally nervous disposition made worse by its own encouragement, started and almost parted company with his monocle.

'My word, my word,' the little man blustered, 'you are surely in a tremendous hurry, Mr Learmonth. An affair of the heart, no doubt?'

John gave an uneasy laugh. 'In a manner of speaking, but with little romance to it.'

The other man's face fell. 'Oh. I am sorry to hear it.' Mr Fordyce had never recovered from his first reading, in its original German, of *The Sorrows of Young Werther*, and had spent fifty years nursing the broken heart of his own twenty-year-old self.

'I am going to Kirkmichael,' explained John, 'to begin

sketching the tombstones and noting the inscriptions.' He saw from Mr Isaac's expression that this was no reassurance.

'But not yet, surely?'

'Why not?' The schoolmaster threw out his arm to indicate the fineness of the day. 'The autumn gales will be upon us before we know it and after them the dark of winter. You would not have me waste such a day as this?'

'But the books,' urged Mr Isaac. 'Surely you cannot have forgotten? It is this afternoon that we are to meet in the coffee room and make choice of the books.'

'The books . . .' echoed John, his voice trailing away as it came back to him.

'Indeed! For the circulating library! Mr Gilfeather was insistent we should not arrive a minute beyond two, and I for one would not wish to arrive at the coffee room to discover him consulting his pocket watch!'

John knew it would be in vain to suggest that another – Mr Fordyce himself, perhaps – might give in his choice for him. And in truth, he was in hopes that membership of the library might give him access to works he wished to read but had little possibility of buying. He knew moreover that his invitation to join in the association was something much coveted by others longer domiciled in the town. If he were truly to settle here, he must build around him as strong a carapace as possible. He watched the prospect of his afternoon studying and sketching the ancient graves of Kirkmichael recede into the distance, like a ship passing over the horizon.

Miss Juniper

Miss Juniper was a small, tidy person. She had never over-indulged in the more sensuous pleasures of life and looked a little younger than her seventy-two years. It was wondered about the town and amongst the society of the Black Isle in general, whether she had ever had a suitor. Speculation ranged from an unfulfilled passion for some past employer in whose family she had been governess, to youthful heart-break over a young officer, possibly during the American War. Those whose interest was sustained thus far were in the habit of deciding her tender feelings for the tragic officer had not been reciprocated.

That Miss Juniper had once known better days could be seen from her carefully mended clothes, in fashions more than ten years, perhaps nearer twenty, out of date. The lowered waistline, the tightened corset, sleeves puffed like gigots of lamb – all were unknown in the wardrobe of Miss Juniper, where light muslins and silk still held sway in preference to heavier cottons, and over which a spencer or full-length pelisse might still be fitted to afford protection against the cold northerly winds. Miss Juniper watched waists tighten, hems widen and sleeves expand so that a woman could barely get through a door, and be hardly fit for much once she did so. She warned her girls against allowing themselves to be trussed and immobilised in such a manner.

Her girls. Only two now, on the brink of womanhood, and lucky she was to have them. Alicia Middleton and Mairead Buchan, the one the daughter of a tenant farmer sliding ever closer to penury, the other that of a widowed half-pay captain of the Highland Regiment.

Miss Juniper closed the front door of her cottage and stepped out onto Little Vennel. The fisherfolk of the vennel were kindly enough, and the slight suspicion with which they viewed her was of a different order from that which the better society of the town harboured. The smell of the sea was everywhere in Cromarty, perhaps only a little more pungent here than elsewhere. Besides, Miss Juniper's was a pretty cottage, with whitewash on the walls and bright blue for door and window frames. The thatch was tidy and her step well-swept. Marigolds and asters tripped along the front where it met the public path, nudging and bumping each other like excitable schoolgirls. Her own girls, in comparison, were a picture of good deportment as they went up the lane ahead of her, dipping their curtsies to Mr Isaac Fordyce, who was in animated conversation with the schoolmaster. Well, Alicia at least. Mairead did her best, poor child, and certainly she had much improved in her three years under Miss Juniper's instruction, but the analogy of silk purse and sow's ear sprang uncomfortably to mind.

The girls had left the cottage in the highest of spirits for their Saturday's half-day holiday, which they were to spend in the company of Rachel Mackay, the minister's wife, whom they adored. Rachel was one of Miss Juniper's own former pupils, from better days, and almost her favourite. Almost, but not quite. Rachel would manage life on her own wits and merits, but Miss Juniper had always been more drawn to a challenge. Her favourite had been, would always be, Charlotte.

The girls were greatly relieved to hear the minister was not to be at home, but for different reasons. They discussed the matter with Miss Juniper on the short walk from Little Vennel to the Causeway. It was Mairead who introduced the subject.

'Will the minister be there, do you think, Miss Juniper?'

'I think not. I believe Mr Mackay will be engaged on matters of the new library.'

At this the girl puffed her florid cheeks and let out a sigh of relief. 'Thank goodness! When he leans forward in the pulpit on a Sunday and fixes his eye upon me, I am certain he knows every bad thing I ever did. I cannot believe that Rach— I mean, Mrs Mackay, is not terrified of him.'

'He's not looking at you, silly,' Alicia said. 'He has three hundred people at least, who are much, *much* worse than you, on whom he might fix his eye.'

'You are right, Alicia,' said Miss Juniper. 'Cromarty is awash with people who have indeed much greater cause to fear the minister's censure than does Mairead. I can assure you both, however, that Mrs Mackay is not one of them.'

Mairead pursed her lips and looked steadfastly at her own feet. It was as well Miss Juniper did not know the thoughts that sometimes raced through her head. She was sure that was why her cheeks flamed so much more readily than Alicia's, why her red hair curled in so unruly a fashion.

After a moment's silence between the three of them, Alicia spoke again. 'He is handsome, though, isn't he?'

'Who is, my dear?'

'Mr Mackay. I mean, well, if he were not a minister of course, and if he were a great deal younger, one might perhaps think him quite handsome.'

Such an idea had never entered Mairead's head, but Miss Juniper seemed to agree. 'Oh, a great many people did. The first Mrs Mackay was quite a society beauty, you know, and of very good family, but her eyes once set on Alasdair Mackay she would look at no other. Her mother, sensible woman, was very much against the match, but her father was indulgent and . . .' Here, Miss Juniper's voice had trailed off, as it always did at this point in the tale. All the girls knew for a certainty was that the first Mrs Mackay had died within four years of her marriage, having produced one son who had been given into the care of her family, and that after a widowhood of a further ten years, the minister had married their own Rachel. 'There was many a disappointed matron with an unmarried daughter the length and breadth of the Black Isle on that day, you may be assured,' she said, 'but having chosen unwisely in his first wife, Mr Mackay made certain not to do so in his second.'

The girls had seen the portrait of the first Mrs Mackay, of course, hanging in the manse dining room. She had indeed been very beautiful, and it had to be conceded their Rachel would probably not make so fine a portrait, but then, as Alicia had pointed out, a man could hardly be married to a portrait.

At the manse, Miss Juniper refused Rachel's invitation to join in the afternoon's picnic on the hill. She had 'other fish to fry'.

Rachel raised an admonitory eyebrow. 'You would not be thinking of taking your tea in the parlour of the Commercial Hotel now, would you, Miss Juniper?'

Miss Juniper was the personification of innocence. 'As you know, my dear, I am often in the habit of going there on a Saturday afternoon, to consult the quarterlies and reviews, which Mrs Cameron is good enough to take in. I am sure there is no reason why I should not do so today?'

Rachel laughed. 'On, none whatsoever, I am sure.'

On leaving her charges at the manse, Miss Juniper set off briskly back towards town, and the Commercial Hotel. She had hardly turned the foot of the Causeway when the sound of carriage wheels coming down from Cromarty House made her look back to see Lady Charlotte slow the gig and bring the horse to a halt.

'Charlotte. You are going out for a drive.'

'It's such a fine afternoon, I thought I might take a run out along the bay.' She indicated the small easel and her paintbox on the seat beside her. 'I thought to paint the thistledown amongst the old walls of Kirkmichael, before it is all blown away.'

'Kirkmichael? Oh, my dear, I wish you wouldn't. The place has so many sinister associations.'

Charlotte leaned down and touched the old lady lightly on the cheek. 'You must not worry about me, Miss Juniper.' Then, lifting the reins again, she urged the horse forward at a trot that was really too fast for the cobbled causeys of Cromarty.

It was not long after the sound of Lady Charlotte's gig passing had faded into the distance that Miss Juniper's girls, each now with a basket, left the manse in company with Rachel Mackay. As they turned off the Causeway for the path up Cromarty hill, Alicia asked Mrs Mackay, 'Are you and the minister to join the library?'

'Yes,' Rachel smiled, 'we are.'

'I am surprised you need to,' said Mairead. 'Still less the minister. I am sure he must have read almost every book there is.'

Rachel laughed. 'Well, I don't think even he has read every book there is. Besides, the library is to be a respectable, social association, and so the minister would be expected to form part of it.'

'So,' Mairead continued, choosing her words as carefully as she was able, 'will he have read Miss Juniper's book?'

'Mairead!' Alicia said.

They had just crossed over the burn at the start of the coastal path leading to the hill. Mrs Mackay stopped. 'Who told you about Miss Juniper's book, Mairead?'

Mairead felt her cheeks flame and found that her courage failed her. Alicia glanced at her then answered for her. 'Everyone knows about it. They say it is why Miss Juniper was disgraced, why she had to leave Fortrose, why no one that can afford any better will send their daughters to her . . .'

Rachel Mackay's face became stern. 'I am surprised, given her kindness and care for you both, that you pay any heed to such gossip. There are few girls in Scotland, be their fathers never so rich, who will have as good an education as you will have from Miss Juniper.' She put down her basket. 'Come, girls, we'll sit down over here.' She led them to a wooden bench at the side of the path. 'It's only to be expected that you are curious, and unfair to leave you to imagine the worst. Miss Juniper's book, as you must know, was an account of her time as a village schoolmistress.'

The girls nodded. 'But how could that be so bad?' asked Alicia. 'Surely she could not have been a very scandalous person?'

'Oh, she wasn't,' agreed Mrs Mackay. 'Her mistake was to tell the truth. She showed her pupils, her neighbours, the great and the good of the society of Fortrose, as they really were, and in doing so she failed to take enough care in disguising the identities of those people about whom she told the truth.'

Alicia's eyes widened. 'She wrote about real people? From Fortrose?'

Mrs Mackay nodded. 'I'm afraid so. And some of them were not at all pleased about it.'

Mairead was now agog. 'But what did she write?'

The minister's wife looked as if she might admonish her again, but then she leaned a little closer to them. 'She wrote about people who were nosy – who spied on their neighbours and crept up to listen at their windows at night.'

'She didn't!'

'Oh, but she did. Moreover, she portrayed people who were lazy and slovenly. She took care to give them assumed names – but such was the precision of her descriptions that no one was in any doubt as to whom she was talking about. She took aim at the arrogant, the avaricious, the mean; she exposed duplicity, cruelty, vanity, greed and dishonesty. In short, she described the society around her exactly as she found it, all in her little book.'

The girls were both now open-mouthed and waiting to hear more.

'Now, as you know, the book is dedicated to Sir Walter Scott himself.'

The girls knew. There was no figure more greatly venerated in the cottage on Little Vennel than was Sir Walter. The letter from Sir Walter, congratulating Miss Juniper on the publication of her own book, was taken out and read every year, on his birthday. They would have been astonished to learn that her book had been dedicated to anyone else.

'Well,' continued Mrs Mackay, 'Sir Walter Scott's is only the first amongst many names of the highest quality on the list of subscribers to the publication of Miss Juniper's book, from one end of Scotland to the other. In drawing so precisely the society and manners of the town of Fortrose, Miss Juniper made it a national laughing stock. For that she was chased from her position and her home and has sought refuge here.'

'But why did she come here, where she was known and was bound to be shunned? Why not somewhere far away where she might have started again?'

Rachel took Mairead's hand. 'Because she had nowhere else to go. No home, no money, no relations who might have helped her. She came here because of me, and because of Lady Charlotte – as you know, we had both boarded at her school in Fortrose. We cannot stop the tittle-tattle, we cannot regain for her what she has lost, but Charlotte is able to see to it that she has a roof over her head and that her hearth is never cold nor her larder empty. That she is welcomed by me at the manse means that others must at least acknowledge her in the street, and that fathers like yours might with propriety leave their daughters in her care.'

But the girls were no longer following Mrs Mackay. They should have guessed, of course. Where else would the baskets of game, eggs and vegetables that regularly appeared in the cottage kitchen come from, if not the larder and gardens of Cromarty House? Their own meagre fees would not have paid the half of it.

As they resumed their walk up the hill, each pursued her own thoughts. Alicia, always the romantic, tried to imagine

Lady Charlotte as the schoolgirl she must once have been and whether some lost love had interposed itself before she had been condemned to life in the house on the hill, and marriage to Sir William. Mairead, on the other hand, was more interested in the matter of Miss Juniper's pen, and the story it might write should she decide to turn her attention to the people of Cromarty.

TWO

Choice is made of the Books

James Craig, the clockmaker, looked up from his workbench as his shop door opened to admit Sanders Gilfeather, manager of the Caledonian Bank and session clerk to the kirk of Cromarty. Sanders was still in his banking suit, even though by this time on a Saturday afternoon it was his habit to be in waders and gansey and making his way out to Donal Deacon's lobster boat.

'All is well I hope, Sanders,' said James, as Gilfeather set on the counter the bracket clock he had had under his arm. It was a fine piece – quality without frippery – and this only the second time Sanders had brought it to him. The first time had been sixteen years since, when the news had come to the town of Cromarty that his son, Ensign Alexander Gilfeather, had fallen at the Battle of Waterloo. Gilfeather had brought it to him then, setting the clock, its well-made mahogany case, with flawless glass and the maker's mark of Ritchie of Edinburgh, upon the counter, informing him it had stopped. James had observed the mechanism, moving seamlessly, keeping perfect time. 'Aye, Sanders,' he'd said, 'you're right enough. It's stopped.'

'It'll not mend right, I don't think.'

'No,' James had conceded. 'But we'll make the best of it.'

Sixteen years ago, and now here the clock was back on his counter. But this time the thing really was going slow.

'You're not away fishing this afternoon then?'

'Chance would be the fine thing,' said the bank manager. 'But today the members of the library are to make choice of their books. I'll bid you good day, James.'

James recalled the list of the library members Gilfeather had shown to him only a few days beforehand. 'Good day to you too, Sanders. And good luck.'

Just then, Stanislas appeared through from the back shop, where he had evidently been hovering. 'Why is Mr Gilfeather in his business attire? I did not think the bank was open on a Saturday afternoon.'

'It isn't,' said James. 'But the great and the good of the town have set themselves up as a circulating library, and they've settled on poor Sanders to be their clerk. He's away to make note of their choice of reading.'

'But why are you not there?'

Despite the young man's great intelligence, James often had to remind himself that Stanislas had much to learn about life in a Scottish town. He laughed. 'Me? Because I am neither great nor good. And there are amongst the chosen ones a goodly few whose memories stretch back forty years and are not inclined to forgive what they have been so careful not to forget.' What they would neither forgive nor forget was James's youthful enthusiasm for the French and their revolution that had, in his younger days, drawn him to Paris itself.

'But you have read more than those people. You have read more than anyone in this town.'

James took out his eyeglass and pointed it at Stanislas. 'Not quite, Stan. Miller, the stonemason, has read more than anyone else in this town, and I can assure you, they haven't invited him to join in their number either.'

'Then what is the point of their association?'

'The point, my lad, is that others might know they are in it.'

In the small front parlour of the Commercial Hotel, Janet Cameron set down the coffee pot in front of Miss Juniper, who had positioned herself by the window. 'I'll have Hester light the fire for you,' she said.

'I am quite comfortable, thank you. The ladies and gentlemen will be wanting it lit though – in the reading room, I suppose?'

'The fire there is already lit, though it is only the gentlemen. As the Misses Rose could not attend, being at a cousin's wedding in Rosemarkie today, it was not thought right that the other ladies should be there either. Now, can I bring you anything else?'

'No, thank you. I shall be quite content here with my

coffee and the *Courier*. I am most obliged to you for bringing it through.'

Janet Cameron had known what Miss Juniper was about the minute Hester had hurried through to the kitchen to tell her the schoolmistress was out in the front hall. There would have been nothing unusual in this – Miss Juniper habitually appeared at the Commercial Hotel on a Saturday afternoon, to take her coffee in the coffee room and to peruse the *Inverness Courier* and the *Quarterly Review*, but her accustomed time was three o'clock on the dot, not a quarter to two. It was plain that she had got wind, somehow, that the gentlemen of the library were to be gathering there at two, to make choice of the books, and that she was determined to interpose herself in some manner. Mrs Cameron had swiftly told her the reading room was reserved for a private function and deposited her instead in the parlour.

But despite the crisp sunshine outside, the parlour was chilly, it being now October, and Mrs Cameron rang through for Hester to come and light the fire anyway. She was about to leave when her eye was caught by the article the other woman was now reading, a report of the murder trial just brought to its conclusion in the High Court of Inverness.

'Guilty,' said Miss Juniper. 'It's a puzzling thing to me all the same, why a schoolmaster in Assynt should murder a pedlar – all for the sake of thirty pounds.'

'Not an insignificant amount of money, though.'

'No, but a schoolmaster? And for a life?'

'I suppose a schoolmaster is a man like any other,' said Mrs Cameron, straightening the hearth rug. 'Perhaps he just had it in him.'

Miss Juniper took a sip of her coffee. 'Yes,' she said, 'perhaps he did.'

Across the hall, Mr Gilfeather opened his leather attaché case and took out the library minute book. Opening it at the correct page, he read:

List of the Cromarty Citizens who have formed a Circulating Library, Books being Precious, Carriage costly, and Communication slow and expensive.

Sir William Mackenzie
Lady Charlotte
Rev. Dr Micah Fraser
Rev. Alasdair Mackay
Mrs Mackay
Mr Isaac Fordyce
Miss Elspeth Rose
Miss Anna Rose
Mr John Learmonth
Mrs Cameron
Mr Ludovic Cameron
Mr Hossack

That would put Willie Hossack's nose out of joint, he reflected, to see himself so exactly at the bottom of the list, and not to be able to do a blind thing about it, for there could be little debate about the order of precedence: aside from a brief hesitation over whether Mr Fordyce should indeed come before the Misses Rose, the list had as good as written itself.

Miss Elspeth Rose, of course, was behind it all. Whatever she might claim, he knew her aim in the establishment of this association was that it should allow her greater oversight of the society of the town. 'Things are slipping, Mr Gilfeather,' she had said to him, and who knew but she was not right?

There had been a great deal said, at that inaugural meeting, and much of it by Miss Elspeth and her sister, about the rules by which the library should be governed, but Mr Gilfeather had used his own common sense and minuted accordingly. He was, nonetheless, ill at ease. For a start, there was Arabella Juniper, just across the hall, in the parlour. There had been some discussion, *prior* to the first meeting of the members of the library, as to whether Miss Juniper should be invited to become one of their number. The discussion had not taken up a great deal of the committee's time: the ancient, if somewhat tenuous acquaintance of Miss Juniper with the parents of Sir Walter Scott gave her a claim, of course, to entrance into every literary society. And indeed, her possession of a congratulatory letter from Sir Walter himself on the publication of her own book might in other circumstances have made her the first name on Mr Gilfeather's list. It was, however, the nature of that very book which made the discussion of her potential membership a matter of such short order. Every one of them had read *The Memoirs of a Fortrose Schoolmistress* but could scarcely publicly admit the fact. Sir Walter notwithstanding, it had quickly been agreed that Miss Juniper should *not* be invited.

And then here was Dr Fraser, minister of Resolis, the neighbouring parish and a full six miles away, but here he was, ensconced in Mr Gilfeather's own preferred chair in the coffee room. Mrs Cameron herself had been put out by it, but it was not the place of either of them to tell a minister to shift. Alasdair Mackay of Cromarty kirk had made no such mistake, of course, and was leaning contentedly at one end of the fireplace, puffing on his pipe while Sir William Mackenzie, scanning *The Scotsman* for the latest news of the Reform Bill, leant on the other end in an accommodation of Church and State which Mr Gilfeather could not but approve.

'What news of the Bill, William?' asked Mr Mackay.

Before Sir William could well get his response prepared, Isaac Fordyce had let out a shrill cry. 'No, minister! I cannot allow it. Surely, it was one of the first rules of our new association that politics should *not* be discussed?'

Sir William looked to Mr Gilfeather who consulted in his ledger. 'Although such an interdict does not constitute one of the actual *rules* of the library, it was certainly agreed in spirit that discussions of an overtly political nature, and touching on the present times, should be discouraged.'

'Thank the Good Lord for that,' drawled Farquhar Hossack. Mr Gilfeather was greatly put out by the presence in the coffee room – or reading room as several of the members had now taken to calling it – of Willie Hossack's son. Farquhar Hossack was *not* a member of the library, and on this one occasion Mr Gilfeather was mildly regretful that Miss Elspeth Rose was not here to bother him about regulations. Willie Hossack, proprietor of Cromarty ropeworks, was bad enough, but his son was infinitely worse. Farquhar, Mrs Cameron had confided, had been annoying the maids in the reading room half the morning, and had made no shift to leave as two o'clock approached, despite her best efforts.

With just a minute wanting of two o'clock, Willie Hossack himself finally arrived. Farquhar accorded his father little more than an uninterested grunt, and Hossack was forced to wedge himself onto the small sofa already occupied by Ludovic Cameron, son and heir to the proprietress of the Commercial Hotel.

Sir William cleared his throat. 'Well, we are all assembled. Let us proceed to business. Mr Fordyce, I understand, has been in communication with his cousin in Elgin with regard to the supply of the books.'

The little man leaned forward. 'Indeed,' he said, 'and you may be assured, my cousin deals only with books of the finest quality, bound to the highest standard.'

Willie Hossack sniffed. 'Aye, but will he give us as good a price as might be had from Morrison in Inverness?'

Isaac Fordyce bristled. 'The goods in Morrison's establishment have been rifled by a thousand pairs of hands and made the tour of half the Highlands. I for one am more inclined to pay for a volume in mint condition, rather than some cheap edition, no doubt reeking of mutton fat and peat.'

It was for eventualities such as this that Mr Gilfeather, and he alone, had been approached to fill the position of clerk to the library. All eyes turned to him.

'In the matter of cost,' he began, 'the question of transportation must also be considered. And I'll tell you this, there's a sight more chance of getting a box of books taken cheaply across the firth from Elgin than paying to have them on the Kessock Ferry from Inverness then trundled here in a cart. That is, of course, only my opinion.'

But that opinion once given, there was no more to be said. Mr Fordyce's dignity was upheld and no further mention made of booksellers in Inverness. Willie Hossack sat back, ill-pleased, and Sir William pressed on to the choice of the books. At least the women weren't here – that would save some time.

'I believe you are in receipt of the ladies' selection, Mr Gilfeather?'

Mr Gilfeather nodded. He was in receipt of the ladies' selection, all right. Miss Elspeth Rose had handed it to him in the street, as if presenting him with an overdue butcher's bill. He proceeded to read aloud the list.

'Lady Charlotte: De Bourrienne's *Memoirs of Napoleon*.'

Willie Hossack snorted and Mr Gilfeather, while privately deploring anything associated with the Corsican, shot the man a look charged with forty years of contempt. Sir William asked whether he was quite certain that had been his wife's choice. 'I wonder whether she did not mean rather to ask for a biography of the Empress Josephine?'

'No, no,' he said. 'Both title and author are written out quite exactly, and the translation recently brought out by Constable specified.'

Sir William said something to the effect that he would never quite understand his wife, and the listing of the ladies' choices continued. Mrs Mackay had requested Sir Walter Scott's *Anne of Geierstein*. It was the general apprehension of the community that the minister might not have his young wife entirely under his control. Rachel Mackay had been too clever for a lady's maid and governess, and she might be too clever for a minister's wife as well, but Sir Walter Scott could hardly be objected to.

Next came the choice of Miss Elspeth Rose. There would be no grounds for concern here: if something were to be disapproved of it would be Miss Elspeth who would do the disapproving. Her choice must be therefore, *de facto*, acceptable to all. 'Miss Elspeth requests Mrs Hemans' *Records of Woman: with Other Poems*.'

'Heaven preserve us,' murmured Farquhar Hossack from behind a copy of the *Inverness Journal*, 'poetry! Don't tell me the old bluestocking has discovered she has a heart. I had half-expected she would ask for *Frankenstein*.'

Willie Hossack coughed as if he had a beetle in his throat and Mr Fordyce hastened to fill the moment of awkwardness. 'Miss Rose has made a fine choice, and I daresay that she has already read Mrs Shelley's novel in any case.'

Dr Fraser turned to Farquhar Hossack. 'No doubt *Frankenstein* is required reading amongst the anatomy students at Aberdeen, Fachie, if only as a warning against meddling with things that are better left alone.'

Farquhar lowered his newspaper. 'You would have us remain in ignorance, sir?'

'I would have our kirkyards left unmolested, sir,' responded the minister.

No one in the room could have been unaware of what it was that Dr Fraser alluded to. The horrors perpetrated only three years since by William Burke and William Hare in the closes of Edinburgh were still fresh in the minds of everyone. How could they not be? Every week the papers continued to tell of suspected abductions and murders up and down the country, all to meet the insatiable demand for corpses of the anatomy professors that even grave-robbing could not satisfy.

The imputation was all too clear to Farquhar, who cast aside his newspaper and stood up. 'Your kirkyards? It'll be your pews that are unmolested, if you persist in your slavish devotion to superstition in the place of science.' Having shocked the room, Fachie left, giving no farewells, even to his stupefied father.

Willie Hossack attempted to bluster something, but Mr Gilfeather ignored him and, as if there had been no unfortunate interruption, passed from the choice of Miss Elspeth Rose to that of her sister Anna, who had requested a copy of Miss Ferrier's *Marriage*. The gentle amusement at this settled the company and threatened to start conversations, but Mr Gilfeather hurried on: Donal Deacon's lobster boat would not wait in the harbour for ever. 'Finally, we have the choice of Mrs Cameron, who has requested *The Youth and Manhood of Cyril Thornton*.'

On hearing his mother's selection, Ludovic Cameron groaned.

'Bear up, Ludo,' murmured the schoolmaster, from behind the sofa occupied by his friend.

'Bear up? *Cyril Thornton* is a cautionary tale of a young man who, a disappointment to his parents, neglects the studies for which he was sent away and learns some bitter lessons by a career in the army. He returns home, a little too late to be of any great use to those he left behind, but in time to marry the dependable girl he should have married in the first place.'

'Perhaps,' persisted the schoolmaster. 'But Hamilton writes an excellent comic character. He'll soon have your good lady mother in fine form.' The sequence of looks provoked around the room by this remark suggested that the idea of the austere Janet Cameron being elevated to the condition of 'fine form' was not one that persuaded anybody.

Sir William hastily suggested moving on to the gentlemen's choices.

'For myself, I should say Croker's *Boswell's Life of Johnson,*' he began, 'if only to see whether there is anything in the controversy stirred up amongst the reviewers.'

'Ach, they are all so tight in with the booksellers,' said Dr Fraser. 'They do nothing but puff their favourites and manufacture controversies. It's all contrived in order to sell more books.'

This point conceded, the selections continued. Isaac Fordyce, predictably enough, requested the first two volumes of Moore's *Life of Byron*; Dr Fraser, to general surprise, asked for Heber's *Poetical Works*. Mr Gilfeather turned now to Ludovic Cameron. His assistant clerk at the bank could be relied upon to be sensible. Ludovic requested Basil Hall.

'The *Travels in North America*?' queried Willie Hossack, alert that mention was finally made of something he had heard of. How on earth had the fellow got himself in here? Mr Gilfeather wondered. And then Hossack himself was piping up that he would like The *Aberdeen Magazine* ordered on his behalf. On his behalf! It would be his wife who was after it, thinking no doubt that she might one day read of Fachie's exploits amongst its pages. As if there weren't enough periodicals brought into the reading room as it was. Mr Gilfeather did not waste time on quibbling, however, and with a sniff at Willie Hossack's choice, wrote it down.

Things were cutting along quite nicely, but then the minister announced he would wish to be purchased James

Justinian Morier's *Hajji Baba*. Mr Gilfeather stayed his pen. He was not an unreasonable man, but he *was* an elder of the Kirk.

'*Hajji Baba*, minister? You are aware the fellow is an infidel?'

Alasdair Mackay attempted a conciliatory look. 'The book is a satire, Sanders, on the Persian society and on our own.'

Satire! Djinns, and sorcerers and carpets that flew were one thing, but to introduce *satire* into the society of Cromarty would be to insert the thin end of the wedge. Sanders gave his minister a look to make clear that he inscribed this particular title into the books list of the Cromarty Circulating Library under duress.

Last to give in his choice was the schoolmaster, Mr Learmonth, who said he thought he would like a look at MacFarlane's *Constantinople in 1828*. 'It is a light thing, I believe,' he added. 'Part travel memoir and part novel. Something the ladies might enjoy too.' Mr Gilfeather wrinkled his nose. This was the start of it, if a schoolmaster barely arrived in Cromarty thought it his place to be suggesting reading matter for the ladies of the town. Good luck to him with that! And then the schoolmaster was on his feet before Mr Gilfeather had set down his pen.

'We are keeping you from some engagement, Mr Learmonth?'

The young man laughed slightly. 'No engagement, only a visit to Kirkmichael. I believe there is much of interest to be found amongst the gravestones there.'

'Well,' said Dr Fraser, at last heaving himself out of Mr Gilfeather's accustomed chair, 'as long as what you find isn't Fachie Hossack, with a shovel.'

It was several hours later that Charlotte was looking out at her casement as she pulled a brush through her hair. The sea and the sky had both turned to grey on her journey back from Kirkmichael, the one seeming to dissolve and disappear into the other so that soon they would be black. In the cold space of her bedchamber, she felt the chill air on her neck. The fire was unlit. She had told the girl to leave it because she did not have it in her to manage the ten minutes the child would be in the room, lighting the fire, closing the curtain drapes, attempting to talk to her. Not tonight, not with the great dark emptiness of the world outside that made her want to disappear. She could not manage it tonight.

It would be all she could do to manage the dinner at the manse. The men would talk about the library, and the prospects of the Reform Bill. Someone would say something of the cholera, which had now reached Vienna. Rachel might talk of Miss Juniper's girls.

Charlotte put her hand against the windowpane and imagined for a moment what it might be to dissolve, like the light, into darkness. She could hardly make out the sea now. Over the town, lights were appearing at windows. The schoolhouse was there somewhere, past the vennels of Fishertown, down by the shore. She wondered if the schoolmaster was returned yet from Kirkmichael, where he had come upon her this afternoon, ruining her solitude. Perhaps he would reproduce his drawings on the blackboard for his pupils, a little of the arm still tanned from the summer past showing above the wrist where his cuff had begun to fray. He had offered to go, to leave the place to her, but she had demurred and began to gather up her things instead. He had insisted on helping her and as he'd bent to pick up her easel their hands had touched. Those tanned fingers had been on her skin. The rough material of his sleeve had brushed her cheek. A current had gone through her, from him to her and back again. She had stepped back, stunned, and he had turned away, murmuring an apology. He should have been the one to leave.

Charlotte traced her fingers over her own lips then shook herself. Her eyes travelled from the schoolhouse, past the courthouse and the kirk and the grand merchant houses, until her gaze fell upon the manse down below. Rachel would have been back hours since from her picnic on the hill, to give orders for their dinner and to make herself sit and sew or read in Alasdair's first wife's parlour. Or perhaps she had waited, winding her hair in anticipation of his return later in the afternoon from the meeting of the library. How was it they could have made such different marriages? Once, when Charlotte had spoken to Rachel about the blessed darkness that enveloped her as William paid her his – thank God – ever less frequent attentions, Rachel had said quietly, her eyes lowered a little, that she liked the afternoons.

THREE

Wednesday Evening

Supper among friends

Ludovic Cameron picked his way carefully along the middle of the street and wondered about Boston. 'The streets of Boston are not paved with gold, Ludovic,' his mother had only just informed him. Perhaps not, but it would be something if they were paved at all. And lit at night, as the streets of Inverness were lit. Surely he might hope for that? Ahead of him, small creatures scuttled from one alleyway to another while behind him lurked the dark bulk of yet another ship, within its decks a mass of people and all their worldly goods, waiting to be carried westwards, across the ocean. Most of them had had little choice in the matter, forced to the edges and finally the sea by improvements, and sheep. Ludovic, though, would not have to be forced. Ludovic would be off, at the first opportunity. Further out in the bay still, a ship in quarantine, for fear of the cholera that had now crept from the east into Europe. East to west, was that the way the world turned?

Ludovic tried to recall his mathematics lectures, from his one year of study at the Marischal College in Aberdeen, but Dr Jamesone had been so constantly befuddled that Ludo had hardly been able to make sense of the old fellow at all. Mrs Cameron, back in Cromarty, had soon seen that her money was wasted in pursuit of her son's academic deficiencies, and called him home. Five years ago, and Ludo had been intent on getting away ever since. His father had gone westwards to Sir William's plantation in Demerara many years ago and never come back. Hester had come here instead. James Craig had left many years ago too, for Paris, only to pitch up again one day in Cromarty, where he had started. Ludo was quite determined he would not finish back where he had started.

He was almost at the door of the clockmaker's when he saw John Learmonth turn the corner at the bottom of the Paye and emerge onto the street ahead of him. He lifted an arm in greeting, but John, in some reverie of graveyards and old memorials, no doubt, didn't notice. Ludo whistled.

John looked up and his face brightened. 'I hadn't noticed you there.' They were now at the clockmaker's door. 'By the smell of that goulash, I should say we have arrived *precisely* at the proper time. Come, Ludo, Stan will be dishing up.' Soon, they had passed through the front shop and workshop, on the trail of aromas of herbs and stewing pork, to the comfortable back room which James Craig shared with his young Polish apprentice. Stanislas was indeed occupied in stirring the contents of a large pot suspended over the fire. He set down his spoon and without any other greeting said, 'Have you brought it?'

Ludovic held out to him the copy of *The Scotsman* that had just that day come into the hotel's reading room, and James lit the lamp above the table. The glow spread to the corners of the small room, illuminating the stack of well-thumbed books in the corner and the small oil painting of Notre Dame that hung above the hearth, as well as the old terrier dog that lay in front of it.

'Page two,' said Ludovic as Stanislas spread out the newspaper.

The Pole frantically traced the columns then began to read aloud. 'From Cracow, on the fifteenth. "It is now certain that the Polish army has not submitted . . ."' He turned towards his friends with glee and John clapped him on the shoulder.

'Go on, go on,' said Craig.

'". . . has not submitted to the Russians and that the spirit of resistance is still alive in the country."' His excitement grew as he read, only to fade again. '"Strong hopes are entertained that the severe weather will set in before Paskewitch can reduce the two or three fortresses which the Poles still hold, and that by the independence of the brave people . . ."' His voice dwindled to nothing and he turned away.

Ludovic was mystified. 'But surely, that's good, Stan, is it not?'

'Good? It is hopeless. '"two or three fortresses", and they

expect them to hold out until spring? They think Russia will cower before the onslaught of a Polish winter as Napoleon before the gates of Moscow?' He abandoned his reading of the paper to return to his pot. 'They know nothing.'

'But bear up, old fellow,' said Ludovic, scanning the columns once more. 'Surely, the mediating powers . . .'

James shook his head as he laid down a dish of potatoes. 'All their concern is to prevent the insurrection of their own people.'

'The people,' said Stanislas. 'The people are so enslaved by their masters they don't even know what they want. If the people had but risen . . .'

Stanislas' father had lost almost all in his resistance to their Russian masters, and with the little that remained to him he had sent his son to the university in Warsaw, where Stanislas had learned to repeat his father's mistakes. The previous November's uprising had given the Tsar the excuse he wanted for ordering his armies to crush the Polish revolt. Stanislas' subsequent adventures, his close encounters with near-certain death in fleeing before the Russian army, had held them spellbound on many an evening. Their friend had made his way to the Baltic coast, thinking to take ship for England, his experience of having been tutored at home by a young Englishman having led him to hope he might engage the sympathy of like-minded liberals for the cause of his homeland. He had somehow instead boarded a ship loaded with hemp and bound for Cromarty. What series of accidents had then brought him to the door of the only other inhabitant of this town to have participated in a European revolution was not quite clear to Ludovic, but the upshot was that the highly educated son of a Polish count sat in the back room of a shop in Cromarty on the edge of the North Sea learning how to mend clocks.

John Learmonth put an arm round Stanislas' drooping shoulders. 'There is hope, Stan. The piece says Warsaw has not fallen, does it not? There is always hope.'

As James Craig doled ladlesful of the rich stew into wooden bowls, their talk, the purpose of these evening gatherings, was of the news. The Reform Bill could not be avoided. Craig dismissed it as an irrelevance that would serve only to further enrich the masters and more thoroughly enslave the people on whose labour their wealth was built. What good to enfranchise tenants if they must cast their vote in full sight of their landlord? What of the labourers and artisans who would still have no vote at all? What of the Highlanders in the ropeworks, the slaughtermen and curers and coopers and packers at the piggery, the fishermen risking death every time they took to their boats? Much good the great Reform Bill would do them!

'Or us,' John Learmonth pointed out. 'Other than Ludo, of course.' Ludo was the only one of them who could claim a property valued at £10 per annum. Janet Cameron's saving and determination for as long as Ludovic could remember, to build up the trade and reputation of the Commercial Hotel, would, should the Lords in Westminster be so inclined, give Ludovic, man of property, the vote.

They spoke of the devastation said to have been wrought in the West Indies by the coming of a hurricane. Stanislas asked whether the 'losses' reported by the newspaper referred to lives or to profits. John checked again. 'Both.' Below the news of the hurricane was printed a letter, from a planter in Demerara, complaining of the effects of the speeches of the abolitionists on the slaves who were thus rendered indolent and hardly to be kept under control. There was talk of the distribution of arms and ammunition amongst the white brethren. Ludo hoped that Hester would not have had time to read the paper yet, for he knew such things upset her.

They plundered the newspaper for anything that might distract Stanislas' thoughts from the closing down of his university and the deaths and losses of his friends and family at home, those who had not got away ahead of the inexorable Russian advance on Warsaw.

At last they spoke about the stew they were eating, and of the pigs from whom the pork had come, until John Learmonth, whose schoolroom lay close to the piggery, begged them to stop.

'The pigs have no choice but to be in Cromarty,' said Ludo, 'to be reared, slaughtered, salted and sent in barrels to Barbados. You, on the other hand, have a choice. You do not need to be here at all.'

'Everyone must be somewhere, Ludo.'

'But why here? You are not even from Cromarty! Look, look here.' He pointed to a column on the front page of the newspaper, filled with the advertisements of Edinburgh writing, arithmetic and music masters. 'You took your degree in Edinburgh, and might have made your name there, like all these fellows are busy doing. *You* might have taken rooms in some elegant and respectable New Town address from which to launch yourself upon the world, and yet you banish yourself here. Look' – again he pointed – '"Prizes were awarded to *young ladies*." John, your life might have been a delight – you might have attended recitals, the theatre, societies . . .'

'But here I have the Northern Institution in Inverness, with their many fascinating lectures, and there is the Mechanics' Institute, which Stan talks of joining . . .'

Ludovic wasn't sure whether he was supposed to take this seriously. He often felt, when he was with his friends, John especially, that more was meant by their conversation than he fully understood. That they sought out his company was a matter of some astonishment to him who, until first John Learmonth and then Stanislas Jeszewski had arrived in Cromarty, had had no friends at all. The coincidence of his birth, within a few months and in the same small town with that of Farquhar Hossack, had plagued him his whole life.

His childhood had been a litany of bruisings, drubbings and humiliations at the hands of a laughing Fachie, the only respite coming in their years at the grammar school of Fortrose, where Fachie's interests had increasingly turned to menacing the young women of the town. Their simultaneous advancement to the Marischal College in Aberdeen, greeted with relief in Fortrose, made things worse again for Ludo, for Fachie let loose amongst the brothels and gambling dens of Aberdeen had been a nightmare, the responsibility for which was as often as not laid at Ludo's door, for the mere fact that they had arrived at the college together. Ludo had never told her, of course, but his mother's summons home following his failure to pass the first year of his courses had come as a blessed relief. Fachie, however, by some miraculous sequence of events beyond Ludo's comprehension, had passed his courses and was now embarked upon higher studies with a view to entering the medical profession. The only explanation Ludo could think of was in Fachie's oft-repeated drunken vow that he 'would go to Hell before he went to the Cromarty ropeworks'. And so, for at least eight months of the year, Ludo was free to walk the streets of the town without fear of being subjected to the mockery and abuse of Farquhar Hossack. That in itself would have been enough – it had never entered his head that he might one day actually have friends. But friends he now had, and he was determined to keep them. He made a point, every week, of reading the paper from end to end in order that he would know what it was they were alluding to when they began to discuss the news.

Tonight, having again evaded the question of why he had abandoned life in the Athens of the north to languish instead behind a schoolmaster's desk in Cromarty, John now turned the conversation onto Ludovic himself.

'Did you notice the "Letter from Ontario", Ludo?'

'I did.' Now he was on firmer ground.

'And?'

'It is evidently not Boston.'

'They will be as much in need of worthy bankers in Ontario as they are in Boston, I should have thought.'

'I have no doubt of it, but at least in Boston a man might hope to make a living as a bank agent without also being expected to milk his own cow!'

James Craig exploded with laughter. 'Do you not think Sanders Gilfeather has milked a cow or two in his time?' Ludovic was head clerk to Mr Gilfeather in the bank, a position which was the delight of his mother's life.

Still laughing, James went on. 'Your mother has made a fine gentleman of you indeed, and I daresay she would run as sound an establishment in Massachusetts as she does in Cromarty.'

Ludovic felt his shoulders slump. 'She will never go to America, because of Hester. It's bad enough here, but she fears that there, even in the northern states, it would be worse.'

James began to clear away their bowls. 'I daresay she might be right.' He brought out the whisky and got down his fiddle from its place on the wall. He was soon playing some of his favourite airs while John sketched him and Stanislas carried on with his translations of some poet from his homeland whose name Ludovic could never remember. 'I do it so that you might understand,' Stanislas said. Week after week the son of the Polish count went at those translations, till his volume of his countryman's poem was in danger of coming away at the spine, but he was never quite satisfied, always promising them that another few days and he was sure he would have it. The more the conclusion was put off, the more Ludovic was coming to think that his translation told Stanislas a story of his homeland somewhat different from the one he wished it to.

The friends having bid their farewells at the end of their evening, John Learmonth watched Ludovic disappear into the darkness. How was it that it was Ludo, good, trusting Ludo, who was the only one saw a chink in the reasoning that had brought him here to Cromarty? The rest of the town was merely grateful that so able a scholar should have come at all, to take charge of their parish school. There was Dr Fraser too, John reminded himself. The Resolis minister had also shown some curiosity as to why John should have chosen to come to this northern outpost, hardly the springboard for a brilliant career. John had cited his interest in natural history and the enticements of the fascinating newspaper columns of the 'Cromarty Correspondent' which had found their way beyond the pages of the *Inverness Courier* to a wider national audience. The minister had seemed *almost* convinced by this story, and yet some hint of doubt lingered. John had never been an adept liar, and so, in as far as was possible in a place of this sort, he took care to avoid finding himself too often alone in the company of Micah Fraser. As for Ludovic – John could only hope that he would give up asking.

FOUR

Sunday Morning

Sabbath

Miss Elspeth Rose stood ready at the door of Rose Lodge, the very model of exasperation. 'The kirk bell has been ringing this quarter-hour. I shall have a curtain put over that glass if you look in it another half minute!'

Her sister, already much flustered, became even more so. 'But, Elspeth, my dear, I cannot get this bow rightly tied, and think should my bonnet blow off amongst the gravestones!'

'There would be no one to see it, you silly woman, for every other soul in the town will be in their seats before us.' Elspeth sniffed and straightened her shoulders in a manner that struck terror into her sister's heart. Elspeth liked to be in their box ahead of time, that she might have a good view. Miss Anna gave up her attempt to set the bonnet *comme il faut* and fled out of the door and down the front steps in the wake of her sister. The horror of clattering late and alone, into the family pew in the north loft of the church, for all the world of Cromarty to see, was too much for her.

She need not have concerned herself. Out on the street, the Highlanders were still wending their way towards the Paye and their Gaelic chapel. She sometimes thought she would like to go up the brae with them, just to see. Their Gaelic speech was like music in the ears of Miss Anna Rose, who still held dear to the tales of Ossian, despite her sister's claims that James Macpherson had made them up. After all, how should Elspeth have any more knowledge of the truth of them than did Anna herself? She thought this often, but never said it.

People were emerging, too, from the vennels of Fisher-town, the women in their shawls and good mutches, the men with their boots cleaned. The poor souls – the fishing had not been good this year. Miss Anna determined to pray for them, once she had got safely into the kirk, and their box. But here were Mrs Cameron and Ludovic and their girl Hester coming. To arrive after Mrs Cameron, who wasted not a minute away from her hotel that she did not have to, would be the end of her as far as Elspeth was concerned. It was with relief that she saw that the gig from Cromarty House was not yet at the churchyard gate – that at least was something.

There was a press of people at the door to the north loft, where the Roses had long had their box pew. As she emerged at the top of the stair and into the aisle of the loft, she saw below in the church the grey head of the only man whose eye she had ever wished to catch. As if knowing her thought, he looked up and inclined his head to her. So slight was the movement she was certain that none but herself would have seen it. None but herself and Elspeth, of course.

Her sister pursed her lips and nodded a brisk greeting to Hugh Miller, the stonemason, seated with his family across the aisle. The Millers had fallen somewhat in the world through the loss at sea of Hugh's father at a young age, but they were acknowledged respectable people still and maintained their box. Anna had wondered whether Hugh might be invited to join the library but Elspeth had reminded her that he was the one man in Cromarty *not* in need of literary guidance. She was probably right.

'Is it quite necessary to make such an exhibition of yourself?' Elspeth asked as Anna arranged her skirts around the wall seat.

'But surely I am not late?' She craned her head over the rail to see round to the laird's loft. 'See, Sir William and Lady Charlotte are not yet arrived.'

'I am not talking about your tardiness, Anna, but your lack of discretion as concerns the clockmaker.'

'The clockmaker . . .?' Tears pricked Miss Anna's eyes and she could feel the heat creep into her cheeks. This was too cruel, and unworthy, even of Elspeth. She had not exchanged anything but the most conventional of greetings with James Craig since his return to Cromarty over thirty years ago, when her father had made it plain that the man who had been the beau of her youth was no longer welcome in their house. Her father's intransigence had not died with him, but been bequeathed to their brother who, on his death, had passed the responsibility for Anna's unhappiness to Elspeth, who had looked to her duty with unswerving solicitude ever since. And if she might not even be permitted a glimpse . . . But then she saw Elspeth's mouth tighten, signalling the arrival of the laird of Cromarty and his wife, and she remembered that her sister, too, had had her disappointments.

Anna Rose would content herself that from here she could glimpse not only the top of James Craig's head, but also sometimes his face as he turned to make a point to that handsome Polish boy he had for his apprentice. She might catch the corner of his smile or that slight furrowing of his brow when he suspected his point was not being made, for those expressions had not changed in forty years, and they might still be being made for her.

Down there too, in the very front pew, was Mrs Mackay, the minister's wife, whose story was well-known. One might almost have said tragedy, had not its issue, in time, been that she had been free to marry the Reverend Alasdair Mackay. As if in acknowledgement of this very fact, behind Mrs Mackay, at the head of the elders, was Mr Gilfeather, whose son Rachel had been meant to marry. Miss Anna would not wish to catch Mr Gilfeather's eye, lest he thought her attention wandered. His attention never wandered, and Miss Anna was certain that should anyone ask him, Mr Gilfeather would be able to give an account of every word the minister said. Mrs Gilfeather, on the other hand, had her eyes everywhere. 'All that's proper and to be emulated, and all that's ill-gotten and to be avoided, is to be seen on the pews o' Cromarty kirk,' she had once told Anna. This way of looking upon the world had been a revelation to Miss Anna, and had opened to her imagination whole new vistas down which it might wander, should the Reverend Alasdair Mackay's sermon, as it very occasionally did, become more erudite than her attention was quite equal to.

A brief acknowledgement to Sir William aside, Elspeth Rose kept her eyes rigidly to the front. Doubtless the dissecting of Lady Charlotte's outfit would take Anna half the afternoon. Why did her sister insist on being such a silly woman? It was as if the girl of sixteen had been stopped somehow, kept within the body of a woman who had continued to grow older, so now the girl of sixteen seemed barely to understand that she was fifty-four years old and the blush long-gone from her cheek.

The kirk was near enough full today, as on most Sundays, and that fact went some way towards keeping the place warm. So long as the wind did not blow too strongly from the north or east. Miss Elspeth's bones did not look forward to the winter, although she herself was glad enough that the summer was finally over. The heat of the sun on the collected mass of fish-workers, slaughtermen and brewery-workers, rising on the warm air to where most of their betters sat in the lofts of Cromarty kirk, was not a welcome thing.

Above where the clockmaker sat with that strange young apprentice was Major Munro. Elspeth had been in hopes that the major might join the library, but he had declined their invitation. The major sat alone in his box and always waited until the other occupants of the west loft – even the schoolchildren – had descended at the end of the service, before he started to make his own slow way down the steps and out of the church. A French bullet taken at Albuera, Sir William had told her. The scarring down the left side of his face had been from when the enemy had fired the transport ship taking his platoon home after Corunna or Austerlitz or Castellón, or some other place of inhumanity and carnage. There was talk, as there usually was in these cases, of a fiancée who had abandoned him, but like Corunna and Austerlitz and Castellón, that had all been a very long time ago. Miss Elspeth didn't know, as Major Munro stared straight ahead of him, if he saw across from him Sir William and his wife, or something from that time long past only visible to himself.

Elspeth shook herself. She would be as bad as Anna, if she didn't take care, and here now was Sanders Gilfeather standing up, and Willie Hossack carrying in the Bible.

Afterwards, Rachel stood a little behind Alasdair as he greeted the parishioners at the churchyard gate. Even as a small child, it had struck her as something to be wondered at, that the populace of Cromarty displaced itself so precisely in their allotted places in the kirk, upstairs to their lofts and their boxes, or down to their aisles and particular pews, according to some order of precedence whose origins had long since been forgotten, and yet they all had to go out the same gate. She had mentioned it to Alasdair once, and he had laughed and said that that was what most of his sermons were about.

Mrs Gilfeather, in virtue of her position as wife of the session clerk, felt no compunction in standing beside Rachel as her husband did by Alasdair until Lady Charlotte, followed by Sir William, emerged from the west door of the church, although she had not felt free to do this with the first Mrs Mackay. Then she would give Rachel's hand a squeeze. 'Weel, weel, my dear, I'd better get on, for Sanders, as ye ken, doesna like his dinner to be late, not even on the Sabbath,' and calling her housemaid to her, away she would go, for the short walk to the house at the corner of Oswald Lane.

And so it was today, or almost, but this time, when Charlotte stepped out of the door, there was a pause, an indrawing of breath, and an 'And whit's to become o' *her*, I wonder?' before the housemaid was called to accompany her mistress away.

A little discomfited, Rachel waited for Charlotte while Sir William joined Alasdair by the gate. She had hoped that no one but herself had noticed the fading, the gradual distancing from the world, of her friend.

'Who are you looking for?' she asked as Charlotte, who had been continually looking around her since she'd come out of the church, arrived beside her.

Charlotte hesitated. 'Oh, no one. No one at all.' She slipped a thin arm through Rachel's. 'Who would I be looking for in the town of Cromarty that I have not seen a hundred times before?'

Who indeed? Almost everyone now was out of the kirk. Just outside the gate, Miss Anna was in conference with Miss Juniper, much to the evident annoyance of Miss Elspeth, who seemed at any moment like to hook her sister away by the bonnet strings. The fisherfolk and slaughterhouse workers had already made their murmured farewells to the minister and on the street Mr Isaac Fordyce was making his dainty way home, lifting his hat to every lady over the age of five. Janet Cameron, Hester behind her with eyes firmly lowered, had bid Alasdair and Sir William a brisk good day and was already making her way back up Church Street. Ludovic, however, had dawdled behind, to chat with James Craig and his apprentice. There was the usual commotion of the schoolboys tumbling out into the freedom of the kirkyard, their schoolmaster seeming distracted and more negligent than usual in his attempts to keep them in check. Beside her, Rachel felt Charlotte tense. She looked from the schoolmaster to her friend and back again.

'It is not him you are looking out for?' she said, her voice lowered.

Charlotte looked away. 'I encountered him yesterday, at Kirkmichael. There was something . . . He makes me a little uncomfortable, that's all.'

There was no chance for Charlotte to explain further

because there at last was Major Munro issuing from the central door, to pass by the beadle, who would now be able to begin his inspection of the state of the church after its weekly assault by the congregation.

Sir William came over. 'I have invited Alasdair to come up and take his dinner with us today, my dear. And you too, of course,' he added, turning to Rachel.

Rachel was about to decline, but the look on Charlotte's face forestalled her. Without guests, Charlotte would be forced to endure the company at dinner of Sir William's old nurse, or, 'that old witch, Morag Mackenzie', as she was prone to call her. Miss Mackenzie disapproved of guests on the Sabbath, provoking, as they did, the performance of unnecessary labours on the Lord's Day. Their presence at the dining table would drive her, with her cold cuts and her notes of the sermon in the Gaelic chapel, to her own room, where she would remain until the following morning.

'I will ask the major too,' said William. 'There can be little enough cheer in that empty house of his, looking forever out over the firth as if to the ends of the earth.'

Rachel thought it a poor idea, for that the major was known to avoid social gatherings, even to the size of a private dinner, but it was not her place to say so. Charlotte, however, was altogether alarmed by the suggestion. 'No, William, I don't think—'

But her husband forestalled her. 'Come, my dear, he is not nearly of so forbidding a bent as he might first appear.'

Charlotte was flustered. 'I . . . I did not say . . .'

What she had not said was that she, who had once loved parties and dinners and gatherings, could hardly bear any company at all.

Sir William lowered his voice. 'The man is lonely, Charlotte. It will hardly kill you to sit an hour or two in the same room as him.' He strode back over to the gate and issued his invitation. It was refused, immediately, Rachel could see that. But Sir William pressed, and Alasdair too, and eventually, his face registering defeat, the major accepted. 'You must come up to us now, Rachel,' Charlotte said. 'You absolutely must.'

Major Munro was standing with Sir William at the French windows overlooking the lawns when Rachel and Alasdair were shown into the dining room of Cromarty House. The men had their backs to the room, and Rachel thought the contrast between them was not as she would have expected. The major was a half-head taller than Sir William, and seen like this, standing at rest rather than walking along in his halting fashion or seated in the kirk, he presented a fine, erect figure, unblemished. From her chair by a small side table, where she had laid down her book, Charlotte was also watching the men. She turned, and it was a moment before her watching expression was replaced by a smile of recognition. She got up and, kissing Rachel, whispered into her ear, 'The spell has not worked; the witch has declared she will join us.'

Before Rachel could say anything, Charlotte fled away

to pull the sash by the fireplace to summon dinner, and Alasdair went to join the men by the windows. Drifts of their conversation came to her – the boats in the bay, the emigrations and the quarantine – but she paid little attention. She had always loved this room – the light seemed to drift up off the sea and through the leaves to dapple in at the windows and land quietly wherever it might be needed, even places where it had not been thought of. It had been in this room, on a summer's evening, that Alasdair had first looked at her and then looked back again. She had been governess to a family on terms of friendship with previous tenants of Cromarty House. On that occasion she had only been allowed as far as two feet within the door, ushering in the children to say goodnight to their parents and hosts, before going down to take her own supper with the servants in the kitchen. She could never have believed that she might one day – often, in fact – dine here as a guest herself, still less that it might be of Charlotte that she was the guest. The moment of that second look had changed her life.

The furnishing of the room was different now, everything chosen with so much care by Charlotte. She had had the sense not to touch the silk-painted wallpaper which, aside from the views to be had from the front windows, was the room's glory. Nothing had the heaviness that had begun to creep into parlours and drawing rooms elsewhere in the county. Everything was lightness and elegance. The portrait above the fireplace was of Charlotte herself. The artist, a pupil of Raeburn, had captured her almost perfectly, or as perfectly as anyone could capture that which could not be caught. The whole told the story of Sir William's success as a second son made good, of his discipline from the military, of his wealth from India and the Caribbean trade, and of his luck in marrying a woman who, while she might have been a draper's daughter, was undeniably a person of taste. And Charlotte had been happy too, or as near to happy as Rachel had seen her, for a good year and a half as she'd overseen the decoration and the ordering of the furnishings of Cromarty House, and content for at least six months more in the acquisition and hanging of pictures. She had even spoken of a new design for the gardens before the harshest of winters had set in. Then the beautiful young woman who had exchanged her youth and freedom for everything she'd thought she had wanted out of life, had realised she hadn't really wanted it at all. By spring all hope in her situation had been quite frozen from her heart.

'Her trouble is she's read too many novels,' Alasdair had remarked.

Rachel had replied that the problem was that Charlotte had not read enough of them.

Morag Mackenzie having preceded the servants carrying the dishes of food into the dining room, they all at last sat to table and Alasdair said grace. That done, and despite the dark looks and withering disapproval of the housekeeper, the talk did in fact turn to books.

'I hear from Mr Gilfeather that you will not join us in the library, Major,' Alasdair opened with.

The major took a moment to find his words. 'I fear my tastes in reading would be of too dull a nature to interest the members of your society. I'm fortunate in that my own library at Harbour House is well enough provided that I don't require the assistance of this very laudable association in order to access the books that interest me.'

'And what are those books?' asked Charlotte.

The major looked at Charlotte directly, and Rachel realised for the first time what fine grey eyes he had. The scarring on the left side of his face had stopped within an inch of his eye, leaving it untouched. 'For the most part, I read accounts of military campaigns, from the Ancients to our own times. I consider why some campaigns failed where others succeeded, and what unsuccessful generals might have done differently.'

'And do you consider the hand of God in it?' asked Morag Mackenzie.

There was a sudden stillness in the room. It seemed to Rachel that even their breathing was suspended. At last, Major Munro replied.

'The hand of God, madam? No, I do not. I have often looked for God on the battlefield and failed to find him.'

After a sharp, unguarded intake of breath, Morag Mackenzie stiffened her already stiff back and uttered not another word. Alasdair's right hand tightened its grip on his spoon whilst Rachel saw that the left flexed slightly. Sir William, as was his wont, struggled and failed to find something to say that might please everybody. But Rachel watched Charlotte, and something like a chill went through her. For Charlotte's lips were parted, just a little, and it seemed that some light had at last begun to edge around her deadened spirit. Again, she spoke.

'And do you read nothing else, Major?'

The major addressed himself as if only to her. 'From time to time I have whiled away my hours with the work of Lord Byron.'

A look came into Charlotte's eyes that Rachel had not seen since their girlhood, and she knew from what she saw when she moved her head slightly to observe the major, that he would surely drown in them, him and all who might think to help him. It was only then that Rachel realised that Charles Munro had been watching Charlotte since first they had sat down. As Sir William talked on of horses and the disappointments of the Northern Meeting, Rachel wanted to stop what was about to happen. She wanted to put the clock back three hours and hurry Sir William and his wife back up the hill from the kirk to Cromarty House and lock the doors behind them.

FIVE

The Arrival of the Books

Mr Isaac Fordyce sat in his library in Fordyce House. Laid out before him, on the surface of his large walnut desk, were the books. They had arrived just this morning, sent over the firth by his bookseller cousin in Elgin. Mr Gilfeather, though secretary to the library, had made it abundantly clear that under no circumstances would Mrs Gilfeather consent to have the books cluttering up her house. It had been a joy to Mr Fordyce to watch as they'd been taken by cart from the harbourside to be carried instead up the curving front stair of Fordyce House, finally to be unpacked and inventoried in his library. The room took up the north-east corner on the first floor of his large and, as he prided himself, still elegant home. It was that time of day when the rays of the sun were about to make their departure for more welcoming vistas of the house, but still it sent out a last few beams to light the dust motes in the air and show how the carpet brought from Bengal fifty years since by an uncle was gradually fading.

The house had been built sixty years ago, in the heyday of the town, when Mr Fordyce himself had been about to set out on the perils of adolescence and the great adventure of life. His father, a prominent merchant, had shared in the speculations of the former laird, with much greater personal success than had done the laird himself, and had bequeathed to his son the unintended legacy of a life of leisure. Mr Isaac, having studied at the best universities the conflicts of the age would allow, had then spent an untaxing decade overseeing the family's interests abroad, and had, like many a young gentleman before him, returned home to write his memoirs and never do a day's work again.

By the time Bonaparte had begun his assault on the affairs of Europe, drawing the young men of Cromarty overseas to the armed service of the crown, Mr Fordyce, with his greying temples, had no longer been considered a young man. Never having come close to marrying, he had nonetheless been free in those days to open his house to some of the bright young people of the town and had delighted in watching them dance and in listening to them sing, make plays or read poetry to one another. There had been many gay times in the drawing room, when the carpet (not the Bengal, but another one brought by a cousin from Istanbul that Mr Isaac had always thought a little too vulgar) would be rolled back that the dancing might take place. But the tenor of the times had changed, sadly, as if peace had brought in its train a suspicion of adventure and romance, ushering in the reign of morals, silencing the pianoforte and keeping dull the candelabra of the drawing room of Fordyce House. Mr Fordyce, bewildered, had more and more retreated to his library.

Ludo Cameron had come to help him with the inventorying of the books. Mr Fordyce had watched with pleasure as they were unpacked, and carefully examined each volume as it was handed to him, his anticipation reaching its height when Ludovic pulled from the crate the two volumes of the *Life of Byron* ordered on his behalf.

'You will have some delightful evenings in company with these, Mr Isaac,' Ludo had said.

'Indeed. And several more volumes are expected next year. I have looked out the poems, that I might read them in tandem with their place in the *Life*. My atlas is out on the table there, marked at Missolonghi. And there by the lamp the journal of my own journeys through Germany and the Swiss Cantons to Italy. I was barely twenty! Can you imagine, Ludovic?'

'I think I can picture it. I daresay you cut quite a dash through the continent.'

Mr Fordyce had felt a sudden warmth in his breast. 'Oh, I was not without my adventures, though nothing to rival those of the noble lord, of course.'

The young bank clerk had blushed. 'I doubt the noble lord would have passed muster as a respectable bachelor of Cromarty.'

'No,' Mr Fordyce had said, 'perhaps not.'

After Ludovic had gone, the old man opened the first

volume of the *Life* and began to read the author's introduction, but he found that his mind, determined to glance instead over his shoulder, would not stay on the page in front of him. He laid the book aside and took up in its place a volume of the *Poems*, but did not open it. Memory pulled at him. 'I would recall a vision that I dreamed,' he murmured. Neustadt, 1778. Gunther. Mr Fordyce closed his eyes as the bell of the courthouse clock chimed the hour and the light in the library began to fade.

SIX

Late October

Anne of Geierstein

'Poor Sir Walter.'

Alasdair looked up from buttering a bannock. 'Is there bad news?'

Rachel made a face. 'Really, Alasdair, what news would I have of Sir Walter Scott, sitting here at our breakfast table, that you would not have told me first from your reading of the newspapers in Mrs Cameron's coffee room? No, it's here, in his new introduction to this novel.'

Alasdair glanced over. '*Anne of Geierstein*. Has he said something about the Swiss cantons, in light of recent events?'

'Recent events? The story is set in the fifteenth century.'

'And says much to the upheavals of our own. At least to begin with. The plot wanders somewhat, if I recall.'

'Oh.' Rachel was disappointed. 'I would have picked something else for the library, had I known you'd read it.' Her choice of book had been made at a special tea at Rose Lodge, after a meeting of the Friendly Society, of which all ladies of any standing in Cromarty were members. It had been clear that Rachel's former employer, Mrs Hossack, was *not* pleased that Rachel, as minister's wife, had been invited to join the most select group of ladies in the library, while she, wife of the owner of the ropeworks and mother of the illustrious Fachie, had not.

Alasdair attempted an endearing grimace, by way of apology. 'It was when I was down in Edinburgh last year, for the General Assembly. There was a copy in Mrs Mackintosh's boarding house. But why "Poor Sir Walter"?'

Rachel indicated the open book. 'Because he must begin this new edition with an apology over some minuscule fact of history that he has unwittingly got wrong. The apology, and the detail of the error, go on for many pages.'

Alasdair wiped his fingers on his napkin and reached out a hand to take the volume, but she held it back a little. 'Recall the library rules, Alasdair. If you get crumbs or butter smears on it, there will be plenty to be said by Miss Elspeth, and you'll find yourself on the stool of repentance for a month. You may be sure I will give you up to her at the first suggestion that I am to blame.'

He gave his fingers an extra wipe and murmured, 'I would expect nothing less.' When she relinquished the book to him, he cast an eye over the new introduction and the smile on his face grew. 'I think, my dear, you will find that Sir Walter, in his own gentle way, is making fun of the pedants.' He turned more of the pages, and Rachel could see the adventure come alive in his eyes. He reached for another bannock and examined it. 'Mrs Cramond is back from visiting her sister, I see.'

'And what do you mean by that?'

He gave a genuine grimace now. 'Well, it is just my dinner was late last night. And the meat a mite . . . crispy.'

Rachel bristled. 'You know fine she got back late from Rosemarkie, and I had to see to the dinner myself. A wee bit of burnt mutton will hardly kill you.'

'Just as well,' he muttered.

'If you'd wanted a wife who could cook,' she said, affecting offence, 'you should have married one.' This at least was one accomplishment which her predecessor could not have claimed: as Mrs Cramond had confidentially told her, the first Mrs Mackay had been a stranger to work in any form.

'You are right,' he said. 'Would she have had me, I should certainly have married Mrs Cramond.' Then he looked at the book again. 'It is beautifully done though. You pass it to Charlotte, do you not?'

'Yes.' Rachel took a sip of her chocolate, 'and she is to pass hers to Dr Fraser.'

'Indeed? Well, it will do Charlotte no harm to find herself under Micah's scrutiny once in the month.'

'You don't think Charlotte is under enough scrutiny already, with Morag Mackenzie looming from the shadows at every turn?'

'Morag is just protective of William.' Then he cleared his throat, patently reluctant to say what he was about to say. 'As to Micah – for all his bluster, you know he has a heart as big as himself. His guidance will be animated only by what is for Charlotte's own good. He may be a little forthright for some tastes, a little too rooted in the people to be a natural choice for the dinner table at Cromarty House, but it will do Charlotte no harm at all to come more often into his society.'

'I thought this was supposed to be about the books?'

Her husband reached for the jam. 'This is Cromarty, Rachel. It was never going to be just about the books. And, well, Micah might find it easier to speak frankly to Charlotte regarding her conduct of late than I could, as your husband and William's friend.'

'Conduct?'

'Come, Rachel. You must have noticed she has hardly been out of Charles Munro's company since we were all up at Cromarty House to dinner the other week. The major is a decent man, but you must urge her to caution.'

Rachel opened her mouth to challenge him but stopped. Of course he was right. Charlotte had been lit by a new light since that moment across the dining table when she and Munro had somehow, through the carelessness of fate or the design of some malevolent spirit, discovered one another.

'Micah will only speak to her if he has to. He understands people better than I do.' He glanced at her, uncharacteristically hesitant. 'It was him I went to, when I found myself falling in love with you.'

Rachel was startled. 'I didn't know you had had to go to anyone at all.'

He gestured to himself, at the obviousness of it. 'I was a man of the cloth, almost forty, and you a young woman of barely twenty. I had to be certain that it was not just . . .'

She stared at him, indignation building. 'Not just what, Alasdair? Lust?'

'Lust? God forgive me, Rachel, but how could there not be – I am a man, am I not? But I loved you then for all the other reasons I love you now. I had to be certain though, that our union would be right for you, that I was not just blinded by my own desires. That I was not taking advantage of your youth, your position in the world. Who else could I have talked to – Sanders Gilfeather, whose son you should have married, had he not been blown to bits by Bonaparte's guns in the mud of Flanders?'

She dropped her cup, spilling her chocolate onto the tablecloth.

He pushed back his chair and came over to her. 'Oh, dear God. Rachel, I'm sorry. I should not have spoken like that.'

She didn't lift her head. 'I cannot . . . I have spent sixteen years trying to force that image from my mind. Trying not to think of him that way. And now . . .'

He crouched over her, his arms round her, murmuring into her hair, 'I know, Rachel. I am sorry. I am sorry.'

Rachel sat on the window seat of Charlotte's bedchamber, looking out over the lawns of Cromarty House, down to the town and the sea beyond as Charlotte smoothed a hand over her hair as she had so often done when they were girls. At her feet, unattended, was the basket containing *Anne of Geierstein*.

'Alasdair would never want to hurt you, you know. He will be in an agony just now,' said Charlotte.

'I know.' Rachel had spoken to no one but Charlotte of the black dog of depression that stalked her husband from time to time, the times she had had to hold him in the night as some unnameable despair threatened to overwhelm him. She feared that the black dog might find him, alone, down in the manse this morning, but when the wound of Alexander's death was ripped open in her, it was only with Charlotte that she could find healing. 'I will just have to leave him to it.'

'Then that is what we will do,' said Charlotte with decision. 'Come.'

Rachel wiped a hand across her eyes and sniffed. 'Where to? Where are we going?'

Charlotte pointed beyond the window and the walls of the grounds, towards a place not quite obscured by the pines and birches enclosed within its railings. 'There,' she said.

It didn't take long, going out by the tradesmen's tunnel, before they were at the old burial ground of St Regulus, where the ancient lairds of Cromarty had been laid to their tumultuous rest, before their line had come to grief and the better sort of townsfolk had begun to move their dead in. There were stories of pirate burials, and feuds amongst the dead who lay beneath great slabs carved with *memento mori* designed not to comfort the living, but to warn them. It had been a favourite haunt of Alexander Gilfeather who, as a child, had revelled in those stories. He did not lie there – there had been nothing of him to send home but a bloodied cap and the praises and condolences of his commanding officer. It was here, rather than the confines of the parish kirkyard in the middle of the town, that the Gilfeathers had chosen to erect a simple memorial stone to their only child, over ground in which they themselves would one day lie.

In Charlotte's basket were a dozen white roses, cut from the second flush of blooms in her rose garden. They laid them at the foot of the headstone next to the wall nearest the sea. 'He is here, Rachel. You know it. Not on some foreign battlefield. All that Alexander was is here, his essence is in the breeze. Wherever his bones might lie, he never really left you, or his parents.' She gave her hand a squeeze before retreating to the gate. 'His spirit has never left this place.'

Rachel stood there a long time, summoning her memories of Alexander, his smile, his eyes, the sound of his voice. The scent of him. There came on her too, unbidden, the memory of that disbelief that he could have left her living whilst he himself was gone. She had thought she would never get past it, and indeed hadn't got past it, until Alasdair. The shock and the guilt of it had sent her to Mrs Gilfeather's kitchen, where there had been comfort, and love, and absolution. How could she blame Alasdair if, for his own, different reasons, he too had sought the assurance of a friend before he had declared himself to her? She touched her fingers to her lips, and then to Alexander's stone, then went to join Charlotte where she waited in the gateway.

'Is all well?'

'All is well,' she said.

'Do you want to go back to Alasdair now?'

'He won't be ready to see me yet.'

'Well then,' said Charlotte, 'we are members of the library, are we not? We shall go and take our coffee in Mrs Cameron's reading room, and you can give me my book and we will talk of great matters, as the gentlemen do.'

As the door of the reading room closed behind Hester who had just brought them a pot of coffee, Charlotte relaxed back into her armchair and sighed. 'I wish Hester would not be so ill-at-ease with me, but I don't know how to make it better.'

'I don't think there is anything you or she can do about it, Charlotte. It's not your fault that William took her back here, instead of leaving her in Demerara where, if I understand aright from Miss Juniper, her mother is still alive.'

'Well, you know more than I do. William will not discuss her with me, and I have given up asking him. It's hardly the girl's fault either. I doubt that she or her mother had much say in the matter, and it all happened long before I ever knew him.'

'It's a strange thing, though, to bring her back to Cromarty, and never publicly acknowledge her, when so many others do. I mean, there are those two boys in the school and—'

'I know,' interrupted Charlotte. 'But William will not even acknowledge her privately to me, although Morag Mackenzie likes it to be understood that she is privy to all his doings. She thinks it a judgement on *me* that a slave-woman could give William a child and I cannot. She has made it clear to me that it is my barrenness rather than his past conduct that is to be censured.'

There was silence between them for a moment. Rachel thought she might bear her own lack of a child better if Charlotte had one, for her to love, but fate had been cruel to them both.

'She's a wicked woman,' said Rachel at last. 'But I think you carry her censure more lightly now.'

Charlotte grinned. 'I have quite thrown it off altogether. I daresay it will be there waiting for me, should I feel the need to take it up again.'

'I hope you will not.'

'What?'

Rachel lowered her voice. 'Feel that you must take up her censure again.'

Charlotte put down her china coffee cup. 'You mean you hope I will not merit it? You are talking about Charles . . .? But what can there be to censure? His coming to Cromarty has *saved* me. He has taken me out of – myself. I had been too much inside, the house and myself. I had made the house my prison and come to hate Cromarty and almost everyone in it.' At the 'almost' she leaned across and took Rachel's hand. 'But Charles has *seen* the world and talks of what he has seen. He has no interest in empty things like fashion or commerce or politics. With him I feel I am understood rather than simply looked upon or expected to be entertained.'

'Charlotte, you must be careful . . .'

'If I had not . . . come to know him when I did, I had begun to have thoughts . . .'

Rachel stared at her. 'Of what? You did not think of harming yourself?'

'No, no. Of course not. But there was a point, a temptation – a momentary, animal temptation that would have destroyed me. Destroyed everything.'

Rachel was assailed by dread. 'Charlotte, what happened?'

'Nothing, thank God. And it will not. Charles's coming has saved me.'

After a long silence Rachel said, 'I think, if you are not careful of yourself, you must be careful of him, of his feelings.'

Charlotte looked down at her own hands and spoke very quietly. 'He is too much a man of honour even to *have* feelings for me.'

Rachel shook her head. 'He is too honourable to do anything about them, but the man is in agony every time he looks at you. Perhaps others have not seen it yet, because when you are in a room, everyone is looking at you. But they will see it, you know that. You must be careful.'

'I will never do anything to cause him harm, nor to dishonour William.' Then Charlotte straightened her shoulders. 'But had we not better see to these books? I forget what you were to bring me.'

Rachel lifted the book from her basket.

'*Anne of Geierstein*. Oh, yes. Not one of Sir Walter's best.'

'You've read it too?'

'While we were in Hampshire. William's sister had it in her library. You know, we really have no need to be members of our little Cromarty Library, but William could hardly refuse, once Elspeth Rose proposed it.'

And now they had ventured onto a subject they had barely touched upon before. 'It astonishes me to think that they were once sweethearts,' said Rachel.

'I think he regrets ever telling me. He becomes ill-at-ease if ever I allude to it and says that they were very young.'

'Poor Elspeth. She must have had hopes he would marry her when he came out of the army, and instead he went to the West Indies and left her behind.'

'Yes, he did,' said Charlotte. 'More's the pity.' She picked up the book again and Rachel saw an effort to make her eyes brighten. 'But this is a particularly lovely edition.'

Rachel lowered her voice. 'Mr Fordyce paid his cousin extra, to have the one with those illustrations. He says the image of Anne puts him in mind of you.'

Charlotte's eyes lit up. 'The dear old fellow. Perhaps he is right, you know, for Sir Walter, once having put her in the book, does not appear to be long in realising he doesn't know what to do with her. In one passage he almost suggests she is a ghost. Perhaps I am a ghost of myself, living amongst you.'

Rachel pinched Charlotte's arm, making her yelp. 'See, you are no more ghost than I am, but I should certainly warn Miss Juniper to be circumspect in what she reads to the girls. Mairead's imagination is worryingly suggestible.'

'Mairead? But she looks like she has no imagination at all. She will never make a heroine.'

Rachel set *Anne of Geierstein* and her ghosts back on the table. 'Heroines are of little use to anybody, and we have more than enough of them as it is, when even Sir Walter doesn't know what to do with them.'

Just then they caught the sound of familiar voices coming in from the street. Rachel watched Charlotte's face carefully, but saw in it only anticipation, no hint of anxiety. And then Hester, eyes lowered more than ever, was opening the coffee room door and Sir William and Major Charles Munro were walking through it.

Sir William clapped his hands with pleasure on seeing them, and the major, Rachel could see, attempted to notice her as much as he did Charlotte. The attempt was a dismal failure – some spark had travelled from Charlotte to bring every hidden aspect of Charles Munro's being to life. William, thank God, was oblivious.

'So you are here, the two of you. I can scarcely keep track, such bluestockings that you are! I called at the manse, but did not find you there.'

'No, William, for as you must clearly see, we are here.'

William Mackenzie beamed at his wife. Rachel knew he did not understand *why* Charlotte was happy again after so long and impenetrable a period of being closed off to him and to the world. She knew also that he did not care to know. 'Indeed, you are here,' he said and, with a glance towards the wall clock, added, 'and what Mr Gilfeather will have to say if you are still sitting in his chair a quarter of an hour from now, I would not like to anticipate.'

'Well, he will not find me,' said Rachel, hastening to get up. 'I am expected at Fordyce House at eleven, to have my next book from Mr Isaac.'

Charles Munro gave a hesitant smile, that she had never seen from him before, and that took ten years off him. 'The whole of Cromarty is in a whirl today, it seems, with the passing of books.'

Rachel raised her eyebrows. 'No one wishes to fall foul of Miss Elspeth Rose by disarranging the order laid down. We shall all be quite dizzy by dinnertime. You had a narrow escape, Major, when you declined to join in our cavalcade.'

'Not so!' declared Sir William. 'I have got the fellow by the gills and reeled him in.'

'Oh?' Charlotte only just stopped herself from putting a hand on the major's arm. 'Have you joined us, Charles?'

The major affected a grimace. 'No, your ladyship. Your husband has not so much reeled me in as entangled me completely in his net.'

Charlotte's eyes danced in curiosity from Munro's face to

her husband's. 'William, what trick have you played upon the poor major?'

Sir William bared his teeth like a naughty schoolboy preparing to tell his secret. 'I have persuaded him to accompany you to Resolis today in my stead. I know you will not mind, my dear. *I* am not next to Dr Fraser in the library list and I really don't see why *I* should have to endure his sermons and lectures over the dinner table when it is *you* that is to pass him your book. I happened to encounter him at the inn at Balblair just last week, and the ferry had been across the firth and back before he had finished on the clearance of Strathnaver, as if it hadn't been near twenty years ago and was anything to do with me in the first place.'

'William!' laughed Charlotte. 'That is the third time I have heard you tell that story, and it grows legs every time.'

'Well might it, but Charles here has only heard it once and has agreed on the strength of it to escort you to the Manse of Resolis in my stead, and being a gentleman, he cannot now go back on his word, no matter how far you might provoke him.'

Charlotte again looked to the major whose grey eyes were gazing on her with such longing it was astonishing her husband didn't see it. 'Then I shall study not to provoke him,' she said.

SEVEN

Boswell

Hurrying down the steps of the bank, a leather case of documents under his arm, Ludo was surprised to almost bump into John Learmonth.

'Why are you not in your classroom?'

'I am summoned to Resolis,' answered John, 'to be put upon the rack by Dr Fraser who was unconvinced by the vehemence with which I catechised the children at his last inspection. I have arranged that John Edwards should teach the children something of the geography of Berbice and Demerara in my absence. Then they will have a half-day's holiday, sanctioned by the Kirk session, most of whom live in as much fear of Dr Fraser as do the rest of us.'

'And who can blame them?' agreed Ludo. 'And he is not even *our* minister. I am bound to Resolis today too, once I have finished my business at Cromarty House.'

John's face brightened. 'We will brave him together! You

can collect me at Kirkmichael – I plan to stop there on the way.'

'But Kirkmichael is not *on* the way,' protested Ludovic. 'And I have actual business to attend to today, that does not involve wandering around kirkyards, trying not to step on my ancestors.'

'Oh, it's as near as makes no difference,' said John. 'Besides, Sir William might not be at home. I saw Lady Charlotte and Mrs Mackay going into the hotel a little earlier. Perhaps they were calling on your mother. She is rather pretty, don't you think?'

Ludo stared. 'My mother?'

'No. Well, of course, your mother is an extremely fine-looking woman and I've no doubt she was . . .'

Understanding dawned and Ludo experienced a sensation of alarm rather than relief. John was talking not of his mother, nor of Lady Charlotte, but of Rachel Mackay. No one would call Lady Charlotte 'rather pretty'. It would be like calling the ocean 'rather damp'. Lady Charlotte was a being of breathtaking beauty who would have set battalions of Greek and Roman deities at war with one another. As for Rachel Mackay, the minister's wife, while unlikely to provoke epic poetry or sculptures in marble, she was indeed pretty. Her eyes brought her features to life and her smile was engaging, encompassing the beneficiary in its warmth.

Ludo murmured a reluctant, 'Oh, yes. I suppose, quite,' and resolved that at a more private opportunity he would advise his friend that it was unwise for a schoolmaster to be expressing any such opinion on his minister's wife. For now though, he must get to Cromarty House. Mindful of the dignity of the bank, he went by way of the top gate and the driveway, eschewing the shorter route through the kitchen garden, so familiar to him from childhood days of hiding amongst the cabbages and onions from a marauding Fachie Hossack.

Sir William smiled broadly when Ludo was shown into his study. 'Ludovic! I am just sat down – I'd swear Mr Gilfeather knows when I have the ledgers out and worries that I will try to add the columns up myself.'

Ludo never knew how to comport himself with the laird and his misplaced attempts at familiarity. It was as if Sir William blamed himself for the fact that Ludo's father had gone to the Caribbean to oversee the Mackenzie plantation and eventually died there, without ever displaying the slightest intention of coming home. 'The best thing he ever did for you or me,' his mother had told him once, and not a single soul in Cromarty had ever said anything to him about his father to suggest she might have been wrong in her assessment. It was not Ludo's place to assure Sir William of this, though. Instead, he cleared his throat and gestured towards the ledgers.

'If I can be of any assistance with the arithmetic . . .' he began.

Sir William sighed. 'If only it were a matter of arithmetic. But look, see here . . .'

Ludo bent his head to the columns. They were headed by names familiar to him – places close to home and yet also thousands of miles away, across the Atlantic. Plantations in Berbice and Demerara named by Sir William's and other families to recall the villages and estates on the Black Isle and Easter Ross that their owners and overseers had come from. 'It is all well and good for the abolitionists to speak of emancipation, but it is a question of property. How am I to be compensated?'

'Compensated, Sir William?'

'For the loss of my property. Look.' He pointed again at the columns. 'Each figure here – man, woman or child – represents a unit. How much am I to be paid per unit? Is a slave in Berbice worth as much in the eyes of the abolitionists as one in Demerara? For I tell you, and you may say you have heard this from my own lips, they are not worth the same to me.'

As Ludo searched for some reply, Sir William carried on. 'It's a simple matter of economics, of the value of what each unit will produce.'

'Like the sheep,' said Ludo, his mouth articulating what his head told him, too late, was better kept quiet.

'Exactly,' said Sir William. 'For a Cheviot sheep is worth more to the Countess of Sutherland than the old Blackface. It will produce more wool and of a higher quality from the same ground. By the same token, a slave working on a tobacco farm in Virginia is not the same as one working at sugar cane in Berbice. One is much more valuable than the other, because of the comparative weight and prices of the commodity produced. Do you see?'

Ludo could only attempt a nod.

'And then there is the question of whether the slaves wish to be emancipated at all.' Sir William pushed the ledger aside. 'I tell you, Ludovic, there's hardly a gentleman hereabouts will be able to arrange his affairs properly until the thing is settled. Yet all we hear of from Lords and Commons is the Reform Bill. But you have not come here to talk to me of politics, I think.'

With relief, Ludo lifted a sheaf of papers from his satchel. 'Mr Gilfeather has sent me up with these rent deposit receipts for you to sign, Sir William. Also,' he added, after Sir William had signed the receipts, 'my mother asked that I bring this up for you. As I was coming anyway.' He laid on the table the copy of *Cyril Thornton* that had been his mother's original choice for the circulating library.

'Ah,' said Sir William. 'Did she enjoy it?'

'In parts, I believe. Although . . .' Ludo cleared his throat, 'she became rather exercised over the matter of Thornton's sister, and the brute she was married to.'

Sir William was clearly no keener than was Ludo to interrogate Janet Cameron's thoughts on brute husbands, 'Ah well. Yes. But here I have *your* next book. Boswell's *Life of Johnson*. It runs to eight volumes, so I shall have them sent down to the hotel, to spare you the trouble of carrying them back on foot.'

'Eight volumes,' echoed Ludo, unable to keep a hint of despair from his voice. 'Mr Croker's edition has had a hot time of it in the reviews.'

'Poor fellow,' responded Sir William. 'And he himself, being against the Reform, an even worse time of it in the House. Might as well condemn the flavour of a potato because you don't like the politics of the fellow that grew it.'

'I believe though,' said Ludo, emboldened by discussions in James Craig's parlour, 'that some of the objection to Mr Croker's edition is to his interweaving of the work of others into what Boswell wrote.' The view of the clockmaker's *salon* on this particular matter had been unequivocal: writers of minor talent should steer clear of interfering with the creations of their betters.

'Nonetheless,' said Sir William, 'I doubt anyone could disapprove Croker's inclusion in it of the *Journal of a Tour to the Hebrides*.'

Certainly, Ludo would not. Having ventured one opinion in opposition to the laird's, he was not about to venture another.

'Imagine, Ludovic, to have lived such a life that within fifty years of your death, your biography should run to eleven editions?'

'I can hardly imagine that mine would offer material sufficient for one,' responded Ludo somewhat gloomily.

The older man leaned forward. 'But it *will*, Ludovic. I am certain of it. There is a wider world than Cromarty. And we must get you away into it. If this damned business of the abolitionists would only be settled, I could make arrangements.'

'I would not go,' began Ludo, summoning his courage,

'to the plantations, I mean. When I leave Scotland, it will be for the northern states. Boston, or even New York.' He glanced away. 'I mean no ingratitude.'

Rather than taking offence, Sir William seemed pleased. 'Then you have learned from our mistakes already, for no one returns from the plantations a better man than he went. You have something of your mother's steel in you, Ludovic, and that will see you through whatever may come your way.' He picked up the first volume of the *Life of Johnson*. 'There is value in being a man who poses no one any threat and so is not taken seriously. I do not suggest you should be another James Boswell, but allow yourself to be Ludo, and know that for your friends, the Ludo you are is enough.'

With a lightened heart and forgetting that he was the embodiment of the dignity of the Caledonian bank, Ludo went across the lawns and back down into town by way of the kitchen garden, breathing in scents of a few late roses and crushing between his fingers forgotten spikes of lavender from the summer past, not noticing the onions and cabbages at all.

Some two hours later, at Kirkmichael, John Learmonth watched his friend's awkward progress between the gravestones. 'To look at you, Ludo, you would think that you had never been out of the town.'

Ludovic was supporting himself on an upright headstone, examining the damage after his foot had sunk into a deep clump of moss. 'My shoes and stockings are soaked.' He hopped to the dry kerb in front of the old church and glowered at John.

'You should have dressed more sensibly. Mrs Cameron will scald your ears for you when you go home with your good breeks covered in dubs.'

Ludo was indignant. 'It is only at *your* suggestion that I am here.' Then a happy thought struck him. 'Perhaps you could tell Dr Fraser that the pony threw me, and I had to go home to—'

But John put up a hand. 'Oh, no, you're not leaving me to be interrogated by Micah Fraser on my own.'

Ludo pouted. 'The last time I was there, I was hardly through the door before he was quizzing me about what I intend to do with my life, and what you, Stanislas and every other poor soul in the town of Cromarty to have taken his notice, were up to. You had better be ready to give a good account of yourself.'

John looked at him a moment then began to make his way across the boggy churchyard. 'If you would just assist me in holding the paper over that slab there, I will get a rubbing done quick as you like and then we can be gone.'

The sartorial damage already done, Ludo made no further argument. When they were at last going back out through the kirkyard gate, a gust of wind caught the dead bell of the ruined church and set it to a mournful fading toll. Ludo shivered. 'I can't think why you insist on spending so much time here.'

'The ancient graves fascinate me,' said John. 'The names

fading away until time and the elements render them unknowable, so that those who lie beneath may truly sleep in peace.'

Ludo frowned. 'In peace? Oh no, John. I don't think so. Don't you know that this place is cursed?'

EIGHT

The Manse of Resolis

'It cannot be that day already. It seems not half an hour since you last staged an invasion.'

'It's been a good fortnight, Dr Fraser, as well you know!' Mrs Swanson, housekeeper to the Reverend Dr Micah Fraser, minister of Resolis, and to his father before him, brandished her feather duster in a manner that brooked no further argument.

The minister, nonetheless, was not keen to shift. 'Surely you have enough to be getting on with today, without bothering yourself about my study?'

'Exactly that,' agreed the good lady. 'The dinner to be seen to, and the parlour and dining room to be put in readiness, and Teenie Ross about as much use as a horse with two heads!'

The defects of the manse housemaid were a favourite and well-rehearsed subject of Mrs Swanson's, and Dr Fraser would have to admit that the young woman seemed to be remarkably clumsy and slow.

'Aye, but Bella,' he said, lapsing into the familiarity of forty years, 'what else is to be done with her? I doubt the lassie's much use for anything else.'

Mrs Swanson pursed her lips and considered. 'Well, she has a way with the cow and the hens,' she conceded, 'and can peel a tattie and pull a neep well enough, but she's a never-ending trial in the house. And I'm not getting any younger.'

The minister looked on the kindly face he seemed to have known his whole life. 'You're still the same Bella you've always been to me,' he said.

'Hmmph! The Bella that wiped your nose and cleaned your scraped knees forty years since had younger bones and knew nothing of the rheumatics.'

'But I can't sack Teenie, you know.'

'I'm not asking you to, but we're needing another maid. Once the winter's past you'll need to see to it. If I could get back over to Sutherland a while, get a lassie from amongst my own folk . . .'

'That would certainly be best,' agreed the minister. They both knew Mrs Swanson would not go back to Sutherland to pick a promising young girl from amongst her kinsfolk because Mrs Swanson's home was charcoal and rubble, the rooms grazed by sheep, and her kinsfolk scattered to the four corners of the earth, to try for a living they were no longer permitted to attempt at home. Micah took hold of the old woman's hand and patted it. 'When next I am down in Edinburgh, I will consult with Mrs Mackintosh at the boarding house, and she will find a girl to send up fit to dust the finest manse in Scotland. Will you manage a few months till then, Bella, you and Teenie?'

Mrs Swanson bit her lip and dabbed away the tear that had come into her eye. 'Yes, minister. Thank you. We will.' Then she sniffed. 'But you will get out of my road for half an hour till I get this study put right. If Lady Charlotte should chance to look in here and go back to Cromarty House and tell Morag Mackenzie the state it's in, I'll not be answerable!'

Dr Fraser admitted defeat and, collecting his hat and stick from the front door, he set out. He had forgotten, if truth be told, that it was today that Lady Charlotte was to come, to take her dinner with him and pass on her book. He would not have asked the schoolmaster Learmonth over on the same day if he had remembered, and Sanders Gilfeather had spoken of sending Janet Cameron's boy over with papers for him to sign too. Little wonder Bella was out of humour, with such a crowd to see to.

As he stepped out, he reminded himself that a good walk on a fine day was beneficial to his health. It was, he knew, the real reason his housekeeper so regularly insisted on fussing him out of his study, allegedly that she might get her dusting done. Should he choose to remonstrate, Mrs Swanson's tone would become grave and he would be reminded that it had been 'Mrs Fraser's wish'. Mrs Fraser's wish that he did not set his face to the wall and never look at the light again; Mrs Fraser's wish that he did not collapse into his chair and never get up again; Mrs Fraser's wish that he should live one day and then another and then another until he forgot that all he wanted to do was stop breathing and be laid beneath the turf with her and their newborn child, that had lived a day and a night, before departing this world with its mother. Sixteen years since she had died, and those last wishes of his wife were still the only thing that got him out of the bed in the morning.

As he struck out up the brae of his parish, a cold wind coming down from the Arctic battered the tails of his coat, but the sun was shining. He looked back towards the town of Cromarty, eight miles away, across Udale Bay. It almost sparkled against the clear blue of the sky. And there, too, was the hulk of the last of the emigrant ships for this year, the wind still blowing the wrong way, keeping it in home waters for as long as it could. Best be away and done with, he thought. Be away and forget that they had ever had a home, that they had ever heard the gospel in his father's church in the Strath of Kildonan, that the thatch of their houses was burned and their empty rooms now grazed by the Countess of Sutherland's sheep.

Micah Fraser could feel the years of bitterness rising in him and tried to make himself think of something else – the library, for instance. But that summoned the memory of that devil Farquhar Hossack, baiting him with the claims of science over Gospel truth. The very thought of the fellow put a clench in Dr Fraser's stomach – had done ever since he'd had to pull a half-drowned nine-year-old Ludovic Cameron from the shore mill pool after a grinning Fachie Hossack had held him head down in it. Dr Fraser would never be convinced that Fachie would have stopped of his own accord. He'd told Willie Hossack straight to send the child away from Cromarty before he killed someone, but Hossack's wife would have none of it, and the man could not gainsay her.

He carried with him today the book of poems by Reginald Heber that he had ordered for the library. Had Dr Fraser happened to meet the late Bishop of Calcutta he would have shared a thought or two on some of the blasphemous nonsense of the English Church, but there were verses amongst it that affected him greatly. He lengthened his stride and descended the brae to Cullicudden, where that lovely girl and his bonny baby lay buried, and where he might sit with none but the birds of the air to attend him while he read the comforting words of Heber's 'Innocents' Day' over their tomb.

Returned from his walk ready to welcome his guests, Dr Fraser had found Lady Charlotte and Major Munro already arrived. He had merely cocked an eyebrow at the appearance of the major in place of Sir William, and bid them most welcome.

'And did you see anything at all of Ludo Cameron or the schoolmaster on the road?' he asked them.

'We met them just coming down from Kirkmichael,' said Lady Charlotte.

'Hmmph,' responded Dr Fraser. 'Blundering about, disturbing the dead. They'll be lucky not to bring the curse down on themselves.'

'Do you believe in it, Doctor? That the souls of the wicked can find sanctuary at Kirkmichael, if only they can reach it before midnight, but that otherwise they are condemned to wander the earth in eternal darkness?'

Dr Fraser wasted no time in considering this. 'There is no sanctuary for the wicked,' he said. Just then came the sound of footsteps crunching down the path to the manse door, followed moments later by the appearance in the parlour of Ludo Cameron and John Learmonth.

Charlotte had not seen the schoolmaster at such close quarters since that day at the graveyard and she found herself stepping back slightly, putting Charles Munro between herself and the newcomers. But then Dr Fraser was discoursing on the state of Ludovic's feet and trousers, and speculating as to what Mr Gilfeather might have to say about the condition his clerk was going about in. And then they were all being ushered through to the manse dining room, all thought of curses and lost souls forgotten.

Dr Fraser was not a man keen on rich or foreign food, and his cook a woman to whom such things spoke of immorality. French sauces and mulligatawnies, therefore, such as might grace the table of Mr Isaac Fordyce, or even the Hossacks, were not to be looked for on the dinner table at Resolis. And so the party sat down to kale brose and a good veal pie, cabbage and mashed turnips, a rice pudding with soft fruit and cinnamon – a permitted indulgence – and ewe's cheese with apple puffs.

John Learmonth, whose lodgings were modest and the highlight of whose weekly diet was the stroganoff made by Stanislas, had not eaten so well since he had left Edinburgh, and made the mistake of saying so.

Dr Fraser was instantly alert. 'Indeed, Mr Learmonth? Your landlady in Edinburgh was of a more refined bent than the honest widow of a Cromarty skipper?'

John's eyes darted from one side of the table to the other and then back again. Ludo was bemused to see his friend discomfited by so innocuous a question. 'No, not at all – although she was a highly respectable woman.'

Dr Fraser cocked an interested eyebrow. 'They were decent lodgings you had in Edinburgh, then? You would not complain of them?'

'No, not in the least,' stammered John.

Dr Fraser slapped his knees, making the others around the table jump. 'Excellent! I have been using the same lodging house in Edinburgh for nearly twenty years, and while I would never complain of Mrs Mackintosh's arrangements, I am heartily sick of sharing the board with other ministers. Now, your old landlady, Mrs . . .?'

'Gavin,' said John, after a moment.

'Mrs Gavin does not take in many ministers, I hope?'

'Not as I recall,' managed the schoolmaster.

'Splendid,' said Dr Fraser. 'And where might she reside?'

'In a close off the Canongate, but . . .'

There were to be no 'buts'. Dr Fraser was not satisfied until he had the name of the particular close. Only then had he turned his attention back to his other guests.

Later, as they were the walking up the brae away from the manse, Ludo said, 'I do wonder if the old fellow might be beginning to wander in his mind.'

'Old?' said John. 'He looks barely fifty to me, and strong as an ox.'

'Well, yes, but perhaps having your head in bibles and sermons and other people's business for more than half your life might expose a man's mind to wandering. Certainly, it is the easiest time of it I have ever had from him. It was as if he hardly noticed I was there, such was his interest in securing the details of your Edinburgh lodgings for himself. His interest seemed to increase the more you were bothered by it, although I cannot think why you should have been.'

'Why would a man speak of old lodgings?' replied John, tersely. 'But, what do you think of the major? It seems a little strange that Sir William Mackenzie should allow another man to squire his wife around the countryside like that.'

'Oh,' said Ludo, 'but everyone *knows* Lady Charlotte, and she really has no interest in anything. Besides, Sir William has business to be getting on with and his affairs in the Caribbean to be seeing to, and has to think about the next election, and which of his second cousins shall have his vote. He hardly has the time to go trailing round the countryside, entertaining his wife and subjecting himself to the attentions of Dr Fraser.' He plodded on, unconcernedly.

'But surely a married woman and a bachelor . . .'

Ludo stopped and faced his friend. 'You really have not got the hang of things here yet, have you? Lady Charlotte is Sir William's *wife*. She was the daughter of a respectable Inverness draper and now she is the wife of a gentleman of significant means and unquestionable standing in the county. Did you not hear her yourself, speak of their house in Edinburgh? And I imagine the rest of her conversation at the table would be enough to convince you that she is not a fool. And Major Munro is above suspicion.'

'Because he is so scarred?'

'Scarred? Because he is a *gentleman* – his family own most of the parts of Ross-Shire that the Mackenzies do not. And what's more, he has a valorous name from his army service.' Ludo shook his head at how much his friend still had to learn about Highland society. 'And to be frank,' he continued, 'were he not escorting Lady Charlotte on Sir William's behalf, he might find himself expected to escort *others* in the town of a much less pleasing countenance and disposition. Sir William need hardly concern himself over Major Munro.'

John was not satisfied. 'Did you not see the way he looked at her though? I am certain Dr Fraser did.'

'Don't be ridiculous. Had Dr Fraser noticed any such thing, we should all have heard about it, there at the table. But that was an uncommonly good veal flory, was it not? And the rice pudding, too, uncommonly good.'

'Yes,' said John, quickening his pace. 'Uncommonly good.'

And then the moment was lost, Ludo realised, when he

might deftly have shifted the conversation from the propriety of Major Munro's escorting of Lady Charlotte to the inadvisability of an unmarried schoolmaster expressing an opinion on the prettiness or otherwise of his minister's much younger wife.

The young men having departed with a view to being back in Cromarty before darkness fell, Dr Fraser shifted Lady Charlotte and Major Munro through to his study, where the fire was lit and where he had Teenie bring through the tea while he himself saw to the mixing of punch for himself and the major.

'Well, now,' he said once they were settled and Lady Charlotte had taken over the management of the teapot, 'Bonaparte, is it?' He picked up the first of the three volumes of Bourrienne's *Memoirs of Napoleon* that she had brought to pass on to him. What had been going on in the woman's mind when she had chosen it?

'What were you thinking, I wonder, your ladyship, when you asked for *this* to be ordered for the library on your behalf? I daresay there are other books that might tell you of Josephine's frocks, but perhaps it was not that you were looking for?' He had thrown down his challenge and waited.

'I hope I am not so empty-headed as to care for nothing but dead women's dresses,' she replied. 'I asked for the book that I might better understand how the man could so readily cast aside his wife, as a matter of policy.'

Dr Fraser found himself stumped for a response and was relieved when the major spoke up. 'I would not put too great a faith in what Bourrienne has to say, Charlotte. Those who know him say he is a disappointed man, embittered by the success of one he thought beneath him.'

Dr Fraser registered that 'Charlotte' for later contemplation. 'No doubt you yourself will have seen men promoted to positions of command they had no business holding, Major?'

'Many more times than I would have liked,' conceded Munro, 'but even his greatest enemy could not rank Bonaparte amongst their number.'

'No,' agreed the minister.

'But,' continued Lady Charlotte, 'it is not the hero, but the man, that Bourrienne sets out to portray here.'

Dr Fraser took a deep drink of his punch. 'And so we move from Major Munro's territory onto mine, your ladyship. And what then did you think of the man you found in these pages?'

'I thought we should not have liked each other very much.'

'Well,' said the minister, pleased with this answer and, to his surprise, with Lady Charlotte, 'we shall see if I like the fellow any better.'

They would all have sat together a good bit longer, but the major was conscious of wishing to get Lady Charlotte home to Cromarty House before dark, and even with the gig, they would be needing their time. It was with reluctance that Dr Fraser watched them depart, just as it had been with reluctance that he had passed a hastily penned missive into the major's hand, for delivery to Alasdair Mackay at the manse in Cromarty.

As they sped along past Udale Bay, small lights gradually beginning to glimmer in windows across the water, Charles Munro glanced at Charlotte. 'You are not cold?'

She laid a gloved hand on his arm and drew closer to him. 'I am cold as can be, and happy as can be and alive as can be. I would not exchange this place and this moment for all the firesides in the world.'

Munro smiled, though his eyes, now looking straight ahead, were shot through by a sadness. He felt the softness of her hair brush his jaw, and took in the jasmine scent of her, mingled with the salt of the sea. His hands tightened their grip on the reins, as if he might somehow hold on to the moment, absorb it, relive it long after it was over.

They were within a half mile of the town, and darkness almost fallen when he spoke again. 'Charlotte,' he said gently.

Nothing.

'Charlotte, you must waken. We will soon be there.'

She stirred against his shoulder and gradually came to, rubbing her eyes as she sat up. 'It's almost dark.'

'Yes. I hope William will not mind me having kept you out so late.'

'Oh, William will not even have noticed,' she replied,

arranging her bonnet. 'It is Morag we must look out for, or up for, rather.'

'Up?'

'Yes. A half hour more and she will be out with the bats, on her broomstick.'

Charles did his best to sound disapproving, but the joy of her here beside him, free as he had never seen her anywhere else, took all sensible words away from him. It was so long since he had even sat this close to a woman, or since a woman had looked at him as openly as she did. After a moment he said, 'I shall take you directly to the house and deliver Dr Fraser's letter to Mr Mackay on my way back.'

'You must keep the gig,' she said. 'I will walk down and collect it tomorrow.'

'I will do no such thing and neither will you.'

Charlotte laughed. 'Of course, you are right. The matrons of Cromarty would be falling out of their windows with gossip about it if I did.' Then she opened her reticule, into which he had asked her to put Dr Fraser's letter for safekeeping. 'Mind you, I rather suspect Dr Fraser will have found some fault in my behaviour that he is counselling Alasdair to correct.'

'Impossible,' he said.

'That Alasdair might put right my faults?'

'That you could have any.' Charles Munro geed the horse to a faster trot and darkness enveloped them as they sped back to Cromarty.

NINE

The Friendly Society

Alasdair Mackay picked up letters that had been left on the hall table, only then remembering the one from Micah Fraser at Resolis, delivered last night by Charles Munro. He had invited Munro in, taken a brandy and smoked a pipe with him, and entirely forgotten about his brother minister's letter. Now he saw again Micah's sealed note, buried under other letters, almost forgotten. He was about to go back into his study when he saw Rachel come down the hall, a bonnet in each hand and an expression of irritation on her face.

How happy it made him to see that expression in place of the cold politeness with which they had circled each other yesterday until at last, in the darkness of their bedchamber, he had nuzzled his head into the nape of her neck, through the hair tumbling down her turned back and murmured, 'I am sorry, I am sorry.' Sorry that he had cast up her dead love in so brutal a manner. Sorry that he had then shut himself away, as if he were the victim. His relief when she had reached for his hand and put it on her breast, had been immense. And now, he ventured a witticism.

'Have you lost a companion, or are you setting up a market stall?'

'What?' she said with a hint of annoyance.

'You are wearing your best outdoor shawl and holding two bonnets. I can only imagine you are getting ready to go out, but as you have only the one head, I suppose you have either mislaid a bonnet-less companion or you purpose to sell the one you do not need.'

Rachel huffed out a sigh of annoyance. 'Have you no sermon to write or backsliding parishioner to be visiting? Do I look like I have the time for listening to nonsense?'

He remained in the study doorway, watching her. 'No, my dear, you most certainly do not.'

Rachel made a show of ignoring him. She studied herself in the hall mirror then threw off the first bonnet she had chosen, to replace it with the other. The second bonnet suited her better, but even she could see that it did not go with her shawl. The changing of bonnets and shawls had had a deleterious effect on the hair which she had just repinned as carefully as she could. Alasdair observed all with amusement.

'If I didn't know any better, I might begin to fear I had a rival.'

'A rival?' She let out a small 'tch' as she dropped a pin. 'For what?'

'Your affections, what else?' He crossed the hall and

taking up the discarded bonnet, set it on her head. 'There. This one. This one matches your eyes and the sprigs on the pattern of your gown.'

Rachel looked and saw that it did. She found it not a little irritating that Alasdair should have so much better an idea of what suited her than she herself did. 'And would your rival think so?' she said.

'Undoubtedly,' he said, burying his face in her neck and setting the hairpins once more in peril. 'But I shall best him.'

Rachel looked down towards the kitchen, lest Mrs Cramond or Jane, the housemaid, should suddenly appear. 'How?' she asked, letting him nuzzle her neck a little longer. 'Will you sermonise him?'

'Sermonise him?' He stopped and stood up, looking into the mirror also. 'No, I think I would fight him to the death.'

This time Rachel laughed, but he did not. 'I believe that I would, you know, Rachel. If any other man should threaten to take you from me, I fear I would lose all reason and control. I fear I would kill him.'

She turned to look into his face. 'Alasdair. You must not speak like that. You mustn't even think it. And you will never have a rival for my affections – you must know that.'

He loosened his hold on her and stepped back. Of course he knew it. The only man who might ever have stood between himself and Rachel was long dead. He straightened his neckcloth. 'I know it. But where on earth are you going, that you are getting yourself in such a tizzy?'

'I told you last week. I am to take tea with the other ladies of the Friendly Society, at Marjorie Hossack's.'

Alasdair pulled a face. 'Mrs Hossack? Then I fear I have the better of the bargain today, my dear.'

'What bargain?'

'Willie Hossack was to come here today, to pass on his book from the library, but I see here it has been handed in at the door when we were still at our breakfast – a child from the ropeworks, Mrs Cramond said. From which we are to understand that Willie Hossack is a busy man.' He held out to her the copy of the *Aberdeen Magazine* that had been lying on the hall table with the letters. 'I'd lay a pound to the penny he has not read it, by the way.'

'Hmm.' She took the volume and glanced at the contents page. '"Sir Walter's letters to Mr Lockhart on *Demonology*; A Singular Ghost Story; The Landing of the Danes at Gamrie". We shall have to hope this does not get into the wrong hands.'

'The wrong hands?' he queried, taking the magazine back from her and looking at the contents page himself.

'Some of the younger people are very susceptible to that kind of story. Miss Juniper's Mairead, for instance.'

'Well,' he said, 'given the interdict against poor Miss Juniper joining the library, I think we may hardly fear her pupils falling prey to such light nonsense as the *Aberdeen Magazine* appears to be filled with.'

'I hope not. It is a disgrace that she was not invited to join. She is the best-read woman I know. But as to whether

Willie Hossack has read that publication – I'd say your pounds and your pennies are very safe. The man never had an interest in a thing that was not to do with the making of money, and I never saw a book in his hand the whole time I was in service in that house.'

She finally tied the bow, giving it a sharp tug so it would not come undone, before pulling on her gloves and making for the door. As she passed her husband, who was taking his letter knife to Dr Fraser's missive, she paused to kiss him on the cheek and said, 'I need to know what they are saying, Alasdair.'

The Hossacks lived in a large house fronting the harbour, and beyond it was the hempworks on which their fortune was built. Four ranges, each over two hundred feet long, where hemp was spun into rope or stitched into sacks by the Highlanders who had chosen that over the alternatives of departing for the mills of the south or of taking to the ships that crossed the ocean. Even in her time as governess to the Hossacks' daughters, Rachel had never been into the ropeworks, where the people spoke and sang in a language she did not understand. Alasdair did though, and she knew he went there sometimes, on whatever pretext he might light upon, to hear the singing and talk to men and women in his native tongue. There was singing sometimes at the other end of the journey too, Hester had told them, where the cotton was picked that filled those bags and where the herring and salt pork was eaten, sent in barrels from the piggery beside Cromarty schoolhouse. Singing, far across the ocean in that place where the money was made that sustained the fine houses of this northern Scottish town, and where the people who did the work that made the money had been given no choice at all.

Rachel had to remind herself to ring the bell on the wall by the heavy, black-painted double doors; remind herself to wait to be shown into Hossack House. Remind herself to walk behind the maid who led her up the stairs and into the front drawing room to announce her. Mrs Mackay. The minister's wife. Mrs Mackay, that used to be governess to your two spoilt daughters. Mrs Mackay that you treated like dirt. Here she is now. She sits in front of you in the kirk and takes tea in Cromarty House.

Marjorie Hossack was there, a profusion of ribbons and lace taking up half of a sofa that was the wrong colour for the dress she was wearing. Marjorie was the wrong colour too, and the wrong age, to be wearing such a dress. Twenty years too old and straining every seam. It was all Rachel could do to look at her long enough to make her greeting. Miss Anna Rose was there alongside and would have been in a dress to rival Marjorie Hossack's, had her sister not the good sense to forbid such grotesquery. Miss Elspeth herself was properly dressed for a walk in late October from Church Street to the harbour front and had removed her pelisse in response to the excessive heat of the Hossack drawing room.

'Mrs Mackay!' said Marjorie. 'We had begun to despair

of you, or to think that you had forgot to send along your apologies.'

'Yes,' joined Miss Anna. 'For Lady Charlotte sent hers down, and I did wonder whether you might not have sent yours with them.'

Rachel's heart sank. She had hoped Charlotte might have been at the afternoon tea – a sign, if nothing more, of adherence to convention, something to anchor her to life in the town. For herself, she did not like to be late, but it was not Marjorie Hossack's business to know that Alasdair had kept her back a while longer than she had intended.

Despite being the wife of one of the wealthiest men in Cromarty, Marjorie Hossack had no pretensions, for herself, to membership of the library. She had read some novels in her youth, but owned to not having found them very interesting, the adventure of her own life, from shoemaker's daughter in Dingwall to factory owner's wife in Cromarty, with a fine house overlooking the harbour, being quite enough for her. A pattern book, a new bolt of Paisley cloth, those were more to her taste. It was generally believed that Willie Hossack had read even less than his wife but it was conceded that he could read what mattered: a bill of lading and an inventory. Willie Hossack's membership of the library had been driven solely by his wife's ambition that their son, Farquhar, who certainly had read as much as was required to progress in his studies at the Marischal College in Aberdeen, should be accorded his rightful social standing in the town.

But this afternoon's gathering was not one of the circulating library, instead it was of some of the ladies prominent in the town's Friendly Society, bent upon discussing Good Works. The minister's wife finally arrived, Marjorie Hossack rang to have more coals put upon the fire and set about overseeing the preparation of the tea, making a great show of unlocking the drawer in her tea table that held the caddy, for fear anyone might think she trusted her own servants. Over the sounds of tongs and scuttles, Rachel heard the sound of the world outside, and turned her face towards the window, but of course there was nothing to see. They were on the first floor, and Mrs Hossack, foolish woman that she was, had hung the windows with so many swags of lace that the grey light of day hardly got through. The sea and sky and the whole west stretching out at the other side of the firth could not be seen at all, to say nothing of the road that ran past the front door of the Hossack house and along by the shore. Rachel could remember the joy of summer mornings, opening her curtains in the garret room of this house, looking out over the world, its beauty and its possibilities, or at the end of the day seeing the sun set in splendour beyond the firth, sinking magnificently behind the mountains into the straths of the west. She envied Marjorie Hossack nothing but the views that were to be had from the windows of her house, if only she would pull back the curtains.

The women had begun to talk, and Mrs Gilfeather was saying something of the cholera and the need to make preparations, but Marjorie Hossack dismissed the idea. It would have blown itself out, she insisted, before ever it got to Scotland, and could be no concern of theirs. With the noise the women made and the heat from the fire, Rachel could almost feel herself being sucked down into the swirls of the Persian carpet that covered half the room and clashed with everything in it. She pulled herself out of its grasp and forced herself to concentrate, to catch up.

'Will he stay long in the town, do you think? I hope he will stay for the winter at least. What do you think, Mrs Mackay?'

Rachel accepted a teacup from Miss Anna Rose. The delicate Minton china that was so tasteful she had always thought Marjorie must have bought it by mistake. 'Who, Fachie?' she said, without thinking properly.

Mrs Hossack looked with disdain at her daughters' former governess. 'Farquhar returned several weeks ago to the college in Aberdeen, where he is continuing his medical studies. We are in hopes that he will be home for Christmas, but no doubt he will have many invitations elsewhere.'

'And his sisters?' enquired Miss Anna.

Marjorie took a brisk sip at her tea. 'The girls will remain in Edinburgh for the winter season. There is nothing in Cromarty to compete with the opportunities they will be exposed to in the capital.'

Elspeth Rose, battle-hardened in the matter of afternoon teas in Cromarty drawing rooms, was hardly likely to let that pass. 'I think there is much they might be exposed to in the capital that they would be advised to be kept from, were they here in the town, but then I am sure you know your business, Mrs Hossack.'

'I am sure I do, Miss Elspeth. But in any case, we were talking of the major. Will he stay for the winter season, do you think?'

The question had been addressed, a second time, to Rachel. 'I have no idea,' she said.

Miss Anna spoke into her teacup. 'I do not think it would be the *greatest* loss to our society, should the major go west before winter sets in. He is rather austere, and not at all festive.' This declaration ventured, Rachel saw her peek quickly over at her sister.

'That house is much too large for him,' pronounced Miss Elspeth, to the evident relief of her sibling. 'A man alone . . .'

'I think I have heard talk of a young lady once, a promise, many years ago, but the misfortunes of war . . .' said Miss Anna.

'That terrible visage,' added Mrs Hossack, shaking her head. 'My girls would not like to look on it over the breakfast table.'

Her girls. Her girls would never have the chance. Still there, below the window, was the worktable at which those girls had laboured. A lovely thing, with walnut lid and finely turned legs, the seats of the accompanying chairs embroidered with trailing roses. And still there, beneath the table, was the little drawer and its keyhole, telling nothing of its secrets. A keyhole, but no key. Marjorie Hossack had confiscated the key on the day she'd unlocked that drawer to find the letters written to Amelia Hossack from a naval midshipman long re-embarked. The letters and their scandalous content had been hurled on the fire, Amelia and her younger sister Caroline packed off the next day to an aunt in Ferintosh to await transportation to a girls' school in Edinburgh, whence they would not be permitted to return until they were each of them safely married. 'And all she could talk about,' the housemaid who had told Rachel the story had said, 'was the harm Amelia might have done to Fachie's good name.'

So no, neither of the Hossack girls would be called upon to sit opposite the major at the breakfast table, either in that tall house set high up over the harbour, or in his draughty family keep, deep in the hills of Ross. Neither of them would have cause to look up at that blasted face, or into those fine grey eyes. Rachel had never been in the major's house, but Alasdair had told her of the telescope, trained over the firth to the straths beyond, to where Charles Munro had come from and where he seemed desperate yet reluctant to return to.

Miss Elspeth, a little displeased with the tone of the conversation, reminded them of the major's patriotic service, his suffering in the line of duty and his respectability. Mrs Hossack remembered then his rumoured income. Miss Anna, who knew more than she let on, slyly said it was a pity, after all, that Amelia would not be home for Christmas. Rachel stared determinedly into the swirls of the carpet and wished herself elsewhere, but Marjorie Hossack's voice reminded her that she was not.

'I believe you were at Cromarty House to dine only last Saturday, Mrs Mackay.'

Rachel answered that she had been. It would not have been worth the bother of asking how it was that Mrs Hossack might know this – a minister's movements were far from being his own sole concern, still less were those of his wife.

'And the major was also a guest, was he not?'

'Yes,' answered Rachel, now wary. 'He and Sir William are friends.'

'They surely get on very well.'

'Why should they not?' enquired Rachel. 'As one gentleman of the world and another, they do not want for topics in common.'

'In common. Indeed. They surely had much to talk about yesterday that they had not the time for on Saturday,' pursued Mrs Hossack.

Rachel had no idea what Marjorie Hossack might mean, but what she was certain of was that she meant something. Elspeth Rose was there ahead of her.

'I believe you have some point to make, Mrs Hossack. Perhaps, if we are to drink our tea before it is stone cold, it is time that you made it.'

'Oh,' said Mrs Hossack, taking a dainty sip of her own tea, her fat finger bulging where it hooked the handle of her cup, 'it is just the gig from Cromarty House was outside the major's door yesterday and appeared to call again there this morning where it waited at least an hour, before it scampered off up the Fortrose road. The major and Sir William will have some business on hand together, no doubt.'

Rachel knew, for Alasdair had mentioned it only that morning, that Sir William had planned to leave very early for business in Inverness and was not expected back in Cromarty until Monday. She also knew that he would not have thought of taking the gig and would have been off on his favourite hunter. What she didn't know was that, having at last read Dr Fraser's missive, Alasdair was at that moment walking towards the door of Charles Munro's house, that stood high overlooking the harbour. Marjorie Hossack smiled at Rachel and, as the gilded ormolu mantel clock struck the hour, like a cat returning its gaze to a stricken mouse, she resumed the consumption of her tea.

It was many hours later, after the ladies' tea had been drunk and them all gone home to see to their respective suppers, that James Craig placed an eight-day spring clock in a plain wooden case down in front of Stanislas. It was rare for James to bring a clock through from the workshop to their living quarters, but the problem had been bothering him since Major Munro had brought it in just as they had been shutting up for the night.

'The chime is not right. Listen.'

Stanislas could not hear the problem.

James set the clock again. 'Try now. You will hear it. It does not synchronise quite rightly with the others.'

'I will never have such an ear for these things as you do, James.'

'It's just that I've been listening a lot longer.'

'The major too, I think.'

'A man knows his own clock.'

Stanislas, who had grown up in a mansion full of clocks that he had never been required to do more than glance at from time to time, merely nodded. 'Are you going to work on it tonight? I can set up the lamps in the workshop.'

James shook his head. 'There will be no hurry for it. The major leaves Cromarty tomorrow, he tells me, and doesn't envisage being back for some time. I am to return it to his house when I am finished with it, and it will be returned to him, eventually.'

Not so far from the clockmaker's shop, in the small bedchamber beneath the eaves of the cottage on Little Vennel, Mairead Buchan could scarcely breathe. There was no moon to be seen tonight through the tiny window in the gable, and the light of their lamp had been extinguished hours since. That of Miss Juniper, just through the door, had not been long in following it. Mairead lay staring at the darkness, listening as the courthouse clock tolled the hour over the town. She was too terrified to close her eyes lest the worst of her fearful imaginings should choose tonight to manifest itself. A sudden gust of wind outside set the roof timbers above her to creaking, and at the third creak she could bear it no longer. Heedless of Alicia's many warnings that she was not to be woken, she threw back her own blankets and scurried from her bed to that of her friend. Burrowing to make space for herself, she curled an arm around Alicia's waist and buried her head in her back.

There was a murmur of irritation as Alicia shuffled herself closer to the wall, then the resumption of regular breathing.

Mairead whispered her friend's name, *sotto voce* to begin with. 'Alicia.'

A discontented murmur and an inching a little further away.

'Al*icia*.'

A grunt and a decided pulling of the blankets.

'Alicia!'

A long groan of resignation. 'What *is* it, Mairead?'

'Did you hear the creak?'

'What creak?'

'Just now. Like a wooden beam creaking under a weight.'

'No, I did not hear the creak, Mairead, because I was asleep. It'll be nothing but the wind in the roof beams. Go back to sleep.'

'But it sounded like a weight, swinging.'

Alicia let out a long breath of exasperation. 'Hugh MacLeod is *not* hanging from the rafters of Miss Juniper's cottage, Mairead. He was hanged six days since at the Longman in Inverness. His body will be in Edinburgh by now, where the judge said it was to be sent, to be cut up by the professor of anatomy there. Hester told me. She read it in the paper.'

Mairead's mind would not permit her to believe that the murderous Assynt schoolmaster was as far away as Edinburgh, not in the ways that mattered, at least. 'But what if it isn't? What if his spirit . . .'

'His spirit is in Hell, where else would it be after murdering that pedlar and stealing his money? Now go back to sleep and let me do the same. I was dreaming about Thaddeus . . .'

But whatever sweet dreams Alicia might be returning to, where no doubt James Craig's young Polish apprentice found himself conflated with Miss Jane Porter's fictional hero of Warsaw, Mairead could not shake her conviction that the spirit of the murderous Assynt schoolmaster stalked the streets of Cromarty, or that even worse would be produced when the students of Edinburgh got busy with his bones. For there was a question in Mairead's mind that she was too terrified to ask: what happened to the spirits of the dead who had not had a Christian burial? What point could there be in a Christian burial, were it not to send the spirit of the dead person safely off to Heaven or to that *other* place? And worse, what might the dead so dispatched then do should their final earthly resting place be disturbed? What might they not do should those graves be plundered? Alicia might chastise her for having ignored her advice *against* reading *Frankenstein*, but Mrs Shelley's book had only been the start of it. Every week the newspapers were filled with tales of grave-robbings and Burkings, where the perpetrators did not have the decency to wait for their victims to be dead, still less buried. Not that the girls had untrammelled access to the newspapers, but Hester could be relied upon to relay to them the gist of all the most interesting articles from the publications she tidied up or laid out each day in the reading room of the Commercial Hotel.

Mairead knew she had to stop being so foolish. She was not a child any more and she had to make herself let go of her childish terrors. Yet she did fear the coming winter and its almost endless hours of darkness. Tomorrow night, Hallowe'en, was the most frightening of all but on that one night, at least, no one in Cromarty would laugh at her foolishness.

In another part of the town, Mr Isaac Fordyce was also awake, his eyes directed towards the ceiling. But the ceiling of Mr Isaac's bedchamber in Fordyce House was much higher than that of the frightened young woman in Little Vennel, and it was excitement, not fear, that kept him awake. He scarcely knew how he should get through the coming day waiting for night to fall. There were still many preparations to be made of course, and much to be overseen. A party he was to give, such as Fordyce House had not seen in many years. But this would not be a party of quadrilles and minuets and the pleasant tunes of Signor Scarlatti to accompany the genteel steps and polite conversation of the well-to-do of Cromarty, nor would there be card tables and a cold supper laid out in the dining room. Those parties had their place, and Mr Isaac was generally the first to accept any invitation issued to one such, but the party he had planned was of another description altogether, and most of it would take place not within doors, but outside, in the gardens of the house with braziers lit along pathways and between trees, and there would be a great bonfire, and a tub of apples for dooking sent down from the manse garden, and tatties from Cromarty House for roasting in the ashes, and eerie tales of the supernatural told, all under the glorious stars of the night sky.

The candle by Mr Isaac's bedside still burned, and he knew he should snuff it out, for really, there was much to be done tomorrow, and he could not lie in late – certainly not beyond ten. He reached out a hand for the candle snuffer then changed his mind. He would have a look at MacFarlane's *Constantinople*, that Mr Learmonth, the young schoolmaster, had passed to him from the circulating library. He had been meant to travel there, to Constantinople, when he had made his Grand Tour, but once arrived in Germany had found himself so thoroughly *belonging* that it had been almost impossible to leave, until the increasing urgings of family had drawn him home. And so *Constantinople* was forgotten and his hand searched instead for the well-worn, familiar contours of the volume he had bought as a first edition, and had long known by heart. There! That was it. Now he did snuff out the candle, and holding the comforting book, began a murmured recital of *The Lady of the*

Lake until, the expanse of Loch Katrine behind him and the blazing fiery cross before his eyes, he was fast asleep.

In the tall house overlooking the harbour, light could be seen in almost every window. Had anyone cared to look long enough, they might have seen figures passing back and forth, engaged in packing, stripping, taking down pictures from walls and laying sheets over furnishings. Then, had they looked again in the cold dawn of the early morning, they would have seen Major Charles Munro emerge from the archway leading from the stables behind his house, his horse walking slowly at first, and then picking up speed, until he was out on the road from Cromarty and no longer to be seen.

TEN

Hallowe'en Night 1831

Alicia could see her breath in front of her. The frost was already forming on the stones of the causey and the stars were like splinters of ice in a sky black as pitch. 'My toes are nipping already,' she complained. 'I wish the party was to be in the house. I cannot think why it isn't. Do you think perhaps Mr Fordyce is wandered in the head?'

Miss Juniper, a little ahead of the girls, her arm linked into Rachel's, turned around. 'Mr Fordyce has always been wandered in the head, ever since he was a young boy. He will never be dull and he will never be bored. There are worse things a man can be than wandered in the head. Anyway, I understand that the latter stages of the party are to be held inside, it is only the initial stages – the storytelling, the children's games – that are to be outside.'

'But it will be so *cold*,' protested Alicia.

'Well, why did you not put on your good warm woollen shawl like Mairead there, instead of that silly light thing?

It can surely not be a surprise to you that the air on the last night of October in the north of Scotland is chill. If you are determined to be foolish you must determine also to take the consequences.'

Alicia pursed her lips and said no more, huddling instead closer into the thick woollen wrappings of Mairead, who had a good grip on her arm.

'It will be for the atmosphere,' breathed Mairead.

'Atmosphere, indeed,' muttered Alicia as they hurried along. 'Foxes and badgers and owls and bats to contend with. Dirt on our shoes and the hems of our dresses, all exposed to the light just when the dancing is to begin. And "atmosphere" is the very last thing *you* need. Do not even consider climbing into my bed tonight, waking me up because you think you have died of fright.'

Up ahead, illuminated by a lantern held up by the waiting schoolmaster, they saw James Craig's apprentice step out at the front door of the clockmaker's house.

Alicia let loose an unguarded sigh and Mairead whispered into her ear, 'Look! Stanislas. You will be glad you wore your nice crocheted shawl and not your old heavy tartan one after all.'

'Well, why on earth did you think I wore it?' retorted Alicia. 'Certainly not for the benefit of Ludovic Cameron or Mr Fordyce.' She gazed ahead in the darkness at the ethereal form of the Polish apprentice and gave another sigh. 'It will hardly compare with what he will have seen in the drawing rooms and ballrooms of Warsaw, of course.

And I'm sure the ladies there did not have noses that were blue with the cold!'

Mairead knew no more of the drawing rooms and ballrooms of Warsaw than did Alicia but saw no cause to fret over them. 'Everybody's nose will be blue. You are not disappointed that he is not in his uniform, though?'

Alicia had spent a great deal of time, and wasted an unconscionable number of pages of her sketchbook adorning a very good likeness of the clockmaker's apprentice with her idea of what a Polish cavalry officer's uniform might consist of. Unlike the heroic Thaddeus of Warsaw from the novel she had been obsessing over ever since Lady Charlotte had sent it down for them, Stanislas had not stepped onto British soil decked in full military regalia. Instead, he had made landfall in Cromarty shoeless, in a threadbare jacket that looked as if it had had several previous owners and the arms of which were too short for him, and a pair of rough brown trousers that may once have belonged to a Dutch fisherman. The Ladies' Friendly Society had immediately raised a subscription to provide him with a more appropriate suit of clothing, but they had not run to a full cavalry uniform. Mairead had considered this perfectly generous of the ladies, given that she had never heard of Stanislas to have been anything more heroic than a protesting student, but rather than share this view with Alicia, she had kept it to herself.

It seemed that half the world was streaming into the gardens of Fordyce House. The wide wrought-iron gates stood open to welcome the *bon ton* of the town. Perhaps in other places, a clockmaker's refugee apprentice, an elderly schoolmistress cast forth from neighbouring society and a hotelkeeper's son, might not have been invited to mingle with the laird and his lady, the minister and his, the wealthy merchants and the wealthy others that might constitute *society*, but this was Cromarty, where there were those, most chiefly Mr Fordyce, who still held dear the old, sociable, ways.

Into the broad circular drive, around the magnificent elm at its centre, swung carriages bearing most of the gentry of much of the Black Isle. The Reverend Dr Micah Fraser of Resolis was not there, of course. His ways were older, Highland ways, his memories of Hallowe'ens in now-empty haunted straths where new atrocities, perpetrated in broad daylight, outbid the Devil.

Once through the gates, Mairead and Alicia hastened towards the punch table where Hester, alongside Mr Fordyce's scullery maid, was ladling out cups of hot punch and creamy hot Scotch pints.

'You are here!' said Mairead excitedly. 'I was afraid Mrs Cameron would not allow you to come.'

Hester glanced at her friends then resumed concentration on her work. 'Mrs Cameron would do anything for Mr Fordyce. She says he is the most perfect gentleman on the whole of the Black Isle. When he asked if I might assist tonight, she took great pleasure in saying yes. She is sending Ludo along with buttered apples.'

Mairead closed her eyes in delight. 'I dream of Mrs Cameron's buttered apples.' Then the eyes were discreetly open again. 'And Ludovic is to be here, you say?'

Hester and Alicia exchanged knowing grins. 'He should be arriving any minute.'

'He will need to hurry, or he will miss Lady Charlotte arriving,' said Alicia.

But then there was a collective 'Oh' from the assembly and there she was, being handed down from her carriage by Mr Fordyce himself, a shimmering, sylph-like form hardly of this world. Lady Charlotte's evening dress was out of time, a water-green shift of silk gauze embroidered with tiny white flowers of silk satin. She must have had it from her days as a pupil of Miss Juniper, or not long after. And yet, it was somehow perfect for this most ethereal of nights. She was perfect. Alicia, born too late, ached for such a dress.

Much to the surprise of Mairead and Alicia, Lady Charlotte had Mr Fordyce escort her not to where the other ladies of the gentry were seated by a brazier in what might have been described as a bower, but directly over to where Miss Juniper was. Startled, they hurried over to their schoolmistress, made their curtsies, and leaned in.

'You look a little flushed, my dear,' Miss Juniper was saying. 'I hope you are not ill?'

Lady Charlotte placed her hand over the old lady's. 'Nothing could be further from the truth, Miss Juniper. I think I am better now than I have ever been.'

The look of hope that glimmered for a moment in the

schoolmistress's eye was quickly extinguished by Lady Charlotte. 'Oh, no, not *that*, I am afraid. It is clear to me by now that Sir William and I will not be blessed in that way.'

'Oh.' Miss Juniper's keen gaze clouded a little. 'I am sorry to hear it.'

'You must not be,' replied Charlotte. 'Perhaps I would not have made a very good mother.'

'I cannot agree,' replied the old lady. 'I am glad anyhow that you do so well.'

'How could I not?' replied Charlotte. 'The autumn has been so fine. I have hardly been within doors these past few weeks.'

'Today, even?' enquired the old governess. 'The whole morning and afternoon I worried that Mr Fordyce would not be able to have his party after all. The sea was so very choppy and the gusts coming from the west almost knocked me off my feet.'

'Oh, I am glad they did not.' Lady Charlotte smiled. 'But they were powerful. Yes. And fresh, and clean. The winds blow away all bad and dead things, and will leave a bare canvas for winter, to write what it pleases.'

'Well, *I* wish it were not so windy,' confided Miss Anna Rose, who had somehow slipped her sister to emerge from between a pair of hardy rose bushes and appear at Miss Juniper's elbow. 'I lie awake at night and worry that the wind will blow the cholera from the quarantine ships ashore to us here. I would keep all the doors and windows shut, but Elspeth does not like to be stuffy, and a person cannot remain indoors for ever.'

As Miss Juniper and Lady Charlotte attempted to reassure Miss Anna on the matter of the *cholera morbus*, and that no ship at anchor in the bay had as yet been found to carry the pestilence, Mairead followed Alicia's lead in moving back to the buffet table, where Hester was now arranging the dishes that Mrs Cameron had sent along from the hotel. Safely out of the older women's earshot, she said, 'Has she gone mad, do you think?'

'Who?' enquired Alicia. 'Miss Anna? She is only a little touched – everyone knows that.'

'Not Miss Anna. Lady Charlotte. The way she smiles and takes people under her notice and looks as if everything pleases her . . .'

'It's better than the way she was before,' said Hester, looking up from her setting out of napkins.

'Well, yes,' said Mairead, 'but I worry that she might have gone a little mad.'

Alicia gave thought for a moment. 'Perhaps she's in love.'

Mairead wrinkled her brow and looked again at Lady Charlotte and then at Sir William. 'What? With Sir William?'

'Sir William?' hissed Alicia in disbelief. 'Don't be ridiculous. He must be over fifty and he has no interest in anything but horses and his investments. How could she be in love with Sir William?'

'Well, he is her husband.'

Alicia shook her head. 'That has nothing to do with it.'

Mairead wondered what it was that Alicia found in the books she read that made her so much better informed on the complexities of the married state than she herself was.

The girls all looked about them, but they could see no one in the milling crowd of gentlemen arrived for Mr Fordyce's party that Lady Charlotte could possibly be in love with.

All through the garden, braziers burned at interludes along walls and winding pathways. The bonfire – not too large, for fear of confusing the shipping – was enough to send warmth out through the garden and to cast dancing shadows where the lights of the burning torches could not reach. The smoke of well-seasoned wood drifted upwards to mingle with the taste of salt perennially in the air. Seating of various sorts had been arranged for the ladies, and rugs laid out at intervals on the grass. In a corner with a small fire lit at its centre, a sort of grotto had been contrived. Already there was music playing, two Highland lads from the ropeworks adept with fiddle and flute. Mr Isaac had thought of everything.

Charlotte was now flitting across the garden towards Rachel, so light she might have been borne on the music that drifted around her. The gleam of a torch briefly illuminated her face, the sparkle in her eyes, the smile almost there, the anticipation.

'She does not know,' said Rachel, the cold reality of the thing only now dawning on her. She had only just discovered herself – what Dr Fraser had written in his letter two nights ago to Alasdair, what Alasdair had done about it yesterday afternoon, when she was enduring tea at Marjorie Hossack's.

'He decided to leave quietly, I think. No good could have come of prolonging his leaving by attempting to make her understand.'

'No good . . .?' As Charlotte came towards them, her face open with the possibilities of the evening to come, Rachel was taken by a dreadful certainty of what would unfold. 'She might at least have heard it in the privacy of her own home, rather than here, before all the world.'

And then Charlotte's lips were brushing her cheek, and Sir William was greeting Alasdair with a remark on the cold and the suggestion that they go and fetch some punch for the ladies.

'Come,' said Charlotte, pulling Rachel towards the grotto. 'Hugh Miller is to tell stories of Hallowe'ens past that I am assured will make our hair stand on end. But tell me, have you noticed Charles anywhere? I cannot see him.'

Before Rachel could answer her, Charlotte had started to move through the crowd and their hands had become disentangled. Then Miss Elspeth Rose was standing in front of Rachel and talking, and Charlotte was lost to her view.

'I'm sorry, Miss Rose,' she said, a little distractedly, 'I did not quite hear—'

'No, because you weren't listening,' returned Miss Elspeth. 'I was talking of soap, the importance of soap. The minister can lead us in prayer against the cholera until we are blue in the face, but you and I well know that the Good Lord has already provided us with the means to combat the contagion. Soap, Mrs Mackay. We cannot be too soon in adopting preventative measures.'

Rachel was not entirely sure what her role in this laudable undertaking was to be. 'Perhaps the town council . . .'

Miss Elspeth made a 'pfft' sound out of the side of her mouth. 'The town council will do as it's told, if it does anything at all,' she said. 'Anyway, I must see Mrs Gilfeather . . .' It was with some relief that Rachel watched the elder of the Rose sisters disappear once more into the darkness.

Rachel eventually found Alasdair and Sir William, punch cups secured, positioned behind one of several old sofas that been carried out into the garden to form an arc around the fire. Illumined by the torches on the wall at their backs, the men cast elongated shadows over Charlotte, seated in front of them. Nearest to the fire itself, in a grand old chair that looked as if it might have found its way down the street from the courthouse, sat Hugh Miller, the stonemason. The fiddle and flute slowed from the hectic jig that had had the children in the company running and whirling about like sprites to a more sedate, but somewhat discordant air. Rachel accepted a cup of warm punch and took up her seat by Charlotte.

'I still cannot find Charles,' said Charlotte. 'I think I must have William go to look for him.'

Rachel glanced at Alasdair. 'I don't think the major is—'

But then, of a sudden, the music stopped and the torches around the walls were almost simultaneously extinguished, plunging the guests into a darkness and illuminating only the stonemason on his story-telling throne. 'It is time,' said Mr Fordyce, from his place at the edge of the grotto, 'for Miller to begin his tale.'

As the fire crackled and the conversation stilled, the stonemason leaned forward a little in his chair, warning the gathered company that what he told them would be no fables, but true accounts handed down by their forefathers, of strange beings, spirits and fairy folk that had passed through their doors, by the streets of this town, over the moorlands above and the hills beyond. Green ladies, wraiths, who brought death or disease wherever they visited. He told of sinister, lonely places where the foolhardy had been known to go to consult their fates on Hallowe'en, only to return mad, if they returned at all. He had dared it once himself, but no amount of pleading from the children or offers of whisky punch from the matrons of Cromarty would induce him to tell what he had discovered on that terrible night.

Though the children and some of the elderly maidens showed appropriate signs of terror at the stonemason's tales, Charlotte and Rachel had heard them all before, so many times that they might have relayed them themselves. Rachel let herself sink back a little into the sofa, so that Charlotte gave her shoulders a jiggle. 'Come on, sleepy head! Don't nod off here or we shall get stuck with Miss Juniper and

Miss Anna or, Heaven help us, with Marjorie Hossack! We must find Charles before the dancing starts and William drags him off for a game of cards. I'm sure I saw him slip a pack into his pocket as we were leaving.'

Before Rachel knew it, Charlotte had pulled her up and was trailing her into the house and up the great stairway towards the room where a more formal music recital was to be held, and dancing to take place. 'Charlotte,' she breathed, struggling to keep up. 'Wait, you must listen . . .'

Upstairs, in the drawing room, Mr Fordyce announced a travelling teacher who was to tell them a sinister musical tale, lately heard in Paris.

Alicia was usually agog to hear anything of Paris and its fashions, but tonight was not the time. 'I shall die of tedium if the dancing doesn't begin soon, and what if Stanislas should leave before then?'

Mairead was tempted to reply that in that case he would miss a dramatic and exceptionally well-rehearsed death, but she thought this hardly likely to lighten Alicia's mood. 'We had better listen. Miss Juniper is bound to quiz us about it on the way home.'

With practised determination, the two girls skilfully outflanked the girls from the ladies' boarding school in the new part of town to position themselves close to where Stanislas, Ludo and the schoolmaster John Learmonth were congregated amongst a group of the town's most respectable young gentlemen.

The music teacher began to talk of the Opéra, and on hearing Stanislas whisper to John Learmonth, 'my father took me there often, when we were in Paris,' Alicia could not have been dragged from the drawing room. There followed an account of the *Symphonie Fantastique* of M. Berlioz that, interspersed with musical illustrations, shocked and terrified the audience in equal measure, until the account of the climactic diabolic orgy that carried the soul of the symphony's protagonist to Hell was brought to an abrupt halt by the decided thump of a swooning Mairead falling to the floor.

'Is the child all right?' asked Alasdair. Rachel had found him outside, where he had gone when the fuss was at its height.

'Yes,' she said. 'Some air and a dash of brandy have restored her to her senses.'

'Might we all be,' said Alasdair. 'That was no tale to tell before children.'

'Mairead is hardly a child. She is sixteen, just past. I am more worried about Charlotte. I have not seen her since shortly after the musician began his recitation. She left me to go in search of the major. I tried to tell her, but I could not make myself understood.'

'I told her,' said Alasdair. 'I met her on the landing there. I told her that Charles has left for his estates in Ross and has no plans to return to Cromarty. I told her he did it because he is a man of honour who has too much respect for her, for William and for himself to meddle with the laws of God or the morals of another man's wife, and that she should give thanks that it was to him and not some man of lesser scruple that she had as good as thrown herself.'

Rachel was astonished. 'Thrown herself?'

'What else would you call it?'

'She had . . .' She searched for the words, but in her horror at what her husband had said, she could not articulate them. 'She did not "throw herself" at him, Alasdair. Over these last few weeks she showed him a sympathy of feeling, of understanding that he clearly did not find elsewhere, and she accepted that same understanding from him in return. William encouraged her, for God's sake!'

His face grew grim. 'Rachel, I would ask you not to blaspheme nor to invoke the name of the Lord in such a matter. William was glad to see a lonely man enjoy some companionship, and to see a discontented wife begin to take an interest in the world around her. He was too naive and trusting to see that Munro was falling in love with Charlotte, but I know you were not. And Micah Fraser was certainly not. You should give thanks that a catastrophe has been averted, and your friend's good name preserved.'

Rachel stared at him. 'Catastrophe? What do you think will happen now? How is it, Alasdair, that you still do not know her at all? She was becoming lost to us all before Major Munro came to Cromarty. The man took her by the hand and led her back into the world. Now you tell her the fault is hers that he has gone away. I must go to her. Where is she?'

But Alasdair didn't know. No one knew. A discreet search was made of the gardens and the house, but no sign of Charlotte was found. Some children waiting at the back gate for some treats from Mr Fordyce's kitchen reported having seen a lady going alone along the street. They thought at first it had been a ghost, but then one of them had said it was only Lady Charlotte, and it was a wonder if she didn't freeze to death with nothing but that floaty shift to keep her warm.

Rachel and Alasdair went with Sir William to Cromarty House, all in darkness save the kitchens where the servants kept their own Hallowe'en, Morag Mackenzie being safely gone to bed. Morag was soon wakened and the whole house lit up, but Charlotte was not found. William had his head in his hands. 'Where can she have gone?' he kept asking. He did not ask why. Alasdair had told him why.

Every suggestion had its attendant dangers. To the harbour and a boat to ferry her across to Ross, after Charles Munro. But dear God, other things might happen at the harbour, the pier jutting out into so stormy a sea. Or there were the cliffs – Charlotte knew the cliffs from childhood. She knew where was safe to walk and where was not. She knew hiding places, caves. But in the darkness, with the paths already ice? Or up out of town, over Cromarty hill, onto the Mulbuie, that desolate moor stretching over the spine of the Black Isle, and God knew what.

Rachel's heart raced. 'You must send out search parties, William. She will do herself a damage.'

Rachel herself, in desperate hope, went to Miss Juniper's cottage, but Charlotte was not there. The girls were still up and engaged in the old Hallowe'en game of breaking an egg into a glass of water, that they might interpret their futures in the patterns of the white as it rose. 'Foolishness, I know,' whispered Miss Juniper, 'but I have allowed it, to take Mairead's mind off the terrors of the *Symphonie Fantastique* and to make up for the disappointment of them having no dancing tonight after all.' For all her concern for Charlotte, Rachel's attention was momentarily arrested by what she saw in the glass into which Alicia Middleton was gazing. Miss Juniper and Mairead saw what she did, she was certain, and Alicia's own face showed confusion mingled with dismay. 'It's a shroud,' she said.

Rachel was struggling to find an alternative that might persuade the girl that she had not seen what they had all seen, but it was Mairead, recovered from her earlier unfortunate episode, who managed it. 'Nonsense, Alicia. What are you thinking of? It's a veil – look, could anything be clearer? Miss Juniper . . .'

The old lady had by now collected herself. 'Oh, it is most certainly a veil, Alicia. A bridal veil. Mrs Mackay, you see it, do you not?'

'Yes,' lied Rachel. 'A beautiful bridal veil. Soft as gossamer, ethereal as silk. Oh my, to think that young people still play these silly old games.'

'Did you play them when you were a girl, Mrs Mackay, you and Lady Charlotte?'

'I believe we did,' said Rachel.

'And what did you see?' asked Alicia.

Rachel remembered. She remembered the shroud she herself had seen, that invisible shroud that within two years had wound itself around Ensign Alexander Gilfeather. 'Oh, nothing,' she said. 'Nothing at all.'

Death or joy. Hugh Miller's Hallowe'en tales told themselves again in Charlotte's head, and she could not shake that one of the madness brought at Hallowe'en to those who attempt to discover their own fate. Charlotte would not allow that she only had one possible fate. She had two, and the choice was hers. Death or joy. She had been living a slow death, married to William, immured in Cromarty House, not even a child to hold, her friendship with Rachel her only release and she had had a moment where she might almost have fallen to the schoolmaster. Dear God! But then Charles Munro had come into her life and that man, that everyone thought so damaged, had taken her by the hand and begun to show her a world of texture, of colour, of books and places that came alive in her mind. A glimpse, she had had. But even that had been too much for the society around them, and now he was gone and she once more a pretty nothing.

The shock of it, when Alasdair Mackay had told her, had taken the breath from her, taken the possibility of words, but she had them now. Death or joy. She would find Charles or she would not. But if that death-veil must blind her vision once more, let it envelop her entirely. She would not be an ornament.

He would have gone to Balblair to take the ferry to Easter Ross and his own country. Perhaps she would reach him before he crossed and the hills folded him away from her sight again. She would make him take her with him. Seven miles to Balblair. She would reach the inn before midnight. They could sail at dawn. The sounds of games and music grew fainter as she drew closer to the shore where the sea creeping over the stones on the beach was soft and insistent. There was no light at Hossack House but the burning lantern by the door. The ropeworks were silent and still as Charlotte moved past. Soon, she was on the open road and the town behind her. She wished it were not so cold and that she had not left her shawl on Mr Fordyce's sofa. She wished she had on her good boots and not her dancing slippers. She wished she had a lantern to guide her, and not just the part-light of the moon as it glimmered off the softly shifting waters. Owls were out, and bats, swooping too close. She thought of Morag Mackenzie, chasing her from town. Twice, parties on horseback came along the road from the direction of Cromarty and she slipped off the road to conceal herself amongst the trees and bushes. Her skirts snagged on brambles, but it didn't matter. She would be with Charles soon.

The stories of the night began to jumble themselves in her head, the voices of brownies and water-wraiths and green ladies arguing with one another, becoming more hectic. She tried to make them be quiet and so they began to murmur, which was worse. They whispered to her the story of the Brownie of the Black Haggs that had driven mad a wicked woman, sent her distracted and tormented to her death on the moor. Charlotte told them she would not be wandering up onto the moor, whatever they said. She would stay close to the road. She would be with Charles soon.

The Reverend Dr Micah Fraser threw another log into the brazier and stamped his feet in an attempt to keep warm. His housekeeper had threatened to bolt the doors on him when he had told her of his intention to stand guard in the burial ground of Kirkmichael tonight, but he had told her he would simply climb through a window and trample the rose beds if she did. Poor Katy Ross was hardly twelve hours in the ground and it was well-known the resurrectionists were creeping about all over the country. Her corpse would be on a boat and off round the coast to the anatomy professors in Aberdeen before Mrs Swanson had their breakfast out, and Hallowe'en night was the very night they would think no watch would be kept on the burial grounds. Let them try Micah Fraser, if they thought he had not wrestled with worse!

It had been a quiet enough night though, only some of the young ones from the surrounding farms out and about at their Hallowe'en nonsense, but none of them brave enough to approach too close to Kirkmichael and its restless spirits. The shifting clouds let the moon play shadows upon the jagged broken walls of the kirk and lent sudden, sinister life to the yew trees amongst the tombstones. Dr Fraser did not doubt that there were restless spirits in this kirkyard, but he had his Bible by him and had challenged the deep silence with the rendering of many an edifying psalm.

It was well past eleven and the firth a silver dart in the moonlight when he became aware of lights approaching and the sound of horses on the road. Dr Fraser took a draught from the bottle he had brought with him, then strode up the path to the kirkyard gate, brandishing his staff in a manner that could not leave any doubt that he was ready to use it.

When they were yet twenty yards away, he saw there were two horsemen. 'I am armed and will not hesitate,' he shouted. 'Halt there and state your business!'

An exclamation of fright escaped one of the horsemen while the other was forced to steady his own horse which had threatened to rear up in front. Dr Fraser held up his lantern.

'Ludovic Cameron! John Learmonth! What devilment has you out here on this road tonight? You are not in league with Fachie Hossack?'

The young men, both vehemently protesting their innocence, dismounted and led their reluctant beasts the last few yards to where he stood. Dr Fraser was relieved to see they had not shovels or sacks with them. 'Well?' he demanded. 'Explain yourselves!'

And they told him that word had been sent down from Cromarty House that Lady Charlotte Mackenzie had gone missing from Mr Fordyce's party. It was feared she had taken fright at Hugh Miller's stories, or at the musician's, or maybe been taken by a sudden chill or fever and wandered off and got lost. All anyone knew was that she had disappeared into the night with not as much as a shawl over her shoulders. 'She has not been past this way?'

'She has not.' But Charles Munro had, many hours earlier, in the morning. Teenie had had the news from the gamekeeper's boy at Newhall. Major Munro had got the ferry at Balblair, and travelling cases had followed him. He was leaving Cromarty, the gamekeeper's boy had said. Dr Fraser wished to ask another question but found himself hoarse. 'We will pray,' he said at last. They all three removed their hats and prayed beneath the broken walls of the old kirkyard, that Sir William's wife might be found, if God so willed it. As Dr Fraser was finishing his long and fervent prayer, the wind started to get up and the old bell of the ruined kirk swayed a little, threatening to toll. Ludovic, whose fleshy cheeks had glowed paler than ever in the night, opened his mouth in something like fear and pointed down the road. 'Look,' he said.

Charlotte didn't know why the wind had got up so suddenly. It was gusting around her, making the light material of her dress stick to her bones and flow out behind her. Her hair had come loose too and whipped crazily across her face. The clouds rushed so fast across the surface of the moon now that they might have been being chased by demons. Charlotte thought of all the lost souls hurrying to reach Kirkmichael before midnight. She was sure she could hear the bell now. If only she could get past the old kirk, to Balblair. She could hardly drag one foot in front of the other, so exhausted was she from arguing all the way against the voices. She wondered if she just sat down whether she might die there and then, and if it might be peaceful in the dark nothingness, yet she stumbled on. She would get as far as the kirk, and then the night creatures might take her as they willed. She had nothing left.

There were lights though, moving towards her from the kirkyard. Fairy lights. Or wicked little sprites, dancing around. 'The Good People', her grandmother had called them, wicked old woman that she had been. The lights were spreading out now, three of them, weaving and waving in the wind, coming towards her. Charlotte smiled as she closed her eyes. Let them come.

ELEVEN

November

Speculation

The night was very still and all that could be heard from the darkness outside Miss Juniper's cottage was the rumbling sound of the stones on the shore as the sea rolled over them and back again. Inside, from their beds, the girls listened to the scratch of Miss Juniper's pen.

'What is she writing, do you think?' whispered Alicia. 'Do you think she is writing about Cromarty?'

Mairead shook her head. 'It's a letter. As I bent to kiss her goodnight I saw the superscription, "My Dearest Charlotte,".'

Alicia sat up, mindless of the care she had taken over the disposition of her curls across her pillow only two minutes earlier. 'She's writing to Lady Charlotte? Did you see anything else? A line, or a word even?'

'No.'

Alicia let out a grumble of disappointment. 'Well, that tells us nothing.'

'It tells us Lady Charlotte is alive, Alicia.'

'Well *of course* she's alive! How many times have I told you that Sir William is infinitely too dull a person to have murdered her, and what in the world would he have murdered her for?'

'But if she *was* in love with someone – it was you, at the party, who thought she might be . . .'

'Well, if she was in love with someone, Sir William would not have murdered *her*, he would have challenged *him* to a duel. And if that had happened, we would have heard about it. Not even people like Sir William can keep a thing like *that* out of the newspapers.' Having recently read *Zelucco*, the girls were thoroughly versed in the conventions of duelling. Alicia was already at the limits of her patience though. 'Lady Charlotte is merely unwell, as Mrs Mackay has already told us. And it is hardly to be wondered that she caught a chill at Mr Fordyce's party and wandered off, disorientated, when everyone else was having a carry-on about you fainting and landing on Ludo Cameron's foot! Ever since Dr Fraser found her half-dead at Kirkmichael, Mrs Cameron has been sending bone broth up to Cromarty House every other day. Hester said so. And Mrs Mackay would hardly have told us Lady Charlotte was safe and well if she were not.' Alicia herself would have preferred that a secret lover had swept Lady Charlotte away to some romantic fastness, but given the profile of the available gentlemen of Cromarty, she had reluctantly decided that this could not be the case.

'Perhaps Sir William has duped Mrs Mackay too,' offered Mairead, in defence of her unshakeable conviction that Lady Charlotte, who had not been seen in the town since the night of Mr Fordyce's party some three weeks earlier, had been murdered.

'Oh,' grumbled Alicia as she pulled on her blankets and thumped her head back down onto her pillow, completely forgetting about the disposition of her curls, 'you really are intolerable, Mairead.'

In Cromarty House, Sir William Mackenzie sat by the dying embers of the drawing room fire and stared at the French windows, opened onto the lawns. He had taken to having braziers lit at night, at intervals around the grounds. Charlotte had been in a fever almost a week, after the messenger had come from Dr Fraser at the manse of Resolis. She had remained there a few days more until she had been strong enough for William to have brought her home. Since then, she had begun to rise from her bed at night, and to wander. He'd tried to follow her, the first night, but he had lost her somewhere between the grounds of the house and the town. She knew every pathway, every nook and cranny from her schooldays here. She had come back that first night though, and each night since. She had promised him that she would always come back, and that would have to be enough.

William's old nurse, Morag Mackenzie, also knew of Charlotte's wanderings. She seemed satisfied by the fact of them, proof, somehow, of the justice of her antipathy to the woman he had married. William suspected that Morag was sorry Charlotte had not died that Hallowe'en night, or in the following days, when Rachel Mackay had taken herself to Resolis to keep vigil at her bedside, determined that hers should be the first face Charlotte saw when she woke. When at last Charlotte's fever had broken and her hallucinations had left her, she had pronounced herself 'recovered, now', and begged her friend to go back to her own life.

She had not gone back to hers, though. The Charlotte that William had known, the one that he'd been married to for ten years, had never returned from Kirkmichael. The woman who had come back in her place bore his wife's form, but little else. Better he had been cuckolded by Charles Munro than have been left with this stranger. The fragile butterfly of a woman Munro had set to dancing in the air around them had gone, blown off course by the winds of convention, and been replaced by some other being. First the fine gowns had been abandoned for old, simple things that might have fitted better for a housekeeper or an elder's wife, and then the night wandering had begun. William didn't know where she went, this replacement woman. He did not really care: it was not her return he watched for, in the near-darkness of this room, but for some sight of the spectral beauty she had replaced.

The conversation around the clockmaker's kitchen table was all of the coming visitation of John Learmonth's school by the Ladies of the Friendly Society.

Stanislas could not see John's difficulty. 'But surely you

can have nothing to fear from the Ladies of the Friendly Society, John?'

The three other men stared at him.

It was Ludovic who spoke first. 'These are not "ladies" as you might have encountered in Poland,' he explained. 'They are the Ladies of the Cromarty Friendly Society – Mrs Gilfeather, Mrs Hossack, Miss Elspeth Rose, to name but three, and I say nothing of my mother.'

'But your mother is so good – letting us have the newspapers and sending down sweetmeats and the like with you when you come to us. I cannot speak of Mrs Hossack, of course, but Mrs Gilfeather is the very soul of kindness, and as for Miss Elspeth Rose . . .'

Everyone waited as Stanislas scrambled in his mind for some positive aspect to John's impending scrutiny by Miss Elspeth Rose. Finally, he lit upon something. 'You need not fear Miss Elspeth berating you. Most certainly, had she fault to find with you, she would already have told it, to your face.'

James Craig burst into laughter. 'At last, my boy, you begin to understand this place. But at least the woman is honest.' He waved the newspaper at them. 'Better her way of going about things than this.'

The Scotsman, like every other newspaper in the country, was full of the Bristol riots, begun in protest against the city's anti-Reform representative and extending to days of violence, vandalism, looting and arson that raised the spectre of the French revolutionaries in the imaginations of the sober shopkeepers and property owners of Britain. Twelve protesters killed, most of them under twenty, almost a hundred injured, and countless homes and public buildings destroyed. The clockmaker was firmly of the view that the riots had been engineered deliberately.

'You cannot really believe the government would provoke such unrest on purpose?' said Ludo, whose days spent under the eye of Mr Gilfeather rendered him less susceptible to radical ideas than were his friends.

'Of course they would, Ludo,' said Stanislas.

'But I read that article from beginning to end. I knew it would be of interest to you,' Ludo was giving himself away, but it was too late now to retract, 'and I did not see one word that suggested these riots had been provoked deliberately.' Deflated, he looked to his friend. 'I don't understand.'

Stanislas came to sit by him. 'I have seen this before. The enemies of liberty deliberately provoke to violence those who call for freedom. They create a state of fear and uncertainty amongst people who were previously indifferent, that they might present themselves as the only safeguard of order. In this way they crush dissent and establish control. I saw it with my own eyes, in Warsaw.'

Ludovic appealed to the clockmaker. 'But surely, James, it would not be allowed to happen here, in Scotland?'

'Would it not?' said the clockmaker. 'Already political societies all over the country are holding meetings to pledge non-violence, to the degree it becomes non-action. There is a great deal of talk of the militias.'

'Much good might the militia do protecting us from the cholera, which is what everyone *should* be worrying about,' said Ludo. 'It's at Sunderland now. It could be here in no time.'

James Craig shook his head. 'Not possible. Should the disease somehow outwit the new Health Board at Inverness, it will meet its match in Cromarty, when it comes up against the Ladies of the Friendly Society.'

'Perhaps,' agreed Ludo. 'For the minute Mr Gilfeather saw the price of soap and chloride of soda rising, he put in orders enough to scrub and dose everything within a six-mile radius of the town. I don't know if it was the price rises or the pestilence that scared him more. And he has had a great deal to say of dung-heaps lately, too . . .'

Everyone laughed.

'What?' asked Ludo, perplexed.

John Learmonth smiled. 'Just that you are the greatest of tonics, Ludo. Your company never fails to cheer. I shall think of the dung heaps of Cromarty as the beady eyes of the Ladies of the Friendly Society sweep my schoolroom. If I survive to see the Visitation at all.'

'But why should you not?' asked Stan.

John grimaced. 'Because I am summoned to take my dinner at Cromarty Manse a week beforehand. For advice.'

'But Alasdair Mackay is excellent company,' said James, 'and his wife one of the most intelligent women you could hope to meet. Don't be fooled by her plain demeanour.'

'She is hardly plain!' protested John, much too enthusiastically for Ludovic, who still remembered John's worrying comment about the prettiness of Rachel Mackay. He glanced away. 'And I find her very – interesting. But Dr Fraser is to be there too.'

'Rather you than me.' Despite his sympathy for his friend, Ludo resolved to keep his wits about him over the coming days. He had no intention of finding himself drafted into yet another dinner table duel with the Resolis minister. His ears were still recovering from the rollicking Dr Fraser had given them both for having missed Lady Charlotte on the road.

'But what of the library?' asked Stan. 'What book have you now, Ludovic? I think it must almost be your turn for Miss Ferrier's *Marriage*, is it not?' he went on, innocently.

Ludo was about to explain that he was not on the rota to receive that particular book until May, when an exchange of amused glances between his friends alerted him to the fact that he was being made fun of. 'Oh!' he gave off in exasperation. 'Surely we are not to return to this? I mean, Miss Buchan is barely sixteen and . . .'

Since the night of Isaac Fordyce's Hallowe'en party, when the sturdy form of Miss Juniper's red-headed pupil had fallen at Ludo's feet, his friends had teased him mercilessly on the subject, and he knew he was expected to be outraged at their teasing. But the fact was that in the brief moment between Mairead Buchan opening her eyes to see him looking down upon her and her then becoming aware of the rest of the town standing about them, she had murmured the word, 'Ludo,' and the most beatific look had settled on her face. Ludo had never, in all his twenty-one years, been the recipient of such a look, and he had been able to think of little else since.

'Have you really not spoken to her yet, Ludovic?' asked Stanislas.

Ludo threw up his hands. 'What on earth should I say? She would hardly be interested in the doings of the bank, and she must, like everyone else, already know everything that happens in Cromarty.'

'You could always attend them on one of their nature walks,' suggested James.

'But then I would have to feign an interest in rocks and plants and the like, and honestly, James, it is quite beyond me.'

'Thus spake Romeo,' murmured Stanislas.

James Craig shook his head, smiling. 'But what have you brought to us tonight, Ludovic?'

Relieved, Ludo extracted from his bag two of the volumes he had brought with him, that Stan and James might get to read them too. 'It's Croker's new edition of Boswell's *Life of Johnson*.'

'You have read all eight volumes?' asked Stanislas.

Ludovic was known to trudge doggedly through whatever was put in front of him, a quality that served him very well at the bank.

'Of course I have read them all.' He watched with pleasure as James and Stanislas examined the books.

'I don't think I would like any companion of mine to write down my every saying and doing, in order that they might lay it before posterity,' said John Learmonth.

James looked up from the books. 'We would be interested in the earlier chapters at least.'

'Why the earlier chapters?'

'Well,' said James, 'Stan has opened the book of his life to us, and we have thrilled and wondered at it. You know my own history and Ludo here is hardly a man of secrets, but you . . .'

John took a deep breath and relayed to them what they already knew. 'I have already told you all there is to tell. I grew up in a small village in East Lothian. My father was a schoolmaster who died when I was a child. My mother was supported in my education by the charity of the parish. I attended the college in Edinburgh and am now following in my father's profession. I choose to do it here because I am intrigued by the history of the ancient peoples of the north. My own would barely merit a footnote in any but the most conventional biography.'

'Imagine, though,' enthused Ludo, 'to be even a footnote in the chapter of another's life. To have left some impression that one has existed at all!'

TWELVE

Early December 1831

A Dinner at Cromarty Manse

The Reverend Dr Micah Fraser of Resolis gave off rifling the drawers of his dresser and roared down the corridor, 'And where is my blue waistcoat, Bella?'

'In the press. Where else would it be?' Mrs Swanson left off her sweeping of the landing and came to see what chaos the minister had made of his dressing room. 'But surely you will be looking for your blacks, when you are going to Cromarty to quiz the schoolmaster?'

'I am going to Cromarty to read the newspapers and then to take my dinner with the Reverend and Mrs Alasdair Mackay and I daresay she'll be looking to me to keep up her table, for Alasdair never once knew how to dress himself properly, not even when that first wife of his would have had him a popinjay. Now, the blue waistcoat and my necktie, Bella. We will discomfit this schoolmaster fellow and get to the bottom of whatever he is at – for he is at something. The devil of a job he had to look me in the eye that time he was here, when all I was enquiring about was his time in Edinburgh. Did you ever see such a shifty-looking fellow? But I will winkle it out of him – he will hardly withstand the blue necktie!'

The items fetched and laid over the back of his chair, Dr Fraser looked into the mottled glass that had been gifted to them many years ago by his wife's mother and readied himself for battle. He knew a rogue when he saw one.

'It'll be money he's after, the blackguard. My money! By God, at his age I was earning my own keep, and I did not squander it in taverns and at the dog track, and God knows where else! Unless he's been thrown from the college?'

Mrs Hossack bridled at her husband's harshness. The man had no sensibility, no understanding of Fachie. 'Can a boy not come home to see his own mother, and at Christmas time?'

'To see you? You may tell yourself that as you wish, but I daresay they can roast a goose as well in Aberdeen as they can here. It'll be me he's coming back here for – me and my money. I should have put him to the ropeworks long ago.'

Mrs Hossack's lips worked together to keep in her contempt, but it was not to be done. She brandished the letter that had come, just before breakfast, from Aberdeen. In such a fine hand it was, so beautifully written, if short. 'Farquhar will be a physician and will move amongst gentlemen. Should he spend his days amongst the clash and noise of your Highland paupers in those ropeworks? Did I carry and birth him for *that* humiliation?'

Willie Hossack's eyes almost started from his head. 'Humiliation?!' He threw out a hand to indicate the room and its trappings all around her. 'The humiliation that pays for your foolish flounces and a piano you canna play, that pays to keep our own two girls in Edinburgh, because you hadna the wit to keep your eye on them here.' He crossed the rug towards her and brought his face down very close to hers. 'Humiliation? Oh, but you wait a while, Madge Ross, and I'll show you humiliation!' Again, the hand was flung out, the velvet drapes that kept the wind from rattling in on them through the firth in his sights now. 'I'll show you humiliation. You'll be lucky to have a wax cloth over your windows and a tin plate to eat your dinner off, and brose and kale will be your lot.' His face was twisted in disgust, and his eyes were looking at her as if he would murder her.

Mrs Hossack pressed herself back against her chair and wondered if she could reach the bell, but Willie didn't seem to notice. He carried on talking but it was as if he had forgotten he spoke to her at all. 'Aye, if you're lucky,' he repeated, beginning now to pace the rug, twisting his hands inside each other. His face took on an awful grin. 'Aye, and thon lassie that's married the minister, that you were always so uppit with and looking down your fat nose at, she'll stand with her hand on her hip and watch you walk the road out of Cromarty back to where you belong and the smile will be curling on her lip. Back to Dingwall you'll go, with me in the gaol and your world on your back.'

Mrs Hossack stared at her husband. 'Willie! What are

you saying? Dingwall? I'll not go back to Dingwall but in a coach and four.' She had not come thirty years and the road and the miles across the firth from two rooms behind her shoemaker father's workshop to go back to where that was all people remembered of her.

Hossack stopped. 'What I am saying, you foolish woman, is that your humiliation that your gentleman son owes the fine coat on his back to the ropeworks of Cromarty will soon be over. The trade is done, it's done.'

'But—'

'But nothing. Say what you like for Bonaparte, but it was boom days for hemp when he was sundering Europe. It's been going down ever since the peace, and those works across the firth at Invergordon have drained away every penny I put into them.'

'But the sacking, the Caribbean trade . . .'

He looked at her with contempt. 'Caribbean trade? The cotton plantations are wasted. Any man with an ounce of sense got out of them long ago. The sugar will no doubt be next.'

'But the negroes . . .'

'Can make their own clothes and grow their own food and they're not needing our pork or salt herring or ropes or sacking, and soon enough there'll not be a Scotsman with sense hasn't taken his money out of the whole damned place.'

'But what will the slaves do then, for they must surely do something and not be left lying about going to waste?'

'They will be freed. And we will be ruined.'

★

The Reverend Dr Micah Fraser heaved himself off his knees just as Hester entered the reading room with his coffee. The girl opened her mouth then hurriedly placed the tray on the table by his chair and took the tongs from his hand. 'I would have done that, Dr Fraser, if you would have rung the bell.'

'Heavens, lassie,' he said, dusting his hands on his breeches. 'Setting a few peats on the fire will hardly be the end of me. You know, when I was your age, I walked from the Strath of Kildonan all the way to the King's College in Aberdeen, and never thought a thing of it!' Then he settled himself in the armchair and waited while she poured out his coffee. 'Mind you, that'll not be much to you.'

Hester kept her eyes lowered. What use to explain to him anything about her life, what it had been or what it was? He would not begin to understand it. He was not the worst, though. She set out a plate of the shortbread petticoat tails that he was so fond of, and that Mrs Cameron got up early on a Friday morning to bake specially for him coming in. It was one minute to eleven. Hester suspected that Dr Fraser came in at this time on a Friday expressly that he might antagonise the bank manager, whom a glance through the window told her was at that very moment dodging a cart as he crossed the street towards the hotel. The pair, at whom no one else would dare to take a tilt, seemed to relish their duelling of wits with one another. At least Dr Fraser would not have time to quiz her on her life in Demerara while he was occupied in sparring with Mr Gilfeather.

Dr Fraser had not taken Mr Gilfeather's preferred seat on this occasion, though. She might safely go to the kitchen and be back before a stand-off had ensued. As she closed the coffee room door Mr Gilfeather appeared to be issuing a query as to the meaning of Dr Fraser's blue waistcoat, but by the time of her return with the coffee, the two men were seated across the fire from one another, each rigorously screened from the sight of his opponent by his newspaper.

Hester was not fooled. Her pouring of Mr Gilfeather's milk was accompanied by a 'Humph' from the minister of Resolis. The bank manager lifted his chin a little, behind his paper. 'Mmm?' he responded.

'The Archbishop of Canterbury,' replied Dr Fraser without looking over the top of his newspaper.

'And why in the world would I be interested in the doings of the English church?' enquired the bank manager, a steadfast Presbyterian and clerk to the Kirk Session of Cromarty. Hester had been in Scotland long enough to know that this made Sanders Gilfeather the most important man in the town, believe the laird or anyone else what they might. 'The affairs of the English church are nothing to me.'

Dr Fraser rumbled in admonition. 'An eye should be kept on them, all the same. Look here at the Archbishop, and what the fellow has beneath his apron – absenteeism, pluralism – it might as well be Ireland!' He pointed to a column of his newspaper. 'They are killing folk there, over the tithes. If such as you and I are not vigilant, Gilfeather, it will all go to Hell here too. Intrusion is already creeping in. Where are we if landlords are to appoint ministers simply for that they are a friend, or a relative to whom it suits them to do a favour, and never a word of Gospel truth or the call of the congregation?'

Hester could see that, behind his newspaper, Mr Gilfeather was resolute against the Intrusionists, and the integrity of the Scottish church assured, the two gentlemen returned to their reading. Hester felt it a good moment to step around the back of Mr Gilfeather's chair to add some more peats to the fire.

She had hardly straightened when there was another 'Humph' from Dr Fraser. The bank manager lowered his own paper two inches and waited.

'More Burkings.'

Now Mr Gilfeather lowered his paper even further. 'Where?'

'Bethnal Green, in London.'

Mr Gilfeather had some knowledge of London, from his earliest days as a clerk. It had been many a long day since news from London, of any stripe whatsoever, had had the power to surprise him. He merely sniffed.

'A man and two women – *women*, Gilfeather!' continued Dr Fraser, 'suspected of the murder of a girl seen going into their house, but never leaving. And word of a strange box being carried forth, after cries of "murder".'

The minister and the bank manager agreed that science had gone much too far in its quest for knowledge that belonged only to God, for was not man made in God's image? To open him up and to seek to understand what was inside! Little wonder the Devil had found his way in and was busy at his work. At Bethnal Green, and other places.

Hester thought of how she and Alicia and Mairead had pored over the reports of Burkings and decided no such thing could ever happen in Cromarty, where everyone was so closely watched. 'A murder under darkness, though,' Mairead had said, but Alicia had said murders in Cromarty might as well be committed in daylight, 'Because everyone would know who to suspect anyway, especially if Fachie Hossack was at home.'

Rachel surveyed the table, giving thought to where the candlesticks should be placed, to manage the changing light as the afternoon progressed. She wondered about the orchard and candied fruits Mrs Cramond had selected for the *epergne* at the centre, thinking the whole spoke a little more of luxury and indulgence than befitted a gathering of two ministers, a schoolmaster and a minister's wife. She wished she might not have to be present, but when she had asked Alasdair if he would mind if she were not there he had said of course he would mind and what was she thinking? 'Besides,' he'd said, 'I thought you would like to have someone closer to your own age at the table.'

That had annoyed her more than she could account for. 'I have no idea how old Mr Learmonth is, but I doubt his conversation, or the sight of his face, could be of more interest to me than yours.' She had turned away then, unfolding napkins that she had only just folded. 'I have friends enough of my own age. I need no more.'

And now Alasdair was standing looking out of the dining room window, and the atmosphere between them was heavier than an autumn fog until he uttered a sudden imprecation in his native Gaelic.

'What is it?' she said.

'Come here.' He beckoned her, slipping his arm round her waist as she drew up to the window. 'Look at Micah.'

'What in the name . . .' Their friend was striding up the middle of the road, his hat ever threatening to launch itself in flight, his best tail coat and breeches in good order, but in place of the sober black of a learned and revered Doctor of Theology of the Kirk of Scotland was a startling blue waistcoat with silver buttons, paired, where the ministerial cloth should have been, with a necktie of equally startling blue. Never had Dr Fraser looked more invigorated.

The schoolmaster arriving very shortly after Dr Fraser, and he almost, but not quite, managing to hide his confusion at the latter's unexpected foray into colour, they had soon all four of them sat down to table. Micah, as Rachel had feared, was in the best of form and a danger to the unwary. Mr Learmonth was invited to undergo his first trial – he would say the grace. A trial indeed, for what would satisfy Mr Mackay would not satisfy Dr Fraser, and every one of them at the table knew it. He should have chosen one or the other, Rachel thought, but the schoolmaster attempted to please them both, and so hashed it. She left a beat after the 'amens' before asking Jane to uncover the dishes.

Evidently anxious to put the awkwardness of the grace behind him, the schoolmaster opened his mouth again. 'It is very kind of you, Mrs Mackay, to invite me here ahead of the Visitation.'

Rachel reached for the dish of leeks and began to help Micah Fraser to them first. 'It was not I but my husband that invited you, Mr Learmonth, but I can assure you that the Ladies of the Friendly Society have only the good of the school at heart, and any criticism should only be taken as an encouragement to improvement.'

'I fear perhaps Miss Elspeth Rose will be very encouraging, then,' he offered.

Dr Fraser started at this pleasantry as if the schoolmaster had just produced a unicorn for his inspection. 'You make very bold, Mr Learmonth. Many an errant schoolmaster has come and gone under the reign of Miss Elspeth. I believe there was some rumpus with your immediate predecessor over the lassies' sewing class.' He looked to Rachel. 'Was there not, Mrs Mackay?'

Rachel forked a little cabbage onto her own plate. 'There was some question of the utility of lace handkerchiefs over stockings,' she said, 'but Miss Anna laid herself down in defence of the handkerchiefs, and so the schoolmaster escaped with only a mild censure. Although, as I recall, he did not remain in Cromarty very long afterwards.'

Dr Fraser helped himself to a slab of beef from the platter

being held out to him. 'She has mettle though, the Miss Anna.'

The schoolmaster looked across at him. 'Has she . . .' He seemed uncertain as to how to proceed. Micah Fraser sprang into the gap.

'Has she what?'

'Has she always been,' another hesitation, 'the way she is, or did she suffer some accident?'

It was Alasdair who replied. 'She has always been a pure-hearted soul. The only accident she has suffered is that the world around her is not. Where others might have grown bitter, she has remained herself. Long may she continue, *the way she is*.'

'Of course,' said the schoolmaster. Then a happier line of approach seemed to strike him. 'In the library – the circulating library – it is from Miss Anna that I receive my book each month. I have found her very kind and warm-hearted and have enjoyed our exchanges very much. Her sister is always there too, of course.'

'You will not get one without the other,' agreed Micah. 'And which books has Miss Anna passed to you so far? I have the devil of a job to remember the order Sanders Gilfeather set them all out in.'

Micah Fraser was as nosy as a fishwife and Rachel suspected he had been in cahoots with Mr Gilfeather over the matter of who should be permitted to be in regular contact with whom over the passing of the books.

The unsuspecting schoolmaster appeared relieved that

this new avenue of discussion had been embarked upon. 'Last month Miss Anna passed to me Miss Ferrier's *Marriage* and this time it was Morier's *Hajji Baba*.'

Dr Fraser leaned forward. 'And is it full of djinns and sorcerers and carpets that fly, as the good Mr Gilfeather fears?'

John Learmonth risked a smile. 'I am afraid not. Mr Morier rather uses his portrayal of the Persian ambassador's visit to Britain to tell us something of ourselves.'

Micah slapped a hand to his knee. 'I shall look forward to it. And what does he tell us?'

'Oh,' Learmonth glanced towards Alasdair as if for approval, 'he has things to say on the matter of slavery, on questions of hygiene and the spread of disease.'

Dr Fraser turned and addressed himself to Rachel. 'Surely this Hajji Baba was at the last meeting of the Elgin Board of Health, for they were speaking of the very same thing.' He turned back to the schoolmaster. 'But you were saying, Mr Learmonth.'

The schoolmaster took a sip of wine, as if to fortify himself. 'Morier talks also of the morality of our . . .' He glanced at Rachel. 'But perhaps it is not a subject for discussion in front of ladies.'

'Well,' said Rachel, 'as Miss Anna Rose must already have read and discussed the book with her sister, and it has not been jettisoned from the library, I am confident I will not be so appalled as to have to get up from table. Or is it that you think we ladies will not *understand* what we read unless the meaning is explained to us by the gentlemen of our acquaintance?'

A rumble of amusement came from Micah Fraser's throat. 'You have set her to it now, young man. How do you answer? Think carefully – you will have the bluestockings of Cromarty upon you.'

John Learmonth set down his knife and fork and looked intently at Rachel. His eyes were a pale green under thick brown lashes. She had noticed them before. Her question had given him licence to do this and she wished she had never asked it. She forced herself not to look away.

'Morier draws comparisons between the morals of Persian women and of our own, for that Persian women cover their faces and show themselves only to their husbands, whereas,' he cleared his throat, 'whereas our women expose themselves for all to see.'

Rachel felt a flush shoot up her neck but before anyone else could say anything, Micah Fraser brought his hand down so hard on the table that the first Mrs Mackay's cutlery jumped and the candles trembled in their sticks. 'I will not allow *that*, Mr Learmonth! Whatever debaucheries might parade themselves about in London or wherever else Mr Morier might be acquainted with, *our* women dress with the height of propriety, of which Mrs Mackay here offers an unimpeachable example. A face that the Mussulmans, for whatever reason seems best to them, cover up, is often all a man here might see.'

Learmonth was not to be cowed on the matter though. 'I only tell you what Morier has to say, Dr Fraser, and I do not think he is entirely wrong. It is the *face* of a woman that will bewitch a man. The look in her eyes, the motion of her lips that will entice him . . .'

Here Alasdair, to Rachel's immense relief, cleared his throat in a manner not to be misunderstood, and said, 'Morier takes aim at many of the hypocrisies of our society. I do not think it entirely fitting that we concentrate on what he has to say of women.'

Learmonth looked momentarily startled at this intervention, as if only now aware of what he had been saying and where he was saying it. He sat back in his chair. 'I meant no impropriety. Please forgive me.'

Again, there was a rumble from Dr Fraser. 'We shall see what Morier has to say for himself when I have my turn. Though I daresay I shall find the book does not hold a candle to Miss Ferrier's. A clever woman, that.'

The schoolmaster grasped at the opportunity to extract himself from the quagmire he had stumbled into. 'Yes, certainly Miss Anna preferred Miss Ferrier's book although, of course, it was a little awkward when it came to the discussion of the aunts.'

'Oh?' enquired Dr Fraser, still on the alert. 'How so?'

'Well, they are old maids.'

Rachel could not help herself. 'Than which no greater fate can befall a woman.'

'I mean no disparagement by it,' said Learmonth. 'But in her painting of their characters, Miss Ferrier at first seems to invite us to laugh at them, and it is possible to discern in them characteristics familiar in ladies of our own acquaintance.'

'Like Miss Anna herself?' enquired Alasdair.

'Perhaps,' said the schoolmaster. He picked up his fork then set it down again. 'I wonder though at the pains Miss Elspeth takes to regulate her sister's behaviour, and whether Miss Anna would be less childlike were she treated less like a child.'

'Elspeth has only her sister's well-being at heart,' said Alasdair. 'Anna formed an attachment in her youth of which her family did not approve, and they strove to ensure she could not persist in it. It may seem harsh now, but they have lived that way so long that I doubt either would know how to go about living in any other. Anna would be lost without Elspeth, and Elspeth without Anna.'

'The pity is there are not more Elspeth Roses in the world,' declared Dr Fraser. 'There is too much these days of young people entering harum-scarum into associations they would do better to avoid. Yourself, for instance, Mr Learmonth . . .'

The schoolmaster, who had begun to relax, was so startled by the remark that he knocked over his glass, sending its ruby liquid across the pure white linen tablecloth. He jumped up, blustering apologies and flapping his napkin frustratedly at the mess.

'The girl will see to it, Mr Learmonth,' said Alisdair as Jane began to set things to rights. 'Please sit back down.'

'I'm sorry, Mrs Mackay,' apologised the schoolmaster, looking as humiliated as a petulant boy.

Dr Fraser exchanged a look with Alasdair, then picked up

where he had left off. 'I was about to observe that a young man like yourself might find himself subject to the wiles of a great many ladies and their mothers. Books such as Miss Ferrier's, or Miss Austen's in England for that matter, have not been conjured out of thin air. No doubt your own mother has some plan in mind for you. Is there a young lady with expectations, waiting at home in Dunbar, or have you abandoned the place altogether, leaving a gaggle of broken hearts in your wake?'

John Learmonth looked to Alasdair as if for some intervention at this astounding turn in the conversation. On almost any other occasion, Rachel would have expected Alasdair to say something, but Alasdair merely continued to work quietly at his beef. They were all waiting for the schoolmaster's answer.

'I . . . trust not,' said the schoolmaster, 'and you may be certain that my mother has no notion of young ladies in Dunbar.' This said, he very determinedly gave all his attention to his food.

The room was then given over to the ticking of the clock in time to the scraping of cutlery on the second-best china until, at last, Alasdair broke the silence of the table. 'That is a very fine waistcoat you have on, Micah,' he said. 'I am not sure, for myself, that I could carry off the blue.'

THIRTEEN

10 December

Visitations

Rachel watched as Charlotte's fingers tried to tie the buttons of her coat. Plain grey buttons on a plain grey coat – serviceable, and nothing like the delicate pearl buttons of the silk and velvet jackets and spencers with which Charlotte's dressing room was filled. And yet the fingers stumbled and could not manage their simple task.

Rachel could bear it no longer. 'Let me do it.'

Charlotte let her hands fall to her sides, without protest.

'You do not need to come, you know. No one expects you to come. They know you have been ill. The wind is very sharp today. They will not look for you.'

Charlotte closed her eyes a moment and took a breath. 'I cannot be ill for ever. I must begin to be . . .'

'To be what?'

'Something. Something more than whatever I am now.'

Rachel put her arms around Charlotte and held her close. 'You are something, to me.' Then she pulled back a little. 'And to William, for all he cannot express it.'

Charlotte said nothing.

Rachel pressed on. 'He says that you have taken to wandering, at night.'

'I have promised him I will not leave the confines of the town, that I will always come back.'

'But where do you go, Charlotte? What are you looking for? You know Charles is not here.'

Charlotte gave a desperate laugh. 'I know that, if I know nothing else at all! I wander at night because I can be free. I am not watched in the darkness. I wander paths that I have walked all my life and think what other routes they might have taken me. I fill myself with the thoughts and the freedom of them, and then I come back here, where those thoughts sustain me through another day.' She looked down at her coat and tied up a button Rachel had missed. 'But I cannot be for ever in the darkness. And besides, I must face the schoolmaster.'

'You will not have seen him since that night?'

'No. Nor poor Ludovic either, since they carried me to Dr Fraser's manse. But Ludo – well, he and Dr Fraser and I belong, do we not, to this little world of ours? If I were to be found, it is right that they found me. I am theirs to look after, as they would be mine. Mr Learmonth, though, is an outsider.'

Rachel slipped her arm through Charlotte's. 'I think by the end of today, he may wish he had never come here at all.'

*

John Learmonth stood by the door of his schoolroom, a man at the gallows, awaiting his executioner. He had been having these dark thoughts ever since the awful dinner at Cromarty Manse, at the end of which Dr Fraser had thrust upon him a copy of Hogg's *Private Memoirs and Confessions of a Justified Sinner*, with some ominous observation about shape-shifters. Now John saw sinister shadows everywhere. Last night, as he had taken a turn about the harbour to clear his head, his eye had been taken by a fleeting figure that might have been Fachie Hossack. He would mention it to Ludo, just in case, but for now, all he could think of were those words from the Sermon on the Mount, 'sufficient unto the day is the Evil thereof'.

'They're coming,' whispered young Flora Stewart, standing frozenly beside him, a sad winter bouquet of red-berried branches twined round with ivy gripped in her fingers. Emerging on to Shore Street, like the vanguard of an army on the march, were the ladies of the Friendly Society.

At the front, of course, was Miss Elspeth Rose, her face set like Nigg Hill across the water, battered by storms and yet immovable. Beside her, missing a step for every three of her sister's, and rosy faced in the struggle to keep up, was Miss Anna. Tartan. A bright red tartan to her bonnet and gown, billowing like a declaration, Culloden somewhere at her back. Behind them, in a jostling for precedence that must come to an end once they reached the school door, was Mrs Hossack, who was wont to remind anyone within earshot that it was *her* husband's money that kept the school afloat, or most of it at any rate. John was surprised that she had not tricked herself out with a guard of Highland women from the ropeworks, the ones that did the work that made the money Mrs Hossack was benevolent enough to spend. On they came in a wave and John found himself murmuring, 'And the first shall be last and the last shall be first.' Mrs Gilfeather, as wife of the bank manager or session clerk – he was not certain which bonnet she wore today – walked just a step ahead of Rachel Mackay. Rachel's gown and pelisse were deep blue-green, as the sea against the glittering mica of her eyes. Wisps of brown hair were escaping to dance around her in the wind. A pearl, he thought, like the blue pearl he had found one day in a mollusc taken from the Conon. At her side was Lady Charlotte Mackenzie.

At the door, nodding to Flora's curtsy, Miss Elspeth Rose stepped aside, her sister falling in behind her. Across from them, so as to be first on the *left*-hand side, went Mrs Hossack. The other ladies disposed themselves in order, according to their status and allegiances. Through this guard of honour came the three who really mattered: the session clerk's wife, the minister's wife, the laird's wife. Roddie Urquhart, the school monitor, swept off his cap and looked to his boots as Flora drew from behind her back her sad posy. It was a stark thing, clean and beautiful. Lady Charlotte's lips parted slightly as she took it into her hand. 'Perfect,' she said. 'It is perfect.'

John's eyes alighted briefly on Lady Charlotte, the pale spectre of the woman they had found at Kirkmichael still lost-looking, somehow, but he could not stop his gaze travelling back to Rachel, and there it came to rest. 'Mrs Mackay,' he said, looking from her to the arrangement in Charlotte's hands. 'I'm sorry, we should have . . .'

Rachel's eyes briefly flared then her face became a mask. 'Be assured that I am not in the habit of receiving bouquets, Mr Learmonth. If you would kindly show us in. It is very cold out here on the step and Lady Charlotte is not long recovered from her illness.'

And so they went in, and as Marjorie Hossack stepped past him at the door he could not help but notice the look of some special triumph in her small eyes.

'Poor John,' said Ludo as he finished off the herring in oatmeal Hester had given him for his dinner. His mother was making her final inspection of the parlour, in advance of the arrival of the Ladies of the Friendly Society to take their tea.

'No one has actually *died* during a Visitation,' replied Hester.

'Well, I should certainly die, if I had to face them all like some unfortunate soul before the Vehmic tribunal.'

'The what?' Hester poked his feet with her broom to shift them as she swept the kitchen floor.

'Oh, it's in this book of Sir Walter's that's going around the circulating library. About some old Swiss secret society, that sat in judgement on members of the community and pronounced upon crimes the accused didn't even know they had committed.'

Hester laughed. 'If Mr Learmonth has committed any great crime, he will know about it – there is nothing secretive about the judgement of the Ladies' Friendly Society.'

'We are to have supper at James Craig's tonight, to cheer John up, regardless. Do you mind if I take the old newspapers down, or is there anything you wish to keep back for taking to Miss Juniper's tomorrow?'

'No, there is not,' said Hester. 'The newspapers are full of nothing but reports of grave-robbing and Burkings.'

'Ah, no,' said Ludo, pleased to be on firm ground, 'I can assure you they are full of a great deal more.' He drew in a breath, preparatory to expanding upon this, but Hester flicked the coming lecture away with a wave of her hand, as if at an inconvenient fly.

'We were talking about the Burkings, Ludo. Mairead terrifies herself with such tales.'

'But Miss Buchan seems such a sensible, dependable kind of girl. I would not have thought her prone to superstition.'

Hester frowned. 'She has read too many frightening stories that have stuck themselves in her head. And she is from a seafaring family – disasters and drownings are bound to happen. Might as well be superstitious as not. There is wickedness here on this earth, Ludo, why not in the other realms?'

Ludo shifted a little uncomfortably in his seat. He didn't

like to hear Hester talk of 'other realms'. He feared it might give people round about the wrong idea about her own beliefs.

Hester didn't wait for an answer though. She was four or five years younger than he was, but somehow here at home, if not out in the world – she was the older figure, the one with authority and worldly wisdom. Ludo wondered if she had been like this with her brother Caleb, but he thought not. All her stories of Caleb were of a strong, defiant figure. It was because of Caleb that Ludo tried to keep much of the late news from the Caribbean from Hester. He was careful to scour reports of uprisings, and their putting down, for Caleb's name. He had come to realise it was very unlikely the reports would actually give Caleb's or any other slave's name. But still. As he looked at her now, Ludo wondered if Hester had spent so much time with his mother that she had absorbed more of her ways than she had from her own.

'Anyway,' she was continuing, 'to fear Burkings is not to be superstitious, it is to be sensible. They are murders, by another name, and they are carried on by men and women of flesh and blood that you might meet walking down the street. Grave-robbing is bad enough, but to murder people so that one might sell their bodies to the anatomists – that is no superstition. It is proven in the courts. Wickedness exists and it walks the world in human form.'

Ludo finished his beer and washed his fingers in the bowl of water she had set in front of him, remembering to dry them on his napkin rather than his good work trousers. 'I know that, Hester,' he said. He bent down and kissed her on the cheek before putting on his hat and setting off back across the road, to the bank.

Fachie let the wind bang shut the door behind him as he left Hossack House. The ropeworks, his mother had asked him to go to. He had been home barely a day. He could feel them chuntering in the square of long brick ranges to his left, those half-savage Highland drones that soaked and boiled and pulled and twisted the hemp to make his father's fortune. If his father didn't want him to spend it, let him get another son.

'Get.' Fachie amused himself with the etymology of the word as he strode away in the other direction, laughing at the images that came to his mind. Crossing up Bank Street ahead of him, there was Ludo Cameron, going back to the bank after taking his dinner in his mother's hotel. What a little life, Fachie thought, that extended a dozen yards one way and a dozen back. Ludo had had his chance in Aberdeen and had come creeping back here. He would never leave the place. What a useless lump of humanity. But Fachie's palate was too jaded these days to bother himself with baiting the likes of Ludo Cameron. He did not, himself, plan on staying on in Aberdeen either, once his studies were done, but he sure as Hell would not be going where his father planned to send him. France now, or Italy perhaps, those were the places for a man like him.

For now though, Fachie needed money. He fingered the

pocket watch hanging on its fob at his waistcoat and headed for Church Street. The watch was a rather fine Pinchbeck, of which he had relieved the younger son of an earl in the back room of an Aberdeen tavern, only last week. He had hoped to keep it – the back of the casing was enamelled with the form of an exceptionally attractive young woman, whom the young lord had sworn was a lady of unimpeachable morals, from one of the finest bordellos in Paris. The nobleman, being just returned from the casinos of France, had imagined he would have a tremendous advantage over the less-travelled Fachie. He had soon learned his mistake. As a point of honour and to spare the young lord's blushes, Fachie had promised not to sell the thing to a watchmaker in Aberdeen, where it would be recognised at once.

He was soon pushing open the door of the clockmaker's shop. James Craig, the fellow at the counter informed him, was away, and not expected home before nightfall. This must be the Pole of whom his mother had so many opinions. A count, he was supposed to be, or the son of a count, or something. But, as his mother also said, what would a count or the son of a count be doing in Cromarty, working in James Craig's shop? She was an ignorant woman, but sometimes she asked a good question.

'Count nothing,' his father had said. 'A revolutionary, more like. Chased from Poland by the Russians and now holed up here, planning God knows what with that old Jacobin. I have had extra guards put on the ropeworks. You see what's gone on in Bristol?'

Fachie looked now at the man his mother was consequently convinced would murder them in their beds. Even seated behind the counter he looked thin and long, like a willow, and had all the pallor of a consumptive. The Pole was not a consumptive though, Fachie could tell that much just standing here in the doorway. Dark eyes, hollow cheeks, hair longer than was fashionable. He would snap like a twig in the wind, this clockmaker's apprentice. But then Fachie remembered the little provincial lawyer who had murdered half of France and thought it better to step warily with this Polish Robespierre. He would certainly not be entrusting him with his watch.

'Tell him I will come back tomorrow then.'

He stepped out of the shop and almost right into Rachel Mackay, who had once been governess to his sisters. She still looked like a governess. But what was under that blue-green dress, the shift, the bodice? He looked at the pulse at her neck. He used to think she must be cold comfort to Alasdair Mackay for all she was little more than half his age. But there now was the pulse at her neck and her skin soft and warm-looking. He leaned towards her slightly and she stepped back. He tipped his hat, slowly.

'You're back, then, Farquhar. Are you finished with your studies in Aberdeen?'

He smiled – did that slowly too. 'A lecture or two more and then the examinations, but it has become . . . expedient – shall we say – that I pay my father a visit.'

She looked at him then as she had used to look at him

years ago, when discovering him in some misdemeanour that she had no business concerning herself with. He saw the thought going through her head. It was killing her not to say it. Damn her, he thought. Why bother? He moved still closer to her so that she was forced to step further back into the street. 'That's right, Rachel, I'm back because I'm needing money. The life of a gentleman is not cheap, which you would know, if you were better acquainted with any gentlemen. Gambling and drinking and whores, you know? They don't come cheap.' He looked her up and down. 'Aberdeen isn't Cromarty.'

There was a slight movement of her lips and he could see a quiver of her nostrils before she walked away from him. Fachie laughed and went on down the street, whistling. Life at home did have its compensations.

At the cottage in Little Vennel, the girls were settling to a cosy afternoon of sewing and storytelling with Hester. Miss Juniper had already departed for Cromarty House, armed with a basket containing jars of her own rowan jelly and a flask of beef broth Janet Cameron had sent along from the hotel. 'Poor Charlotte will be exhausted after attending the school today. I wish she had not gone, but oh, she was always wilful, you know.'

Alicia watched the old lady go purposefully up the vennel and disappear around the top onto Church Street. Ever since the events of Hallowe'en, the elderly governess had been taking herself up to Cromarty House on a Saturday afternoon, when the witch housekeeper Morag Mackenzie was known to be in the Gaelic chapel, tormenting the children of the ropeworkers into their catechism. The rowan jelly and the beef broth were because, 'Charlotte loved both as a child, you know, and if she was ever ill, they were the things that would be sure to set her right again.' There had been a shifting in the way she spoke to them of Lady Charlotte, as if Sir William's wife were no longer a person distant, to be alluded to rather than spoken of. Now she had become what she in fact was – an older schoolfellow to Mairead and Alicia, just as Mrs Mackay was, a loved former pupil, a member of their little family who was in need of their care and their prayers.

The nature of Lady Charlotte's illness was never specified. The girls continued to speculate as to whether Lady Charlotte might be lovesick, but were always brought up against the question of who could she possibly be lovesick *for*? From here, it was the work of a moment for Alicia to wander from the subject of Lady Charlotte to that of Stanislas. Even Mairead had eventually admitted that Stanislas was quite beautiful, if your taste ran to a delicate sort of beauty rather than the reliable sturdiness which she preferred. Mairead had, nevertheless, positively forbidden her from writing a letter to the newspaper, such as were beginning to appear elsewhere from the hands of anonymous young ladies in praise of the heroic young Polish gentlemen who had of late months appeared, penniless and friendless, on Britain's streets. 'Everyone would know it was you,' she'd said.

As they settled to their sewing today, Alicia said in a low voice, 'Fachie Hossack is back. I saw him pass the top of the vennel, as I was closing the door just now after Miss Juniper.'

Mairead put down her needle. 'Are you sure? I was hoping he wouldn't be back in Cromarty before the spring, when I'm to visit my aunt Martha in Buckie.'

'Oh, it was him all right, sloping about at the end of the street like Zelucco looking for his next conquest . . .' Alicia stopped. She could have bitten her tongue. They had read *Zelucco* together, the three of them, only that autumn. If Alicia had known of the portion set in the Caribbean, she would not have suggested it. But Hester had said what the author wrote was nothing like the Caribbean, and she didn't think this Mr Moore could have been there at all. They had all agreed afterwards that they really would have done better not to have read the book in the first place, and so had dosed themselves with three of Miss Austen's novels in a row.

'That man Zelucco had a bad end,' said Hester. 'Perhaps Fachie Hossack will do too.'

They all thought that this was a most likely prospect, and then Alicia went to fetch their book. It was her turn to read as the others sewed. Last week they had decided to set aside Mrs Shelley's novel, *The Last Man*, which had been going on for an exceedingly long time and had begun to speak of a terrible plague sweeping the world, which was hardly a thing anyone would want to hear about with the cholera raging across the continent. They had fallen back upon Miss Juniper's own library, lighting at last on Sir Walter's, *St Ronan's Well*, which they all felt was much more the thing. After an hour's sewing they put away book and needlework and settled to their tea and cake, and poring over the advertisements of drapers and perfumiers in whichever Inverness paper Hester had brought down for them.

It was almost five by the time Hester left. There was very little light coming from the small windows of the fisher cottages as she hurried up the middle of Little Vennel. When she turned onto Church Street, the larger windows of the tall merchant houses gave a little more, but there was no moon to be seen and the street was just a progression of darknesses, the edges and gables of houses and ends of narrow lanes merely different degrees of black. She went as quickly as she was able, but suddenly, as she was about to pass the Gilfeathers' house, she felt the grip of a hand around her waist and another covering her mouth. She could see nothing of her assailant but felt herself being pulled backwards and a man's voice in her ear, murmuring about Jamaican ginger.

Hester struggled but his grip was firm, pulling her backwards to she knew not where. She could not cry out and she could not turn but she *could* move her hand. Hester slipped her hand into the pocket of her apron where she had put the jar of rowan jelly Miss Juniper had insisted she take home to Mrs Cameron, and drawing it out hurled it with all her might at the downpipe of the Gilfeathers' house.

The sound of the jar smashing echoed like an explosion in the silent darkness. Seemingly all at once, the doors to the clockmaker's shop and to the Oswald Street entrance of the Gilfeathers' burst open and anxious voices were calling out. Hester heard a curse before she was released and pushed to the ground, the heel of her hand impaling itself on a shard of sticky earthenware from the broken jar. The clockmaker's apprentice was quickest to her, soon followed by the Gilfeathers' little maid, her mistress close behind her. Of her assailant, there was no sign.

Stanislas stood back as Mrs Gilfeather bent towards her. 'What in the world has befallen you, lassie?'

Hester glanced from the kindly woman to the Polish apprentice and back again. Pressing her palm against the brown wool of her shawl, in the hope that the blood might not be noticed, she said, 'A cat. Darting across in the path in front of me. It startled me. I am sorry.'

'No need for you to be sorry, lassie, and— Oh my! But you're bleeding. Bessie, here, you help the poor lassie in and we'll see what's ado with her hand.' Mrs Gilfeather turned then to Stanislas whose dark eyes were fixed on Hester, half a question in them. 'You'll manage to get all this mess swept up now, afore someone else hurts themselves?'

Familiar with Mrs Gilfeather's ways, Stanislas hesitated only a moment, long enough to look at Hester again, to wordlessly ask the question, and to register the tiniest shake of her head. He understood. Thank God, thought Hester. Thank God the Polish apprentice understood that it would bring more trouble on her head, and on his, should either of them try to make the townsfolk of Cromarty understand that the man who had assaulted her was Farquhar Hossack.

By the time Ludo was setting out for the supper at James Craig's, the wind was howling and battering rain against his face. Any sensible person would remain at home and not get themselves a soaking in order to carry to his friend news that would be far, far better kept from him another day, if it need ever be told at all. Ludo, nonetheless, ploughed on, the newspaper tucked firmly inside his coat.

He was glad to see, when he entered the clockmaker's cosy back room, that John Learmonth had indeed survived the Visitation and was now in the midst of relaying the worst of it to Stan and James. Stan looked as if he wished to say something privately to Ludo but John was in full flow, telling of some incident between Mrs Hossack and Mrs Gilfeather. 'Am I to understand that there is some bad blood between those ladies?'

As Stanislas also looked enquiringly at him, Ludo discovered a frog in his throat that required a great deal of clearing and James Craig gave a rueful shake of the head. 'If you are still in the town in another thirty years or so, I might consider myself permitted to tell you. And Lady Charlotte was there?'

'Corporeally at least,' said John. 'Otherwise, I could not say that she took much interest in what went on about her.'

'She always was like one of the Three Graces blown

off course,' said James. 'I think Miss Juniper had been in hopes that marriage to William Mackenzie might anchor her somehow, but I have seen little sign of it, over the years.'

'She is a great deal younger than him,' said Stanislas. 'She would have been an ornament to any ballroom or salon. It seems a pity . . . Although, of course, an age difference need not be an impediment to a good marriage. The minister, Mr Mackay, seems to have the best of marriages.'

John examined the food in his bowl. 'But what of his wife? I know she was meant to marry the Gilfeathers' son. Perhaps, when he died, she thought she would be left a governess for ever. But can the security of the manse roof truly compensate her for her loss of freedom and marriage to a man almost twenty years her senior? And their lack of a child—'

James Craig's face was as stern as Ludo had ever seen it. 'Is not your business! You misunderstand and belittle them both. Perhaps you have not been here long enough to understand whom you might with impunity insult and whom you might not.'

John looked stunned. 'I – I meant no offence, James. I . . .'

Ludo felt his own cheeks burn and was almost relieved when an equally mortified Stan, in a desperate attempt to change the subject, asked, 'Have you brought the paper, Ludovic?' And then Ludovic wished they might have carried on talking for the rest of the night of the marriages of every couple in Cromarty. He laid down his spoon. 'I have, Stan.' Something in his face must have told the rest because his friend simply stared at him.

'Will you read it to us?'

Ludovic brought out the paper and looked to James, who took it from him.

'Let me,' said James.

The item they sought was on the fourth page, in the column marked 'Foreign Intelligence'. James began to read but was taken with a need to clear his throat and so had to start again. 'The Autocrat of Russia is pursuing a case of confiscation and banishment towards the unfortunate Poles, who seem destined to be deprived of a national existence altogether.' There followed a listing of the edicts lately issued by Paskewitch. 'The Polish cockade is also abolished, and that of Russia alone to be worn in future; and several penalties are denounced for any infringement of these orders. By this document, nothing Polish is to remain within the kingdom of Poland but the Poles themselves, who are now to be made Russians.'

None of them spoke, then Stanislas went to the drawer in the sideboard where he kept his translations. 'We are not Russians,' he said. As his friends hastily cleared a space on the table, he laid out the papers of his manuscript and opened his copy of *Konrad Wallenrod*, marked at the place he had last been working on. He dipped his pen in the ink bottle and bent his head over the paper, his lips moving as he read along the next line of Mickiewicz's poem, that national epic by which he sought to grasp hold of his nation's story. He held his pen above the paper for so long that a blob of ink fell from the nib to the sheet below, obscuring the last word he had written. He looked at his pen and at the ink mark and at the bare expanse of the rest of the sheet of paper as if he had never encountered them before. Then he dipped the pen again in the ink, and this time he did begin to write, hardly glancing at the printed volume in front of him and making firm strokes on the page. He said it again: 'We are not Russians.'

Whatever else he might have wanted to tell Ludo earlier in the evening had clearly been put out of his head.

FOURTEEN

24 December

An Evening at the Hossacks'

The Gilfeathers, he in a black arrangement almost identical to his banking suit and she in her good serviceable old brown silk and pearls, stopped first at the Commercial Hotel, on their way to the circulating library dinner at the Hossacks' house, that event having proved impossible to avoid. To her husband's demand as to what in the world Marjorie Hossack could be thinking of, taking it upon herself to summon the members of the library to a dinner on a night in December, his wife had observed that it would be all in the hope of promoting Fachie, and that Sir William might find a place for him somewhere.

'Sir William? I ken fa has a place for Fachie Hossack and it's no' Sir William,' Mr Gilfeather had muttered, slipping into the language of his own fireside. 'As well his mother keeps that hoose as hot as Hades, to get him used till it.'

Usually, on such occasions, the Gilfeathers would leave their housemaid at home to take a quiet evening to herself, set everything right for the morning and get off early to her bed, but since the business of the lassie Hester and the broken jar of jam, neither master nor mistress liked to leave their young Bessie in the house alone. They were sure there had been more to the circumstance of Hester's tumble than she had let on. Sanders hadn't been thirty years on the kirk session without understanding that lassies who took a fall were not always believed when they said they hadn't done it by themselves. So, Bessie would tonight keep company with Hester in the kitchen of the Commercial Hotel, as agreed with Janet Cameron.

'Safety in numbers,' Sanders muttered to his clerk as they followed Mrs Cameron and Mrs Gilfeather on the short journey down the street to the harbour front and Hossack House. 'Safety in numbers.' It was odds though, from Ludovic's face, whether he thought his senior was talking about the housemaids, or about themselves. Mr Gilfeather had in fact overheard Ludovic speculating with a junior clerk, just after the invitations had gone out, on his chances of catching the cholera in advance of Mrs Hossack's dinner. The clerk had lugubriously informed him that the cholera was only at Newcastle and so there probably wouldn't be time.

Eachie Hossack poured himself another brandy. The best stuff, that his father had paid a French *matelot* over the odds for. The customs officers were too busy chasing whisky-smugglers up the glens to notice a stray barrel of brandy being rolled into the ropeworks. Usually, his father would have the stuff under lock and key – the key that he had hanging from his waistcoat where a gentleman would wear a watch. But tonight, it was all about the *show*: the brandy bottle was out and Fachie determined to get his money's worth.

The dining room was set out in its finest. All credit to his mother, vulgar she might be, but she knew how to spend properly. The curtains were a good ten years out of date, but he knew they had cost a fortune and would hang there till the day they carried his father out in a box, feet first, for the old man had said so when he'd got the bill. And that dinner set – Willie Hossack hadn't complained about that. Derby porcelain. A bargain. That and the silverware, all from a roup of the Grants of Rothiemurchus, that had to scuttle away to India, away from the father's debts. The house was rented out now, for the making of money, old man Grant having blown the family fortune on buying parliamentary seats in English counties that had never heard of him. The Grants, that would not have deigned to wear shoes so common as those made by Fachie's grandfather, here now was their plate and silver, laid out by the cobbler's daughter, paid for by the little man from the ropeworks. Fachie toasted the ropeworks, the brandy swilling red gold in the candlelight. There was peculiar pleasure to be had, sometimes, in *not* being a gentleman's son.

The doorbell clanged, and soon the clack and chirrup of the Rose spinsters was drifting up the stairs from the lobby.

He poured himself another measure and swallowed it. He'd better get himself across to the drawing room before the old quizzes had their cloaks off and caught him on the landing.

His parents had posed themselves at the far end of the drawing room – his father leaning on the fireplace as if master of a thousand acres, and she a squashed pom-pom of a woman in silks two shades too bright for her and jewellery that might have suited her twenty years ago but did nothing now but announce the chins wobbling down her neck.

'Farquhar.' His mother beamed at him while his father eyed him as if wondering what he'd stolen. 'Oh, how well you carry off that new coat. I wish there were young ladies we could have asked, but the library is sorely lacking. Never mind. If you play your cards right with Sir William tonight, who knows what doors he might open to you?'

Fachie glanced at his father. 'I can only play the cards I am dealt, Mother, but we shall see.'

'Cards you are dealt?' His father pushed himself away from the mantelpiece towards him, a well-worn lecture ready to spill from his lips, but then the door opened and the Misses Rose were announced. The housemaid did not have time to close it again behind them before Miss Elspeth had drawn herself back as if from a sudden furnace. 'My word, Mrs Hossack, surely you have some fear of the cholera coming in, that you have the fire at such a raging heat.'

Before Fachie's mortified mother could open her mouth, his father had stepped forward. 'She has that, Miss Rose.

As well to drop my money directly on the flames and be done with it.'

Fachie made his most gracious bow and extended an arm to lead the old shrew and her sister to the settle opposite the one occupied by his mother. The show had begun.

Rachel knew of long experience as governess in this house that anyone who *mattered* would find themselves seated at dinner not beside Willie Hossack, but by Fachie. She could have laid out the place cards herself tonight, potential for discomfort and misunderstandings at almost every elbow, and in conversations that would have to battle their way cross-table, past gaudy and overflowing *epergnes*, heavy wine coolers and ostentatious candlesticks. This was the society they had somehow chosen for themselves by the formation of the library, and they would all just have to endure it. Sixteen of them to table, the dozen members of the library, their secretary Mr Gilfeather with his wife, and Mrs Hossack and Fachie. Rachel took a deep breath. So be it.

Once Alasdair had said grace and the servants begun to lift lids from tureens and dishes laid the length of the table, Mrs Hossack set forth. 'What a doubly happy occasion, to welcome the members of the library here to our table at Hossack House, and Farquhar home for Christmas from his studies in Aberdeen.'

It was the flawless gallantry of Mr Isaac Fordyce that rescued the table from its inability to echo their hostess's delight. 'We are most obliged to you, Mrs Hossack. And we shall look forward to hearing young Farquhar's thoughts on our reading, for I am sure a young man out in the world as he is will have enjoyed many of his own *Noctes Ambrosianae*.'

Mr Fordyce's allusion to the rowdy literary nights enjoyed in an Edinburgh tavern by Scott, Hogg and other luminaries of Scottish letters, and published in satirical form in *Blackwood's Magazine*, only served to thoroughly disarm Fachie's mother, who had never heard of them.

'Oh yes, Mr Fordyce,' said Fachie, 'I can assure you that the taverns of Aberdeen are quite as lively as those of Edinburgh.'

'I wonder that you have left them,' put in Dr Fraser, who, at Rachel's right, had to lean forwards and virtually shout down the table at the object of his remark. She pinned herself back against her seat, to facilitate him.

Marjorie Hossack, having placed Dr Fraser so far away from herself, was forced to shout back. 'I am blessed to have a son who will make the effort to come home at Christmas time to see his mother.'

'No doubt,' agreed Dr Fraser. 'But I was just wondering whether Fachie had come of his own accord, or was he chased?'

'Chased?' Mrs Hossack's face was like that of a horse that had dropped its nosebag. 'William . . .' she appealed to her husband.

Willie Hossack, who had already sunk down in his seat, his duty done in having paid for this whole performance, roused himself up. 'I daresay Dr Fraser will tell us what he means.'

'What I mean,' said Dr Fraser, addressing the entire table now, 'is that the good citizens of Aberdeen have taken matters into their own hands to put an end to the godless experimentations of the medical faculty there. I hear the new anatomical theatre is torn brick from brick and the place rendered ashes. The medical students who were so agog to witness the blasphemies performed by their professors will have to find some other way to occupy their time.'

Willie Hossack moved his mouth in a manner to suggest he would like to have agreed with the minister, but his wife looked to be well on the way to a seizure of some sort. Fachie's drawl made its way up the table. 'In Aberdeen, it is the indigent and ignorant whose fears are played upon, until they know no better than to assault the bastions of science, whereas here the ignorance is all on the part of those who really should know better. Never fear, Dr Fraser, whatever *you* might have buried in the ground about Resolis or Cullicudden is far too long dead for *me* to take an interest in it.'

Rachel saw Dr Fraser's hand grip his knife and laid her own over it, to calm him. 'It's all right, Micah,' she breathed. 'It's all right.' Across from her she saw that Alasdair was also struggling to keep his composure.

'Well,' said Sir William, in a gallant effort to retrieve the conversation, 'I blame those damned liberal agitators.

Look at Bristol – the guilty not even brought to trial yet and the country like a tinder box.'

People around the table had started to murmur their agreement when, to the general astonishment, Ludovic Cameron broke in. 'But I do not think it's the same thing. The desire for a greater voice in the running of the country is a question of economic sense. You, Mr Hossack, for instance. You create much of the wealth on which this town prides itself. Should you not have the right to participate in the selection of the government that will spend your taxes?'

Willie Hossack looked at Ludovic as if he had just noticed him for the first time. 'Indeed, I should. And I doubt anyone will accuse *me* of pulling down anatomy theatres!' This should have been the end of it, but it was not the end of it, because Fachie Hossack had got the bit between his teeth and would not let it be.

'Well, well, so Ludo Cameron has caught an opinion. I heard you had been haunting James Craig's place, paying court to that old Jacobin and his aristocratic apprentice.'

Ludo coloured. 'James and Stanislas are my friends.'

At this Fachie made a show of spurting out his wine. 'Oh, Ludo. You have acquired a sense of humour, too, I see. You must warn me next time, though, for the sake of my mother's napkins.'

No one else laughed.

'I too count myself fortunate to be Ludovic's friend,' said John Learmonth.

'My,' replied Fachie. 'Truly, there has been a revolution

in the society of Cromarty. The schoolmaster and the bank clerk. It will not be long until we have the servants sitting to table alongside us.' Here he leaned forward, just as Dr Fraser had done. He raised his glass towards Rachel. 'But of course, that has already happened.'

It was for Alasdair to have said something. It should have been him, and she could see him struggling to find the words, but he did not get there in time, because John Learmonth had pushed back his chair and was on his feet. Rachel felt suddenly frozen. She could not believe what he was doing, but he was doing it. The schoolmaster was lifting his glass to her and looking at her as if she was a woman with no husband. 'Are we toasting the ladies already?' he asked. The rest of the men reached in confusion for their glasses, and mumbled something about, 'the ladies', before Willie Hossack said it was high time they set to their meat, for everybody knew that the time for toasts was after you had eaten your fill, and what was the point in paying butchers a fortune if your meat was to be stone cold by the time you got to it?

Plates were passed and neighbours helped neighbours to whatever dishes were closest. In her mortification, Rachel accepted and dispensed spoonsful and slices of she knew not what. Consumed with shame and anger, at Fachie Hossack for his venom, at Alasdair for doing nothing, at John Learmonth – for what, his act of insanity? If the rest of the table believed it to have been an act of gallantry in the face of Fachie Hossack's insult, all well and good, but she had seen the look in the schoolmaster's eyes and knew that that was not what it had been about at all. At least Alasdair, on the same side of the table as him and separated from him by the substantial forms of Ludo Cameron and Mrs Gilfeather, could not also have seen it, or understood what it meant. Thank God, Rachel thought, for the cack-handedness of Marjorie Hossack's cook, who could render meat so tough that there was nothing for the company to do for the next while but chew on it.

At last, though, the dinner guests took respite from their eating and fell again to conversation. Miss Elspeth, who ate sparingly and accusingly, was the first to speak. 'It is all well and good to dine on Mr Hossack's hospitality, but the point of this gathering is to discuss the books, is it not? It's a stormy night to go out for your dinner, when you might have had as good if not better at your own table.'

Rachel had to suppress a grin, and to try not to catch sight of the desperately reassuring smile Miss Anna was beaming upon Mrs Hossack, in mitigation of her sister's rudeness. Miss Elspeth, unabashed, continued, addressing her neighbour to the left. 'Mr Fordyce, you selected the *Life of Lord Byron* as your first choice, I believe. Did you find it to your liking?'

'Oh yes,' enthused the old gentleman. 'What a delight it has been, to feel that one has been able once again in the imagination to accompany the noble lord. I am sure Lady Charlotte and Mrs Mackay, who have had the book since, I believe, and Dr Fraser, who has it now will—'

'Indeed, I have it now, Mr Fordyce, and I have to say I am not certain it is a thing I would have advised for the attention of these two ladies here.'

Charlotte looked up, showing an interest for the first time in the evening. 'Oh, but I enjoyed it very much, Dr Fraser, and do not think I am any the worse for it. And Rachel too—'

But she got no further, because from the opposite end of the table, Fachie Hossack interrupted her. 'I wonder how much one would profit from reading the *Life* that had not read Byron's poems? I cannot believe that so *moral* a person as Mrs Mackay could have read so scandalous a work as *Don Juan*, for instance.' He turned then towards Alasdair. 'Surely Mr Mackay does not think *Don Juan* fit reading for the lady of the manse?'

'My wife is a woman of sense and education, Farquhar. I do not find it necessary to censor her reading.'

'No? But even in the first canto – and I'm sure you will forgive me, Mother, for lowering the tone at your table – but in the first canto, the cuckolding of Don Alonso, even that does not give you pause for thought? That an older man who has been foolish enough to take *so much younger* a wife finds himself cuckolded by her young lover?'

'It is a poem,' said Alasdair. 'A work of fiction. And Cromarty is not Seville.'

'Of course not,' said Fachie. 'But enough of the cuckolding of older husbands. Mr Learmonth, what on earth can you find to do in Cromarty, once the school day is done?'

There was a stunned silence around the table. Rachel could scarcely breathe for impotent rage. Alasdair had gone white as chalk. Mrs Gilfeather began to say something that sounded like, 'I dinna think this quite . . .' But it was Dr Fraser who put an end to it. 'Mr Hossack, your son is drunk and making himself deliberately offensive. You will understand if we do not stay for the rest of the performance.' He looked around the table, his granite gaze landing on one library member after another.

Mr Gilfeather was the first to join him on his feet. 'Come, Maggie, this is not fit talk for your ears.'

One by one, the guests arose and making their muted apologies, made their way from the table. The parlourmaid, who understood enough to know that some disaster had occurred, scurried to open the dining room door ahead of her mistress's guests and could be heard hissing down the stairs, 'Matthew, they're needing their coats.'

Icy air from a cold north wind had got into the Hossack house at each opening of the street door and breaths of it had reached the half-empty dining room. Last of the Hossacks' guests to leave were Sir William, Lady Charlotte, Alasdair and Rachel. Sir William cleared his throat. 'Thank you for your hospitality, Mrs Hossack, Willie, but if you could have our carriage sent around to the hotel, we will wait for it there.' He looked over at his wife and at Rachel, both already standing, before laying a hand on Alasdair, who remained seated and grey amongst the ruins. 'Come, Alasdair. It is time for us to go.'

PART TWO

Spring 1832

FIFTEEN

March

A Wrathful God

It was perishingly cold inside the kirk. Within the stone walls and beneath the high roofbeams it was never warm. The winter had been mild but now, at the beginning of March, the gods of snow and ice had decided to take their revenge upon the north of Scotland and it was chill as death.

Mairead looked at Alicia's delicate lace gloves, that exposed her fingertips. 'I told you they would go blue. And for what? Stanislas will not see them from where he is sitting unless you take to waving your arms in the air, and this is *not* that kind of church.' There had been much in the papers lately about 'that kind of church', the Caledonian church in London having actually been shut down on account of its minister having taken a very peculiar turn, and the girls had heard of astonishing behaviours in churches in America, although they were fairly confident such would never find a foothold in Cromarty.

It was a source of great disappointment to Alicia that

Miss Juniper's accustomed place in the church was four rows behind that of the clockmaker rather than directly across from him, beneath the laird's loft, which would have given her an almost perfect view of Stanislas's face throughout the service. At least she could glimpse the back of his head, his long, fair locks, and she had learned to content herself with that.

'You know very well that he will see them when we come out into the churchyard and Miss Juniper stops to speak to Mrs Gilfeather,' she said to Mairead. 'You are so tetchy today. If you are like this after only missing your breakfast, what will I be having to put up with by suppertime?'

'Suppertime,' sighed Mairead. 'Don't even speak of it. But are *you* not ravenous without your porridge? And at least it would have kept us warm. I doubt I will make it past dinnertime, never mind until suppertime – and we are not to have anything even then!'

'You will prevail,' replied Alicia, not unkindly. 'Look about you – Cromarty is full of elderly people who must have endured many fasts before this one. Besides, we have not the whole day to go now, just another twenty-two hours.'

'Hmmph,' said Mairead. 'You may wait until eight o'clock tomorrow morning for your breakfast, but I will be taking a store of apples and bannocks up to bed with me tonight, and they will not survive many minutes beyond the first strike of the courthouse clock at midnight.' She huffed out a great breath. 'How in the world is starving the populace supposed to protect us from the cholera?'

The door opened behind them to reveal Mr Gilfeather carrying the Bible and the minister following. 'I daresay we are about to find out,' whispered Alicia, as the congregation rose to its feet.

Mr Mackay ascended the pulpit, looking about him grim-faced as if he had ordered the cold in specially. Mairead could not put this down to the fast though – he had been like this since Christmas, and Rachel had not been herself since then either. They looked as if they had forgone their fire at the manse along with their breakfast. The minister had certainly not had *his* kipper and had a look on his face fit to curdle the stomach of any who had. Mairead was momentarily glad that Miss Juniper had followed to the letter the government's instruction that the people of Scotland should observe today as a fast day, on account of the cholera. She steeled herself, and as anyone who had ever sat on a cold bench in a Scottish kirk might have predicted, the minister took his text from Isaiah.

'Behold, thou art wroth; for we have sinned . . .'

The populace of Cromarty, the collective empty stomach notwithstanding, settled itself in anticipation of hearing of the sins of their neighbours, and their minister did not spare them. He named no names, but every soul there knew who were the blasphemers, the adulterers, the fornicators, the usurers and the thieves. Had they not seen them for themselves, publicly shamed in this very kirk, or before the magistrate in the courthouse only yards along the road? There was much righteous satisfaction amongst the congregation. Mairead wished that she might join in it, but she was waiting to see if the minister said anything about landowners who drove people out of their villages and burned the roofs of their cottages, because she was sure Dr Fraser in Resolis would be saying plenty about *them* at this present moment, but perhaps Mr Mackay meant them to be encompassed in the common run of sinners against whom he had already fulminated, as well as the slave masters Hester had told them about, but whom he had also failed to mention. The wrath of God had lately manifested itself as a hurricane in the Caribbean, and Hester had said that perhaps it was better that Cromarty had to take its chances with the cholera, because the thatch of Miss Juniper's cottage roof would hardly withstand a real hurricane.

Her mind wandering around the various lofts and aisles of the kirk, stuffed full as they evidently were with sinners of every description, Mairead was able to forget her growling stomach for the most part of the sermon to the extent that she was able to join enthusiastically in the final, urgent prayer that the Lord's 'wroth' should not be very sore and that He should not 'remember iniquity forever'.

Alicia, on the other hand, was of a different mind. As the last psalm dwindled away and they waited for Mr Gilfeather, the Bible, and Mr Mackay to process out of the church again, she whispered into Mairead's ear, 'The hypocrisy of it – to ask the Lord to forgive the transgressions of Cromarty when the self-same town will not forgive Miss Juniper for her book!'

A glance towards their schoolmistress suggested that these same sentiments were going through her mind, too.

Outside, Rachel bade farewell to Mrs Gilfeather and watched her go off down the path in the company of Janet Cameron who hardly bothered to lower her voice as she said, 'A fast, indeed! They'd do better to hand everyone a cake of soap.' Rachel knew, nonetheless, that Ludo Cameron, who appeared to be in sympathetic conversation with Miss Juniper's Mairead, would be going home to a bare, if scrupulously clean, dinner table.

She wished she were not. Not for herself, although her stomach was growling enough, but for Alasdair. He was not well. Ever since the night of the terrible dinner at the Hossacks' house, and through the disconcertingly mild winter that had followed, she had noticed the shadow of his black dog stalking him. She had told him outright, when they had got home that night, that what Fachie had implied in relation to the schoolmaster and to herself was utterly untrue, and he had said he believed her. She had nonetheless avoided every possible encounter with John Learmonth since then, because she understood well enough the meaning of the look he had given her across the Hossacks' dinner table. And yet, Alasdair's black dog had stalked, and now, with the sudden banishment of the expected spring, she could practically hear it panting behind him as he entered a room.

The snow had started while they were in the kirk and whirled around the gravestones now. No one was tempted to linger by the church door today but hurried instead back to homes and workplaces. Soon they were all gone, and Sanders Gilfeather, in his heavy black winter coat with its fur trimmings, was ushering Alasdair down the path.

'Get this fellow home in front of the fire, Mrs Mackay, and get a dram of brandy inside him. It'll do no good to anyone should the minister fall ill.'

Alasdair, hunched in on himself, shook his head, but allowed Rachel to slip her arm through his as they bid farewell to the bank manager and started back along the street to the manse, the bitter cold wind swirling snow into their faces. She persuaded him to sit by the fire, and to take a brandy as directed by Sanders Gilfeather, but he refused her urging that he take some broth, the sick being excused the fast. 'God is not mocked, Rachel. I am not ill and He who knows all knows it.' The look in his eyes terrified her.

The day had at last neared its end and the girls were in their beds under the eaves of Miss Juniper's cottage. Mairead was determined to stay awake until midnight. She had, with Miss Juniper's tacit approval, secreted an apple, three bannocks, a piece of cheese and a slice of cold mutton in her largest handkerchief and carried them upstairs, to be consumed the moment the courthouse clock struck twelve. She had no fears that she would fall asleep and miss the tolling of the bells, such was the emptiness of her stomach.

Alicia had declined the suggestion that she should follow Mairead's example, saying that she was sure if she just went to sleep, the morning would come around all the quicker. Besides, she had said, gorging on mutton and apple and cheese in the middle of the night would bring nothing but bad dreams and a sore belly and she preferred to take her chances with an empty one. They said their prayers and within minutes of getting into bed, Alicia was asleep.

The wind was still battering the rooftops, and Mairead could hear the sea as it hurled itself at the shore. She was glad they did not live right at the front, and so at least had some protection from the onslaught, here in their little row of gable ends. A girl who lived in a cottage facing directly onto the shore had told them how, on nights like these when storms raged and the sea threw up its wares, the sound of the wrack and other seaweeds being hurled against the door and windows was like the knocking of drowned men demanding entry. The firth was full of the drowned. Four men had been lost on the short crossing between Cromarty and Balintraid only a few months ago, four women on the same crossing the year before, and a family of eight coming down the coast from Caithness a few months before that. Mairead knew the ghosts of those taken by the deep were eternally trying to get home. She forced her mind away from the sea and instead set her thoughts on the path to Cromarty hill and summertime walks and picnics, but every time she got her mind halfway up the hill, the wind would start and the sea below the cliffs would boil up. She would need to get away from the sea altogether. Further up then, onto the moor, but there it was worse – the moor was filled with malign spirits and should

Mairead wander there on a night like this she might be dead of exposure long before morning. What would she do, she thought, should ever she find herself up there, alone, in a snow storm? Mairead had all but forgotten about her empty stomach and her eyes were closing as she imagined herself lying in a gouged out hollow on Cromarty hill, where the snow and the wind and whatever the sea might give up could not reach her. But then the wind caught up debris from the ground and hurled it all around so that twigs, leaves and sods and clods of earth landed on her arms, her legs, her face. Soil covered her eyes, filled her mouth, blocked her nose. Into Mairead's head roared a story she had read in the paper many months ago and had tried very hard to forget. She sat bolt upright in her bed and she screamed and screamed and screamed.

The snow and the wind had continued all night and lay thick around the streets of the town, the wind turning it into drifts against buildings and across the fields and roads higher up. Rachel wrenched open the back door, swollen as it was with the damp and cold She was startled, as she did so, to see the back gate of the garden edge open at the same time, and Miss Juniper trying to get herself through it.

She hurried over to help the old lady before the door banged shut again. 'What's wrong? What has brought you out in this weather, at this hour of the morning? Come, let us get you into the warmth.'

Once safely in the kitchen, Miss Juniper began to speak. 'It is Mairead, my dear.'

'Mairead? She is not ill?'

Miss Juniper shook her head, while accepting a cup of the hot currant gruel Mrs Cramond had been preparing for the minister. 'Not ill, precisely. But I fear she will become so if I do not get her some help.'

'Is it the nightmares again? I thought they had lessened of late?'

'They had. And this is not quite what the others were. It was – a waking nightmare. Alicia and I had great difficulty in calming her. We eventually got her settled and off to sleep with a little warmed milk and grated nutmeg. She is of such a very suggestible nature, as you know, and I fear the effects of yesterday's fast on her too fertile imagination, combined with some of the more – admonitory – aspects of the minister's sermon, have convinced her that some dire evil awaits her.'

'But Alasdair would never have wished . . . he would never have meant Mairead.'

'I know that, my child,' said Miss Juniper, 'and I have told her so. Although,' she hesitated, 'Mr Mackay has been unwontedly severe in his preaching of late.'

In spite of her shawl and the fire and the cup of gruel in her hand, Rachel felt suddenly cold. She had hoped that no one but herself would have remarked the change in Alasdair. 'He – he has been much troubled, in his spirit, about what the cholera might mean, how the will of God is to be understood in it . . .'

Miss Juniper reached for her hand. 'Oh, my dear. Mr

Mackay is so great a pillar to us all that we forget sometimes that he is but a human soul, like the rest of us. We expect him to carry what we cannot.' She began to stand up. 'I would not trouble him further. A day or two in her bed, with good food and the occasional company of friends, will be all Mairead needs.'

Rachel put out a hand to stop her. 'You wouldn't have come out in the snow at so early an hour if you believed that. Alasdair would not forgive himself, or me, if he thought you had not called upon his help because I have been fussing about him. He will come to you this morning.'

It was just as the clock in Miss Juniper's small parlour struck nine that a knock came at the door and the minister and Mrs Mackay were being ushered in out of the cold. Alicia was seated by Mairead on the settle where they usually did their sewing and reading in the evening. She couldn't leave Mairead to face the coming interrogation alone.

Alicia had never encountered the minister at such close quarters, in so cramped a space, and he was certainly as handsome as he appeared to be from a greater distance, but for all his smile he looked weary, and not entirely well. Mrs Mackay, whom they had not seen so much of these last few months, looked almost as bad. She was probably worried about Mairead, or maybe about her husband.

After they had prayed, Mr Mackay leaned in towards Mairead, hands clasped at his knees. He had eschewed the comfortable armchair that had been meant for him and instead pulled a spindle-legged stool out from under Miss Juniper's sewing table.

'Now, Mairead,' he began, 'Miss Juniper tells me you have been having frightening dreams.'

Mairead nodded but kept her eyes firmly on her knees.

The minister dropped his own head a little lower, as if to find her out beneath her bedcap, she still being in the clothes of an invalid. 'Have you perhaps taken up your old reading habits again? Mrs Mackay tells me you have been frightened in the past by the novels you have read.'

Mairead lifted her head a little, her face that had been pale now gaining colour. 'Oh, no, Mr Mackay, I promise I have not.'

He turned an enquiring glance on Alicia.

'Miss Juniper put all those sorts of books out of the house and completely forbade us to read *Melmoth* when we came across a copy at the roup of the Macraes' place on the High Street last year. Aside from the usual tales of brownies and bogles and the like at Hallowe'en, we have really only been reading nice things like *Thaddeus of—*'

'Thank you, Alicia,' the minister said before turning his attention back to Mairead. 'Do you think perhaps it was the fast yesterday that occasioned your dreams?'

Mairead looked up fully now. 'But I wasn't dreaming, Mr Mackay. I was wide awake and the thing felt as real to me as . . . as . . .' she looked about her, 'as you are.'

'And what was this thing?'

'It felt like evil, wickedness, pressing upon me.'

Mr Mackay sighed a little. 'Mairead, your attention to my sermon yesterday does you credit, but I hope you know I was not accusing *you* of wickedness. There is wickedness enough about the town that I am perfectly aware of, and in the country at large, and you do right to eschew it, but you must not think the evil in the world will find its focus on you. I know you read your Bible—'

'Every morning and night.'

'Good. Let that be your shield against these imaginings of evil. I daresay the desolation of an empty stomach made you more susceptible to them.'

Mairead nodded. 'I do try to forget all the terrible stories,' she said.

'And you must remember that,' interposed Rachel. 'They are simply stories, that have been made up for some entertainment. The creatures and characters in these books that so terrify you are not real.'

'Oh, but this one was not from a book, Mrs Mackay,' interposed Alicia, 'it was from a newspaper.'

'Since when do you girls read the newspapers?' asked the minister.

A little taken aback to have spoken at all and now to find herself addressed so directly, Alicia thought best to continue to look at Mrs Mackay, and to answer the question as if it had been she, and not her husband, who had put it. 'We don't exactly read them. Hester brings them to us from the hotel, when everyone else is finished with them. We look at the notices of concerts and recitals in Edinburgh and imagine ourselves there.' She was about to add that they also looked at the notices of plays and comedians, but thought it best not to mention those in front of the minister, for she thought it unlikely that Mr Mackay was of the party who approved those things. Thinking of her scrapbook, she returned to safer ground. 'And the advertisements by the dressmakers and furriers – sometimes I cut them out and paste them into my scrapbook. And the poems . . .'

'And anything you can find out about Poland,' put in Mairead, as if having forgotten that *she* and not the contents of Alicia's scrapbook was the point of the whole interview.

'And what,' said the minister, who was beginning to look as if he felt his time was being wasted, 'among this parade of advertisements and the travails of Poland had you screaming in your bed last night?'

'Oh,' said Mairead, suddenly remembering her own distress, that had brought the minister here in the first place. 'It was a piece of news that I had not set out to read but that caught my eye.'

Mr Mackay turned to his wife. 'The Burkings. I have said time and again they should not be so much reported. And Micah Fraser should not make such a noise about it. It leads to nothing but hysteria.'

'But it wasn't a Burking, Mr Mackay,' pleaded Mairead, anxious that he should understand. 'She wasn't dead.'

'What?' he said a little sharply. 'Who wasn't dead?'

Alicia could see that Mairead had taken fright at the minister's sudden change of tone, the strangeness that had crept into his voice. She took it upon herself to speak up again and bring an end to the confusion. 'The girl mentioned in the article, at least she had not been dead to begin with.' The minister had now turned his darkening look on herself, but she was too far in to go back again. 'I – I have brought it down, in case you might need to see it, because I thought it must be this that had given Mairead the waking nightmare.' She put her hand into her apron pocket and brought out a narrow, folded strip cut several months ago from a newspaper.

The minister took it and unfolded it, then frowned, before handing the cutting to his wife. 'Here, Rachel,' he said. 'You read it. I have forgotten my spectacles.'

Rachel began. '"From Austria: a Tale of Horror".' She gave Alicia a look of disapproval and continued. '"The eldest daughter of a carter died suddenly of apoplexy and on the fourth day she was interred. Three or four hours after the ceremony, a hunter who was shooting near the village perceived that his favourite spaniel had suddenly left him and was nowhere to be found. The following morning, to the surprise of everyone who heard it, the dog was found beside the new grave, scratching away with great eagerness and howling piteously. The circumstance excited an immediate and painful interest. The churchyard was filled with the population. Horrible suspicion circulated in whispers, but none dared to act without advice and authority from the *bürgermeister* – the mayor. The latter, insensible to the entreaties of the people, ridiculed their apprehensions and declared that he would permit nothing to be done but in the presence of the physician of the department. Before the latter had arrived, two days had elapsed and the dog still continued sentinel and howling at the grave, upbraiding as he well might, those who looked idly on. The coffin was disinterred and opened in the presence of the physician. They found the ill-fated young woman turned with her face downwards, her grave clothes soaked with blood, and her person covered with bruises and lacerations! The *bürgermeister* was apprehended and is now in the fortress of K___, but the circumstances produced a dreadful sensation in the commune.'

Alicia had stopped paying attention to Mrs Mackay's reading sometime before she reached the end of the narrative, because her attention had been taken by the minister who, at an early point, had begun to exhibit symptoms of an agitation not greatly divorced from Mairead's. Mr Mackay was not emitting occasional squeaks of distress as Mairead was, but there was a movement in his jaw and in his clenched lips together with a whitening of his knuckles. He had gone paler, too. Even in the lamplit room Alicia could see that.

The minister was starting to get up. Alicia looked frantically to Mrs Mackay who had at last noticed the disarrangement of her husband.

'Alasdair – whatever is . . .?'

But she got to ask no more, because in that instant Mr Mackay pushed back the spindly stool, knocking it to the floor as he stumbled to the cottage door. Rachel was still trying to call to him when a blast from the blizzard swirling in off the sea banged it shut again after him.

SIXTEEN

The Pearl

Charlotte looked out at her casement and thought of Alasdair Mackay's sermon, of the great need for propitiation. The snow had gathered around the edges of the windowpanes, piling up in corners, limiting her view to steamed curves of glass. The trees shook their bare branches angrily in the park and she could make out the grey and white of the sea, rising up and crashing onto the shore. It was as if the town was encircled by fury.

Charlotte put her hand to her own bare neck and fingered the chain that lay there, the pearl drop her mother had been so proud of. How she used to disdain that chain, that paltry pearl. She turned slightly now, and in the cheval mirror to her side she saw that the pearl sat very well on her skin, just resting at the indent of her collarbone. Clavicle, she remembered. How had she not seen it before? The plain white shift and grey woollen gown that she had not known she still possessed set it off very well. After her illness of the winter, William had written to Edinburgh, to his sister, to have new gowns sent up for her because her old gowns hung so from her, as if the dresses were the problem. But this morning, when her hand could find nothing to content her eye, she had sent away her maid and plundered the chest herself and found it.

William, not daring to oppose his old nurse in the matter of strict adherence to yesterday's fast, had ordered breakfast be served early, and was already at his letters by the time she went down to the dining room. He glanced up at her and then back down to his letters, in his accustomed fashion. But then he looked back up at her. 'Charlotte – are you not well today?'

'I am well, William. Thank you.'

Morag Mackenzie looked at her with suspicion. 'That is an old dress, Lady Charlotte,' she said, pouring Charlotte tea brown as peat water. 'Had you nothing else in your dressing room?'

William looked up again, wary.

'Nothing that pleased me as well as this, Miss Mackenzie,' she said.

She found, to her surprise, that she was ravenous. Her observation, when first the fast had been announced, that she had not understood cholera to particularly seek out fat people who had plenty to eat, had not gone down well with her husband's housekeeper. There had followed a long homily about the need to propitiate God in His wrath, to humble themselves before Him in the face of the plague which He had chosen to visit on so Godless a people. Alasdair Mackay might have saved himself the bother of yesterday's sermon and had Morag deliver hers instead.

Alasdair had looked ill and so had Rachel. In fact, as Charlotte had gradually become stronger over these past few months, it seemed to her that Rachel had become more withdrawn, more vulnerable. It was all the fault of Fachie Hossack and that terrible dinner on Christmas Eve. Rachel had as good as admitted that this was what was wrong. Or rather, it was the fault of the schoolmaster, John Learmonth. Charlotte had told William he had to get rid of the man, out of the school and away from Cromarty, but William had said he could not do that without the approval of the kirk session and probably the presbytery, and should he drag Rachel's name up before them all, before Alasdair himself? It would blow over, he had said. Here they were now in March, the winter had returned, and the matter of the schoolmaster had not blown over. Perhaps the pestilence would come at last and bring it to an end. The disease was already spreading in the south of Scotland but had not yet made its presence felt here. Probably though, it would take such a terror at the cold and the Calvinism that it would never reach them at all.

Charlotte had just pushed away the cup of brackish tea poured for her by Morag Mackenzie and rung the bell for coffee, when they heard a rapping at the front door and soon the footman was in the dining room with a message from the manse.

William quickly scanned the note. 'Alasdair has been taken unwell. Rachel asks that I go to him and that I send for Dr Fraser.' He turned to the footman. 'Go to the stables. Tell Jimmy Dunn he must ride to Resolis and fetch Dr Fraser to Cromarty Manse, and to lose no time. He must take Foula and Stoura Baa – only the ponies will make it through in this weather.'

Within half an hour, near-frozen and soaked through with snow, Charlotte and William were being shown into the parlour of the manse. 'I have sent for Dr Fraser. But what is the matter with Alasdair? What does Dr Smith say?'

Rachel shook her head. 'He has forbidden me to send for a physician. He asks only for Micah and has locked himself in his study.' She twisted her apron in her hands. 'He keeps talking about Elizabeth, his first wife. He will not let me into the room. Can you try, William?'

As William went to Alasdair's study, Rachel told Charlotte of what had happened at Miss Juniper's cottage.

Charlotte couldn't temper her anger. 'Little wonder the girl was half-delirious. The hunger and the bleakness of the sermon would have played upon anyone's resilience, to say nothing of how cold it was in the kirk. Half the town will be taking pneumonia and . . .' But then she saw the distraction on Rachel's face. She leaned forwards and took hold of her friend's hands. 'Oh, forgive me. None of that is the point. But tell me, though – what can Mairead's story have to do with Elizabeth? It is fifteen years since she died, is it not?'

'Eighteen,' said Rachel. 'It was while we were away with Miss Juniper, do you recall? We went across the firth on a visit to one of her former pupils, in Elgin. Mrs—'

'Oh yes,' interrupted Charlotte, 'and we saw the cathedral ruins, and Spynie Palace . . . But, yes, I remember. Alasdair went away for a time afterwards, did he not?'

'He had to take young Charles to Elizabeth's people and help to settle the boy. But I think he was ill, Charlotte, after Elizabeth died. Disordered in his mind. I think that is when his black dog first began to stalk him. It has come back. It found him out again that night of the Hossacks' dinner and something in Mairead's story has it unleashed and lashing out like a thing wounded.'

Charlotte dropped Rachel's hands as if she had suddenly found herself holding a block of ice. 'I have let you down.'

'You have never let me down, Charlotte. It has never been *your* task to lift me up. You must simply *be*, and that is enough for me.'

'But it is not enough for me. I have failed to notice your troubles because I have had nothing in my head but my own. And who do you have to confide in but me? But now I am here and you must tell me. He cannot truly believe there is anything between you and the schoolmaster. But—'

Rachel stopped her. 'Elizabeth was unfaithful to him, Charlotte. She flaunted her infidelities in his face. Even the birth of young Charles . . .'

Charlotte stared at her. 'He is not Alasdair's son?'

'She told him Charles was the child of an old lover. He

has told me that the circumstances, and the way the child looked, made it likely enough. It's why he gave in to her family after Elizabeth died, when they insisted the boy should be put into their care.'

Charlotte cast her mind back eighteen years, trying to remember the small boy who had been gone from Cromarty within days of his mother's death. Fair, that was all she could think, white-gold hair like his mother's, hanging about his face like a silken curtain. There had been none of Alasdair Mackay's swarthiness, his rebellious curls. Perhaps he had not been Alasdair's after all. 'But why would she tell her husband such a thing? And with his position – the risk?'

'To punish him. For having taken her to so humble a life as that of the minister's wife in Cromarty.' An unaccustomed bitterness had come into Rachel's voice. 'She played at peasants and cottages, like Marie Antoinette, and then she grew tired of it. When she realised there was no Versailles waiting for her, nothing but this manse, she grew to resent him as the cause of her being here. She spent more and more time with her family in the south, where she sought other diversions. Charles no longer even bears his name – he has taken his mother's family name, for inheritance purposes. They think by this means that the family's temporary foray amongst the lower orders may be quietly forgotten.'

'But what bearing can this have on you? You cannot reciprocate the schoolmaster's feelings?'

Rachel stood up, furious. 'How can you ask me such a thing? You *know* how I love Alasdair. The only other I have ever loved was Alexander and, oh, Alexander was only a boy. I would never . . .' She was wracked with helpless sobs. 'I would never.'

Charlotte was appalled at herself. 'Forgive me, forgive me. I have been so desolate in my marriage that it is hard to believe that other women are not.'

Rachel closed her eyes and sank down onto her seat again.

Charlotte kissed Rachel's hands in relief. 'But,' she said, after a moment, 'I still don't see how this all connected with Mairead and her nightmares.'

'Neither do I,' said Rachel. 'We must pray he will talk to Dr Fraser when he comes.'

It was almost dinner time by the time Dr Fraser, sodden as he swung himself down from the doughty Shetland pony, was being admitted through the front door. Divesting himself of his dripping riding coat and handing it to the maid who had scurried in after him, he clapped his hands together. 'Have you a dram?' he said, and Charlotte instantly crossed to where Alasdair kept his whisky and poured a good measure, which the minister took with thanks.

'Now, Rachel,' he said, 'before I go in to your husband you will tell me what in the world has befallen him.'

And so again Rachel spoke of Alasdair's strain, of his spiritual struggle to discern God's will in the cholera, of the cold of the kirk and the effects of the fast and at last of the call to Mairead Buchan. She did not mention the schoolmaster.

'I see. And what did the lassie Buchan do, to bring so low this man of God?'

Rachel shrugged helplessly. 'It was just a story from an old newspaper that had been giving her waking nightmares.'

'And the nature of this story?'

'It was of a girl, in Austria I think. It was discovered too late that she had been buried alive.'

Dr Fraser put down his glass. 'Dear God,' he said. 'I must go to him.'

A moment or two later, William had appeared in the parlour. 'Dr Fraser asked that I might leave them alone.'

'How is Alasdair?' Rachel asked him.

William simply shook his head.

It was a long hour before Dr Fraser came out again. He begged Sir William and Lady Charlotte their pardon, but he must speak to Mrs Mackay alone. 'Perhaps your ladyship might wait a while, to stay with Mrs Mackay after I have gone.'

'There is no need for Charlotte to—' said Rachel.

'But aye, my dear,' said Dr Fraser, a gentle but firm hand on her arm, 'her ladyship is your friend, and I doubt not that she will sit with you a wee while. But you and I shall speak first, just the two of us.'

William went back up to his stables, to give orders for having the sleigh made ready, as Micah had asked him to, and Charlotte took herself first into the cold dining room, but there she caught sight of the portrait of Alasdair's first wife who appeared to look down upon her and to be not a little pleased. Charlotte took one of the embroidered satinwood dining chairs from the table and took off her boots, which were still sodden from the walk in the snow. Glad that she had put on such a simple dress, she stepped up onto the seat of the chair and reached up to take hold of the edge of the gilt frame. 'This is not your house, Elizabeth Mackay. Time you were gone.' She lifted the portrait from the wall, and went through to the kitchen, still in her stockings, to hand it to the astonished scullery maid, telling her to see it was put out of the house and never let back.

'Now, my dear,' said Micah Fraser, settling himself across from Rachel into Alasdair's armchair, 'God has sent you a trial, but it is no greater a trial than you can bear, or he would not have chosen you to bear it.'

Someone had lit more candles, Rachel noticed. This day was already dying. She nodded, to show that she understood what in reality she did not.

'Alasdair is a good man,' he continued, 'a great man, an unwavering servant of the Lord.'

She waited.

'Yet even great men, resolute men, are afflicted from time to time by human weakness. Did the Lord not come down to us in human form that he might share in our troubles? The Lord tests us all, and it is to His most faithful servants that he gives the most severe tests.'

'Alasdair is being tested?'

'He is.'

'But by what? The advance of the cholera?'

Dr Fraser shook his head. 'He knows, as I do, that the cholera is sent by God because of human wickedness. It is the nature of the wickedness that we must question, not the wrath of God in answering it. But that is for another time. Alasdair's test is of different nature, and more particular to him.' He cleared his throat, and Rachel thought he was itching to take out his pipe.

'Please, Dr Fraser,' she said, 'take out your pipe. The smoke will not bother me at all.'

'Ah.' He smiled, already reaching for his tobacco pouch and commencing the operation. 'You know, I think, that your husband's first marriage was not a happy one.'

Rachel felt herself colour. 'He has never hidden from me that he loved Elizabeth, for all that they had their difficulties.'

'Difficulties?' Dr Fraser pushed the tobacco into the bowl of his pipe with some vigour. 'The woman was a Jezebel and she near enough destroyed him.'

Rachel had not expected this. 'He loved her, all the same.'

'The best of men can be fools,' he said, lighting a spill from the fire and putting it to his pipe.

'Dr Fraser,' she began.

He looked up at her from under bushy brows.

'After she died, Alasdair was ill, wasn't he?' She didn't need to say any more. This was not a game they were playing.

'I think it was the manner of her death that shocked him. The suddenness of it,' he said.

And not, thought Rachel, that she was out riding with another man at the time. An officer from a naval frigate anchored in the bay, waiting for its orders. Elizabeth's horse had thrown her over a dyke near Newhall and she had broken her neck.

Dr Fraser carried on speaking. 'He would not believe it at first and insisted on seeing her. Her body was carried to my house, at Resolis, to spare her son the sight of it. Alasdair would not leave the side of her coffin. I took her funeral myself and as you know, she was laid to rest at Kirkmichael. Her family had refused to allow her to be buried in Cromarty. It was the burial itself that put him wrong.'

The ticking of the clock on the mantelshelf suddenly sounded very loud to her. 'How so?'

'He had had a carry-on at the manse when they screwed down the lid of the coffin, but he went near-distracted when she was lowered into the ground. I had to keep hold of him myself. Folk put it down to an excess of grief, nothing more, and I got him bundled into a carriage and taken back to my manse before anyone could understand what he was at.'

'What he was at?' asked Rachel.

Dr Fraser let out a long sigh. 'He wouldn't believe she was dead. He thought she had been just sent into some kind of stupor by the hit she had taken on the head.'

Rachel put her hand to her mouth, picturing his desolation in that isolated kirkyard. 'He thought you were burying her alive?'

Dr Fraser nodded. 'He didn't go to Edinburgh to settle

the boy with his grandparents. My Mary accompanied the child and Alasdair stayed at Resolis manse with me and Bella Swanson. We kept him there six weeks till he was fit to go out in the world again and return to Cromarty.'

'And nobody in Cromarty knew?'

The minister shook his head as he kept his pipe going. 'Sanders and Maggie Gilfeather knew. We could hardly have let Alasdair go home without someone there to keep an eye on him, and who else could it have been but Sanders?'

Rachel didn't know if it was this news or the revelation that Alasdair had believed Elizabeth to have been buried alive in the first place that shocked her more. She recalled Mrs Gilfeather's face the night she had gone to tell them that she was to marry Alasdair Mackay. She recalled the momentary look of sadness in Mrs Gilfeather's eyes, the slight hesitation before the congratulation that she had put down to grief for the boy Rachel should have married. At Mr Gilfeather, she had not dared to look at all, for fear she might see that grief writ too plainly on the bank manager's face. But now she thought it might have been concern for herself that had stayed their congratulations just a moment too long.

Dr Fraser continued. 'It was hard going to start with. Bella and I took turns at sitting with him, watching him, even when he slept. He would cry out that she was still living and he had to get to her and dig her out. There was one night Bella fell asleep, poor soul, and he must have been halfway to Kirkmichael before she awoke and we realised he was gone. I found him there digging at the ground with his bare hands.' He closed his eyes a moment at the memory. 'The job I had getting him away. He had the strength of a madman.'

There it was now, out between them, the word. 'And do you think, now that he . . .'

Micah Fraser shook his head. 'He's not mad, lassie, just exhausted. But I think you must know better than I that he has times when a sort of darkness comes upon him.'

'I should go to him.'

Dr Fraser gave a heavy sigh, and she could see there was something he didn't wish to tell her. 'Rachel, he believes if she is alive, he cannot be married to you.'

Rachel was on her feet. 'Alive! The woman has been mouldering in the soil of Kirkmichael eighteen years. She will be nothing but a ruckle of bones in a rotting silk dress. Even if he was right when first she—'

Dr Fraser also sprang up and took hold of her shoulders. 'Right at first? Are you as bad as him? From the moment she hit the ground after that horse threw her, the woman was dead. You knew just by looking at her, but the physician made sure nonetheless. I bent over her corpse and there was not the merest hint of a wisp of breath from her blue lips.' As if alarmed by his own passion he let go her shoulders and took a step back. 'I have seen dead often enough and I tell you, Elizabeth Mackay was as dead as the rest of them.'

'But he would discount our marriage? He would turn me into a—'

'It's not him, Rachel. The Fiend is at him, but he will not have him. I am staying here tonight and tomorrow I am taking Alasdair back to Resolis and I will wrestle his demons until I have chased them into the sea.'

'And what shall I do?'

'You will stay here and have all ready for him when the battle is won and he is able to come home. You will put it about that Alasdair has taken a chest infection and that his physician has insisted he come away from the coast and the harsh winds. You will tell people he is recuperating at the manse of Resolis, with me. I will make all right with the presbytery, and Sanders Gilfeather will see that the kirk session looks to its business. The schoolmaster can do the sermon on the Sabbath.'

Rachel had been swept along by Dr Fraser's authority, but here she stopped him. 'I don't think Mr Learmonth has ever spoken of going into the ministry.'

'I never met a schoolmaster yet that didn't aspire to it, and John Learmonth is an able fellow. Too able to bury himself in a schoolroom near enough tipping into the German Ocean. But never mind. Let him fill Alasdair's pulpit for now. Test his mettle.'

'No,' said Rachel. The word shot out with more emphasis than she had intended. Dr Fraser, who had been in the process of closing the window drapes, turned around. 'Is there some particular objection to the schoolmaster?'

She bit her lip. Micah Fraser knew enough of their secrets. To tell him more could hardly do any harm. 'The insinuations of Fachie Hossack – at Christmastime. Alasdair was – shaken by them. If he should somehow get wind that Mr Learmonth was in his pulpit, I dread to think what his sick mind would make of it.'

Micah Fraser's face, usually so mobile, had gone almost to stone. 'Has the schoolmaster spoken to you – in any way out of the ordinary course of his duties?'

'I have had no dealings with him, other than in my capacity as the minister's wife.' She paused, then corrected herself. 'And as a member of the library.'

Dr Fraser ruminated. 'But there is something about the fellow, all the same.' He tapped out his pipe. 'Well, there is a student at Fortrose just now can preach a few weeks, until Alasdair is recovered.' He touched her on the shoulder. 'All will be well, my dear, and you will have your husband back with you before the primroses are out on Cromarty hill.'

SEVENTEEN

April

A Tea at Rose Lodge

Miss Anna Rose was fluttering about the drawing room, getting in her sister's way at every turn. 'What a pity the young officers are not able to join us. I am sure the very best of hygiene is kept aboard the naval vessels. Surely there is no need for such young *gentlemen* to be subject to the quarantine.'

Elspeth sighed, and attempted to explain to her sister, yet again and with as much patience as she could muster, the quarantine regulations as they applied to the vessels at anchor out in the bay. If Anna would but read the newspapers, beyond the advertisements of haberdashers and perfumiers in Edinburgh, she might establish some grip, however tenuous, on matters of the wider world. As well ask her to go out and catch hold of the wind.

'Of course you are right, Elspeth,' Anna continued, 'but, oh, do you remember the parties we used to have when dear Pap was still alive, and all the officers making our house their first port of call, that they might pay him their respects? The places they told us about, the dances we used to have? And that young naval lieutenant who was so particularly attentive to you . . . what was his name now?'

Elspeth stopped in her arranging of the candelabra. Of course she remembered. 'Lieutenant Whiteside.'

'That's it. Lieutenant Whiteside. Did he not ask Pap for permission to speak to you? I believe you broke his heart, you know.'

Elspeth remembered the young man, handsome, hopeful. The second son of a wealthy English gentleman. A better prospect than might have been expected, for one of her plain looks and her family's diminishing fortune. He had asked her, in this very room. Thirty years ago. She might have given him her hand. She had thought about it, for a moment or two. She had already given her promise to another though, a foolish promise, secret and given too young and yet she had felt bound to honour it. She looked past Anna to her last image of the young lieutenant, to where, dejected, rejected, he had made his bow to her and passed out of the door and of her life. 'He fell not long afterward, I believe,' she said, resuming the placing of the candelabra. 'At Algeciras. Has the cheese arrived from the farm?'

'Yes,' said Anna, a little startled, not so much at the change in their conversation, but at the look on Elspeth's face when she had recalled the young, dead lieutenant. Anna had never known any other man to pay court to her sister, aside from Sir William of course, before he had taken up his commission, but then they had been very young in those days, little more than children, and the idea had been almost as ridiculous then as it would be now, even had he not married.

Anna thought it was a pity, too, that they could not invite Miss Juniper and her girls to join their party. The girls were both very fond of reading novels, she knew, and Miss Juniper had such connections. But when she had suggested it to Elspeth earlier that morning, her sister had crushed the idea before it had fully escaped her mouth.

'Must I remind you of the content of the woman's book?'

Anna had felt her cheeks begin to pink. Elspeth had thrown their copy of *Reminiscences of a Village Governess* in the fire, and she had been obliged to get another from a friend in Rosemarkie, where twice as many copies were read in secret as were publicly thrown away.

'No, Elspeth, but she was not wrong, in what she had to say of—'

Her sister had swept round upon her. 'That is exactly it! Would you have her mock and ridicule us and our arrangements and the behaviour of our guests, in print and for all the world to see?'

'Oh, Elspeth, I am sure she would not think of it, for what in the world could she find to mock here? Everyone knows this is the most respectable house in Cromarty. Saving the manse, of course.'

'Hmm.' Elspeth was not altogether persuaded of the

respectability of the manse. 'I am convinced there is more to the minister's absence than the illness his wife pleads, but no matter. No doubt Dr Fraser will have something to say about it. But you must not forget that this evening's assembly is not in the nature of a domestic tea party, Anna. It is a gathering of the circulating library, membership of which comes with certain responsibilities and expectations. To have been invited to join the library is an acknowledgement of our standing and the respect accorded our family name in this town. Should we expose our fellow library members to the pen of Arabella Juniper we might find ourselves as ostracised as she is.'

Anna was appalled, unable to conceive of what her sister might mean. How could they be cut out of a society of which they were at the root? Surely, there could be no respectable society at all in the town that did not include the daughters of the late Captain Rose, the present custodians of Rose Lodge? Perhaps she herself might be dispensed with – she knew she was foolish, although she was conscious of the kindness of many friends – but surely Elspeth could not be. Anna resolved to say no more in defence of Miss Juniper. It would be useless to argue that the elderly schoolmistress was on familiar terms with Mrs Mackay at the manse and with Lady Charlotte at Cromarty House, for Elspeth had already made clear that she in no way viewed those connections as unimpeachable. They had never, of course, mentioned the unsavoury allusions of Farquhar Hossack at that unfortunate Christmas Eve dinner, yet the rumours that had begun to swirl around the town and country had nonetheless come to rest on the steps of Rose Lodge, like so many dead leaves. Elspeth was a very model of discretion and indulged in no gossip, but she could occasionally let loose a barb which unintentionally encouraged others to be less so. Anna hoped indeed that Dr Fraser might put in an appearance at their tea, for he could be relied upon to crush any malicious conversation as surely as a schoolboy might be relied upon to stamp on a beetle.

Ludo had been astonished when his mother had accepted Elspeth Rose's invitation to the tea at Rose Lodge. Janet Cameron was as much a member of the circulating library as he was himself, of course, but following the debacle of the Hossacks' dinner, she had decreed that it would be a cold day in Hell before she exposed herself again to such company. But when Ludo reminded her of this, she dismissed it.

'There are things I wish to discuss arising from some of the books,' she said, donning the gloves usually reserved for the walk to the kirk on the Sabbath. 'In addition, the minister's illness has provoked idle speculation which has naturally found its way to the coffee room.'

Ludo didn't need to ask about the nature of the speculation. John had been living under its lengthening shadow for months, and the minister's absence from the manse had people practically pointing at him in the street.

'Rachel Mackay,' she said as she gave a sharp tug to the

ribbons of her bonnet, setting the bow in a manner that not the wildest winds the German ocean had to offer would think of dislodging, 'does not deserve to be so traduced. You have brought the newspaper with you?'

For a brief moment, a horrified Ludovic thought the travails of his friend must have found their way into the *Inverness Courier*, but then he remembered. He nodded and patted his coat beneath which he had slipped the column cut from Wednesday's *Scotsman*, to keep it dry. His mother had noticed it when the paper had come in that afternoon and she had been about to lay it in the reading room. It was a small item, a last-minute piece of news like an afterthought thrown down before the paper had gone to print, much to say but no time to say it. And yet his mother, usually such a stranger to sentiment, had known that for someone in the town that small item would say everything and she had instructed Ludovic to cut it out and pass it to them.

Meeting Dr Fraser of Resolis at the front steps of Rose Lodge, Ludo's mother asked after the health of their own minister.

'He is on the mend, but it may be a little while yet.' Dr Fraser glanced up to the windows of the lodge, panes aglow. 'The gulls will be cawing over it up there already, I don't doubt. Let us to battle, Janet, and we shall best them.'

Relieved that Dr Fraser had no apparent expectations of himself, Ludo followed the formidable pair up the steps.

Miss Elspeth was first on her feet, Miss Anna soon afterwards. Mr Fordyce was already ensconced by the fire in the place of honour, that grotesquely carved oak armchair from which old Captain Rose had been wont to issue his thunderbolts. Ludo remembered the terrifying, gouty old man who roared at his daughters as if they were pressed men on some vessel under his command. On a more recent visit to the Roses' drawing room, Miss Anna had invited him to 'take the captain's chair', only for an arctic glance from Miss Elspeth, to whom he had felt supremely grateful, to direct him to a less august seat. There was no sign yet of Sir William or Lady Charlotte, and it could hardly be supposed that Mrs Mackay would come. Willie Hossack was there, looking about as comfortable as a trussed turkey, ready for the roast. Ludo issued a silent prayer of thanks that Fachie was still in Aberdeen. He would not have put it past Fachie to impose himself even at Rose Lodge, member of the library or not, just for the devilment.

For a moment, Ludo thought that John wasn't there either. The candles had been placed about the room in such a way that some of the inhabitants were illuminated in full, whilst leaving other corners almost in darkness, and it was in near-darkness that John stood, like a shape shifter awaiting his moment. Ludo ventured an encouraging smile. John had, understandably, become less comfortable amongst this company over the last few months. Ludo started towards him but was stopped in his tracks by the voice of Miss Elspeth, indubitably addressing itself to him.

'Mr Cameron!'

Startled, he made a second bow in case he had forgotten

to make a first. She brushed away his civilities like a day-old dish of whelks. 'I take it, given that Mr Gilfeather declined my invitation on the grounds that he is a functionary and not a *member* of the library, that you will deputise for him in his clerical duties this evening?'

Despite this having been posed as a question, everyone present would have been perfectly clear that an instruction had been issued. Ludo, startled, was still attempting his response when, to his horror, his mother spoke up.

'I am afraid, Miss Rose, that Ludovic's position in relation to Mr Gilfeather at the bank is not something that can be translated, willy-nilly, into every walk of life. It should not be expected that he is to be taken for Mr Gilfeather's representative while partaking in social engagements in private households in the town. I hardly think Mr Gilfeather would think that fitting to the dignity of the bank.'

Miss Elspeth had gone a shade of granite but Ludo's mother hadn't finished.

'You will, moreover, be aware that Ludovic is a member, and not a *functionary* of the library and that in such a capacity he will be no more able to deputise for Mr Gilfeather's clerical duties than would Sir William.'

Ludovic felt he might be sick. A glance towards John showed that his predicament had gained his friend's sympathies and he saw the schoolmaster begin to peel himself away from the window preparatory to coming towards him. But before John had fully emerged from his shadows there came a hearty bark of amusement just behind Ludo's back. 'Well, well, Miss Elspeth,' declared Dr Fraser, 'I'd say Mrs Cameron is able for you. A grand start to our entertainment. Never fear though, should anything worthy of notice be said this evening I *myself* will make certain to take note of it, that Mr Gilfeather might record it for posterity.'

A bolt from the sky could not have had such an effect upon the company as did Dr Fraser's announcement of himself. Miss Elspeth's nostrils contracted and her lips pursed themselves so thoroughly that a pin could not have passed between them. Miss Anna actually let out a squeak and had put her hand to her mouth in a vain attempt to suppress it. The rest of the members of the library were momentarily paralysed with shock. What might have been said when Miss Elspeth finally managed to unpurse her lips was mercifully lost to conjecture by the opening once more of the drawing room doors, and the announcement of Sir William and Lady Charlotte Mackenzie. The company was just rising amid a murmur of relief when the housemaid added, 'And Mrs Mackay.'

Ludo looked to the door and immediately saw the perplexity in Rachel Mackay's eyes, as if she didn't know what could have brought her here. He could sense the bulk of Dr Fraser begin to turn itself towards her, but some voice in his head told him that she deserved to find more than one protector in this room. He stepped hastily in front of Dr Fraser, who shot him a look of curious wonder. 'Mrs Mackay,' he heard himself say, 'permit me to give you my arm. Look, there is Mr Fordyce who has kept a seat just for you, near the fire. Let me take you to him.'

Rachel Mackay looked at him with little less wonder than had Dr Fraser, but then her eyes softened and her mouth relaxed into something more akin to its usual smile. 'Thank you, Ludovic,' she said. 'That's very kind of you.'

The diversion of the new arrivals having given Miss Elspeth the time to recover herself, the process of welcoming Sir William and his wife and seeing them seated was sufficient to restore her to her mettle. She at last made her response to the minister's barb.

'I had not thought you would be able to join us this evening, Dr Fraser. We were given to understand that Mr Mackay was still under your care at Resolis. He surely cannot be home seeing as Mrs Mackay is here, by herself.'

Ludo saw Rachel colour and wished he could again charge to her aid, but he had not the words required for so deep a battle. Dr Fraser, though, appeared to have been ready for it. He might have been in his pulpit. 'Your concern for your minister's health is perfectly proper, Miss Rose. Alasdair Mackay is indeed recuperating in my care at Resolis, his physicians having ordered him to a sheltered spot, away from the sea, that his chest might recover from the infection it took in the relentless pursuance of his duties. I am glad to say, *though you have not asked*, that he is very much on the mend and safely in the care of my housekeeper, Mrs Swanson, this evening. You do not question the capabilities of Mrs Swanson, I hope?'

'I . . . no . . .' Elspeth Rose was a second time defeated.

'Good.'

The woman, to her credit, looked genuinely ashamed. 'I am sorry, Dr Fraser,' she said. And then she turned to Rachel Mackay, 'And I am sorry too, Mrs Mackay, that we have not given you the assistance you have needed in easing the burden on your husband, to whose spiritual care and guidance we owe so much. I hope you will always know that you have friends at Rose Lodge.'

Rachel's response was lost in the fervent assurances of Miss Anna that her sister spoke for her also. The rest of the company murmured in agreement with Miss Elspeth's astonishing contrition. Ludovic's mother had told him once, though he had not believed it, that 'for all her severity, Elspeth Rose has a good heart when it can be brought upon her to remember she has one'. Dr Fraser had turned the situation in the room around with all the strength and dexterity of a helmsman turning a boat coming in to harbour. His work thus done, the minister sat himself down beside Sir William and began to quiz him on the progress of the Reform Bill, and whether he believed the King actually would resort to creating new lords to get it through the Upper House at last.

His great act of chivalry performed, Ludo went to join John Learmouth by the window.

'You were her knight,' said John.

'And would be again. She has done nothing to merit the calumnies put out about her.'

'No.' John looked out into the black deepening outside the windows. 'It is I who deserve the calumny, for being too unguarded in my admiration . . . even after you tried to warn me. And I am powerless to protect her.'

Ludo attempted optimism. 'You must not dwell on it, John. It will pass and they'll soon find something else to talk about. Or the cholera will arrive and no one will have any interest in the business of anyone but themselves.' He knew this wasn't true. Speculation that the parish schoolmaster had harboured inappropriate feelings for the minister's wife would linger about the town a hundred years at least, long after they were all dead. You only needed to ask James Craig or Anna Rose how long the memories of the people of Cromarty could run. 'Now,' he said, 'we had better join the body of the kirk, as Mr Gilfeather is wont to say. I think the discussion of the books is about to begin, and we may not get our tea at all if we don't show at least some interest.'

Miss Elspeth, from a very early stage of the library's existence, had been clear that she was not pleased with the private nature of the transferral of books from one individual to another – it had denied the members the opportunity for a full discussion of their reading. It was for this, and not the investigation of rumour, that she had decreed this tea party. Miss Anna's suggestion that their evening might also encompass a table or two of cards, and who knew, perhaps even a little dancing, had not been welcomed.

By dint of careful study of Mr Gilfeather's ledger, Elspeth had established for herself who should, by that particular evening, have read which books. She had selected the three titles she esteemed most profitable for discussion and instructed her guests to join the specific group she had chosen for them, in order to discuss a particular book that she knew they ought to have read. 'Nothing,' she announced to her bewildered audience following her explanation of her scheme, 'could be simpler.'

Miss Anna smiled brightly, and indeed a little desperately, at this, and Ludo thought she looked as if she wished for nothing more than to ring for the tea to be brought in, but Miss Elspeth hadn't finished. 'The books we shall discuss tonight,' she was saying, 'are as follows: Group One, *Hajji Baba*, by Mr Morier; Group Two, *Marriage* by Miss Ferrier; and the *Travels in North America* of Mr Hall for Group Three. If you could all dispose yourselves accordingly, we might begin.'

After some hesitation, people started to get up from the places in which they had not long settled themselves and cast about for some indication of where they should now go. This movement was accompanied by audible grumbling – most notably from Dr Fraser and Mr Hossack, who found themselves in a rare instance of agreement. At last, everyone came to a halt, having somehow resolved themselves into one group of seven and two of two.

'Oh, dear,' said Miss Anna from the midst of the largest group, 'I fear I have miscalculated.'

'Indeed, you have. Anna!' said her sister. 'You are in Group One. You must join Lady Charlotte's group.'

Miss Anna, tears prickling her eyes, looked beseechingly

at her sister. 'But I did not like Mr Morier's book at all, Elspeth. I thought it cruel, not clever.'

'You are quite right, Miss Anna,' said Lady Charlotte, who Ludo had hardly heard utter a word in months. 'Morier makes some salient points with regard to our society but—'

'Indeed, my dear?' interrupted Sir William, clearly delighted to see his wife engage in company.

'Yes, William. His views on slavery, for instance. I cannot help but feel the criticism he levels at the Turks on the matter is actually intended as a comment on slave-owners in *our* country who oppose the calls for emancipation.'

Sir William coloured and Willie Hossack harrumphed. 'Well, if they be Turks, I am proud to call myself a Turk!'

'Then we must hope for a sturdy carpet,' said Dr Fraser, not entirely *sotto voce*.

'Nonetheless,' continued Lady Charlotte, 'Morier's creation, Hajji Baba, is cruel with regard to women.'

'Such as?' enquired Willie Hossack, who looked as if he thought the book might be worth reading after all.

Lady Charlotte hesitated, but Miss Anna stepped in. 'He paints a most disagreeable picture of the dress of ladies at court, for instance – he affects to think them all so fat as to be pregnant.'

Sir William, the only one amongst them who had ever been to court, looked pained. 'Well, the fashion in court dress was, until very recently, quite ridiculous.'

'He goes on,' continued Miss Anna, her voice trembling a little, 'to suggest that the large numbers of old women he encounters should be veiled, and that the vast number of *superfluous* old women he sees everywhere should be got rid of.' Reaching for her handkerchief, she laid the book aside. No one spoke until Miss Elspeth laid a gentle hand on her sister's shoulder and said, 'Thank you, Anna. Now, my dear, I think we might ring for Jemima to see to the tea.'

The rosewood teapoy unlocked and the accoutrements brought out, all suggestion that the members of the library should dispose themselves into separate groups was forgotten.

After a decent interval of tea-drinking and the consumption of macaroons, Miss Elspeth invited Mr Isaac Fordyce to offer the company his views on Basil Hall's *Travels in North America*. A palpable sigh of relief went round the members of the library. Not a one of them had ever heard the old man utter an unkind word nor give voice to a malicious opinion. Mr Fordyce, whose feet had been tapping a good five minutes, gallantly demurred for another three taps before springing to his feet and adjusting his monocle.

'Now,' he began, 'I believe it was young Mr Cameron who ordered this for the library, was it not?'

'Yes,' admitted Ludo. He thoroughly regretted ever having asked for the book, and as Mr Fordyce began to prattle about it, Ludo's mind went back to the awful evening in October when he had been reading it with Hester. His mother's objection to his suggestion that they all move to North America to see what the New World might have to offer them was the effect such a move might have on

Hester. 'But Hester will come with us of course,' he had said. 'I would no more think of travelling halfway across the world without her than I would without you.'

'And what kind of welcome do you think she might find there?' his mother had asked.

'But we would go to the north, where they have no slavery,' he had protested, and he had ordered Captain Hall's book in order to allay his mother's fears and to set Hester's mind at rest. When the book had come into his hand, it had not occurred to him to read it first before sharing it with Hester.

All had gone well enough in their first evening's reading of Captain Hall's family's voyage across the Atlantic and of their reception in New York. But on their second, wherein Hall recounted his visits to the city's schools, Ludo's terrible mistake became only too evident. They had laughed, at first, at Captain Hall's difficulties with the pronunciations of the pupils at one school, but they had stopped laughing when he had recounted his visit to a school '"for the education of Negro and Mulatto children"'. Ludo had felt Hester tense a little beside him. How he wished he had not gone on to read aloud, '"Poor little wretches!"' His voice had halted but his eye had run along the next two lines and he did not know how he could deliver them. 'Oh, it's tedious,' he had said at last, closing the book and making to stand as if he had somewhere to go. But it had been no use – he never could deceive her. Hester had reached out to take the book from his hand.

'I may find it more interesting,' she said.

The more he had tried to dissuade her, the more clear it had become that she knew he wished to spare her something unpleasant. 'Give me the book, Ludo,' she had said. 'There can be nothing in it worse than I have heard and seen with my own eyes.'

And so he'd sat down again and taken up his reading where he'd left off. '"Poor little wretches! Their whole souls – if, as Uncle Toby says, they have souls – were thrown into their lessons; and it was delightful to see them under the guidance of a man, whose particular hobby was to teach blacks; and who had devoted many years of his life exclusively to this subject . . ." Really, Hester, I think we have heard enough.'

'Go on, Ludo.'

And so he had, until he had read, '"We naturally begged to know whether or not he had discovered any material difference in the intellectual powers of the blacks and whites at these schools. His answer was, that up to a certain age, that is to say, as long as they were little children, there was no difference perceptible. As they played about together, and studied together, the blacks were not made to feel any of those distinctions by which in afterlife their spirits were sure to be crushed down. I was told that even in the state of New York, where Negro slavery has been abolished by law, a black man meets with no real and effective sympathy on the part of the white lords of the creation."'

She had laid an arm on his hand then. 'That's enough,

Ludo, I do not need to hear any more.'

He had shut the book and had not picked it up again.

Hester was not here tonight, of course, in the Misses' Rose drawing room, but Mr Fordyce was not long in laying forth the episode of the schools and that was enough for Ludo's mother to give him a look that said she had suspected as much. But then Sir William had interceded, and spoken of having met Captain Hall only last year at a dinner in Edinburgh, and what good company he had been, and how unjust he thought the Americans to have been in having taken such exception to Hall's account of their country.

Sensing that the conversation was drifting away from literary matters, Mr Fordyce tried to retrieve it by enquiring whether Ludo had read any of the American, Mr Cooper's novels, and Ludo had gratefully begun to babble of the very genteel portrait of life in Boston delineated in *Lionel Lincoln*, for instance, but no one but Mr Fordyce was really listening. Dr Fraser enquired whether Sir William had ever encountered Diedrich Knickerbocker, whose *History of New York* he had found highly entertaining. Sir William replied that he was not certain that that was the gentleman's name at all, and this led into a discussion of the use of pseudonyms, and what in the world an author might mean by not owning to their works.

'Well,' said Miss Elspeth, 'there is one work come new into print, and by a *lady* at that, whose author shows *no* reticence in owning her work, and which I think might be of great interest to any sensible person thinking of emigrating to North America.' She looked very pointedly from Ludo to his mother and then went on. 'There is a most entertaining review of it in the *Aberdeen Magazine*, that I have just had my turn of. Let me see . . .' Anna passed her the magazine. 'Ah, yes. Mrs Frances Trollope's *Domestic Manners of the Americans*. Apparently, Mrs Trollope does not mince her words, and I for one would not think of setting foot across the ocean without having read it.'

The notion that Miss Elspeth would ever consider leaving Cromarty was ludicrous, but that was insufficient for her hint to be ignored. Besides, the idea of any author who did not 'mince her words' in describing some *other* society was too good to be resisted by the members of the library. Ludo felt certain that Mrs Trollope's unminced words would do nothing to persuade his mother of the virtues of a move to North America, not even to Boston. To his dismay, it was decided that Mr Gilfeather should certainly be requested to order a copy on their behalf. Without turning his head as much as forty-five degrees in Ludo's direction, Dr Fraser said, 'Ludovic, you will make a note.'

EIGHTEEN

An Excursion is Planned

Mr Gilfeather was home for his dinner, and Mrs Gilfeather could see the minute he was through the door that he wasn't pleased about something.

'Fit's a dee, Sanders? Is there something no' right at the bank?'

'At the bank, Mrs Gilfeather? Everything at the bank is quite as it should be, I thank you. Which is more than I'll say for the business of the library.' Taking off his jacket, he rolled up his sleeves in readiness to get to his dinner. 'I told Elspeth Rose – no good would come of gathering them all together for the sake of hearing their opinions.' He nodded as the girl set in front of him a dish of minced collops, alongside the plate of shredded onions and a dish of made mustard.

'So,' said Mrs Gilfeather, after the grace had been said and her husband had got down his first mouthful, 'what happened at Rose Lodge last night?'

Mr Gilfeather chewed a while at his food and then swallowed. 'Exactly what I said would happen once they all got together. Not more than half a year through the books they had ordered already for the library, but now they must be getting new ones, before they've as much as read the old ones. Janet Cameron presented me with a list, when I was over for my coffee, that they'd dictated to Ludovic, right in the middle of their gathering, if you please. The lad of course had had the sense to refuse to take it to me at the bank.'

'He kens fit's bank business and fit isna,' observed Mrs Gilfeather with approval.

Mr Gilfeather nodded. 'Just so. But then she tells me – Janet Cameron, that is – that they're all to go on an expedition, to Tain, if you please, to purchase books of their own accord.'

Mrs Gilfeather declared herself flummoxed. 'Can they no' just send to Elgin for them again? Or even Inverness?'

'Any sensible body might, Mrs Gilfeather. *You* would, if ever it entered *your* head you were needing a book. Heavens, the lassie there would.' He flung a hand towards the housemaid, who strove to look as if she would indeed send for any book she required, and certainly would not be traipsing across the firth to Tain in search of it.

'But no,' continued Mr Gilfeather, 'Lady Charlotte has decided they will go *en masse*' – Mr Gilfeather was not above employing a word or two of French when it suited his point, and Mrs Gilfeather was perfectly able to understand his meaning – 'to Tain, where the Dornoch reading club is next month to hold its annual sale of books. Sir William saw the advertisement in the paper, and now there is nothing in her ladyship's head but that everyone must go.'

'Well, I suppose,' considered Mrs Gilfeather, 'it's a good sign she's happy to go oot an' aboot again.'

'Hmmph! She doesna need to take the whole jing-bang o' them wi' her though,' replied her husband.

'Lexy says it's to cheer up Mr Fordyce,' interposed Bessie, in the full confidence that her master and mistress liked to know what titbits of news she might secure in her daily encounters with the other domestic servants of Cromarty.

'Bur Mr Fordyce surely doesn't need cheering up,' said Mrs Gilfeather. 'He's the most cheerful man in the toon.'

'Ah, but a friend o' his is deid, Mrs Gilfeather. It was in the newspaper, and Ludo – Mr Cameron – showed it to Mr Fordyce at the library meeting last night, and he was affa sad aboot it and Lady Charlotte said they should a' hae an ooting to cheer him up.'

Mr Gilfeather frowned. 'But what friend of Mr Fordyce is dead, lassie? I haven't heard anything at the bank.'

Bessie shook her head, her expertise at an end. 'Some old German goaty man that he must ha' known when he was a young loon and travellin' aboot a wye. Lexy says he was aywis spikkin aboot him.'

'Goaty man?' said Mr Gilfeather, and then he understood. 'Ah, dear,' he said, laying down his fork, 'ah, dear me.'

★

The girl Lexy had come in at last and opened the curtains, chastising Mr Fordyce for straining his eyes by lamplight when it was a fine spring day and the sun already at the windows. She had tutted and shaken her head as she moved his book aside to turn out the lamp. *Wilhelm Meister* in the original German. Mr Isaac had no need for Carlyle's translation, although he had heard that Goethe himself was delighted with it. From the window of his bedroom in Fordyce House, he could see up the Cromarty firth, beyond the opposing promontories of the Sutors and out into the Firth of Moray and the German Ocean. How often, these last fifty years, had his mind made that journey, had he promised himself he would go back once more to the land that had told him *who he was*? He had never done it, understanding very young, perhaps, that an ideal can never be, should never be, returned to.

Those days were gone now. War had eaten up the continent and made it into something else. Young men such as Ludovic Cameron now dreamed instead of America and lives that Mr Fordyce could not begin to conceive of. Ludovic who, towards the end of last night's gathering at Rose Lodge, had found a quiet moment to show to him the short newspaper item he had brought with him. Such a short item. Ludovic had apologised for the brevity, as if it was his fault. 'It's Wednesday's paper,' he had explained. 'No doubt there will be more in the Saturday edition.' But what more could be said? Mr Fordyce had brought the newspaper closer to the candelabra nearest to him and read. 'The illustrious

Goethe, the greatest of modern German writers, died at Weimar on 22 ult., in his eighty-second year.'

The chattering had gone on in the room. Glasses and tea-cups had continued to clink, the fire had crackled and spat. There had been some sound from outside too – townspeople passing in the street below, cats fighting. There had been no silence, save that between the old gentleman and the young bank clerk. Removing his monocle, Mr Fordyce had at last thanked Ludo and excused himself, as unobtrusively and politely as he could manage. Expressions of concern had followed him down the stairs and out into the mildness of the early spring night as he had walked home, alone.

Over at the clockmaker's, his breakfast finished, the talk was also of the dead German. 'Well, he will know by now.'

Stanislas looked up from his porridge. 'Who will know what, James?'

'Goethe. He will know if it is God or the Devil that has been waiting for him.'

'You know it was Dr Faustus, and not the poet himself who pledged his soul to the Devil, do you not, James?'

'Oh, I know that well enough. But I don't know how I will ever get *you* to understand that we Scots do not see our souls as our own to promise. From before we draw breath, our eternal fate is predestined to us, be we of the Elect or the Damned. It has the effect of reducing somewhat our scope for manoeuvre. Dr Faustus would have done better to have been born in Scotland.'

'If you are of the Elect you may do as you please then? Hmm, like in that terrible book of Mr Hogg's of the *Justified Sinner* that Dr Fraser forced upon poor John. He was downcast for weeks afterwards. But that, of course, is just a story.'

James gave his apprentice a playful clout on the ear. 'You are too clever for me, Stan.' Then as he gathered up their empty bowls he said, 'You know, you might think of writing your own story. There would be great interest in it.'

'I doubt it. You need only look in your newspapers to see that people have lost interest in the Poles. Just as they grew sick of the aristocratic French beggars who preceded us, they have grown tired of hearing about us and our troubles. In France there are already complaints about the costs of housing so many Polish refugees. They are henceforth to be kept to particular towns. No one will want to hear my story amongst so many thousands. If I could just get my translation of Miekiewicz done though, that would be something.'

James wished that Stan might be done with his countryman's epic of the past and look instead to a future that was his own. 'You know,' he said, 'you might join John and Ludo when they go on this trip that is to be taken by the circulating library.'

Stan looked away. 'I think if they had wished me to join the library, they would have asked me by now.'

James made a dismissive, 'pfft'. 'I don't mean go the whole hog, but you might at least travel over to Nigg with John and Ludo and go with them to Shandwick to look at the ancient carved stone John is so keen upon viewing. You could return here in the evening while they go on to meet with the rest of the library. It would do you good to get out of Cromarty, if even for a day.'

Stan smiled. 'I will think about it.'

'I can hardly believe we are truly to go,' said Alicia. 'In the *barouche.*' She articulated 'barouche' in a manner that might suggest the canopied litter of a Roman empress.

'*On* the barouche,' corrected Mairead, buttoning her thickest coat. 'Remember, we are to sit up on the outside.'

'Oh, I don't care,' said Alicia. 'Just imagine, should one of the girls from the George Street boarding school be looking out of the window as we pass, they will know that *we* have been chosen to travel to Tain with the circulating library, that *we* are to spend the night at Shandwick House, in the company of Lady Charlotte and other persons of quality.'

The invitation, issued at the behest of Lady Charlotte in the name of the ladies of the circulating library and delivered by Janet Cameron, that Miss Juniper's two pupils should join in the expedition to Easter Ross, had landed in the cottage on Little Vennel like a cloud of pollen let loose by a lily. Alicia had looked fit to faint with joy and the hint of a tear had appeared in the old governess's eye. Mairead herself had stood steady, but she had not been indifferent. She had, at first, been unable to speak, but no one had noticed that anyway. For a start, there was the matter of the books – to be allowed to go through the books on offer at the Dornoch Library sale was a thing previously only to have dreamed of. But then there was the altogether different matter of Ludo Cameron. Would Ludo, a full member of the library and therefore entitled to go on the trip, actually go? Would Mr Gilfeather approve the necessary absence from the bank? Probably not, Mairead thought. And would his mother engage in the unthinkable and leave the hotel for more than two days entire?

As well as the pollen of the lily, however, an ominous cloud had also followed Mrs Cameron through the door. The invitation had not encompassed Miss Juniper. When this had become apparent, the girls had declared with some fervour that they would not go without her. At this the elderly governess had raised herself to her full five feet and three inches and insisted that they most certainly would go, and that she would not wish to have to write to their fathers of their ingratitude in the face of so gracious an invitation and opportunity for their advancement. She had then gone to make the tea, leaving them to be surveyed by Mrs Cameron. The hotelkeeper, an occasional, if rare, visitor to the little cottage parlour, had told the girls quite firmly that they must accept the invitation. Their presence on the expedition would be a visible mark of the regard in which their schoolmistress was held by several members of the library. Mrs Cameron did not waste her time on meandering delicacy but told them frankly that it would be at best uncomfortable and at worst impossible for Miss Juniper herself to circulate in a world that remained suspicious of her pen, and that Lady Charlotte had understood that. To have invited her knowing she could not accept would have been an unkindness, and the girls had better learn to grasp such matters if they were to go out into society without coming a cropper amongst its subtleties. Mairead glanced at Alicia and received an affirmative glance in return. They made their curtsies to Mrs Cameron. They would go.

After they had had their tea and Ludovic's mother had left, Miss Juniper had settled at her writing desk to pen her reply to the ladies of the library. The girls, incapable now of any useful schoolwork, were dispatched upstairs to consider what clothing they would take on their adventure, and what little repairs and embellishments they might be required to make to their 'best' gowns.

'I wish all the same that Miss Juniper was able to come with us. How she would have enjoyed to look over the books,' Mairead said.

'Hmm.' Alicia was targeting a block-printed cotton dress that would have done the better of pearl buttons at the cuffs. 'Ten to one it was Miss Elspeth who wouldn't let her come. The rest of the library members are nice . . .'

'I don't like the look of Mr Hossack very much. He's always very red in the face and annoyed-looking and he wears his neckcloth too tight.'

'Oh, as if anyone would listen to Mr Hossack, or he have an opinion on Miss Juniper anyway,' Alicia replied, deep in the scrutiny of a suspect seam. 'And you heard what

Mrs Cameron said – he declines to leave the factory to his managers for the length of a trip to Easter Ross, when there is no profit involved.'

Mairead conceded that that was something. 'You don't think Fachie might go in his place though, do you?'

'Fachie Hossack is still in Aberdeen, slithering about houses of ill-repute.'

'Alicia!'

'Well, it's only what Hester overheard Dr Fraser saying in the coffee room, and if a minister can say it, I don't see why I should not.'

'You know very well why not, Alicia. Because you and I are just a hair's breadth from slipping down the classes. We might more easily go down than up and so we must hold to a higher standard of character at all times. You must, in particular.'

'What?' Alicia let fall the gown she had been examining. 'Why me, *in particular*?'

'Because you are by far the prettier of the two of us, and you know it is always the prettier one who is more destined for a *Fall*.' Before Alicia was able to expostulate, Mairead had reeled off a whole troupe of heroines who had traipsed to notoriety across the pages of their favourite novels, and Alicia was forced to concede that she was right. Mairead was not finished, though. 'And everyone knows that Dr Fraser says what he likes, whereas most ministers do not.'

Alicia, having no interest in ministers, turned the conversation to her preferred subject instead. 'What a pity it is that Stanislas can't go. He would add a great deal to the tone of the company.'

Mairead was tempted to make some reference to Stanislas and the 'tone' of a striking clock, but she had come to learn that reminders that Alicia's beau, however aristocratic his antecedents, was now nothing more than a Cromarty clockmaker's apprentice, were not taken in the good part in which they were intended. She contented herself instead with remarking that if Alicia really was intent upon trying on the enormous and exuberantly foliated hat she had just retrieved from under her bed, she had better first check that there was not a family of mice living in it.

NINETEEN

Late April 1832

Forgotten Lives

Sir William took great care in arranging rugs around his wife's and Rachel's knees and in ensuring they had more cushions than they could possibly require.

'We will be perfectly comfortable, William,' said Charlotte, 'and look what a beautiful day it promises to be.'

'Maybe so, my dear, but you must permit me to fuss a little. The wind can have some sharpness in it, and you know, after your – illness – of the winter, and the burden Rachel has had to carry these last weeks, I should not like either of you to catch a chill.'

Charlotte smiled at him. 'I am quite past all that, William, and much too robust now to worry about a chill. And Rachel, well, all Rachel needs is to be with Alasdair again.'

Rachel put out a hand to him. 'You are very kind, William.'

'Not a bit of it,' he said, colouring. 'It is entirely selfish. Alasdair is my best friend. He would not manage without you, and I would be lost without him. Besides, who else would possibly keep Charlotte company?'

This unfortunate last remark hung in the air a moment until he looked away, giving her hand a gentle pat as he did so. 'Well, as long as you both have everything you need.' Then he closed the door to the carriage and got up front, beside the coachman, a thing he had loved from boyhood.

As they pulled away onto the Causeway, Charlotte gave a short bright smile. 'Poor William. He tries so hard and asks so little.'

'Your happiness is his, regardless of, well, everything.'

'I know that,' said Charlotte. She closed her eyes briefly then made herself sit up straighter. 'And happy I am determined to be, for I have a safe home, and a husband who is kind to me, and I have you, and you are dearer to me than all of it.'

'I could not have managed these last months without you, Charlotte.'

'Just a little longer, and you will not have to manage any more. Alasdair will be home and you will not be alone any longer.'

Charlotte saw some hesitancy in Rachel's eyes. 'What is it, my dear?'

'I . . . am frightened.'

'Of Alasdair? Surely not.'

'No. Not that. I am frightened about him. How he will be. How *we* will be.'

'But all those visits you have had at Dr Fraser's manse . . .'

'Micah has been there, most of the time. It is only the last few visits that we have been alone. Talking, walking. But, oh, Charlotte – he is trying so hard. He is so contrite, as if it has all been his fault.' They were passing the harbour now and Charlotte saw in a glance that Rachel had noticed John Learmonth, the schoolmaster, waiting to board the Nigg ferry alongside James Craig's Polish apprentice. 'I don't need Alasdair's contrition,' Rachel continued. 'I don't want it. I want his anger and his boldness and his strength, for we are neither of us anything without them.'

John Learmonth watched Stanislas step with some trepidation aboard the small ferry boat that would take them the short distance across to Nigg. 'The firth is quite calm, Stan.' The day of the proposed excursion had finally arrived, and Stanislas was joining him and Ludovic on their early morning diversion to see the ancient Shandwick stone, before returning home to Cromarty while the other two went on to meet with the rest of the library members at Shandwick House.

The young Pole cast a nervous eye over the small vessel. 'I have hardly set foot on a boat since I was blown to Cromarty in a gale last March,' he said. 'My mind conjures images of *The Raft of the Medusa*, or of Don Juan's first voyage – the tempest, the shipwreck, the horrors of cannibalism . . .'

After Fachie Hossack's Christmas Eve insinuations about Don Juan's conquest of the wife of an older man, John had had more than enough of Byron's hero, and said so. 'In fact,' he added, 'I would not have mourned his loss. But I think it unlikely that I will feel the need to eat you before we make land at Nigg Bay.'

Once Ludovic had joined them and the ferryman had cast off, John began to talk of the meeting of the Northern Association he had attended in Inverness. 'We heard that the Royal Antiquarian Society of Copenhagen has commissioned a series of sketches of the stones we are to see today. They are greatly interested in them.'

Ludo dismissed the Royal Antiquarian Society of Copenhagen with a wave of his hand. 'Every barefoot schoolboy knows the story of the stones. I will tell it to you when we get there, while we have our picnic.'

By the time they came ashore at Nigg, the morning was in its full late-April glory. Tiny wildflowers were beginning to make themselves known amongst the grasses at the shore and clusters of dainty primroses peeked from amongst the rocks. But as they ascended the hill path, the three friends could not ignore the quarantine ships out in Cromarty Bay or the fact of the constables posted at bridges and prominent crossing places all over the Black Isle and Easter Ross at the behest of the quarter-sessions at Dingwall, for fear of the encroaching cholera.

Ludo looked at the ships and sighed. 'You still hanker for America?' asked Stan.

My mother is more resolute than ever against it. I wish we had never joined the library. Mr Hall's book was bad enough, but Mrs Trollope's has only made matters worse.'

'How so?'

Ludo grimaced. 'According to that good lady, American gentlemen spit at every opportunity, whether indoors or out; for women there is no society but religion, which carries itself off in a very ridiculous manner, with bouts of competitive hysteria; in the states that are "free" . . .'

'Where they have abolished slavery?'

'Yes. To the north. Anyway, in those states, the white servants are so well-apprised of their rights that one is hard put to get them to do anything at all.'

John clapped his friend around the shoulder. 'Don't worry, Ludo. We shall get her persuaded yet – for surely, if anyone can put the faults of that young nation to rights, it will be your mother.'

They walked on a little further and Stanislas suddenly said, 'Do *you* ever think of emigrating, John?'

John hesitated. 'I did, once. But I am too attached to our old volcanic lump of rock, to our bracken and our heather and to the antiquities they have stood sentry to for so many years. Where in North America, for instance, would you find stones as ancient as those we shall see later today?'

'Well,' began Ludo, 'I do believe the natives have . . .'

But John shook his head. 'Let what they have be theirs and let my history be mine. I will not leave old Scotland, whatever the provocation.'

Ludo and Stan exchanged a look, and Ludo cleared his throat. 'Did they ask you to leave – the ministers?'

John strode onwards. They had already, a few days ago, gone over the bones of what had occurred little more than a week earlier, when he had been summoned to the manse of Resolis, to find himself confronted not only with Dr Fraser, but also with the convalescent Reverend Alasdair Mackay. 'I thought we were not going to talk of this any more?'

'It was you who said that, not me,' said Ludo.

John lifted his face heavenwards. 'By God, Ludo, but you can be infuriating.'

'Maybe,' said the bank clerk, 'but I am right.'

John let out a long sigh. 'All right.' He had studied to put the dreadful interview from his mind, along with the sensation of his stomach dropping through the floorboards of Dr Fraser's study when he had walked in there to find Mr Mackay waiting for him.

'On account of you,' Mr Mackay had begun, 'my wife's name is on the lips of half the Black Isle.'

John had known that denial of the essential truth of the thing would be pointless. 'I give you my word,' he'd said, 'I never as much as approached her. I never as much as spoke to her unless in company. And she most certainly never spoke to me in any familiar way, nor encouraged any address from me.' Then, deciding he might as well be hung for a sheep as a lamb, he had taken a deep breath and said, 'I do not deny that I did and do admire that lady very much, and I understand that I allowed that admiration to show on my face and in my conversation more unguardedly than was wise. You may believe me distraught to think that such thoughtlessness on my part has cast any hint of a shadow over her name.'

Alasdair Mackay had stood up and John had feared the man was about to smash his fist into his jaw, but instead the minister had said, 'What is done cannot be undone, but I would counsel you to have a better guard on your emotions – what will pass unnoticed in a city like Edinburgh will not do so in a town such as Cromarty.'

Thinking his ordeal over, John had been about to make his bow and turn for the study door, when the stentorian tones of Dr Fraser had stopped him. 'It would go the better with you, young man, if you were married. There is nothing to put a stop to speculation like the reading of the banns and a houseful of bairns. Think on it.'

These full details now revealed on the walk up Nigg Hill, Ludo was aghast. 'They advised you to get married?'

John nodded. 'Had I not been out of the house as quickly as I was, I have no doubt they would have written me up a list of potential wives.'

'And you have not thought of it? Getting married, I mean?'

John turned away. 'If I had known my private life would be subject to this level of scrutiny, I would have invited Miss Elspeth Rose to join me today instead. Now come on, or the stone will disintegrate and there will be nothing but a pillar of sand awaiting us.'

As they walked, the smell of the yellow whin flowers combined with the urgent trilling back and forth of numberless birds was almost overwhelming to the senses, and John regretted his display of temper. In fact, having at last admitted to his friends the full, mortifying details of his interview with the two ministers, he could almost feel the tensions of the last few long, featureless winter months begin to slip from his shoulders like an old coat.

'It is good though, to get out of the town for a while,' he said, eventually.

Stan gave him a look of sympathy. 'You feel things closing in on you?'

'Sometimes.'

'I think that you, John, were made for the life of the city. Perhaps Ludo is right – you have surely seen what you came for of rocks and tombstones. Perhaps when you have seen this stone we are to see today, you should consider making plans to return to Edinburgh.'

A shadow briefly crossed John's face. 'There are – things in Edinburgh I have no wish to go back to, Stan.' Then he smiled. 'Besides, how could the salons and smoking rooms of the capital compete with the coffee room of the Commercial Hotel? And no doubt Ludo is about to tell us a story that would amaze the learned gentlemen of institutes and societies from Inverness to Copenhagen and every city of note in between. Come, we had better catch up with him.'

Soon they were looking down at the long sweep of yellow sand that was Shandwick Bay, curved round the sea like the blade of a scimitar. Above them, standing sentinel, was the huge, exposed slab of magnificently carved stone they had come to see.

John reached out a hand to the intricate knots, fantastical beasts and hunts and battle scenes that told stories of an unknown people who had been here, centuries before them. 'Incredible,' he said.

Ludo beamed. 'Well, it's one of three, you know, although that at Cadboll has been lost. They are the graves of Danish princes, brothers who drowned on those jagged rocks just off the shore there. They sailed here to rescue their sister from Ballone Castle, where her cruel husband, the wicked Earl of Ross had imprisoned her. It's a ruin, now. A visit for another day,' he added emphatically, looking at John.

Stan was looking out to sea. 'I can picture it. The longship, coming across the water with those three handsome young men standing at the prow.'

'I cannot be certain that they were handsome,' said Ludo.

'Oh but you can,' said John. 'They would have been handsome and brave and tragic. Such magnificent grave markers demand no less.'

They sat then to their picnic, and for John to make his sketches. 'Of course,' said Ludo, when their picnic was almost finished, 'it is said that plague victims were buried here too.' His words broke the spell. A large cloud whose approach they had not noticed began to creep across the sun until it had obscured it, throwing their bright morning into a succession of muted shades that the heart had gone out of. All unseen, the vision of the three tragic brothers dissolved itself into the air.

John said, 'None of it is known though, is it? What was

ever *known* of these people has been forgotten. And yet they lived. And I cannot live unless I am forgotten.'

His friends exchanged a look of concern.

'What is it that are you running from, John?' asked Stan at last. 'We are your friends. You must let us help you.'

But John just packed the last of his drawing materials back into his satchel and stood up. 'You cannot. It is my burden and of my own making. Come, we had better get you back down to Nigg for the ferry boat, then Ludo and I must get on. They will be expecting us at Shandwick House.'

When the carriage from Cromarty House had come to a halt in front of the manse of Resolis, they had been able to hear Dr Fraser remonstrating loudly with his housekeeper over her repacking of his valise, and after he had greeted Rachel and shown her into the parlour where Alasdair was waiting, she heard them resume. Charlotte and William had remained outside, and so now they were alone, she and Alasdair. He was in his best blacks, his neckcloth hanging a little looser than it should do, a little more grey in his hair, but Micah had done what he had promised to do – by sheer force of will and the help of God he had dragged Alisdair back from whatever abyss he had been staring into and forced him back towards the light.

She stood just a foot or two inside the parlour, he at the French window. There was a distance between them in the room and she didn't know how she would get across it.

'How are you?' she said at last.

'I am well,' he said. 'And ready.'

She looked at him. 'Are you sure? We don't need to go on this jaunt. We could stay here a while or go quietly home.'

A small glint of something that might have been anger appeared in his eyes. 'We are not creeping quietly back to Cromarty, apologising for that they nearly broke us. We will go out in the world and it may say what it will, then it can hold its tongue.'

'But are you *sure* you are strong enough?'

'I am strong enough, all right. And ready for them. Micah has conquered my demons and they are not coming back.'

His travelling bag was at his feet, the chest with the rest of his belongings packed and bound, ready to be sent back to Cromarty.

She tried to wet her lips and the words would hardly come out. 'But it is you who must conquer your demons, not Micah.'

His eyes bore into her, something desperate in them. 'Good God, Rachel, do you not want me any more?'

The words went through her like a knife. 'Not want you? Alasdair, I . . . how could I not want you? I . . .'

He was moving across the room and had her by the shoulders. He bent his head towards her. 'Say it, for I have wanted nothing but you.'

She shut her eyes and he closed the last distance between them and she thought if he had not been holding her she could not have managed to remain standing at all.

TWENTY

Shandwick House

Tobacco smoke was already wafting from the dining room as the ladies disposed themselves about the sofas of the drawing room to take their coffee. Alicia had practically wafted in herself. Never, in her life, had she sat in such a room. Miss Elspeth may well have said, as they had trundled here from the Balintraid ferry in one of the conveyances sent by Mrs Ross to collect them, that Shandwick House was not quite so grand as Cromarty House, being somewhat smaller, but Alicia was sure that Miss Juniper's entire cottage would have fitted into the drawing room, regardless. Her delight, as the horses had trotted briskly along the tree-lined drive to turn into the semicircular courtyard in front of the house, had been almost impossible to contain. Even Miss Elspeth, who had scarcely drawn breath in the delivery of her monologue as to how the girls should comport themselves at Shandwick, had remarked that though a little smaller, Shandwick had the greater charm.

Despite its size, the drawing room was pleasantly warm – quite as warm as the parlour of Miss Juniper's cottage, and not so bothered with smoke or the occasional waft of abandoned seaweed to which the vennel was prone. The evening was advancing now, and the sun did not come in at the eastward-facing windows but lit instead the long lawns that swept down to the sea without, as was the case with Cromarty, the encumbrance of a town to spoil the views. Everywhere was rounded elegance – the arched window lights, the circular entrance hall with its domed ceiling, two storeys high, the curving staircase that unfurled itself like a ribbon. 'Neo-classical,' Alicia heard Mr Isaac Fordyce say, and she practised it, for when she might converse with Stanislas on the architecture of country houses.

The dining room across the hall had also been warm, and getting warmer by the minute, and Alicia felt they had got out only just in time for the sake of Mairead's cheeks which had been near enough scarlet by the time the ladies had risen in advance of the arrival of the punchbowl.

Perhaps it had not been the heat of the fire though, that had so heightened the colour of Mairead's cheeks, but rather the proximity of Ludo Cameron, who had somehow contrived to sit himself beside her, leaving Alicia to the surprisingly entertaining company of Dr Fraser. Ludo seemed to be telling Mairead the legend of the Shandwick stone, and Mairead was gazing, fascinated, as if she had not heard the story a hundred times before. While relieved not to have been seated beside Mr Mackay, Alicia was nonetheless pleased to see that, although undoubtedly aged by his late illness, he was not run through altogether. She noticed too that he and Rachel looked at each other sometimes as if they wished they were alone, and that once he had lifted his hand to brush back a lock of her hair that had tumbled from its pinnings. Noticing this made Alicia's stomach strangely warm, and she thought it was perhaps the effect of the wine that Mrs Ross had insisted it was surely all right for her and Mairead to have, with a little water.

Alicia had paid very little heed to the rumours that had circulated in the early spring concerning Mrs Mackay and the schoolmaster. Had Rachel wished to marry a schoolmaster, she might have done it half a dozen times at least before she had become the minister's wife. And besides, for all his acknowledged good looks, there was something in Mr Learmonth that seemed to Alicia to be not quite right. And whatever that was, Mairead did not like it either, though neither could tell what it was about him that left them uneasy. What a pity, she thought for the hundredth time, that it was he and not Stanislas who had been invited to join the library.

But then she became aware that Lady Charlotte was asking Mrs Ross about the particulars of her decorating scheme for the house, and Alicia put thoughts of Stanislas aside for the moment to pay attention to this new and important matter.

'Well, there was enough to be done as you might imagine, your ladyship,' Mrs Ross was saying, 'and scarcely a thing needed that was to be found in Inverness.'

Miss Anna looked genuinely concerned for Mrs Ross's difficulties. 'You would have had to send to Edinburgh, I suppose?'

'Indeed I had, Miss Anna. I was never done writing to my sister Belle in Charlotte Square for this and for that. I keep my design and pattern books in the chiffonier in my sitting room – I will get them out for you tomorrow.'

Miss Anna beamed, and Alicia determined that she, too, would be in attendance when the books were brought out. She also made a note to employ the word *chiffonier* as often as she saw an opportunity, and certainly in any future exchange with the girls from the George Street boarding school.

'Most of it had to be got up from London though,' Mrs Ross was saying, 'and at such an expense that I would blush to tell you of. But Mr Ross is so much amongst the other gentlemen of Caribbean interest that his taste has quite run away from that he was born with and I am left with no option but to go after him.'

Alicia risked a glance around the matrons and spinsters of Cromarty who, she knew, waited every moment to be scandalised, and was rewarded by the critical beam that darted from Miss Elspeth's eye, speaking silent volumes of Mrs Ross's indulgence of her husband's profligacy.

It was Mrs Hossack though, her face nearly turned green by the luxury on display, who got in first. 'Well, we must hope his fortunes follow the same route, for the fortune he was *born* with would hardly pay the hundredth of it.'

Mrs Ross treated Mrs Hossack to the most gracious of smiles. This was not her first encounter with the factory-owner's wife. 'Well, Marjorie, my dear, if anyone could testify to that it is yourself, for many the times has Mr Ross reminisced about himself and your brother running barefoot over the gutters and dykes of Dingwall, near on fifty years ago, when your mother was laundrywoman to his.'

The scarlet that came over Mrs Hossack's cheeks rendered Mairead's pale in comparison. Alicia wondered whether Lady Charlotte might have to get out her smelling salts, but a glance at Lady Charlotte told her that *she* was in danger of erupting into most unladylike laughter at any moment. It was Rachel Mackay who stepped in to move the conversation on, managing not to trip over the origins of either Mrs Hossack or Mr Ross.

'I'm sure you are very happy here at Shandwick, now that you are settled, Mrs Ross.'

'Oh yes, my dear, although Mr Ross cannot settle himself while this emancipation business weighs so heavily on him.'

'Oh?' enquired Mrs Cameron.

Alicia heard a distinct chill in Ludo's mother's tone. It was known that Ludovic's father had gone out to be overseer on Sir William's plantation many years ago and never come back. While Mrs Cameron was not a person prone to the expression of emotion, Alicia supposed that any discussion in this direction was bound to awaken painful memories, even in her.

'Well,' said Mrs Ross, encompassing the generous proportions of the room with a sweep of her hand, 'talk of emancipation threatens the very roof over our heads, for a property such as this must be paid for. How is my husband's plantation to function, pray tell me? Who is to do the work if the negroes will not? It is hardly to be expected that our own people will provide what labour is required.'

It seemed that Mrs Mackay had something to say, but Mrs Ross was not ready to cede the floor. 'I grant you,' she continued, 'that the late improvements in many parts of the Highlands are a great encouragement to the landless classes to cross the Atlantic in search of better fortune, but they are loath to go into the south, the most of them, where they are most needed. And if they are logging in Nova Scotia, they cannot be cutting sugar cane in Demerara, can they? And such being the case, I ask again, who is to do the work?'

No one appeared to have any solution to offer, and eventually Lady Charlotte spoke. 'Sir William tells me Mr Ross has added his name to the letter lately written on behalf of the gentlemen hereabouts, praying Parliament to let drop all talk of emancipation.'

'Indeed he has,' confirmed Mrs Ross. 'But if their pleas should fall on deaf London ears, how is he to be compensated for the loss of his property?'

'I believe it is the people, and not the properties that are to be emancipated from the planters, Mrs Ross,' said Lady Charlotte.

Their hostess gave her a benevolent smile. 'But the people *are* our property, my dear. I am sure Sir William has the same concerns.'

Lady Charlotte took a sip of her tea. 'I believe he does.'

'I think,' put in Miss Elspeth, 'we might leave the politics to the gentlemen.'

Miss Anna, who had a horror at the very hint of unpleasantness, brightened. 'Yes! Perhaps the young schoolmaster will share more of his theories about the Shandwick stone, although I have always inclined to the story Mr Cameron told, of those brave Danish princes. And their poor, imprisoned sister. I cannot think I would be happy to spend even an evening at Ballone Castle, with such an unhappy shadow hanging over it.'

'You would be very unlikely to, you silly woman,' snapped her sister. 'There is not a roof or a window to the place and has not been these last two centuries at least.'

Mrs Ross gave Miss Anna a kindly look. 'You know, Miss Anna, Shandwick House has its own shadow, although I have done what I can to banish any gloomy association with the . . . *unfortunate* . . . things that may have occurred here in the past.' She mouthed 'unfortunate' with a meaningful glance towards Miss Juniper's girls, but Miss Anna failed to take her hint and said, 'Oh, my, yes, I had quite forgotten! We were very young, of course, and Pap would not have liked us to hear of it, would he, Elspeth? But then the servants tattle so.'

Her sister glared at her, but it was too late, for the cat was out of the bag and slinking around the room, paying especial attention to those who might prove most receptive to it.

'I cannot think that some Gothic adventure can have attached itself to somewhere as elegant as Shandwick House,' said Lady Charlotte.

'I think it better not to resurrect the tattle of servants,' said Miss Elspeth, giving Lady Charlotte a sharp look.

To Alicia's disbelief, Mrs Cameron, who had been extremely tight-lipped during the discussion of emancipation, weighed in on the side of disclosure. 'If it were no more than the tattle of servants, Miss Elspeth, I would agree with you. But the thing that took place in the environs of this house was a terrible thing, and a warning whose lesson ought not to be lost on any young woman about to step out into society. I think as well that those who have not heard it should do.'

'But these young girls,' protested Miss Elspeth, indicating Mairead and Alicia. 'I hardly think even Arabella Juniper would have entrusted them to our care had she thought they would hear—'

At this, Alicia felt herself emboldened to interject. 'Oh, yes, Miss Rose, you are right. For Mairead is *so* suggestible, and the nightmares consequent on some of the novels she has read have kept Miss Juniper and me awake no end of nights, and I am sure Miss Juniper would not—'

But even as Alicia began to feel the warm and unaccustomed rays of Miss Elspeth's approbation, Janet Cameron chased them off in an icy blast. 'It is not a question of novels or the usual Gothic terrors. The monsters of this story are of flesh and bone, blood and skin, and as real as we who are sitting here.'

Alicia, feeling Mairead tense beside her, made no further attempt to speak. There was nothing to do but let their elders battle it out, and to hope that Miss Elspeth would win.

But Miss Elspeth did not win, for Mrs Cameron had continued speaking. 'I think Miss Juniper would acknowledge we do these young women a better service by forewarning them of what awaits them in the world they will soon set out in than by leaving them ignorant of it and allowing them to be guided only by novels. There is a class of people amongst whom they will move that do not always face the justice they should, and it is important they understand that.'

Whatever other conversations might have been in train when the ladies had entered Mrs Ross's drawing room all came to an end now. It was Rachel who finally responded. 'I think you had better tell us what you are talking of, Mrs Cameron. With Mrs Ross's permission,' she added, looking to their hostess.

Mrs Ross, who clearly regretted having introduced a hint of the tale in the first place, merely nodded.

Mrs Cameron began. 'It happened what, forty years ago?'

Miss Elspeth gave a brief nod of confirmation. 'Forty-three, I believe. Most of the world was agog with news of events in France, but here, there was a tale of notoriety relating to Shandwick House . . . oh, of course, we were not permitted to hear of it, but as my sister says, the tattle of the servants.'

It was a sorry story, and names were not used so they could not know, really, to whom it alluded. A young woman, not much older than was Alicia herself, had been taken advantage of in the most outrageous way by a young gentleman of good family while they had both been guests at Shandwick House. The young woman had, in the course of time, discovered herself to be carrying a child. Despite the urging of her family, the young man had refused to marry her. She had been sent away to somewhere in England, to hide her shame and to give birth far from her friends and anyone who knew her. The fate of the child born of so unfortunate an episode was not known, but its mother, having survived the birth, was not long afterwards consigned to a lunatic asylum, whereupon her brother, infuriated at the treatment of his sister and the degrading of his family's honour, tracked her assailant to London and challenged him to a duel. The duel took place on some heath or common of the metropolis, but while both men were injured, neither was killed. The young woman's champion, having failed to put to death the man responsible for his sister's ruin, published the entire story for the world to see. There had, however, been no further retribution, no justice. The guilty party had denied all, and the world found things to interest it elsewhere.

At some point during the telling of this tale – she was not certain whether it was in childbed or at the asylum, but it had certainly been before the duel – Alicia had become aware that Rachel Mackay had left her place at the side of

Lady Charlotte and moved across to sit between herself and Mairead, and that she had hold of one of each of their hands.

'And so I hope you will take the lesson from this, girls,' Mrs Cameron concluded, 'that you can trust to nothing and no one but your own virtue and resilience, for to trust in anything else risks losing more than you could ever imagine.'

Alicia looked down at her lap and felt her cheeks flame as hot as Mairead's ever had done. A glance to the side told her that her friend, by contrast, had gone a deathly pale. They might have thrilled to the tale of the Danish princess, locked by her wicked husband in a castle on a stormy headland, but no one would thrill to the tale of the desolate young woman whose story Janet Cameron had just told them. That story could not be banished to the realm of folklore and perhaps the Danish princess should not have been either. Miss Anna – she was sure it was Miss Anna – was sobbing. A burst of laughter from the dining room across the hall broke into the room and seemed to chill all the women for a minute, until Mrs Ross put her hand to the bell to summon the servants she had told to leave before Mrs Cameron had embarked on her tale.

The maid who had come at the ringing of the bell bent down to whisper something to her mistress.

'Ah,' said Mrs Ross to the assembled ladies, 'I believe the gentlemen are on the point of joining us.'

The reception of this news was more muted than might otherwise have been the case. Alicia reminded herself that the events of which Mrs Cameron had spoken had taken place over forty years ago, and that gentlemen were different now, but when the drawing room doors opened and the men began to enter, she thought they looked bleary-eyed and most of them a little red in the face and she was glad that none of them sat near, or attempted to speak to her.

TWENTY-ONE

Unwelcome Guests

Ludovic and John, who had been accommodated at Shandwick Inn rather than the house itself, were enjoying an early breakfast when a loud rapping on the parlour door heralded the unexpected entrance of the two ministers, Dr Fraser and Mr Mackay, declaring their intention of accompanying them on their walk to the nearby burgh.

'A fine day to discourse upon the Lord's creation, is it not?'

Dr Fraser planted himself beside John on the bench and helped himself to a pickled herring from the dish.

'You did not breakfast up at the house?' Ludo asked, concerned for his own.

Dr Fraser made a pout before answering. 'A morsel in the kitchen – the others were not yet up and about – but the herring here in this inn are always of the best, do you not agree, Alasdair?'

'Indubitably,' said the other minister, taking up his place by Ludo.

The two young men, who had previously been discussing where they might visit in Tain when able to divest themselves of the company of their fellow library members, fell silent, each attempting to think of some polite conversation he might make. 'My mother tells me Mrs Ross has offered the ladies the use of her barouche,' offered Ludo at last.

Dr Fraser nodded as he chewed. 'Some of them, some of them.'

'Poor Mr Isaac. I would not wish to be stuck all the way to Tain with my mother and Mrs Hossack and the Misses Rose. They will never travel five miles at once without falling into some dispute or other.'

Dr Fraser glanced at Mr Mackay, who took his cue.

'You need not concern yourself on that head, Ludovic,' he said. 'Mrs Hossack is not going on to Tain.'

'She isn't?'

'No, she is not,' said Dr Fraser. 'The plain truth of it is that after yourself and Mr Learmonth left the company last night, a late visitor arrived at Shandwick House – no less a person than Fachie Hossack.'

'Fachie?' Ludo put down his fork, his relish for his breakfast at an end. 'Should he not still be in Aberdeen?'

'He claims to have come home for a visit with a friend near Inver, but it is my view that he's steering clear of Aberdeen while the trial of the anatomy theatre rioters is afoot.'

'I am the last man to defend Fachie Hossack,' said John, 'but I hardly think he would have been amongst those who *destroyed* the anatomical theatre. He has been one of its foremost proponents.'

'That he has, and against all the lessons of Scripture as I have not failed to tell him. But you may take it from me, he'll have been amongst those who were breaking the heads of the rioters, and that might come out at the trial too. Fachie Hossack has come home to lie low a while till the whole thing passes, I am certain of it.'

'And we are to endure him for the rest of this excursion.' Ludo was despondent.

Mr Mackay shook his head. 'No, his mother has asserted herself for once. She is determined on getting Fachie back to Cromarty before his father hears the news of his arrival from anyone else.'

Dr Fraser rubbed his hands in anticipation. 'There will be storm clouds over the town tonight. I am only sorry I won't be there to see it. Willie Hossack has quite a different idea of how that fellow should make his way in the world than does his wife. The pity of it is that he didn't stand up to the woman long ago.'

'Amen to that.' In the vehemence of his agreement, Ludo had forgotten for a moment whose company he was in. The ministers exchanged a look and he lowered his eyes.

'Well, whatever might occur tonight in the Hossack household, it seemed wise to us that yourself and Mr Learmonth should set out for Tain before Fachie is up and about and takes it into his head to come down here to work mischief.'

'And,' added Dr Fraser, examining a bannock before popping it and one of its fellows into his pocket, 'we can take the occasion to try you two young men on any point of religion you may be having difficulty with. Those *reviews* I have observed you both reading are awash with the deluded musings of would-be philosophers. An hour or two's walk with us will allow you both to profit from the deeper understanding of the world Mr Mackay and I have accumulated over the years; is that not right, Mr Mackay?'

'That is exactly so, Dr Fraser, I have read the reviews too, and I would not like to see the minds of young bank clerks and schoolmasters led astray by misinterpretation.'

As the party from the inn were setting out to walk, some more enthusiastically than others, the guests at Shandwick House were sitting down to their breakfast. If Mrs Ross had been flustered by the unexpected arrival, late the previous evening, of Fachie Hossack, she had not shown it. Mairead and Alicia, however, had already retired for the night before the uninvited visitor's arrival. Their delight at sinking together into a large, canopied bed beneath an embroidered silk counterpane matched by voluminous curtain swags that *someone else* had drawn across the window, was a little tempered by the shocking story they had heard that evening. 'It made me think about poor Gretchen in *Dr Faustus*,' whispered Mairead, as they carried their candles to the bedchamber at the end of the north wing of the house.

'Me too,' said Alicia. So keenly had she felt the unnecessary cruelty of Goethe's treatment of Gretchen that she had refused to read the rest of the tale, which Mairead had later confided had got much worse.

Tonight, they locked the door of their bedchamber. Both had understood from Mrs Cameron's story that a threat to a young woman's honour was as likely to come in the gentlemanly guise of a predatory person of her acquaintance as it was to take the form of a malevolent stranger. They knew that to be thought to have encouraged the attentions of such a person was to render oneself complicit. Neither girl had a brother, as that poor young woman or in fact Goethe's Gretchen had had, to fight a duel for the sake of her honour. They would guard each other's honour, and from this day on, Mairead would be on the alert. For now though, they would write in their journals of the day and the evening they had had, they would say their prayers and snuff out their candles and sleep as sound as they could amidst the luxuries of the canopied bed. And tomorrow they would wake refreshed, and Mairead would be on her guard.

So it was that when the girls walked into the breakfast room of Shandwick House next morning to see Fachie Hossack seated by his mother, they stopped stock-still for a moment. Of all the people they might have wanted to see after hearing what they had heard last night, Fachie Hossack was the very last.

Behind her, Mairead heard Alicia give a sharp intake of breath. Even Alicia was not taken in by his fine coat, his well-made shoes and his fashionable cane.

'Alicia, Mairead, come and sit here by me,' said Mrs

Mackay, smiling very brightly as she motioned the girls to sit alongside her, far down the table from where the Hossacks had lodged themselves on either side of their hostess.

The girls had only just begun to go towards their places when Fachie's voice came down the table at them. 'How fortunate the young ladies are here. You must be in want of company, Mrs Mackay, with the minister having abandoned you already. Or has he taken ill again? I trust it is not the same illness my mother wrote to me of in so many of her letters. I believe she quite began to fear he had left Cromarty for good, with no plan to return.'

As panic wrote itself across Marjorie Hossack's face while she tried to find some formulation of words that might eradicate what her son had just said, Rachel's smile drifted from Mairead and Alicia to rearrange itself into something else for Fachie. 'As you must have observed last night, Farquhar, my husband is restored to the best of health.' There it was, the 'Farquhar' to remind him that she still regarded him as little more than a son of the house in which she had years ago been governess, and a person of no consequence to her. 'He and Dr Fraser decided to walk to Tain in the company of Ludovic and Mr Learmouth.'

Mairead thought that something in her words seemed to bother Fachie's nostrils but before he could make any reply, Mr Fordyce joined in the conversation. 'Oh, that I were twenty years younger, and to have been able to join them. There is nothing better for a young man than to be out with his fellows at the break of day.' He beamed at the women. 'I impute no criticism to the gentle company of you ladies, of course, far from it, but you must excuse the nostalgia of an old man for the more vigorous pursuits of his youth.'

The implication that Fachie, here with his mother and the other women, rather than out walking with the men, thus fell short of proper manliness in some way, was lost on no one.

Fachie's riposte was not long in coming. 'Your Goethe, I hear, is dead.'

Mr Fordyce looked down at his lap a moment, composing himself, Mairead thought, then raised his head with a remarkable dignity. 'Not mine, not mine. But, yes, he is dead. His last acts, I understand, were to express his pleasure on the arrival of spring, and to call for his pen and paper. I cannot think of a better way for a man of letters to die. But while he may be dead, his work, his name, never shall be.'

There were murmurs of agreement from all round the table. Mairead even thought she saw Miss Elspeth reach out a hand and pat that of Mr Fordyce, but then she convinced herself that a trick of the light must have made her imagine it. The rest of the breakfast party was ready to fall to conversation about the coming book sale, but Fachie had got his taste for invective early this morning, and he had yet to satisfy it.

'I quite agree, Mr Fordyce,' he said, over Miss Anna's musings about whether any of Miss Edgeworth's work might be found amongst the Dornoch Library's books. 'Herr von

Goethe's work will never die because it addresses the universals of the human spirit. You see, Mother, I can read the *Edinburgh Review* and the *Quarterly* and *Blackwood's* with the best of them, library member or not. Anyway,' he somehow seemed to have shifted his attention from Mr Fordyce back to Rachel Mackay. 'The story of poor Werther, for instance, in love with another man's wife. Such a tragic tale. And she of course – the woman – while protesting conjugal fidelity, is yet absolutely complicit. What guilt must she have had at his suicide, having so blithely encouraged his affections with no regard to the consequences. She had destroyed him, of course.'

The company was stunned into silence, but Fachie, enjoying himself, had more to say. 'I always thought poor Werther should have had some other object or study that took his interest, and then things might not have been brought to such a pass. Mr Learmonth now, there is a young man with interests. Not at all the sort of man to destroy himself over another man's wife. You will agree, I'm sure, Mrs Mackay.'

Mairead could see Rachel's jaw grind a little under the firm line of her mouth. 'I am not in a position to comment upon Mr Learmonth's character nor on his interests.'

Fachie looked at her a moment, cocked an eyebrow as if in amusement and merely said, 'No?'

Mrs Ross began to say something, but Fachie put down his fork with something of a clatter and spoke again. 'I understand that Mr Learmonth and Ludo Cameron went together yesterday to look upon that heathenish lump of sandstone at Shandwick Bay. I wondered whether Mrs Mackay had gone too, or you perhaps, Lady Charlotte? You must find the days long, with the major being gone.'

'Mrs Mackay and I have seen the stone often enough before, Mr Hossack.'

'Ah.' Fachie feigned disappointment. 'Quite wise on your part, though.' He looked around the table and leaning forward, fixed his gaze on Mairead. 'You know, it is said that in past times, plague victims were buried beneath it. It is to be hoped that, in making their sketches and etchings, Mr Learmonth and his friends have not unsettled the earth beneath their feet, to the extent of disturbing whatever noxious substances lie below. Who is to say what may not been released by such thoughtless trampling upon these plague grounds? Who is to say that they have not brought the germ of the infection into this very house in the dirt of their boots—'

'Oh!' cried Miss Anna.

Rachel Mackay was on her feet, hands pressed on the tabletop and leaning towards Fachie, but it was Miss Elspeth who could articulate her words first. 'You will stop that talk this minute, Farquhar Hossack, or I will be constrained to ask Mrs Ross to put you from the house.'

Fachie stood up, letting his napkin drop to the table. Without acknowledging Elspeth Rose he addressed their hostess. 'I will thank you for your hospitality and save you further trouble, Mrs Ross.' Then he turned his head slightly and said, 'Come, Mother, your company is no more wanted here than mine. Better we get us back to Cromarty to face that old Devil your husband and be done with it.'

Mr Isaac Fordyce had actually got as far as getting to his feet and opening his mouth to remonstrate by the time Fachie went past him, his affronted mother having no option but to trail him in his wake.

'He said *that*? To his mother?' Dr Fraser shook his head. 'The fellow is out of control. 'They'll be lucky if he doesn't end up swinging from a gibbet on the Longman.'

'Come now, Micah,' said Alasdair Mackay, 'surely we cannot give up on him?'

'You wouldn't say that if you had been in his company this morning,' said Rachel, taking a sip of the chocolate that had been ordered to warm herself and Charlotte after the ride to Tain in the gig. 'The man is thoroughly wicked.'

'He will come to a bad end, no question,' said Dr Fraser. 'The trick will be in seeing he takes no one else with him.'

'He would not have behaved in that way had William been at the table,' said Lady Charlotte. 'I wish he had not had to ride to Lochcarron this morning.'

The report had been in the newspaper, laid out in the library when they had arrived the previous evening at Shandwick House. An outbreak of typhus in Lochcarron, amongst the tenants of an absentee Mackenzie cousin, had been mistaken for cholera, and the reporting of it risked causing hysteria. Being near at hand, William had gone west in the hope of calming the fears of the people. A letter-writer to the newspaper had given the blunt reason for the typhus taking hold where it had – the people had not been able to get enough salt the previous herring season. With heaps of rotting fish being left lying on the beaches, they had attempted to preserve something for the winter by hanging as much as they could from the roofs of their houses, hoping thus to smoke them, with the predictable, lamentable, result.

So, because the poor people of Lochcarron had not had enough salt to preserve their fish, Sir William Mackenzie was not with his wife when she accompanied the members of the circulating library into Tain on their book-buying expedition, and he was not with her afterwards, either.

TWENTY-TWO

Pilgrimage

'I do hope we will not be too late,' worried Miss Anna, as she hurried along the street from the hotel to Douglas's bookseller's on Tain High Street. 'The best volumes may already be gone, and I had been looking forward to reading Bishop Heber's *India*, having enjoyed his *Poems* so very much.'

Her sister pursed her lips on her irritation. 'I told you, Anna, nothing is to be sold in advance of twelve o'clock. The advertisement in the *Courier* was quite clear, and Mrs Cameron has brought the cutting with her, at my request, lest things not be done as they were advertised. Besides, who do you think will be able to outbid us? For an individual to purchase books already used by a reading club such as Dornoch's would suggest they had not the wherewithal to purchase them new for themselves, but for our circulating library to do so bespeaks a shared interest in the merits of literature.'

Anna did not see, but she knew from long experience that the more she tried to and the more Elspeth attempted to explain to her, the less she would understand. She felt her spirits begin to droop but then caught a wink from Mr Fordyce who, when Elspeth was a safe distance ahead whispered to her, 'I shall be very much surprised if I do not make some purchases today for my own collection, and I hope it shall not be thought that *I* am on the slide.' And here he executed a forward glide that would not have shamed the most elegant of ice-skaters on Duddingston Loch.

Anna covered her giggle with one hand and accepted Mr Fordyce's arm with the other and they proceeded very happily to the bookshop, remarking on the fine new honey-coloured buildings being erected in the principal parts of the town. She was pleased to see that Mr Isaac had not been too much affected by the unpleasant remarks addressed to him earlier by Farquhar Hossack. She and Elspeth had spoken of it as they had prepared for their journey that morning.

'He has always been such an unpleasant boy. Remember when Pap allowed the boys of the school to come and examine his sea charts and his spy-glasses? Farquhar was caught in the act of stealing Pap's sextant and he tried to blame poor Ludovic.'

'Indeed,' Elspeth had said. 'Marjorie Hossack is much to blame, but the boy has been wicked through and through since the day he was born. I have advised his father to send him very far away, and I know that Dr Fraser and others have done the same.'

Anna could just imagine the scene and was glad she had not been there in person to witness it.

Douglas's bookshop was not as spacious as MacGillivray's in Inverness, and there was just the press of other people in to look at the books and to look at who else was looking at the books that Anna had anticipated. Several of the young men in the shop eager to purchase something were of the mechanic class. Anna remembered how James Craig had loved to read as a young man, and how their father, despite James's lower social standing, had been happy to discuss books with him when James had come to see to the household clocks and to observe the workings of Pap's cherished chronometer, which James had shown such a talent in helping him maintain. Elspeth did not approve of too much reading on the part of the lower orders, asserting that it was to blame for almost all of the political tumults of recent years. This was another connection that Anna failed to see – reading Miss Austen's novels had not resulted in *her* wishing to parade on the street, or to take up arms against the government, but then perhaps she was reading the wrong books.

Then, risking the censure of her sister, she waved a glove to attract the attention of Ludo Cameron and the schoolmaster, whom she had just seen step over the door.

'Miss Rose,' said Mr Learmonth, doffing his hat, 'Miss Anna. Have you found anything of interest?'

'Very little that we have not already got,' replied Elspeth in a slightly louder voice than was necessary. One of the ladies from the Dornoch Reading Club was standing only a few feet away, and Anna understood that this was what had occasioned the raising of Elspeth's voice. 'I mean to say, who has not read *Anne of Geierstein* or . . .'

Anna tapped on her elbow. 'But Elspeth, we ordered that for our—'

Elspeth ignored her and carried on. 'And the *Memoirs of Thomas Jefferson*, well, I think anyone who has read Mrs Trollope's late account of her travels in America will already have formed their view of *him*. But of course, that is a more recent publication and will probably not have reached the more backward reading societies yet.'

The woman from the Dornoch Reading Club was sucking in her cheeks preparatory to some retaliatory remark when Miss Anna spied a diversion in the shape of a quarto edition of MacTaggart's *Three Years in Canada*, laid out just in front of her. 'Look, Ludovic,' she said, plucking it from the table, 'have you considered Canada?'

Mrs Cameron, positioned just behind her son, gave Anna a warning glare and Elspeth took the book from her and laid it back down in its place. Mumbling an apology, though she was not certain to whom, Anna felt tears pricking her eyes, but then Ludovic moved a little closer to her and murmured, 'Thank you, Miss Anna. It is very good of you to think of me.'

They all set to quietly examining the books for a while. To Anna's disappointment, her sister was right, and there were not many volumes amongst those for sale by the Dornoch

Reading Club that their own library did not already possess. Mr Learmonth nonetheless expressed an interest in Buckingham's *Travels in Assyria, Media, and Persia*, and Lady Charlotte had been commissioned by Sir William to bid for Hamilton's *Annals of the Peninsular War*, which would, Miss Anna feared, be a great deal less amusing than the same author's most entertaining novel, *The Youth and Manhood of Cyril Thornton*.

The sale once over and all the Dornoch books sold – MacTaggart's *Canada* to a thin young man in the garb of an agricultural labourer who Miss Anna thought must have gone without a good few dinners to save the shillings required to make his purchase – the shop emptied of almost all its customers save the members of the Cromarty Library. Mr Fordyce was deep in conversation with the bookseller and Miss Juniper's girls had come upon an annual, *The Keepsake*, that was fascinating them, and which they were showing to Lady Charlotte. By the time they all left, the girls were in possession of the annual and almost falling over themselves in the profusion of their thanks to her ladyship. Mr Fordyce had Heber's *India* securely under his arm.

'Oh, Mr Fordyce, have you bought it for the library?' asked Anna, her hopes rising.

'In a manner of speaking,' said the old gentleman. 'It shall come to the library in due course, but for the instant I wish to offer it to Mr and Mrs Hossack, in the hope that they might think of putting Farquhar to the Indian Academy.'

'India is a great distance away,' agreed Miss Anna, 'and would no doubt suit Farquhar very well.'

'Not as well as his going would suit everyone else,' murmured Mr Learmonth, a comment which, while meant only for the ears of Ludo Cameron, found much approbation from the party as a whole.

Lunch was to be taken in the hotel, then the various members of the library were to fill an hour and a half of their own accord before gathering to be transported back to Shandwick House. The ministers announced their intention of taking a walk down to the links, to see if any golf was being played, and Mr Fordyce, a great devotee of the game, was eager to go with them, assuring them that he was perfectly able to walk that distance, especially with the day being so fine. Mrs Cameron and the Rose ladies were intent on making the rounds of the other merchandising establishments the town had to offer, with the Misses Rose deep in dispute with one another over whether it was a new pepper pot or sugar tongs they had agreed to commission at the silversmith's, along with a punch ladle with the Rose crest on the handle. Rachel Mackay was engaged to visit an old school friend with whom she had got on very well but Lady Charlotte had not. Lady Charlotte said that she would prefer to take Miss Juniper's girls to visit the collegiate church, abandoned now but which had once been the pride of the burgh. 'It was a place of pilgrimage for James IV,' she told them, 'the most resplendent and tragic of our Scottish kings.' In an unwonted burst of chivalry, Ludovic offered himself and Mr Learmonth as escorts to the party. While Alicia feared the schoolmaster's presence might involve them in having to listen to tedious historical lectures, she was nonetheless very keen to see the inside of the church or anything else Lady Charlotte chose to look at, and she would not for the world have deprived Mairead of the chance of gazing at close quarters at Ludo Cameron for the best part of an hour. Besides, the girls were hardly in any position to say no to any offer made to them, and so off they all went.

'Can you imagine, the king came here?' said Mairead, looking along the street which, despite boasting a number of very elegant new houses, was still dotted with dwellings every bit as humble of those of Fishertown. The tolbooth and clocktower were not as well kept as those of Cromarty, and Mairead imagined that any prisoner who did not like their surroundings could contrive their escape without great difficulty. She was deep in the imagining of such an event when she realised that Lady Charlotte was talking, and she had better listen. Lady Charlotte talking, especially to themselves or Miss Juniper, had become an increasingly common occurrence over the later months of spring. You could hardly imagine her now as the lost woman of Hallowe'en night, although Mairead, always attuned to such matters, did still see glimpses of it sometimes.

'Yes,' Mr Learmonth was saying in response to some question of Lady Charlotte's. 'King James came on pilgrimage to the shrine of St Duthac once a year at least, as penance for his role in the uprising that killed his father. The relics of the saint himself are unfortunately now lost.'

'His bones, you mean?' asked Mairead.

'Well, those, yes.'

Ludo frowned. 'Would they not just have been buried?'

'They were, at first,' said John. 'Or at least, he was entombed. But several years after his death, the tomb was opened, and his body found not to have decayed in the merest detail – he was exactly as he had been on the day of his death.'

Alicia made a grimace in Mairead's direction, only to see that Mairead was looking vastly interested and likely to encourage the schoolmaster in the perilous direction in which his history lesson was tended.

'How gruesome,' said Lady Charlotte.

'At some point,' continued Mr Learmonth, 'the bones were put into reliquaries of gold and silver for their protection. The head was placed in a reliquary of silver . . .'

'The head,' breathed Mairead.

'Yes. There is also a legend about the shirt he had been buried in and its protective properties for anyone who wore it.'

Alicia's heart sank. It was too late now, much too late, to retrieve the situation. The look on Mairead's face was exactly as it had been on an ill-advised excursion to see *Macbeth*, when the ghost of Banquo had appeared. Yet on the schoolmaster went.

'The reliquaries were given into the safe-keeping of Alexander Ross of Balnagown in 1560, at the time of the Reformation – the head encased in silver, the breastbone in gold and a silver-engraved gilt shrine. What happened to the shirt I don't know, but the rest haven't been seen since.'

'Hmmph,' said Ludo. 'If Ross had any sense he'd have melted down the silver and gold and thrown the bones on the midden.'

'Mr Cameron!' Mairead's sudden exclamation made Alicia jump.

'Well, I'm sorry, Miss Buchan, but the plain facts are that they were papist relics and the reformers were busy up and down the country smashing such things to pieces. It would not have gone at all well for Alexander Ross to have been caught with the items. Better melt the things down for a profit and throw out the bones for the dogs or bury them in a pit with others.'

Alicia thought that perhaps Ludovic had been too long at the bank, under the influence of Mr Gilfeather.

'If it even was his head,' Ludo continued.

Now her friend was looking thoroughly alarmed, and Alicia began to wish that they had gone with Mrs Mackay on her visit instead, or even with Miss Elspeth to the silversmith's. There were bound to be consequences to this talk of burying heads and bones, of which she would bear the brunt.

'Who else's head might it have been?' Mairead asked.

Ludovic shrugged. 'Well, anyone's. How would they know it was his bones and not some other dead monk they were digging up, after all that time?'

'But if they were his bones . . .'

Ludo stopped and turned to look at Mairead, at last realising that his opinions had caused her concern. 'Oh, well yes, I'm sure they would have been, for all that . . .'

'Then that is worse.'

Ludovic looked utterly perplexed, and Alicia thought he had much to learn about the management of Mairead if they were ever to make an enduring union.

'Well,' continued her friend, 'if Alexander Ross did cast the bones of a saint into a pit or midden at Balnagown, and take their gold and silver casings for himself, would the ghost of the saint not wish to exact some terrible revenge?'

Ludo, evidently unused to receiving such questions at the bank, was at the end of his eloquence.

'Oh, don't be silly, Mairead,' said Alicia. 'Ghosts of saints exacting their revenge, indeed! Imagine if Dr Fraser should be just around that corner and overhear you?'

'Oh, we should certainly have known by now if Dr Fraser was just around the corner, Alicia,' said Lady Charlotte, a picture of innocence, 'for he would surely not have been able to hold his peace this long. But you are right – we do better to occupy our minds with rational things, that can be known, rather than allowing ourselves to fear what cannot. Come, let us see if there is anything left of this church that so entranced King James.'

They continued down the street, but passing traffic caused them to rearrange themselves and go in file at points, and before twenty more paces had been taken, Mairead and Ludo found themselves beside one another again. After a brief moment of awkwardness, it was she who broke the silence. 'It's just that, well, if the bones were thrown away at Balnagown, the spirit of whoever they belonged to cannot be pleased.'

'Ah, no,' conceded Ludo. 'I am sure they would not. But *you*, Miss Buchan, can have no cause to worry about it.'

'Oh, but I do, Lud— Mr Cameron. For Balnagown is the very next estate to Shandwick where we are to stay again tonight. And who knows but this Alexander Ross that threw away the saint's bones may be some relation of our Captain Ross at Shandwick, as must be more than likely. And what if, we having come to his sanctuary today, the spirit of St Duthac should choose *us* as the medium of signalling his discontent?' Mairead had almost exhausted herself with her declaration and rendered herself quite out of breath.

Ludo's mouth was open and Alicia, turning to see where her friend might have got to, thought she had never seen him look so much like a fish. To think he was an intimate of Stanislas, and yet it was the fish-faced bank clerk and not the porcelain-featured Polish count who was here! It was all she could do not to share her disappointment with Lady Charlotte.

Lady Charlotte though had followed Alicia's eyes and guessed her thoughts. 'Ludovic is a very good sort of a young man, if unromantic in nature. I think he is exactly what Mairead should look for.'

Alicia sighed. 'But he is so . . .'

'Stolid?' offered Lady Charlotte.

'Yes, that is it exactly,' said Alicia. 'Stolid.' Like a lump of lard, she thought. Or an old boot.

'And at least he is unlikely to write poetry,' continued Lady Charlotte. 'There are few things as excruciating as having to pretend admiration for execrable verse. Mr Learmonth,' she called after the schoolmaster, now several paces ahead.

'Forgive me, your ladyship. I'm so used to striding about the countryside on my own that I have forgotten how to modulate my pace. Ludo often complains of it.' He looked back to where Ludovic and Mairead were now walking awkwardly together in a fury of blushes. 'Although I don't think he minds that I have left him behind today.'

'I don't think he does,' said Lady Charlotte. 'But it was Ludovic I wanted to ask you about. We wondered whether he indulges himself in poetry?'

The schoolmaster gave a very decided shake of the head. 'Not in the least, although he makes a very polite face when Stanislas reads his.'

Alicia, unthinking, put her hand on Lady Charlotte's arm as if to detain herself in the moment. 'Mr Jeszewski writes poetry?'

'Not of his own accord. As far as I know. But he spends many hours wrestling with a great epic of his country, attempting to translate it into English, but somehow his translation never satisfies him.'

Within half a minute, Alicia had extracted the name of

the poet and of his epic and resolved to somehow acquaint herself with the work.

'But Mr Cameron does not write poetry, I hope?'

'Oh, absolutely not, your ladyship. Ludo knows his own competencies and is loath to go beyond them,' said the schoolmaster who, Alicia thought, slipped very easily into conversation with Lady Charlotte. But then, of course, Lady Charlotte had started out in life a shopkeeper's daughter, for whom a schoolmaster with a university degree would have seemed an excellent prospect, had not Sir William with his wealth and his title and his fine house overlooking the firth come along. 'In fact,' Mr Learmonth was saying, 'bad poetry can be fatal.'

'What's that, John?' Ludovic and Mairead had now finally caught them up.

'I was telling the ladies that poetry can be a perilous occupation, particularly when the poem fails to please its audience, such as King James, for instance.'

'He did not like poetry either?' asked Alicia, a little disappointed.

'He did not like *bad* poetry. Once, when he was coming into the town by the King's Causeway, a local poet took it upon himself to recite a poem of welcome. The poem affected to be an epic of some sort, and the king, impatient and irritated, eventually ordered that the fellow be thrown off the bridge.'

'A little harsh, I think,' said Lady Charlotte.

'A bad poem is a bad poem. Your ladyship.'

'True. Please go on.'

'The poet was killed, and strange lights are said to appear about the bridge at night, accompanied by eerie, tortured noises, thought to be the ghost of the poet determined on finishing the recital of his poem.'

'Mr Learmonth!' Alicia could not restrain herself. 'Is it not enough that you have already filled Mairead's head with the bones of dead saints?'

'I, ah . . .'

'But now we must have dying poets, groaning all the night!'

The schoolmaster looked astonished to be addressed in this manner by a young woman, more a girl still, but a look to Ludovic offered no help from that quarter – his friend had adopted his most pompous demeanour, as if the ludicrous story of the poet, which had been meant entirely for their entertainment, shocked him as much as it had done Miss Juniper's young charges.

He bowed his head, biting back a comment on how ridiculous he found the situation. Lady Charlotte was also biting her lip, amusement dancing in her eyes – he couldn't say whether it was at Ludo's affected outrage, Mairead Buchan's silliness, or his own discomfort. The desperate creature of Hallowe'en night, who had still seemed a lost soul on the day five months ago of the school visitation, had gradually come back to some sort of life as spring had advanced. It had been on the night of the Misses' Rose gathering that he had begun to see the change. It was almost as if the fading of Rachel Mackay from society had forced Lady Charlotte back into the light, as if one must always somehow balance the other. Whatever it was, John Learmonth thought she looked happier and more carefree today than he had seen her since first he had arrived in Cromarty, and he felt something in himself lighten too.

As they passed beneath the archway into the church, Charlotte imagined King James, that striding, striving figure, beset by guilt, by the sin he'd carried with him. That driven *man*, who'd gamed and drunk and loved and danced and thought to take his kingdom from the dark edges of Europe and make of it a glittering jewel for all the world to admire. Cut down, with the flower of his nation, on Flodden Field. He had tried to expiate his sins, to build up credit with his God, here in Tain, this little northern town at the shrine of St Duthac, its ancient Celtic saint.

She could see that the church was in need of some repair, the burgesses having abandoned it some years previously for their large and elegant new place of worship on the other side of town. Perhaps they had been right to do so: this was not a place for the living, but for the dead. An assortment of old furnishings – some chairs, what might once have been a communion table, and an old oak pulpit, some of whose steps were missing – crowded close to the door, as if they had been intended for the move to the new church, but at the last, forgotten. The rest was emptiness. That emptiness, here, on the margins between town and sea, enhanced the sense of a time beyond history, a time when the lines between this world and the next were blurred. It was not so long since Charlotte herself had been caught between those worlds. Not now, though. Realising how much Rachel needed her, that someone actually needed her, had given her something to live for.

Birds fluttered about amongst the high rafters as the party from Cromarty wondered about the magnificence of the place, before the Reformers had smashed the coloured glass of the windows and replaced it with Protestant plainness. What glancing colour there must have been. How the light must have danced like jewels on the red sandstone flags of the floor as the King had listened to the singing of the mass.

John Learmonth spoke only of the architecture, studiously refraining from any further reference to saints' bones or the ghosts of murdered poets. Even the empty alcoves and ledges that once would have housed effigies of the dead tempted no further sinister tales from his lips. They all, in fact, spoke in hushed voices. This was quite another sort of church from their own in Cromarty, dedicated, Charlotte thought, to the worship of a different sort of god. On a pedestal at the east end, beyond where the altar must have been, was a roughened stone sculpture that looked as if it must have spent a good deal of time outside, perhaps camouflaged amongst the grave markers of the burgesses of Tain. St Duthac, she realised, still welcoming sinners to his sanctuary.

Then a sound from Alicia brought Charlotte out of her

reverie. The girls were standing in front of a grand marble memorial set into the north wall of the church that Charlotte, in her curiosity about the old saint hiding in his dark corner, had missed.

'How beautiful she was,' Alicia said, gazing at the profile of a young woman, sculpted in relief above the inscription, beside which a handmaiden and a child, both got up in the Roman or Greek manner, mourned her.

'Arabella Rose,' said Charlotte. 'She died when I was a very little girl. William knew her. Her husband is some distant cousin to Miss Elspeth and Miss Anna, although they never speak of him. Because of the tragedy, I assume.'

John Learmonth was reading out the inscription. '"Sacred to the Memory of Arabella Margaret, wife of Hugh Rose Esq., . . . who, in the Act of preparing Medicine for the relief of a sick and indigent Family, suddenly expired on the 9th of November 1806, aged 27 years." Hmm – remarkably precise about the manner of her death.'

'Ah, well . . .' began Ludo, but then, apparently remembering Lady Charlotte's presence, stopped himself.

'Please go on, Ludovic. Neither I nor Sir William have any tie of affection or admiration for Hugh Rose. He is a litigious, self-serving person, and Sir William does not trust him.'

Ludovic cleared his throat and proceeded. 'Well, it is still spoken of sometimes, in the coffee room. There were rumours that she was murdered by her husband's mistress, whom he had carried home with him from the Caribbean and installed in their home, at Bayfield House.' He glanced again at Lady Charlotte. 'All nonsense, I'm sure.'

'Oh, certainly,' said Charlotte, keeping her eyes on the young, marble face of Arabella Rose, an inconvenient wife. 'I think I will stay here a little longer though, but do not let me keep you from exploring the kirkyard.'

John Learmonth was indeed keen to look at the many flat slab tombs that lay above the grass and wildflowers of the graveyard, but Ludovic, saying he thought they had perhaps talked enough of graves and tombs for one day, offered to escort Mairead and Alicia to inspect the small ruined chapel by the east wall of the kirkyard. The girls quickly agreed to join him and so Charlotte was left alone in the church, keeping vigil over Arabella Rose, all under the watchful stone eye of St Duthac.

Hearing the doors *almost* close after the four young people, she closed her eyes and breathed in the air that held in it centuries of faith and doubt, the echoes of the chanting of the religious and the desecration of the iconoclasts. And yet still the place stood. She felt herself at one with the flagstones beneath her feet, surrounded by space and emptiness.

Outside, gulls and crows were noisy in their dominions. The voices of Mairead and Alicia chatting, the lower voice of Ludovic in response, faded. She heard the tolbooth bell chime twice as the town clock struck two. They were all to be assembled at the hotel ready to travel back to Shandwick in half an hour. She would join the others soon.

A door opened somewhere behind her. She opened her

eyes and turned towards the sound but could see nothing for the bright beam of sunshine that at that very moment streamed through the window.

'Did you find them, Mairead?'

'What?' said Mairead, looking startled.

Alicia had known it was a mistake to let her go back into the church by herself, whether Lady Charlotte was still in there or not. 'Your gloves, you ninny.'

'My gloves,' Mairead murmured, as though hard of understanding and having forgotten that only five minutes earlier she had declared herself to have left those very items in the church.

Alicia let out a great sigh. 'You can't have looked properly. Come on.' She turned around, as if to go back down the path to the collegiate church.

'No!' Mairead said suddenly. 'I am sure I left them at the hotel, just when we had taken our dinner.'

'You didn't,' said Alicia. 'Remember, Mr Cameron picked one of them up for you that you had dropped as we came through the kirkyard gate?'

'I really don't want to go back into the church. The thought of the saint, his bones . . .'

'Oh,' retorted Alicia, setting off, 'you are being ridiculous.'

'Alicia, there is no need,' Mairead called after her, almost desperately.

But at that moment, the church door opened again, and

Lady Charlotte emerged from the darkness inside. She saw the girls then lifted a hand to them, waving a pair of grey leather gloves. 'You left these in the church, Mairead,' she said, stepping out onto the path towards them, her eyes shining.

TWENTY-THREE

A Second Night at Shandwick

John Learmonth finished cleaning the dust of the walk from Tain off his boots. It was almost time to go up to Shandwick House for their supper. 'What are you writing, Ludo – not poetry, I hope?'

Ludovic looked up from his work at the small table beneath the window of their room in the inn. 'Indeed I am not. I am writing my report.'

'Report?'

'For Mr Gilfeather. He has deputised me to produce an account of purchases and expenditure on behalf of the library today.'

'I thought he was clear that your roles at the bank and at the library were not to be mixed.'

'He is. Under specific and particular circumstances. But he also wishes to know if anything occurs on this excursion that might, in some manner, reflect on the reputation of the circulating library, and therefore himself, as session clerk and manager of the bank.'

'You are to *spy* on us?'

Ludovic reddened. 'I am merely to forewarn him of anything likely to cause gossip, rumour and the like before it is blown across the firth to land on the steps of the bank.'

'Well, I hardly think you can have much to report from today, unless you wish to resurrect the rumours about the poisoning of Arabella Rose.'

'I have absolutely no intention of as much as mentioning Arabella Rose. Hugh Rose is one of the wealthiest and most powerful men in the county, and not a person to get on the wrong side of.' Ludo gave a slightly defeated sigh. 'But I feel I must inform Mr Gilfeather of Fachie Hossack's appearance here at Shandwick . . .'

'But Fachie and his mother will be in Cromarty by now. Mr Gilfeather will be perfectly aware of his arrival.'

'Which is why I do not wish to lose any time in warning him that Fachie is intent on malice.'

John shrugged. 'That can hardly be news to anyone.'

Ludovic put down his pen. 'It seems that at breakfast this morning he – alluded – to the recent unpleasant rumours – about you. And Mrs Mackay.'

John felt suddenly sick as Ludo hastened on.

'It was Miss Buchan, Mairead, who told me of it this afternoon. She was not gossiping, but indignant in the defence of Mrs Mackay, as it appears was everyone else. She said Fachie was as good as asked to leave Shandwick House. This being so, given Mr Gilfeather's position as clerk to the kirk session . . .'

'The left hand of God,' murmured John.

'In as far as Cromarty goes, yes. Given that, I thought he should be forewarned of what Fachie is about and generally made aware that he has come back from the college no better than when he last went away.'

John sank down on to the bed. 'Thank God Mr Mackay was down here by the time they were taking their breakfast up in the house. But he will have heard of it by now.'

'Quite possibly,' said Ludo.

'Perhaps I should leave Cromarty, after all. I thought, today, that that business had been allowed to fade into the past and be forgotten, but I begin to wonder whether it will ever go away.'

Ludo blotted his report and turned to face him. John waited to be told he was being foolish, to be implored to stay, but something in Ludo's face told him he was not going to say those things. Instead, what the bank clerk said was, 'It won't go away, John. It will be brought up again every time it suits someone to do so. The only thing you can do is stifle the rumours so thoroughly that they can hardly draw breath.'

'But how?'

'It is as the ministers suggested: you need to get married.'

'But, Ludo, I—'

'There are plenty of perfectly nice young women in Cromarty, and lots on the farms too. Really, you only have to look about you a bit in the kirk on a Sunday. Obviously, there is one young lady I would prefer you did not . . .'

Despite everything, John managed a gentle laugh. 'I promise not to interfere in your courting of Miss Buchan.'

'Oh, there is no courting,' replied Ludo, very matter-of-fact. 'But I think it quite possible that at some future point, when my own plans are more decided and she a little older . . . but anyway, we were talking of you. Mrs Gilfeather, you know, is a tremendous judge of a good housewife and I'm sure if I were to ask—'

John stood up. 'Ludo, you are *not* to ask Mrs Gilfeather or anyone else to find me a wife!'

Ludovic was not in the least put off by his reaction. 'Well, I'm sorry, John, but you did ask if it would ever go away, and this is the only means I can see of making it. You need to marry.'

John felt the fight go out of him, and all anger with Ludovic with it. He sat back down again, his head in his hands. 'But I can't, Ludo,' he said.

Rachel turned around on the dressing stool and began to scan the floor around her.

'What have you lost?' said Alasdair, as he finished tying his neckcloth.

'The shoes I brought to wear with this dress. I am sure I had Jane pack them, but I cannot see them anywhere. They are the same blue silk satin as my sash and have a cream-coloured bow. The green ones will not go at all.'

Alasdair bent down and retrieved the blue shoes from

beneath the bed. 'You threw them under here this morning when you were trying to find your walking shoes.'

She put out her hand to take them but he said, 'No. Let me.'

Kneeling down in front of her, he said, 'Lift your foot.'

Rachel lifted it and he took the stockinged foot in his hand and raised it to his lips, looking at her directly all the while, before kissing it so softly that the charge that went through her almost took her breath away. He ran his fingers up from her ankle towards her knee, then said, 'The other one.' She did as she was bid and a moment later he had his hand behind her head and was bent over her, kissing her hard on the mouth. Rachel felt as if she might pass away and then the gong rang for dinner. He let slip an unaccustomed curse and kissed her more urgently.

'No, Alasdair,' she said. 'We must go down.'

He groaned and stood back. 'If you insist. But I warn you, before the punchbowl is out I will declare myself over-fatigued from today's walk, and will require you to attend me.'

She feigned disapproval, checking for any disarrangement of her hair. 'Before the punchbowl?'

'Before the second course is set out, if you are not careful,' he said, leaning down to give a soft bite to her ear. 'Now get down those stairs, you minx, before I change my mind.'

As they walked down the stairs the front door was opened and into the circular entrance hall of Shandwick House walked Ludovic and the schoolmaster.

Alasdair bent towards her and murmured into her ear, 'And I hope you don't expect me to remain anything less than terrifying to the man who thought he might raise his eyes to look at my wife.'

Downstairs, there was a degree of bustle and excitement amongst the servants and in the drawing room, they found their hostess greatly excited. 'Word has come from Tarbat that the captain made land at Portmahomack this afternoon and will be home by nightfall. He was not expected back from the Orkneys before next week! He will be so pleased to find the house filled with so congenial a company. And not at all sorry that Marjorie Hossack is gone,' she confided to Miss Elspeth in an aside that was not as quiet as she might have intended. 'It can be dull enough here with the boys grown up and both in Bombay but how delighted he will be to find gentlemen for a game of billiards and to take a glass of punch with.'

'And not one, but two ministers of the kirk also of the party!' said Dr Fraser, a mischievous smile upon his lips.

'Oh, now, Dr Fraser,' beamed Mrs Ross, 'the captain knows you of old, and is able for you! And of course, Mr Mackay is a bonus to any company.'

'Does Captain Ross know he is coming home to visitors?' asked Charlotte, who, Rachel thought, was glowing as she had not seen her glow in a long time.

'Well, no, my dear. He has been up as far as Shetland, and by the time I might have sent him a letter telling him of the library's visit, he would be bound to have shifted from one island to the other and the letter following him all the way. He will be sorry to have missed Sir William – I am sure he would have pressed him for his thoughts on the Reform. He is sure there will be nothing but trouble from it. But you will not mind if we wait a little yet before calling for the tea? He is bound to be here soon.'

And in fact, Mrs Ross had hardly finished speaking when the sound could be heard of horses coming down the driveway towards the courtyard. Lights were being lit and lanterns held by stable hands hurried past the windows, and then there they were, two horsemen coming out of the gloom.

As the riders came closer to the door and a halloing set up from one of them, Rachel recognised the tall, strongly built man with the unruly sweep of grey hair as Captain Ross. The other rider, coming up behind him, was not shouting, but something in his bearing made Rachel grip her husband's arm. No, she thought. It cannot be.

Alasdair's eyes, though, had moved to where Charlotte sat, showing no interest in the newcomers, her attention on the annual that Alicia Middleton had brought down for her to look at.

'Alasdair,' Rachel said.

He shook his head. 'There is nothing we can do.'

Mrs Ross was already moving towards the front door to meet her husband. Forgetting herself, Rachel stood up and went past Alasdair so that she could see into the hall. From a nearby sofa the eyes of Elspeth Rose were also trained on the door.

Rachel heard the captain's enthusiastic response to the news of their guests, and then she heard, as clearly as if Alasdair or Micah Fraser had been announcing it from the pulpit, 'But look who I found in the stable yard of the inn at Tain, thinking to slope off over to Ardross and never an idea of calling upon his friends at Shandwick. Devil of a job I had to get him to agree to take potluck with us here tonight.'

Rachel felt herself go cold as she heard Mrs Ross's loud exclamation of welcome to her husband and his companion, the unexpected guest: Major Charles Munro. She looked at Charlotte, but knew that all her friend saw from her beaming, brimming eyes was the tall handsome man with the scarred face, who was halt of step and who had no option but to follow his host into the room and make his bow to the last group of people in the world he must have wished to find assembled there.

'I thought it would never end.'

'You didn't enjoy the evening?' asked Ludo, his head emerging through the neck of his nightshirt, his bed cap already on.

'I should never have come on this expedition. I was never intended to mix with such people.'

'Oh, come now, John. Admittedly, Captain Ross and Major Munro are the masters of many acres, but really, your origins cannot be so very much more humble than my own. Or Lady Charlotte's, indeed. Or Mrs Mackay's.' Too late did Ludo realise that it had been a mistake to mention the name of Rachel Mackay.

'Mrs Mackay could hold her place in any company she chooses. Did you not think she shone tonight? Did you not see it? Did you not see the way her husband looked at her?'

'Ahm, well now, I don't think it's quite the thing to consider the way a man looks at his wife, especially a minister . . .'

'It was as a man, not as a minister, that he looked at her.'

Ludo gave a cough, and then another one, eager to get away from the subject of how a minister might look at his wife. 'I did think Lady Charlotte looked very fine tonight. Her jewels became her particularly well. She seemed to be greatly animated by our visit to the church. I always think it does a person good to get out of—'

'Oh, Ludo, don't be so stupid!'

Ludo stepped back as if John had struck him. He looked about for somewhere he might retreat to, but their small room at the top of the inn offered very few options. 'I'm sorry, John. I do not mean to be stupid. I have not been out in the world as much as you, I suppose.'

'Oh, God.' John put his head in his hands. 'Forgive me, Ludo. That was unconscionable. Of course you are not stupid. Just innocent, perhaps.' Then he looked up. 'But do you not realise – it was the presence of Major Munro that made her sparkle so. Did you not see the way she almost seemed to dim, when the supper was ended and he said he could not stay?'

'He is a busy man,' said Ludo. 'The Commissioners for Roads and Bridges have much—'

'It's because he is an *honourable* man that he didn't stay, Ludo. It must have been evident to everyone how Lady Charlotte felt to be in his presence. Her husband is away. He could not have stayed.'

'But—'

'Go to sleep, Ludo,' said John, snuffing out one of the candles on the mantelshelf of their room and taking up the other. 'I'm going out for some air. I'll try not to disturb you when I come back in.'

As Alicia had predicted, Mairead lay awake, staring up at the canopy above their bed, long after Alicia had fallen asleep. What Alicia could not have guessed, though, was that it was neither dead poets, nor the restless bones of desecrated saints that filled Mairead's mind, but what she had seen when she had gone back into the collegiate church in Tain that afternoon, to look for her gloves.

The main door to the church, which they had come out of only a few minutes before, had been ajar enough that Mairead had been able to squeeze through without making a noise to disturb Lady Charlotte. It must have been Ludovic who hadn't shut it properly, she'd thought. He had been last out – save for Lady Charlotte – and she had often heard Mrs Cameron berate him for not closing doors behind him. 'Born in a barn,' she would say, which Mairead did not take literally, because it seemed very unlikely that

Mrs Cameron should have found herself in *that* situation, although of course the Virgin Mary . . .

So Mairead's thoughts had occupied her as she'd slipped quietly into the church. She could see Lady Charlotte, still in front of the memorial to Arabella Rose, her eyes closed and the light from the windows beaming down on her upturned face. She looked like one of the Madonnas Mairead had once seen in a Catholic aunt's prayer book, although, of course, that was not the kind of thing you could say out and about in Cromarty.

Mairead's gloves were still where she had laid them down, on the back of an old chair near the door. She had tiptoed halfway across to get them when a creaking noise from the small door opposite, that she hadn't noticed before, made her look that way. Without fully understanding why she did it, Mairead slipped behind the old pulpit with the broken step, from where she would not be seen. She realised almost instantly how ridiculous this was, and how Alicia would chide her for such behaviour, but now the newcomer was right through the door and beginning to move up the aisle. Mairead almost let out an exclamation of surprise when she saw who it was but managed to keep silent.

Lady Charlotte, however, had turned around, so that the sun was now in her eyes. She had lifted her hands up to shade them and said, 'Hello . . .?'

And then Major Charles Munro, in a strange, strangled voice had said, 'My God. Charlotte.'

Mairead wished, for everything she was worth, that she had closed her eyes then, but she hadn't. Lady Charlotte was moving her head slightly and looking as though she might faint. Mairead was on the point of running out from behind her pulpit to catch her lest she fall when the Major strode quickly towards her and took her by the arms and then *in* to his arms.

The passion of their embrace would have made Mairead sway on her feet too, had she not been supported by the solid old pulpit. It was over quickly, the Major stepping back and saying, 'Charlotte, forgive me. I should not . . .'

Mairead knew he was old, at least forty, she thought, and that he bore the scars of soldiering in foreign lands, but at that moment she could not help agreeing with Alicia's long-ago assessment that for all his drawbacks of age and the slight hesitation in his walk, something in his bearing was very handsome.

'Charles, what are you doing here? Have you come looking for me?'

He shook his head. 'I was – at the courthouse in Dornoch, seeing about the placing of watchmen. I had some business to transact with my agent in Tain. I thought to have a moment's prayer here before . . . But Charlotte, what on earth are you doing here? Where is William?'

She explained everything, and then said, 'We stay tonight at Shandwick House. You could come too.'

The Major looked away then, but Lady Charlotte touched his arm and made him face her. 'You could, Charles.'

'Tonight?' he said, in disbelief. 'Are you mad, Charlotte? I could not think of it.'

'But why? There was never anything improper between us – we might put today's lapse down to the shock of the moment. Why should we not spend an evening, a few hours, in one another's company?'

'Because,' he began, looking at his hand in hers, as if it were an extension of himself, 'because of what has just happened, and what would have happened had I not left Cromarty.'

'But you did leave,' she said. 'And you left such a gulf in my life that I thought I should die. Will you not let me look at your face for a few hours, hear your voice? You need not even speak to me, more than the necessary civilities. Just to be in the same room with you again, I ask no more.'

'You ask more than you know, Charlotte.'

'How so? I ask so little.'

He looked pained. 'You ask everything. Don't you know why I stay away? Do you not know that it kills me to know you are living on this earth and that you are not mine?'

'But I am yours,' she said. 'I have always been yours, from the moment you looked across the dining table at me that Sunday afternoon . . .'

Mairead screwed shut her eyes and pressed herself as hard back against the pulpit as she could. She was so scared to breathe she thought she might suffocate, but at last the major was saying that he had to leave and Lady Charlotte was begging him to at least let her write to him and by the time he was at the door he had conceded and was kissing her again. Then there was the sound of the door closing and Mairead opened her eyes to see Lady Charlotte, standing with her back to it, eyes closed and a look like heaven on her face.

Taking hold of every piece of courage she possessed, Mairead slipped as quickly and as quietly as she could back through the main door of the church, leaving her gloves behind her.

And now here Major Munro had come to Shandwick after all, and neither he nor Lady Charlotte had said a word about having seen each other in Tain earlier that day, for all that Mairead could have told anyone their meeting had been by chance.

Alicia had been quietly furious when their newly obtained copy of *The Keepsake* had landed on the floor, the very minute the major had walked into the drawing room of Shandwick House. No damage had been done to the book, but Alicia had said that in future, Mairead would only be allowed to look at it when they had it opened out on a table in front of them. Mairead had refrained from saying that it was not she, but Lady Charlotte who had actually let go the book at the fatal moment. No one had noticed this exchange between the girls because all the men had then been on their feet and the ladies exuding an arpeggio of delight at seeing the major again after his long absence from Cromarty. Lady Charlotte, for the second time that day, had looked as if she would faint, but this time it was

Rachel Mackay who went to support her, and Major Munro made no move towards her whatsoever.

Mairead had found herself sitting to table at supper next to Ludovic. Before the events of the afternoon, this might have flustered her, as being near to him usually did. Instead, she found herself calmed and reassured by his solid, reliable proximity. In a world when even the best people seemed hardly to know how to behave, there was always Ludovic. Hester had mentioned only the other day how engrossed Mrs Cameron had been in Mrs Trollope's *Domestic Manners of the Americans*, and Mairead tonight decided that she must set her mind to getting hold of it.

When not in conversation with Ludovic – quietly enough so that Mrs Cameron might not hear – about his hopes for America, Mairead watched Lady Charlotte. If she had not known better, and she *did* know better, Mairead would have said Lady Charlotte was a fey child touched in the head, gazing down the table at the major as Aladdin must have gazed upon the magic lamp, or Juliet on Romeo. Nobody else appeared to notice – they were all listening to Captain Ross's stories, and his views on the benefits of clearing impoverished Highlanders from the land and replacing them with sheep. Dr Fraser was practically scraping his foot on the ground as a bull does his hoof before charging, and much of Mr Mackay's evening appeared to be taken up with preventing him from exploding across the table.

Rachel, though, was watching Charlotte like a hawk, murmuring things to her, her eyes almost flashing, and at one point they caught Mairead's, and in that moment was formed a sacred trust, an alliance, that bound Mairead's lips as tightly as if they had been sealed together with molten gold.

The supper had been got through. The gentlemen had had their punch, whilst the ladies had spoken of county news and listened to Alicia sing and spoken of the health of Bonaparte's son. And then the gentlemen had come in and Alicia had sung some more. Cards had been played and hopes for this year's Northern Meeting voiced, if only the cholera might abate. Mr Fordyce had read to the company Sir Walter's latest missive in *The Scotsman* from his Mediterranean tour and discussion had turned to volcanoes, which Mairead did not like the sound of at all. But by that time, Major Munro was gone. He had left before the punchbowl had been brought out. No urging from his host or hostess would dissuade him, and Mairead had watched as something inside Lady Charlotte seemed to die, right before her eyes.

Now, as Alicia slept beside her, the occasional murmur escaping her pretty lips, Mairead went over it all again, set aside shock, surprise, astonishment and looked at the order of things, as Ludovic would no doubt have done. She found she liked this accounting, this system of balances that he had explained to her over supper. She put each event in its place and put the major and Lady Charlotte in their columns and totted up the debits and the credits, and found, at the last, that all was well: Lady Charlotte had declared herself for the major and he for her, not good. But, on the credit side, the major had resisted her entreaties, and left the church telling her it could not be. Good. But then, the major had unexpectedly appeared at Shandwick House – a debit on his account, most certainly, balanced though by Captain Ross's assertion of the difficulty he had had in persuading him to come back with him at all. Then there was the impeccable conduct of Lady Charlotte (the dropped album aside) from the moment Major Munro had entered the house. More, her face, her eyes, her conversation – everything had spoken of the happiness she had early claimed she should feel, simply to spend a few hours more in the same room as him. But then there had been the look on Rachel Mackay's face. At least though, when he had left, Lady Charlotte had not embarrassed herself or descended into a state of collapse, such as those who did not know what Mairead knew would have noticed. This, Mairead felt, not only balanced the account, but closed it, and on this happy thought she at last began to drift off to sleep.

Mairead didn't know how long she had been asleep, or whether she'd fully gone off at all, but suddenly she was sitting bolt upright. There had been the sound of a crash in the courtyard beneath their window. Alicia, of course, slept on. Mairead's thoughts instantly turned to the bones of the dead saint, stripped of their golden reliquary, cast into some pit hereabouts. The wind had got up so that it howled down chimneys and made trees creak, but surely she also heard the clanking of chains?

They had snuffed out their candle, but beyond the drapes of the canopy, Mairead could see a blue-white glow of the moon falling onto the Chinese carpet of their room from where the housemaid had failed to close their curtains completely. She looked at Alicia. She could simply screw shut her eyes, and burrow in behind her and not turn around again or open her eyes until morning. The very thought though, of suffering the creeping, growing terror of unknowing through endless hours of darkness, was almost unsupportable. Pulling on her shawl, Mairead slid from beneath the covers, dangling her feet over the side of the bed until she had found her slippers. The drapes of the canopy swished back into place, hiding Alicia from view. Almost rigid with terror, Mairead stood in the narrow beam of light like a hare transfixed by the poacher's lantern. There was nothing for it now, though – she must go forward, for she most certainly could not go back behind the drapes and hope to endure the night. As her eyes began to see their way about the room, they fell upon the candlestick on top of the rosewood cabinet a few feet from the bed. Mairead took hold of this, snuffed candle and all, and began to advance as softly as she could to the window.

The branches of nearby trees creaked and sighed, and the wind continued to roar down the chimney. Still, though, Mairead was certain she could hear the clanking of a chain. She stopped at the window and pushed the drapes a little further apart. The lawns of the house, stretching out towards the sea, were completely illuminated by the moon, and the swirling trees made crazed shadows dance on their perfect surface. She tore her eyes away from the frenzied shadow dance and sought out the source of the clanking sound. She let her gaze pass over the shrubs and specimen trees, left to right, until at last it fell upon a summer house near the edges of the wood, and a swing that had lost its wooden planking seat, leaving the long chains to clank and twist with one another in the wind. Mairead had never felt such overwhelming relief and was on the point of turning away from the window, telling herself that she had been foolish, when a sudden white apparition that could be nothing but the ghostly shroud of St Duthac came flying from the trees and hurled itself at her window. The scream was out of her mouth before she could think to stop it.

In no time at all, Alicia had leapt from the bed and was behind her. 'What on earth? Is it a nightmare?'

Mairead could not speak, but only point in horror at the flapping white eminence trying to get in at the window.

Alicia looked, and for the briefest moment there was fear on her face too, but then her features transformed themselves into the long-suffering look they were so often wont to assume. 'Oh, Mairead! It is nothing but a shawl, a white silk shawl that the wind has taken up and that has now got caught on the rhone pipe there.' She pointed upwards, and by craning her neck Mairead could see that she was right. It was indeed a shawl, that the wind must have blown away – but from where? – to catch on a jutting piece of ironwork. Another gust in the right direction might tear it or set it free.

Alicia was already trudging back to bed, and Mairead, feeling foolish, had just started to turn away from the window when a slash of white, this time just at the edge of the courtyard where the drive gave onto the lawn, caught her attention. It was all she could do not to let out another scream, but she kept her lips clamped shut and steeled herself to look again.

It was no flapping shawl this time, no phantom, but a woman in a white nightgown, her arms and feet bare, her shawl having blown away. Her hair was loose and at times covered her face, but Mairead knew who it was. The woman was staring down towards the sea, and then she began to walk. Lady Charlotte, out in her nightgown, in the grounds of Shandwick House. Mairead thought she must go to her, dissuade her of whatever she had in mind, but then, emerging from the path out of the wood from Shandwick Inn, came the dark figure of a man. He stood gazing up at the windows and then made to turn back in the direction he had come from, but at some point in his turning the figure walking down the lawn took his eye. He hesitated a moment and then started to walk after her, slowly to begin with, but then quickening his pace until he was only a few yards behind her. Mairead thought he must have called something to her because Lady Charlotte paused suddenly and turned around. She screwed up her face as if confused, displeased, and then carried onwards, towards the sea. Whether the man called her again or not, Mairead couldn't tell, because Lady Charlotte had begun to run. The man also ran and in a moment he had a hand on her shoulder, making her turn around. Angry and upset-looking, Lady Charlotte tried to shake his hand off and move on. He appeared to be remonstrating with her, trying to persuade her back to the house, but she just shook her head and tried to carry on towards the sea. He took hold of her by the shoulders now, and she struggled against him, beating his chest until he pulled her tightly to him, forcing her to stop. She began to sink to her knees and he lifted her up. She was defeated, desolate. And then he leaned towards her and she did not resist.

PART THREE

Summer 1832

TWENTY-FOUR

Late May

Hyacinths

The town of Inverness was heaving and the talk everywhere was of the Reform. Promising to join John at the coffee house in plenty of time for the march, Stan had set off down the High Street and made his way to the premises of Messrs Tait and Cameron, perfumers. It had all started one winter's evening, several months ago, when Ludo had apologised for the holes cut in the copy of the *Inverness Courier* he had brought them, explaining that Hester took the old newspapers down to Miss Juniper's cottage, where the girls pored over the advertisements. 'And Alicia Middleton cuts them out, to paste them into her scrapbook,' Ludo had declared in a manner to prove his own credentials as a serious observer of world affairs, who could not conceive of anything so silly as pasting advertisements into scrapbooks.

There had followed, for Stanislas, a long and delicate process of incidental conversations, seemingly accidental encounters with Hester and downright subterfuge which had at length brought him to the point of knowing the precise item that Alicia Middleton most dreamed of possessing. In the course of obtaining this information, he had come to understand that there was very little hope her father – absent and only intermittently attentive – would buy her the gift on which she had set her heart. And now, at last, Stanislas was in Inverness, standing in front of the perfumer's shop, a pouch of coins in his pocket carefully saved out of the small wage James Craig could afford to pay him.

Stanislas was no stranger to such establishments. He could still, sometimes, imagine the cologne he had been fond of wearing, in the early days of his studies at Warsaw University. He could still remember the French soap his mother liked to use, the pomade that had been his father's favourite. Of course, cologne and perfumed soaps were not things unknown in Cromarty, but for him, they were now luxuries beyond his means. Even laundry soap, as every housewife could be heard saying on the street, was growing more expensive by the day. Prices of all sorts of products rose at the rates the boards of hygiene recommended them, in the face of the relentless advance northwards of the cholera.

Stan was not here to buy laundry soap. He couldn't have said why it mattered so much to him that Alicia Middleton should have a set of the almond oil soaps that she had hoped for. Perhaps it was simply that she was beautiful, a delicate, graceful creature in a world where he had seen too much cruelty and boorishness, too much contempt for beauty. Perhaps that was all she was to him, and why it mattered to him that she should have something fine and lovely. He wasn't even certain how he would effect the transfer of the soaps to her without making some sort of declaration or engendering some sort of assumption that he did not even know might be correct. And yet he pushed open the door of the perfumer's shop and strode through it, remembering he was Stanislas Jeszewski. Brushing aside the curiosity and frank surprise of the perfumer's assistant, he bought the soap.

Back at the coffee house, he managed to jostle his way to a place beside John. 'It's a pity James didn't come,' he said. 'How he would have enjoyed this, but I think he fears raising old suspicions amongst those in Cromarty with long memories.'

'Perhaps he is right,' said John. 'Given what has happened in Bristol and other towns, I don't think these febrile times are the ones in which to expect James's past follies to be forgiven.'

'Past follies?' Stanislas cocked his head a little. 'You should have come to the meeting at the Mechanics Institute with me last night. If you could have heard the hopes of those good honest fellows that they might influence the future and make better the world for their families, and all by their own labour and an acknowledgement of their rights. They say the condition of mechanics elsewhere in the country is appalling. I think if Parliament does not pass this Reform Bill soon, there will be little need for James or anyone else to stir up protests in the streets. Come, though, people are leaving. I think the march will soon start.'

Out on Castle Hill, pennants of endless designs fluttered in the wind behind the men of the Incorporated Trades as they processed down into the town, knights gathering for the tournament. Behind them, the new castle with its planned prison and courthouse was rising against a clear blue sky. The sound of the band preceding the marchers was almost drowned out by the cheers of the people lining the streets and filling every possible window for a vantage point.

John shouted into Stan's ear. 'I would hardly have believed there were so many people in the Highlands.'

'I would not have believed there were so many people in Scotland,' laughed Stan. This was liberty. To be allowed to process joyfully in the name of freedom and reform. As the Russian cavalry had ridden into Warsaw, trampling everything good underfoot, Stanislas had not thought to be part of such a moment again. They joined in the good-natured jostling of the crowd processing past the Town House and the Tolbooth and past Queen Mary's house.

'Do you believe it, Stan, the garrison of Inverness would not let Mary Stuart into her own castle without the authority of the Earl of Huntly. That is the Scottish spirit, we bow down to no one!'

'Apart from the good Dr Fraser of Resolis,' said Stan, although he was not certain that John had heard him. They gave up trying to make one another heard and entered instead into the joy of the music. The river Ness itself seemed to dance, its progress to the sea unhindered by the obstacles of man or nature. Stanislas began to shape a metaphor of the Reform, but a dunt on the back as a crowd of apprentices launched themselves into the parade behind him interrupted his train of thought. By the time the front of the crowd had reached the Caledonian Hotel, where the members of the Reform Committee awaited it, its tail had swollen in number by several thousand. Huge cheers went up in salute of the Committee. Stan tried to remember who John had said they were, but it was no use: Mackintosh of Mackintosh, Fraser of this, Fraser of that, Fraser of the next place. Mackenzie of wherever at all. Descendants of the men who had blown up the castle on the hill they had just marched from or of those who had attempted to defend it. Their grandfathers and great-grandfathers had had different choices to make and ridden out after different banners in a war that could not be won. These grandsons and great-grandsons were thorough Whigs with a different foot upon the world, the smell of victory in their nostrils and the people still theirs to command.

John was completely carried along with the enthusiasm of the whole thing. 'Surely it cannot be long now. With Wellington's failure to form a government, the passing of the bill is all but certain. It's a pity all the same that James wouldn't come. Perhaps he feels he is too old now for such crowds.'

Stan snorted a laugh. 'You had better not let him hear

you say so. He says he has seen too many false dawns to become excited yet and that when the bill passes into law will be the time to celebrate. Though as for these gentlemen' – he indicated the august Mackintoshes, Mackenzies and Frasers who had taken their place at the front of the procession and were now leading the crowd onwards to the meeting in Academy Park – 'he is not convinced they speak for the people.'

'James still imagines himself behind some barricade in Paris. Old fellows whose glory days are behind them do not always see clearly.'

'Old fellows? John, the barricades from last summer's uprising in Paris have scarcely been dismantled.' Stan looked back towards the cramped archways the crowd had squeezed itself through on its way from Castle Hill to the river. Even here, in this town so far from anywhere, it would not take much.

'Don't you think it ironic though,' said John, 'that you and I may agitate all we wish, but it is Ludo, dutifully behind his desk at the Caledonian Bank in Cromarty, with the income his mother's industry has secured upon him, who will get the vote? And you, Count Stanislas Jeszewski of a place I can barely pronounce, and I, Mr John Learmonth, MA of the University of Edinburgh, must celebrate the good fortune of our friend who has nothing in his head but leaving the place where we, unenfranchised souls as we are, have chosen to make ourselves anew?'

Linking arms, the friends fell into step with the crowd

that had set off again, marching boldly on towards the great meeting, Stan smiling to himself, the little packet of soaps secure in his satchel.

Alicia tied on her bonnet, and wondered if they might have time to take a stroll up the Paye before they went to Mr Fordyce's house for their drawing lesson.

'What on earth for?' said Mairead. Alicia had never before volunteered to walk a step further than she absolutely had to.

'I thought perhaps we might find some bluebells in the Gaelic kirkyard, or perhaps some of those tiny hyacinths that stray from people's gardens . . .'

Mairead groaned. Ever since a picnic arranged two weeks ago out at the Shore Mill burn, at which Ludovic's friend Stanislas had picked some hyacinths and remarked they were the very same colour as Alicia's eyes, there had been talk of little else beneath the rafters of their small bedchamber. Well, hyacinths and Lady Charlotte.

'You do know, don't you, that Stanislas and Mr Learmonth are not expected back from the political meeting in Inverness until tonight?'

Alicia was undaunted. 'I thought, if we did come upon some, I might pop them into the ribbon of my bonnet, and then should they return before dark, and the clockmaker's door be open as we pass on our evening stroll . . .'

It was no use. Mairead knew they would be trudging up the Paye and then back down again in order to walk *very slowly* past the clockmaker's door come evening time. She consoled herself by recalling that the last time they had done that, they had lingered so long that Mrs Gilfeather, happening to come out of her own front door across the street, had asked whether Alicia was all right, because she was 'lookin' affa vacant'.

Usually, Miss Juniper would accompany them to their lesson with Mr Fordyce, so that she might listen to his reminiscences as they drew. They believed their schoolmistress had once or twice been out of Scotland in her younger days – she spoke sometimes of Cheshire, and there was some idea that she might even have been to Wales, but she had never crossed over to the continent, and thrilled as much to Mr Fordyce's lectures on the German and the Italian culture as Alicia did. Mairead did not mind these lessons – Mr Fordyce was very kind, and his cook made the most excellent sponge biscuits – but her own thoughts were more often on America, the very existence of which seemed to be an expression of poor taste to Mr Fordyce. Miss Juniper would not be joining them today though. Miss Juniper would be waiting in, in case Lady Charlotte arrived.

Lady Charlotte's unannounced appearance at the cottage door had been happening more and more often since the library had made its trip into Easter Ross. The girls had assumed at first that she came there because Rachel was not at home, but soon it became clear that the public nature, the busyness of the manse was more than Lady Charlotte was equal to, for she had faded again from the bright and lively creature whom they had accompanied to Tain. Alicia put the renewed air of sadness that clung to Lady Charlotte down to the tedium of being home again, with the cholera encroaching ever closer and little to look forward to. Perhaps it was only Mairead who saw a new deadness in Lady Charlotte's eyes. Perhaps no one but Mairead had seen her on the lawn of Shandwick House that night, or the man who had stopped her walking into the sea, where she had appeared intent upon going. What had happened next had not seemed right at all and Mairead had scurried to her bed and not spoken a word of it to Alicia but kept it to herself in the hope that it might disappear, like the relics of St Duthac.

At first, Lady Charlotte had appeared with a basket of eggs and butter, or some preserves from Cromarty House kitchen, but now such gifts were incidentals rather than pretexts to her visits – she came almost every day. Sometimes, she would talk to them about Edinburgh, or the duties of running a large house. Sometimes, she would pore over the advertisements Hester brought them from the newspaper and advise them on which haberdashers or clothiers or perfumers were be patronised and which not, as if either of them would ever be in a position to make such a choice. Alicia took these pronouncements as gospel proclaimed on Sunday from the pulpit, while Mairead exchanged worried glances with Miss Juniper.

As time had gone on, Lady Charlotte had become more and more simple in her dress, until there was little to distinguish what she wore from what Rachel wore on a normal weekday. Sometimes, she would just sit there with them, while they had their lessons, lessons that had probably not changed in all the fifteen years since she herself had been one of Miss Juniper's girls. Rachel Mackay would also sometimes come down to the cottage and finding her old friend there, they would all take tea, as if Miss Juniper's were a real school like the one on George Street and they all schoolgirls together. Since Mr Mackay had been away at the General Assembly in Edinburgh with Dr Fraser though, Rachel was very much occupied with her duties at the manse or going around the parish with Mrs Gilfeather, visiting the sick and needy. The business of Cromarty House, however, seemed to carry itself on perfectly well, regardless of whether Lady Charlotte was there or not, and so it had fallen to them to 'keep an eye on Charlotte' as they had heard Rachel whisper to their schoolmistress one day.

The cottage door was never locked, but Miss Juniper did not like to go out now, lest Lady Charlotte, arriving and finding it empty, should wander off somewhere else. It had happened twice last week, and on the second occasion, instead of going home, she had taken herself to the coffee room of the hotel, which had really not been quite the thing. It was one thing for an elderly spinster schoolmistress such as Miss Juniper to take her coffee in the reading room of the hotel on a Saturday afternoon, but quite another for the young wife of the laird to present herself there alone, on a weekday. A discreet dispatching of Hester with a message to the manse had resolved the situation, but not before Mr Gilfeather's morning coffee arrangements had been sent somewhat askew. So, today, Mairead and Alicia would go alone to their lesson at Fordyce House and therefore be free to take a short diversion up the Paye, in search of hyacinths.

Rachel felt joy in her stomach at the idea of Alasdair returning. She had not wanted him to go to Edinburgh at all. They had only just put the difficult months behind them, but he had assured her those difficulties had disappeared for good on the walk that April morning from Shandwick House to the book sale in Tain.

'I saw the last remnant of the shadow of that dark beast slink away from me on the road to Tain that day,' he had said, 'and all the false, dark, gnawing, burning suspicion with it. Micah knew what he was about when he suggested we accompany Ludovic and the schoolmaster to Tain that morning.'

She had tried to dissuade him from going away for weeks to the General Assembly of the Kirk in Edinburgh. She had asked him to consider his health, and the tongues that would wag at another absence between them.

'But I must go, Rachel,' he had said. 'There are greater questions at stake than you and I. The freedom of the kirk is assaulted daily by the claims of the landowners. If men like Micah and myself don't make our voices heard in defence of the rights of the people of Scotland to choose their own ministers, then what are we for? Are we meekly to stand back until the intrusion of cousins of Sir this and Lord that, clients and stooges with not a word of gospel truth on their tongues, has become a flood of inanities? Yes, Rachel, I am going to Edinburgh with Micah and there will be no one more ready for the fight than I.'

But now he was coming home, and word had arrived at the manse door that the packet *Jenny* that was to carry the ministers back from Leith had been sighted from Cromarty hill. Within minutes, Rachel had her shawl on and was running down to the harbour, careless of what anyone said about the minister's wife being out without even a bonnet upon her head.

Immovable at either side of the entrance to the firth, the Sutors stood proud against the blue sky, the old red sandstone of their flanks robed in greens and yellows, like young ones ready for the joys of the coming summer. Rachel hoped there might be joy in it. She had got so used to the sight of the emigration ships and the boats forced into quarantine by the cholera regulations that her eye had begun to glide over them, so that she hardly saw them at all any more. Today, because she had her back turned on the town and its doings and her eyes straining instead out to sea, the reality of them could not be so easily dismissed. Clenches of anxiety contended in her stomach with the butterflies of anticipation at the thought of Alasdair's homecoming.

Rachel peered at the entrance to the harbour until her eyes hurt and then at last she saw that the vessel nosing in was indeed *The Jenny*, preceded by a fishing boat. The calling and clacking of the gulls circling above the fishing boat grew in excitement. They were like fishwives, broadcasting their views and their wares to anyone who might hear them. Honest gossips. For a moment the sound of them was almost too much and Rachel had to clench her fists by her sides to prevent herself from lifting her hands to press them to her ears.

Charlotte passed through the gate in the wall of the kitchen garden and smiled at the bright sails blowing out on the firth, at the promise of freedom and of other places they spoke of, just like the sea birds that swirled and soared above them. Oh, for one hour, half of an hour, of freedom. If she did not get away from the confines of Cromarty House she would probably murder Morag Mackenzie. Charlotte pictured herself standing up in Cromarty courthouse to hear herself accused of Morag's murder, and William having to sit there on the bench, in judgement on her. But then William was a justice of the peace, not a lord of the session, and should she truly ever find herself arraigned for the murder of her husband's old nurse, or of anyone else, it would be at the High Court in Inverness and she would not get away with her neck. Perhaps William would let the anatomy professors have her body.

William had gone to Dingwall to discuss the laying of the foundation stone of a new infant school there, at which he and many cousins would require to be seen. He had not gone to the latest public meeting in Inverness, at which as many as ten thousand were expected. It was a mistake, he said, to encourage the artisanal and mechanical classes to meddle in politics. If they hadn't been stirred up by the Whigs they'd never have left their yards and workshops. Charlotte pretended to know or care about very little of politics and the affairs of the world, and William liked it that way. He did not expect that she should give any opinion in response to his airing of his views, but she was a shopkeeper's daughter and she understood perfectly well what was afoot.

She also understood that she was not ill, as William and Miss Juniper seemed to fear she was, nor mad, as Morag Mackenzie had taken to hinting at. Let things take their course. Charlotte pulled shut the wooden door in the garden wall and stepped out into the world. Across the road, the wild roses were exuberant in the hedgerow and in that moment she loved them fiercely. She lifted her head and breathed deep the salt air and all that was in it that made her sixteen again.

Alasdair Mackay stood on the port side of the ship with his hands on the railing and gave a sigh of pleasure. The town was a picture, a diorama such as he had seen in Edinburgh, that would come to life the minute they stepped ashore. A profusion of vanilla scents, wafting on the breeze from the whin flowers blanketing Cromarty hill mingled with the salt of the sea to assail his senses. 'Ah, Micah – could anyone doubt that God is in his Heaven, to look upon this?'

An indistinct mumble manifested itself somewhere near his shoulder. The last twelve hours or so of their journey had been without incident, but the greater part of the voyage from Leith had seen the Cromarty smack tossed on angry seas all the way from the Bass Rock to Rattray Head and round every perilous obstacle in between. No one aboard could have been ignorant of the number of lives lost to these waters, the souls gone to eternity as bodies settled without Christian burial on the ocean bed or washed up on beaches miles away. As *The Jenny* had struggled through the raging swell, none had been more fervent in prayer or the offering of psalms than was Dr Fraser, and few had been greener at the gills. Micah now steadied himself at the rail before he replied. 'Had God not been in His Heaven we'd sure as death have been lying smashed about the rocks below Dunnottar by now, the carrion already at our eyes. You island fellows have stomachs of iron. We men of the hills like to feel the ground at our feet. Do you know, I was six years old before I ever saw the sea? I thought it was a hill and couldn't understand why it was moving.'

Alasdair smiled. Those who really knew Micah could still see something of that lad from the Strath of Kildonan who'd run barefoot around the glens and rivers of his father's parish. But that had been before his father's people had been driven from their homes to make way for sheep and forced to try to scrape a living at the margins, gathering kelp or learning to fish from scraps of villages barely clinging to the edge of the sea. Those that would not bear or could not master such an existence took ship and travelled oceans to escape the shadow of the Duchess of Sutherland's grace. Micah's fury, his certainty that there would be retribution in the next life if not this, seemed to drive him onward almost as much as did his faith in God.

Beyond Cromarty Bay, the mountains of Ross and Sutherland still stretched gloriously away to the north and west, their beauty unchanged and their heart ripped out entirely. Alasdair put a hand on his friend's shoulder. 'Come, we had better see that our baggage is all ready to be disembarked, and then we can get those feet of yours onto solid ground again.' He looked back at the town. 'We have a work to perform here, and a fight coming.'

Dr Fraser left off his contemplation of the Sutherland hills and set his eyes on Cromarty, his face grim. 'We have more than one fight, Alasdair.' Then he sniffed. 'But no doubt Mrs Mackay will be down at the harbour, waving a lace handkerchief, so we had better get a brush pulled through that hair of yours or she's like to signal to the pilot to turn around and take us back out to sea.'

TWENTY-FIVE

Knights

Fachie Hossack straightened his necktie in the glass by the front door, then, satisfied, he stuck out his hand for the housemaid to hand him his hat. Pity his father hadn't been there to see it. The first time the old man had witnessed the girl waiting in the hall merely to hand Fachie his hat, he had almost taken a stroke. 'Did Fachie think the lassie had no work to be getting on with? Was there something wrong with his own arms? Was that what they taught in the college of Aberdeen that had cost me a fortune? What use in the world was a man who could not lift his own hat?'

Fachie's mother, hurrying to the top of the stairs at the sound of all the commotion, had been given short shrift when she had protested that Fachie was a gentleman.

Well, his father was not back from the ropeworks yet and Fachie would do as he pleased. So would the housemaid – up to a point and Fachie had learned not to test that point too far. It was six years since his father had taken him by the neck and pinned him to a wall when he'd found Fachie exploring the mysteries beneath a protesting kitchen girl's skirts. Fachie had been surprised by the strength of the hands that had almost choked the life out of him and left him black and blue in places his mother would never see. Old Willie Hossack had not forgotten the lessons learned as a barefoot boy brawling and scrapping in the backlands of Dingwall, and his accumulated wealth had been no barrier to a day's labour in his own ropeworks if such was required. Arms like hams and fists like boulders – Fachie made sure never to risk coming into close contact with them again.

Perhaps old Willie would have lost some of his speed, his strength in the intervening years, who could tell? But he had other weapons to deploy. Money. What little of her own Fachie's mother had was long gone into the pockets of young gentlemen who had bested her son at cards or laid their money on faster dogs, and she could help him no more. He had stretched out his studies in Aberdeen for as long as he could but, until some position as the private physician to an elderly dowager or sickly child being toured round Europe presented itself, he had been left with no choice but to return to kick his heels in Cromarty, and to keep out of his father's way.

That had worked for precisely five hours, from the moment of his making land yesterday afternoon to the moment his father had come into the parlour last night, looking for his supper. The first cutlet had hardly been halfway down old Willie's throat and the grey meat still visible as he chewed, mouth open, when he had demanded, 'Well, sir, and what do you propose you will do for a living?'

'Willie,' his wife had said, 'Farquhar is to be a physician. You know that.'

'And who will he physick?' was his father's retort, as he'd picked a thread of mutton from his teeth. 'Are you to set up practice here, then? We have always called in Dr MacNeil ourselves, as well you know.'

'MacNeil is an old charlatan whose answer to everything is bleeding and a dose of salts. Little better than the latest quack advertising his powders on the front page of *The Courier*. No wonder my brother never made it beyond childhood.'

Mrs Hossack had let out a soft cry then, and turned away, looking for her handkerchief. Willie Hossack had thumped the table, making the silverware rattle.

'You'll not talk of your brother in that light way, sir! It upsets your mother. William was a fine boy, a fine boy.' The old man's own lip trembled, half in rage, half in suppressed grief that could leave Fachie in no doubt, should he ever have had any, that the wrong son had survived that childhood bout of scarlatina. He had grieved for William too, in his way. But his brother's death, in elevating him to the position of only son and heir, had brought for Fachie inconveniences that a second son would not generally have been expected to put up with. William would have gone into the ropeworks – he'd liked nothing better than being in there amongst the bales of hemp, racing down the ranges as ropes were stretched and twisted, and being made a pet of all the Highland women. And then Fachie would have been left in peace to do as he pleased and not be pestered about going into the ropeworks instead, or how else he would make a living.

'I'm sorry, Mother,' he said. Then he turned to his father. 'I have no intention of setting up practice in Cromarty. There are some amongst my associates from college who have offered to introduce me to persons of consequence and thereby find an opening for me to travel abroad as the private physician of some person of—'

'*Consequence*,' his father finished for him. 'Well, I've seen none of them here, and all that lands with the Aberdeen post are bills and demands, not an invitation amongst them. But never you worry, Fachie, you'll travel abroad all right.' So saying, he had thrust out towards his son a newspaper that had been folded at the side of the coal scuttle.

Fachie had examined it. 'This newspaper is almost two months old. What do you wish me to do with it?'

His father had leaned across, wiping his mouth with his napkin, then pointed a rough finger at an item in the third column of the second page. 'I wish you to take cognizance of *that*.'

Fachie had begun to read. '. . . all vessels carrying fifty passengers . . . crew and master to the British possessions in North America or to the United States are . . . to carry a surgeon in order to prevent, as far as possible, the disease called cholera reaching these places . . .'

He'd looked up to find the old man fixing upon him a look of long-delayed triumph.

'Is this a joke, Father?'

'I hardly think the *cholera morbus* is a joke.'

In spite of her husband's unaccustomed lapse into Latin, shock had caused Fachie's mother to revert to her native speech. 'Willie, you're no' serious? Those boats are death traps. You wouldna put a dog on them.'

Her husband had given a dismissive 'pfft'.

Fachie had been on his feet. 'They are breeding grounds of disease. Once the cholera gets in below decks, you might as well sink the thing.' He'd realised he was shaking and had taken a step back to compose himself. 'But this is nothing to me, Father. I am a physician, not a surgeon.'

Willie Hossack had opened his snuff box and snorted a big pinch. 'Makes no odds. If your anatomy classes didna tell you one end o' a corpse from another, there was little point in them. There's half a dozen skippers take my cargoes across the ocean that would take you on, as an obligement to me.'

It had been all Fachie could do not to pick up the kettle from the hearth and throw it in the old man's face. He'd forced the old copy of the *Inverness Courier* under his mother's eyes.

'Look, Mother. Look what your husband would send me to,' he'd said, pointing to a different item.

Marjorie had been flustered. 'You know my eyes are bad in this light, my dear, and the print is so small. You read it.' And so, turned towards his father the whole time, he had read out an account of the late mutiny on the English brig *Jane* and the murder of all her officers on a voyage from Monte Video to Havana

Fachie's mother was in a state of near collapse before he ever reached the end of the piece and her salts called for and her woman sent for to help her to her bed. Willie Hossack had left the room in disgust, shouting that his toddy should be brought to him in his office, and Fachie had been left alone in the parlour to contemplate his homecoming.

But this evening, as Fachie walked along the harbour front, boys and men knowing nothing of his father's contempt touched their caps if he caught their eye, and women hurried. God, the idea that he'd be interested in one of *those*, reeking of peat smoke and fish guts! He glanced out at the ships. This was quite as close as he intended on getting to any of them, unless a steam packet to Leith or a smack to Gravesend. There were people who owed him money and he had their promissory notes in his pocket, with an undertaking that he would burn the said notes on the securing of a position as attendant to some wealthy elderly or widowed relative of the debtor. The others would be exchanged for the specified money, or letters of introduction to persons of real quality. Not long now, and Fachie would be done with Cromarty for good.

Fish guts, ropeworks and smokehouses aside, the place nonetheless offered a pretty enough prospect on this fine

May evening. The sun was sending pinks and purples over the sky as it sank slowly beyond Ben Wyvis, and the waters of the firth were still and golden. Even the gliding of the gulls overhead was lovely, at a distance. The tight bonds of authority he usually felt wrapping themselves around him whenever he returned had been somewhat loosened by the news that Alasdair Mackay of Cromarty Kirk and Micah Fraser of Resolis had gone to Edinburgh for the General Assembly. Fachie thought he might pretend he did not know this, take a stroll up to the manse, ask to see Mr Mackay, see what happened next.

The idea amused him greatly, and he was building upon it as he turned up Bank Street. The front door of the bank opened, and Ludo Cameron emerged. Fachie consulted his watch. Two minutes past six. Gilfeather would be out a minute later, locking up behind him. Gilfeather, his father's old enemy, though Fachie had never yet learned why. Going home to that ignorant woman and their lumpen kitchen maid. God, what a place. What a life.

Fachie missed Ludo, sometimes, in Aberdeen. He'd got used to him, throughout his life, this accident of a creature with whom he might amuse himself if there was no one more interesting around. No one, in childhood or since, had ever been as easy to make fun of as Ludovic Cameron. He could have quickened his pace but there was little point – before he ever caught up with him, Ludo would be over the door of the Commercial Hotel and home. Next time, perhaps.

It seemed, though, that Ludo was not going home. He had continued past the hotel and on towards the High Street, a document of some sort in his hand. All thought of imposing his company on Rachel Mackay drifted away on the breeze now, and Fachie touched his hat to a scowling Sanders Gilfeather, before crossing the street to step through the door of the Commercial Hotel.

Ludo often had to carry items of importance from the bank to various citizens of Cromarty and indeed the wider county. He had even, on occasion, when escorting large sums of money to far points on the Black Isle and beyond, had to carry the box with the bank's pistol in it, but seldom had he felt such apprehension as he did about the letter he had now been instructed to deliver to the clockmaker's house.

Mr Gilfeather had wrinkled his nostrils in a manner that Ludovic knew to betoken surprise. 'A count,' he had said.

Ludo had waited, but Mr Gilfeather had apparently had nothing to add.

'Ahm, which account do you require, Mr Gilfeather?' he had ventured at last.

'Require? No, no. Not "*account*", but "*a* count". You must learn to listen, Mr Cameron, or you'll not get far in the Caledonian Bank.' Mr Gilfeather had brandished an unopened letter. '*A* count. Your friend, Mr Jeszewski, or His Excellency, as we will no doubt now be expected to call him.'

'Stanislas? Oh yes, Mr Gilfeather, he is certainly a count.'

'Hmm.' Mr Gilfeather had appeared not altogether pleased. 'I thought that was just some nonsense made up by the women.'

'Oh no,' Ludovic had said, somewhat uncomfortable at being the possessor of information previously unknown to the bank manager. 'He is the count of some place in Poland. He does not draw attention to it though.' On an afterthought he had added, 'Although I am sure he would not expect anyone in Cromarty to address him as "Your Excellency," especially not *you*, Mr Gilfeather.'

Mr Gilfeather's next 'Hmm', had been of a higher register. 'What the fellow expects, Mr Cameron, is neither here nor there. As regards the business of the bank, I shall address him as is proper.' He had handed the sealed missive to Ludo. 'As you will see, whoever has sent this epistle, "Care of the Caledonian Bank, Cromarty," is particular about the *Excellency*, and so shall we be. You may take it to him at James Craig's this evening. Once you have handed the thing over, the bank's business being thus done, you may address the fellow as you please.'

The idea that Mr Gilfeather, who lived directly opposite the clockmaker, could himself quite easily deliver the letter on his way home might have occurred to another, but it never entered Ludovic's head. Ludo was quite clear that the manager of the Caledonian Bank and clerk to the kirk session of Cromarty was nobody's message boy, howsoever *Excellent* that nobody might be. 'I will take it there directly the bank closes,' he had said.

Despite his apprehensions about the contents of the letter, Ludo was glad of the opportunity to call upon his friends whom he hoped might be returned from their trip to Inverness and the great rally of the Reform Committee. They had been keen that he should accompany them, but he had known in advance what Mr Gilfeather's response to any request for leave for such a venture might be and had not even asked. That morning, when all talk at the bank had been of the rally taking place in Inverness, Mr Gilfeather had commented, 'I am glad to see that you have not mixed yourself up in that nonsense. I hear the greater number of shops in Inverness are to be closed for the day. Closed! How is this *Reform* to benefit anyone, if the very word of it brings commerce to a halt? And then there is the drinking and the toasts that you may be certain will follow in the hotels and taverns of the town. Wickedness and ungodliness will be the attendants of the fine speeches made in Academy Park this day, and the prison cells of Inverness will be filled by morning.' It had been a sermon to which Ludo had understood he was not required to respond.

Although Stan and John were in fact not yet returned from Inverness, James had nonetheless invited Ludo in to take a dram.

The clockmaker was in a humour to talk of meetings and marches that he himself had been on, and of his old schoolfellow, James Mackintosh, whose book on the early days of the French Revolution had persuaded him to take off for France in the first place. 'I was so fired up by the nobility of his argument,' he said, 'I wanted to see what I could learn, that I might bring it back to Scotland.' He laughed. 'Mackintosh, of course, had the good sense to remain at home, and is now a Member of Parliament and Knight of the Realm.'

'Whereas your adventure put an end to your prospects.' The words were out of his mouth before Ludo could stop them, but James only smiled.

'I never really had any to put an end to. I was born to a ships' instrument maker in Fortrose and wished for nothing more than to be an honest clockmaker in an honest town. James Mackintosh was born in a castle to the flower of Highland society. How could our fates have been otherwise? There was only one real loss to me.'

Ludo was suddenly consumed with dread that James was about to vouchsafe details of his personal history considerably more intimate than he would ever care to enquire about, when to his immense relief he heard Stan's familiar whistle in the yard. In a moment Stan was dropping into an armchair and James was pouring out three more drams that a toast might be drunk to Sir James Mackintosh before Stan relayed to them all the sights and sounds of the great meeting in Inverness. This being at last done, James went outside to take the air with his terrier, and Stan opened his satchel and showed to Ludovic a small package purchased that morning from Messrs Tait and Cameron, Perfumers. 'Almond soap,' he whispered. 'Do you think she will like it?'

'Oh,' said Ludo, recalling the advertisements Hester often

took down to Miss Juniper's cottage for Alicia's perusal, 'she is certain to.'

It was after eight o'clock before Ludo remembered the mysterious letter that had brought him here in the first place. With profuse apologies, he handed the letter to Stan. The look that came over the young Pole's face when he saw the direction on the front, and the hand it was written in, spoke of another place, another world. Quietly thanking James for his hospitality, Ludovic left.

There had been some diminution in the trade of the hotel as the *cholera morbus* had drawn ever more surely northwards. Shipping and trade up and down the coast had been hampered for months, since first the disease had been reported at Sunderland and then Newcastle. By February it had crept across the border and begun to spread in the southern counties of Scotland. The newspapers were filled with advertisements for products claiming efficacy in disinfection for the prevention of contagion. Petitions were raised for the removal of duty on soap. Newly instituted health boards saw dung heaps removed, the homeless banished and additional hospital spaces secured. And yet the cholera marched on. By March it had entered Edinburgh and Glasgow, where the people raged against burial measures that took the bodies of their loved ones from them within hours of death. It had all got mixed up, somehow, with their fears about the Burkers and the Resurrectionists. Prejudice against the surgeons and anatomists was growing. Watches had been put on tolls and turnpikes to guard against vagrants who might carry the pestilence from one town to the next. There was rumour of cases amongst the soldiers at Fort George, barely a few miles across the water. Letters in newspaper columns complained of the loss of profit through cessation of trade and the general frightening of the populace. Ludovic's mother was not greatly concerned – her best trade lay in the town itself and country people coming into town – yet the hotel was quieter, all the same.

So Ludovic was surprised at this time to see light still glowing through the reading room window. Hester appeared in the hall as he was hanging up his hat. 'It's all right,' he said, 'it's only me.' Then he caught something in the expression in her eyes. 'Is something wrong?'

Hester said nothing, but her eyes travelled towards the reading room door.

He went closer and whispered, 'Who's in there?'

'Mr Fordyce,' she began.

'At this hour?' Mr Fordyce would on occasion take his dinner at the hotel, but he had never been known to stay this late. 'Has he met in with someone?'

Hester opened her mouth as if unsure how to reply. 'Farquhar is there,' she said at last. 'Farquhar Hossack.'

All the pleasure of Ludovic's evening left him. 'Right then,' he said. 'You go and join my mother upstairs, or go to bed, whatever you like.'

'But what if the gentlemen need . . .'

'If the gentlemen need anything, I will fetch it for them. You may tell my mother. Besides, there is only one gentleman in there. Go on now.' Ludo waited until Hester had disappeared into the private part of the hotel. Fuelled with resolution after his evening in the edifying company of James Craig and Stanislas, he pushed open the door to the reading room and walked in.

Mr Fordyce was seated in the chair at the far side of the fire. The back of the dark head of Fachie Hossack, unmistakable to Ludo, was visible in the chair opposite. Over Mr Fordyce's face spread a broad smile of relief. 'Ludovic! How pleasant to see you. I have just been here these last two hours, keeping company with Farquhar.'

Farquhar Hossack part-turned his head, a queer, irritated look on his face. It was a look Ludo recognised. Fachie had not got his way in something.

'Mr Fordyce, Fachie,' Ludo said, nodding to each. 'Can I bring you anything? More coffee? A toddy?'

Fachie reached a hand towards the sash at the end of the bell. 'We will ring for the girl if we need anything, Ludovic. Unless you are reduced to playing housemaid?'

Ludo did not allow this to bother him. 'I've sent Hester to her bed. You can let me know if you need anything.'

Fachie gave him a long look of contempt and got up. 'Nothing you might have to offer, Ludovic.' Then he made a curt bow to Isaac Fordyce. 'Mr Fordyce.'

The old man, his face uncharacteristically grim, gave an equally curt nod in response and said nothing until the sound of the front door banging shut ricocheted from the hall. As Ludo breathed a sigh of relief, Mr Fordyce stood up. 'I fear Farquhar Hossack has not grown up a gentleman, Ludovic. I did not like the way he spoke to young Hester.' He cleared his throat. 'Nor the way he looked at her.'

'And that is why you stayed so long beyond your usual time.'

Mr Fordyce glanced away.

'Thank you, Mr Isaac,' said Ludo. 'Thank you.'

Mr Fordyce said nothing more, merely pressed Ludo's hand and allowed him to open first one and then the other door for him, as he went out into the street. Ludo watched the old man until he disappeared from view, his stick tapping on the cobbles, a stooped knight, his honour echoing through the darkening town.

TWENTY-SIX

Late July 1832

The Gardeners' Procession

Mrs Gilfeather beamed. What a fine figure Zander cut, marching in the front with his fellow office holders of the Union of Gardeners. The procession had just set off from the front of the Gardener's Lodge, a little way down the street from the Gilfeather house. The band played bravely, and Mrs Gilfeather's foot was soon tapping. Across the street, James Craig and his apprentice stood outside their shop, each with a bloom in his buttonhole. The young Polish lad had a posy in his hands too, and Mrs Gilfeather, who kept her eyes open upon the lingerers about the kirkyard after the sermon on a Sunday, made a shrewd guess as to who it might be for. She smiled to herself, and turned her attention back towards the approaching parade, and Zander. To think that Willie Hossack, forty years since, had thought she would as much as glance his way, when Zander Gilfeather had asked for her hand!

Now here was the town decked out in garlands and

evergreen arches, and Zander to the fore right in the front row of the Gardeners' Union. All the men wore their best clothes, with bright blue sashes across their chests and in their hands carried bits of branches all wreathed round with blooms. Zander had a garland round his hat and carried a staff all twined with flowers he'd grown with his own hands. 'There's nothing that man canna do,' said Mrs Gilfeather to her kitchen maid. 'You mind an' no' tak the first loon that asks for you.'

Behind the procession, there was the gig from Cromarty House. The grooms must have been half the morning with the curry comb, tricking out the horse's mane and bridle all in ribbons and blooms. Sir William held the reins, a sprig of gardenias pinned to his lapel and beside him sat Lady Charlotte, a pale pink rose whose petals might blow off in the breeze. A spray of white lilies lay, unattended, in her lap. Sir William was to be chief judge of the displays. 'Him that canna tell a cabbage from a chrysanthemum,' Zander had muttered. The presentation of the cup for best roses to Willie Hossack the previous year had been a bitter blow.

Behind the gig walked the minister and his wife. Rachel was looking bonny and Mr Mackay himself was a picture of health again – lean and tanned where the winter had seen him gaunt and pale. The troubles of the winter would be, God willing, behind them. The schoolmaster and his pupils brought up the tail of the procession proper, and after them came running and skipping every barefoot lass and urchin in the town, waving whatever piece of greenery they could get. A gala day it was, when troubles might be forgotten.

'Now, girls,' said Miss Juniper, surveying the grassy swathe of the links, 'where shall we sit?'

Alicia turned pleading eyes on Mairead and squeezed her hand. Please let Miss Juniper not spot Rachel, laying out her rug next to Mrs Gilfeather. She had no objection to Mrs Gilfeather, who was nothing but kindness to them, and it wasn't Rachel, in herself, that she wished to avoid. How could it be? She and Mairead had picnicked with her half a dozen times this summer already, and on more than half of those occasions they had happened to encounter Stanislas, out exploring the local rocks and flora. Today, however, Rachel was not *their* Rachel but Mrs Mackay, the minister's wife, and as such was accompanied by her husband, the minister. Alicia had no wish to sit anywhere near the minister, with everyone being guarded and polite, and where no fun could be had at all. She knew Mairead was at one with her in this view.

There was Mr Isaac Fordyce and some of the other gentlemen of the golf club, setting up in the shade of an elm just below his house, whence they might view any potential damage to their course. Mr Fordyce was always a possibility, but the presence of the Misses Rose and some other ladies of the Friendly Society on the border of his little group precluded *that* as a location for Miss Juniper. Alicia began to feel panic rising, but Mairead, whose eyes were sharper than hers, had also been scanning the links. 'Over there,' she said suddenly. 'With M. and Mme Perrin.'

Alicia dared scarcely breathe and then, 'Oh, yes,' said Miss Juniper. 'How very pleasant that will be.'

Alicia could have hugged Mairead. Right next to where the French consul and his wife, with whom the girls had French lessons, were settled, Janet Cameron and Hester were at that very moment setting a basket on the rug they had just laid out. Sauntering along towards his mother and Hester, not a care in the world, was Ludovic, and chatting happily with him were James Craig and Stanislas. As Miss Juniper wove her dainty way between groups of the town's citizens, her girls followed, the one carrying a rug, and the other a basket. When their schoolmistress was safely out of earshot, Alicia darted a kiss at Mairead's ear. 'You clever thing, you have managed things perfectly.'

And so it was. The three separate groups of French Consul, elderly governess and rebellious clockmaker with their young attendants soon merged into one large one, the consul relishing the opportunity to converse in his native tongue with the clockmaker, a man who actually *knew* Paris. As they discussed the insurrection said to have taken place very recently in the western departments of France, the question of which side of which barricade each man might have been on over thirty years beforehand was never broached between them and no one present would have dreamt of asking.

Mrs Cameron and Hester, as it turned out, had hardly

time to nibble a strawberry or swallow a sandwich between them before they had to return to the hotel. There was a great deal yet to be done in preparation of the supper for the evening's Gardeners' Ball, Mrs Cameron having been contracted to supervise all. At Mairead's disappointed look, Mrs Cameron said, 'Mrs Gilfeather has organised half a dozen farm girls for the clearing. Once the supper is served, Hester may dance as much as she pleases.' Hester showed no sign of paying attention to any of this, although Alicia was certain she had seen a distinct dimpling of her friend's cheeks as she passed.

Mrs Cameron thus departed, Mme Perrin and Miss Juniper regrouped, in order to continue talking about whatever it was ladies of that age found to talk about. As a result, Alicia found that she and Mairead had somehow gravitated to the far edge of Mme Perrin's blanket, almost to where it touched that occupied by Ludovic and Stanislas.

A little way up the slope from them, Alicia could see that the schoolmaster had finally shed his charges for the day. He would no doubt soon be over to join them, having first carried out his obligations around the minister's group. It could not be helped. She had never entirely seen whatever it was about the schoolmaster that set the girls of the Ladies' School on George Street aflutter, but she at least could tolerate him. Mairead, however, had developed a holy horror of the man in recent weeks, which even his association with Ludo Cameron could not assuage and which had altogether supplanted the Gothic fears that had previously so tormented her. Mairead denied any such aversion, of course, but Alicia was not to be fooled. Luckily, at that moment her eye was caught by the familiar sturdy form of Dr Fraser interposing himself into the group around Rachel and Mr Mackay. Alicia smiled. They would not be troubled by Mr Learmonth for some while yet.

On the ground at Stanislas's side lay a posy of blue flowers. Alicia had been casting furtive glances towards it from the moment they had sat down. They matched the small spray pinned to his coat and were absolutely as close to hyacinth blue as was to be got at this stage of the summer. Stanislas at last seemed to remember the posy and reached out a tentative hand to pick it up. He looked directly at her, appearing to make some sort of resolution. 'I think this is the most perfect day I have known since I arrived in Scotland, Miss Middleton.'

'Because of the parade?' Ludovic was eating a pork pie, flakes of which had already landed on his waistcoat and would attract the gulls if he wasn't careful. He clearly had not been listening properly to what was being said, or to whom. 'But you were here for it last year, Stan.'

Alicia found this insupportable.

'Yes,' said Stanislas, 'but I had not so many friends, then.'

The look that floated from his dark brown eyes directly into Alicia's own blue ones – hyacinth blue – made a small 'oh' escape her throat. Mairead pinched her and Ludo at last understood enough that *he* coloured.

'I – I think in fact,' continued Stanislas, 'that I will find it rather difficult, painful in fact, under certain circumstances, to leave.'

Alicia stared at him, speechless.

'Leave?' demanded Mairead.

Stanislas looked to Ludovic as if for assistance, but Ludovic was resolutely occupied with his pie and could offer none.

'I had a letter, some few weeks past. It had been sent several months ago but took some time to find me here.'

'From Poland?' asked Alicia, fearing many things.

Stanislas shook his head, a little sad. 'No, London. My old university teacher from Warsaw, Mr Lach-Szyrma. He spent time in Scotland about ten years ago, as tutor to two young noblemen. He conceived a great admiration for this country and made many kind and influential friends. In our rising against the Russia tyrant, Lach-Szyrma commanded the student regiment – he was my commanding officer as well as my teacher.'

Alicia allowed herself a vision of Stanislas in uniform, arm outstretched, sword drawn.

'Well,' he continued, 'Lach-Szyrma was, like myself, forced into exile on the failure of our rising and has made his way to London, where he has renewed his acquaintance with some gentlemen who were kind enough to take notice of him on his first visit to these kingdoms. They are forming a committee of support for the Polish cause and he is hopeful that one will be formed in Edinburgh, too. He says he has written to Professor Pillans at the University in Edinburgh . . .'

Alicia paled. 'You are to go to Edinburgh?'

Stanislas's face registered his distress at her misunderstanding. 'Mr Lach-Szyrma has made the acquaintance, in London, of Dr Joseph Hume, MP, an ardent friend of Poland and supporter of our cause. I have, in sum, been offered the position of under-secretary in Dr Hume's office.'

'London . . .' said Alicia. 'But . . . the clocks . . .' She looked around to James Craig as if pleading for the clockmaker to come to her aid.

James Craig gave off his conversation with the consul. 'I have given him my blessing to go, Miss Middleton. There are plenty of young lads here I might take on and train up. Stanislas is fitted for other things.'

'But . . .' protested Alicia. She could feel tears pricking her eyes and looked desperately around. 'Mairead,' she said, grasping her friend's arm and making to stand up.

Stanislas stood up too, thrusting his posy at her as he did so. 'But Miss Middleton, you are not leaving?'

'Well, *you* are!' she said, angry through her tears.

'No,' he countered.

'What? You are not going?'

Stanislas looked at a loss. 'Yes, I am going to London. I must do something. You have heard of course of the recent disturbances in my country occasioned by the great cruelties practised by the Russians on my people. Only last week came news of the closing of the university of Wilna, the removal of its library of two hundred thousand books to Russia. *Two hundred thousand.* Petitions have been presented in Parliament, and I can hope, if I am in London, that I might be able to exert some little influence, do *some* good for my suffering country.'

Alicia, eyes brimming, nodded. 'Of course. Of course you must go.'

'But,' continued the young man, resolute, 'I do not go without, I hope, the good wishes of my friends, perhaps some understanding, permission to write . . .'

'Permission to write . . .' echoed Alicia as a change in the breeze suffused the party with the scent of almond oil and Mairead readied herself to receive her friend gracefully back down on the grass.

'You are tired, Charlotte.'

'Really, Rachel, I am fine. I can be no more tired than you. I was paraded around in a gig whilst you had to walk.'

'Yes, but I am not . . .' What? What was she not that Charlotte was? Ill? Wasting? Fading? Rachel was saved from finding an end to her statement by the appearance of the Misses Rose, who were clearly headed right at them.

'Miss Elspeth, Miss Anna,' said Rachel, hastily prodding Charlotte down into a chair on her left whilst indicating to the ladies the two on her right. 'What very charming outfits. And your headdress, Miss Anna. It is quite . . .'

'Extraordinary,' finished the elder sister. 'There is hardly a carnation left in the garden. What John Patience will make of it I would not like to think.'

'But John said I might pick what I pleased, Elspeth.'

'He could hardly say other, given it is we who pay him to tend the garden. What he might privately think is another thing entirely.'

Rachel could not help but think that Miss Elspeth was right. Miss Anna did look extraordinary whilst she might simply have looked pretty, but always there was a little too much. She was tempted to reach out a hand and remove a few flowers, 'Here . . . so . . . and here,' but she didn't, because she would not have hurt Miss Anna for the world.

With Miss Elspeth, it was usually the other way. Not too much, but too little. Too little colour, too little lace, too little freedom. Not tonight though. Elspeth wore a gown of midnight blue satin that matched the dark blue of her eyes exactly and gave definition to the clean lines of her profile. Whereas Anna's plumpness had been pretty in her youth, it now rendered her a little doughy and added to a sense of the ridiculous whereas Elspeth's stronger features hinted at the striking young woman she must have been. Why had Sir William not married her? Even as the thought flashed through Rachel's mind, she sought to silence it. William *should* have married Elspeth Rose, but he had gone away and stayed away too long, and by the time he had returned whatever bloom Elspeth might once have had had faded and he had not married her. And now, here he was, married to Charlotte instead.

William and Alasdair were still with the men downstairs at the punchbowl. Only the eager, younger men had ventured yet up to the ballroom where the flower of Cromarty's womanhood awaited them bedecked in new blooms, those of the day, of the parade, of the afternoon picnic in the searing July sun now wilted and cast onto the compost. New, fresh stems, the petals come to perfect flower, had been draped around circlets and bracelets and even long, slim necks. They would go on the waste heap tomorrow. But not Alicia Middleton's flowers. Rachel had seen her grasping them earlier in the day and now those same wilted blue flowers, a match for those pinned to the jacket of the young Pole, were twined in her hair and Rachel thought nothing could have been more lovely. She pictured the girls later, in that little room beneath the eaves of Miss Juniper's cottage, undressing each other's hair, Mairead carefully taking the blue blooms one by one from Alicia's tresses and handing them to her, to be pressed between the pages of a journal.

And there was Mairead bravely wearing a tartan gown of green and red, her cheeks already flushed, and Ludo Cameron in a waistcoat that might soon need letting out circling her at a distance, no idea in the world what to do. Outside, the sky over the firth was darkening, although it was not much past nine. The heat of the day threatened a tumultuous, electric night. The emigration ships and those in quarantine began to rock and bob in the bay, but here, in the ballroom, all was well and all was safe. The band had started up a dance – there was Hugh Miller, the stonemason, spruced like a laird's factor and leading the young schoolmistress, Lydia Fraser, whose mother did not quite approve of him, to the floor. All things were possible. The cholera, the fear, the coming storm were all outside and could not touch them.

There was no sign of Fachie Hossack, she was glad to see. She had last caught sight of him downstairs, drinking, and prowling about the trestles where Janet Cameron and Hester were setting out the supper. Upstairs, the young men picked their partners, but none dared as yet approach the laird's wife or the minister's wife. Alasdair and William would be up soon. They would all dance then.

Suddenly Rachel realised that Miss Elspeth and Miss Anna were no longer seated beside her, but up on the floor, making a set with Mr Fordyce and the physician who had come to Cromarty in early summer and somehow not got away. She had not noticed them go. Charlotte took hold of her hand.

'I think you have been dreaming.'

Rachel smiled. 'I think I have.'

There was a moment's silence then, before Charlotte said, so quiet she almost didn't hear her, 'Rachel, I am with child.'

TWENTY-SEVEN

The Storm Breaks

The thunder preceding the first crack of lightning over Mount Fyrish, a few miles down the firth, brought the dance to an abrupt halt. Farmers in from the country had already left, much to the disappointment of their sons and daughters. Town-dwellers were keen to get in behind their own doors before the storm reached Cromarty. Willie Hossack, worried about his storerooms being struck, had hauled his foreman out of a reel and bustled him down the stairs, leaving his wife to depend on the questionable gallantry of Fachie to see her safely home.

Sir William, brosey-eyed and red of cheek, preceded Charlotte into the street in front of the Gardener's Lodge but remembered to step aside so the coachman might hand her first into the carriage. They raced the thunder up the brae. Rachel and Alasdair, refusing the offer of a lift, ran home, she pressed into his side, his arm around her and almost lifting her from the ground as the first flash lit up the town and its scurrying people. 'I think God does not like our bacchanalian ways,' she said.

'Likely not,' he replied. 'Or perhaps He has some other argument with Cromarty.' They all but flew up the road, past the brewery and along by the estate garden wall until finally they were in through the door to the manse garden. As it banged behind them, the heavens broke open and had drenched them before they reached the warmth of the kitchen.

The cook and housemaid, having got home before them, were readying hot possets but Alasdair said, 'No. It's a toddy we're needing on a night like this. Let us have the parlour fire lit, and Jane, bring towels for myself and Mrs Mackay, then you and Mrs Cramond shall have a toddy too.'

The fire lit and the towels brought, Alasdair was rubbing his head dry before setting about the preparation of the toddy. His hair was in long black tails over his face, and he had such a grin on him, he looked like a man of thirty rather than fifty. Like a boy, almost. She decided to tell him then. It could scarcely wait in any case because Charlotte was going to tell William tonight.

'I know a secret.'

He hooked an arm round her waist to bring her closer to him. 'What secret do you know, Minx?'

'Charlotte is expecting a child,' she said, finding herself smiling so wide her cheeks hurt.

But Alasdair's eyes went from sparkling to flat the minute she said it. He stared at her. 'That cannot be right, Rachel. You should not speculate on these things.'

She didn't understand. 'I'm not speculating. She told me so herself, only this evening. She is going to tell William tonight.'

Alasdair let drop his arm and took a step back from her, so that she almost fell. His face had gone grey. 'Oh, no, Rachel. Oh, no.'

They were in their bedchamber. Morag Mackenzie had drawn the curtains whilst they'd been out, just one of her daily intrusions, but William had opened them again, so they might watch the storm.

He was grinning, enraptured, at the skies. 'I have always loved storms, have you not, Charlotte? Ever since I was a little boy, I felt so *alive*. And then, in Demerara, there were such storms you cannot begin to imagine!' He turned to her and she saw something of the young man he might have been then, a glimpse of someone she might have loved.

'You miss the Caribbean, don't you, William?'

'Sometimes,' he said. 'Not always.'

She slipped an arm through his and watched as a huge flash lit up the town below them.

'I suppose,' she said, 'when there are reminders, like this storm, tonight. Or when you see Hester, at the hotel, or at the dance this evening . . .'

'Hester?' William frowned. 'Well, I suppose so. Sometimes.'

She pressed her hand on his back, turned him to face her. 'William, I am with child.'

She watched for joy, for a change in his face, but it caught in the very expression it had had when she'd turned him around. She didn't understand.

'William?'

An enormous bolt of lightning, then another, flashed almost directly over the house. The grounds were illuminated, the trees the startled chorus of a Greek play. The features on William's face gradually shifted. His lips moved together as he looked at her in disbelief. He shook his head slowly and then glared at her with a sudden disgust. 'Whore,' he said, so quietly she hardly heard him. Then again, louder as he pushed her away, 'Whore!'

Rachel sat, almost speechless. The fire had been lit but the toddies never made. Jane had been sent to her bed and Mrs Cramond too, and Alasdair had poured two large measures of whisky, straight, into glasses for himself and for her.

'How long have you known this?' she asked him, when he had finished speaking.

'Ever since he returned from the Caribbean with that girl in tow. Everyone thought Hester was his, because why else would he have brought her back?'

'And did nobody question why he didn't acknowledge her? There are plenty of other men who do – I am sure I heard Mrs Hossack speak of it, in fact.'

Alasdair stared into his glass. 'It was assumed that his family wasn't keen on the connection. Can you imagine anyone thinking Morag Mackenzie would bring up his bastard?'

'That doesn't mean that Hester *isn't* William's.'

'No, but he told me himself. Because I did say he should acknowledge her, as a Christian duty and for his sake as well as hers. I laid it out to him quite clearly that God sees all and that what might be hidden from his neighbours was not hidden from God.'

'What did he say?'

'He said that the only neighbour whose business any of it was, was perfectly well-acquainted with the facts of the matter and that as God also already knew the truth, the world might speculate as it pleased because they would learn no more of it from him.'

'And the neighbour whose business it was? Janet Cameron, I suppose.'

'Yes. Hester is not William's daughter. She is the daughter of Duncan Cameron.'

Duncan Cameron had made himself such a nothing to Cromarty that Rachel had forgotten all about him. 'You mean Janet's husband – Ludo's father?'

Alasdair nodded. 'Not that Ludovic has lost anything by his absence. When Duncan left Scotland it was to be an overseer on William's father's plantation. Ludovic was a matter of months old, and I doubt Janet wasted a tear or a minute in missing Duncan Cameron. Anyway, Hester's mother was a slave on the estate – a field slave, I believe. She bore Cameron several children, but only Hester and a boy survived. The boy was sold on, I understand. Hester was allowed to stay with her mother. When Duncan was dying, he asked if William might free the girl, and take her back to Scotland, to be brought up by Janet.'

'And her mother?'

'He made no request concerning her.'

'She is not free?'

Alasdair looked away. 'I think not.'

'And she had no say in the matter of what happened to her daughter?'

Alasdair swallowed down what was left in his glass. 'I don't know.'

Rachel stared at him, her thoughts rushing around her head in a medley of incoherence. She looked at the glass in her hand and wondered for a moment how it had got there. None of this was the point, tonight. 'But this has no bearing on Charlotte's situation.'

Alasdair poured himself a second measure of whisky. 'It *does* though, Rachel. Men do not live as monks, in the Caribbean, you know. William did not live as a monk. He told me. He was careful at first – only some of the younger field slaves. And then when it seemed none of them had fallen pregnant, he moved onto the house slaves. None of them fell pregnant either.'

Rachel tried to swallow down her disgust at being forced to confront this new portrait of the man who had married her friend.

'What?' said Alasdair. 'You cannot think this does not happen, or that William was such a paragon?'

'I have hardly thought about it at all,' she answered slowly. 'But still, I do not see . . .'

'Most of the women with whom William had had liaisons subsequently fell pregnant to other men. Do you understand what I'm saying?'

'William cannot father a child,' she said at last.

Alasdair nodded. 'It's why he has only ever taken a lease on Cromarty estate and made no attempt to buy it. He says he knows he will never father a child of his own that he might leave anything to.'

'But Charlotte . . .' she said, stupidly.

'Aye,' Alasdair swallowed down the last of his whisky. 'Charlotte.'

It was sometime after two in the morning and the storm still raging that Alasdair's terrier, Budge, that slept at the top of the stairs, started barking. Rachel, who had been awake the whole night, sat up.

'Leave him,' murmured Alasdair, laying an arm across her. 'He does not like the thunder.'

'No,' said Rachel, shrugging off his arm as she threw back the covers to get out of bed, 'something is banging on the door.'

She lit a candle, but by the time she had reached the top of the stairs, the dog was jumping, half-demented, at the front door. Alasdair went down past her to undo the bolts. Standing there barefoot, the storm lashing a thin silk shawl around her nightgown and the slight swell of her stomach showing through the damp linen, was Charlotte.

Miss Juniper had allowed that the girls might sleep on, the morning after the ball, to recover themselves from the excitements of the previous night. She herself was just sitting down to a simple posset of warm milk and bread when the knocking came at the door. It was Rachel.

'My dear!' The old lady ushered her inside and closed the door on the already bright morning behind it. 'What in the world is it that has you here at this time in the morning?'

Rachel didn't even sit down. 'It's Charlotte.'

Miss Juniper looked at her old pupil, looked into her eyes and at the anguish on her face. Of course, it was Charlotte.

'What has happened?'

'She's with child.'

Rachel's face told her this was no occasion of joy. 'And you are going to tell me the child is not Sir William's.'

Rachel was desolate. 'Alasdair says it cannot be.' Then she looked at her old schoolmistress. 'How did you know?'

'Because they have been married over ten years and never a word of a pregnancy, never as much as a suspicion of it.' Miss Juniper sat across from Rachel. 'And because if it *were* Sir William's child, you would not be here looking as if the world was about to end. Where is she?'

'At the manse. Sir William has put her out.'

Miss Juniper put a hand to her chest. 'Oh no. He has discovered it?'

'She told him last night. She hoped to persuade him the child was his, but it seems . . . Alasdair says . . .'

'Do not be delicate, Rachel. It is past the point for delicacy.'

'He says Sir William has known for some years that he cannot father a child.'

'But Hester . . .' The words died on Miss Juniper's lips. 'Of course. Duncan Cameron. I have thought once or twice that Hester and Ludovic share a look about the mouth, an expression . . .'

A smile briefly flitted onto Rachel's face. 'Yes,' she said. 'I have seen it too, now that you say it. Does he know, do you think?'

Miss Juniper considered. 'Ludovic? I would think so. His mother is a sensible woman.'

'She is more than that,' said Rachel. 'To take on a child fathered by her husband out of wedlock . . .'

'I daresay she would rather have the daughter than the husband. And "out-of-wedlock" does not quite fit for what occurs on those plantations. But as to Charlotte, I fear out-of-wedlock may not be the worst she will hear. Who is the father?'

Rachel was wringing her hands as she had as a child, rubbing them almost red raw. Miss Juniper leaned forwards and gently separated them, as she had used to do in those days.

'She will not tell me.'

Miss Juniper sat back with a sigh. 'Foolish, foolish girl! And has she told Sir William?'

'She says not. She fears he would do something . . . ill-considered.'

'He has already done that in putting her out of the house,' said Miss Juniper. 'Half the town will know of it already.'

Rachel passed her handkerchief over her eyes then blew her nose. Red at the tip, as if it were the middle of winter, and here a beautiful morning in late July. As they sat there the old lady saw the girl of the past more and more shed the guise of minister's wife and revert to her younger self before her eyes.

'No one would have been about to see. It was in the middle of the night – the storm was still at full blast and there was not as much as a dog on the streets. We have told the manse servants they are not to mention her arrival to a soul. They will not think of countermanding Alasdair's warning.' She gave a great sigh. 'Perhaps William will have come to his senses. Perhaps no word of it will have emanated from Cromarty House. Yet.'

'Morag Mackenzie will be in her glory, should she discover it,' said Miss Juniper. 'But what does Mr Mackay say?'

This was the worst, and when Rachel met her old teacher's eye, it was all written there. Alasdair was a minister. Charlotte was an adulteress and the proof would soon be before the eyes of the world. She would face the humiliation and the censure of the kirk session. Charlotte's name and disgrace would be in every newspaper. Sir William would have no choice but to divorce her. She would not be forgiven.

'You must hold him off from informing the kirk session, Rachel.'

Rachel nodded. 'He has given me two weeks, supposing that Sir William himself does not broadcast it in that time.'

'He cannot wish to,' said Miss Juniper. 'But two weeks? What in the world can be done in that time? And if she will not say who the man is?'

Rachel looked down into her lap. 'I have wondered . . . about Major Munro.'

Just at that moment, a creak on the floorboard made them both look towards the stairs.

'Mairead!'

The girl was standing there in her nightdress, her cap askew and no stockings or slippers to her feet. She was staring the way she often did when she had woken from a nightmare, and her lips were slightly parted, as if she were summoning the courage to say something.

'What on earth are you doing standing on the stairs?' said Miss Juniper. 'How long have you been there?'

'I know,' said Mairead. 'I know who the father of Lady Charlotte's baby is.'

TWENTY-EIGHT

The Library Meets at the Manse of Resolis

Rachel had never known Alasdair so stony-faced. It was not like those times when his black dog hounded him and darkness fell over him like a mortcloth that nothing could permeate. This was resolution and conviction, and she could no more get past them than she could the black dog.

He had gone up to William in the night, fearing he would find him with his pistol in front of him, but William had assured him he would be saving his bullets for one more deserving, once he had discovered who the miscreant was. Alasdair had sat with him, watched him drink, reasoned with him through the small hours until dawn, before returning to the manse to inform Charlotte he had almost got her husband persuaded to as quiet a divorce as could be managed. A court case could not be avoided, but she should think herself lucky that she was in Scotland, not England where the dissolution of her marriage must be subject to an Act of Parliament. Her own best course would be to get as far from Cromarty as possible as soon as could be arranged and subsequently to persuade her lover to marry her. So much for the Common Law; as to the Law of God, she would be brought before Cromarty kirk session and he counselled her to look to her soul. Charlotte had faced him stoically; it was Rachel who had gone on her knees and begged Alasdair for a stay of execution for her friend and so he had agreed, through gritted teeth, to two weeks' grace before he informed the kirk session of her transgression. He had advised her then to name the man, for otherwise she would bear the opprobrium alone. This last Charlotte had refused to do.

And now, after her early morning visit to Miss Juniper's cottage, Rachel knew who it was, but she could not tell Alasdair if Charlotte would not. In any case, he all but refused to discuss the matter with her any more. When she'd gone into his study, he'd held up a hand. 'No, Rachel, I will not hear it. I will have no word more of Charlotte until after we have been today to Resolis.'

Resolis! She had forgotten, utterly forgotten that today, this afternoon, had been appointed for the penultimate exchange of books of the circulating library's first year. What had she even been reading? *Cyril Thornton.* A story about a man, of course, and the meek woman waiting until he had finished his military adventures and seeing what he wanted to see of the world before returning to marry her. And now she was to pass it to Charlotte. Perhaps Charlotte would like the humorous sections, though – the old uncle, the Highland funeral, the . . . but this was all nonsense.

'I cannot go to Resolis today,' she said. 'I must stay with Charlotte.'

'No, Rachel. Miss Juniper may come and sit with her. Enough that Charlotte is in this house, but *you* will not disappear from society along with her. God knows, you are already too much implicated . . .'

'*Implicated!* Alasdair, what do you accuse me of?'

He put down his pen and ran a hand over his eyes. 'Nothing. I accuse you of nothing. But you have been associated with Charlotte from childhood and will not easily be dissociated from her in the public mind. You must take every step to – to reinforce the fact that you are my wife. That is why you must come to the meeting of the library at Resolis today.'

Rachel sat down. She could not, in all honesty, have expected him to respond in any other way, and she would be of no help to Charlotte without Alasdair's authority behind her. If there was any word of last night's events circulating the town already, better she hear it where she could try to silence it. But oh, God, Micah!

'Alasdair, you are not going to tell Micah?'

'It will have to be discussed in Presbytery, Rachel.'

She thought frantically for a moment. 'That is three weeks away, a week after the kirk session.'

'Yes. But I will have to tell *him* before that, and before the session meets too.'

'But you promised, two weeks . . .'

'For what, though, Rachel? What is done cannot be undone.'

'Please, Alasdair. Do not tell Micah today.'

He bit his lip. 'I cannot tell him today anyway, with half of Cromarty in his house. Besides, he has some scheme on hand that will take up all of his attentions, and everyone else's.'

'What scheme?'

'Something we came upon when we were in Edinburgh, for the Assembly.' He hesitated. 'It may be nothing.'

'Oh,' she said, 'we are to be lectured on the controversies between the Evangelicals and the Moderates? I think I would rather listen to William discourse on the prospects of Reform.'

'William won't be there today, will he?' Alasdair's voice had an unwonted bitterness to it. 'William will be riding to Inverness, to consult with his lawyers about instituting proceedings of divorce against Charlotte. But no, what Micah has in view has nothing to do with the church controversy. And I think it likely, if his plan comes off, he will not waste two minutes on the matter of Charlotte's absence from the gathering.'

Rachel had no interest in whatever ploy it was that Dr Fraser had on hand. Whatever it was, it was enough for her that he would be too busy with his trick for her husband to think of telling him today of Charlotte's disaster.

They took an early dinner and rode to Resolis. Alasdair kept a little ahead of her, only looking round occasionally to see that she was not too far behind. He sat his horse as ever he did, but she imagined somehow a greater stiffness in his posture, a rebuke to herself. When they passed Ludo Cameron and the schoolmaster, on foot and also headed for Resolis, she kept her eyes rigid on her husband's back.

John watched the diminishing forms of the minister and his wife until they disappeared around a bend in the road. 'What a waste of a Saturday afternoon.'

'Why, what had you planned?' Ludo was perfectly happy walking along the firth road with his friend. There were few clouds in the sky and the breeze really was quite pleasant. He had already pointed out to John three seabirds whose names he had recently made a point of learning and which before their friendship he had never as much as wondered about. He did not even mind that their destination was Dr Fraser's manse. He would simply enjoy the journey there and back and try not to catch the doctor's eye in the intervening period. 'Of course,' he said, without waiting for any response from John, 'it would be more pleasant had Stanislas been able to come with us.'

'I think Stan has a more diverting afternoon planned than listening to Miss Elspeth's ideas on how we might all benefit from a greater understanding of the poems of Mrs Felicia Hemans, or what might be learned from the unfortunate fate of Lord Byron.'

'Mmm,' agreed Ludo. 'I would rather hear about that than what my mother has gleaned from her perusal of Captain Hall's *Travels in North America*, to say nothing of that Trollope woman's tome. There are certainly occasions on which I envy Stan that he has *not* been accepted quite into the first rank of society here.'

John gave a dismissive snort. 'Stanislas is used to mixing with a first rank of society many rungs more elevated than that of the Misses Rose and Sir William Mackenzie, though it were heresy in Cromarty to conceive of such a thing.'

Ludo broke a switch from the branch of a roadside tree and swatted at the verge as he walked. 'I wish he was not leaving.' He gave a decided swish to an early mushroom, cutting off its head. 'I am very happy for him, of course, that he has this opportunity.'

John bent briefly to examine the unfortunate fungus. 'Yes, we shall miss him, you and I.' He straightened again, brushing his hands on the front of his trousers. 'But not as much as Miss Middleton will, I think.'

Ludo said nothing, but began to ruminate his lips in a manner John had come to recognise as a wrestling on the horns of a dilemma. A few yards more and Ludo pursed his lips decisively. A confidence was about to be shared. 'I believe there is something approaching the nature of an understanding, if not quite yet an engagement between them.'

John raised his eyebrows. 'Did Hester tell you this?'

A clearing of the throat and a furious batting of the eyelashes then, 'Ahm, no.'

'Miss Mairead Buchan told you!'

Ludo's cheeks were now almost scarlet.

John clapped him on the shoulder. 'Well, well, we shall come to that later, but first, Stan. And Miss Middleton.'

The cat now out of the bag, Ludo chased happily after it. 'It was really at the picnic yesterday that it all came out. He made mention of his forthcoming shift to London and Miss Middleton took something of a turn and was quite unable to hide her disappointment. Tears had almost been brought into play, but Stanislas asked permission to write and all was well.'

'Permission to write,' repeated John.

'Yes. But *then*, at the Gardeners' ball, you will have noted Stanislas and Miss Middleton danced together quite often . . .'

'I did. They danced together almost the entire evening. I also noted that you and—'

'Well, yes,' interrupted Ludo. 'But at some point between the tasting of the lemon syllabub and the first flash of lightning it seems suggestions were made that Stan hoped to establish himself in the world, and that he hoped whilst he was doing so Miss Middleton might not pledge her heart elsewhere . . .'

'They are engaged!'

Ludo nodded. 'Unofficially. Secretly. Yes.'

'Well, well, well.' John contemplated this happy news for a few minutes before saying, very casually, 'And of course it was very fortunate that you were able to step in, quite so often as you did last night, to ensure that her friend Miss Buchan did not have to play the wallflower.'

'Well,' Ludo was indignant, 'I hardly think there was much danger of *that*. There were half a dozen farm lads at her every time my back was turned!'

John frowned at him. 'I think I only saw her dance once with someone else. But please put down the stick. You are in danger of taking out my eye.'

'What? Oh, yes, sorry.' Ludo cast aside his switch. 'But that clodhopper George Ross *was* inexcusably persistent. If I had not had to keep my eye so much on Hester, he should never have got near.'

'Hester? You mean because of Farquhar Hossack?'

'He was hardly away from her the whole night. It's been the same at the hotel, since he came back from Aberdeen. You know, Mr Gilfeather noticed it in the coffee room and spoke of it to Mrs Gilfeather who spoke to my mother. Even Mr Isaac Fordyce has remarked on it, and said Hester should not be left alone with Fachie.'

'I take it Hester does not welcome his advances?'

It was the first time John had seen Ludovic truly angry. 'Welcome them! How should she welcome them! How could any decent woman welcome them! And I assure you, my s— my mother's maidservant is nothing if she is not a decent and respectable young woman.'

John held up a hand. 'I'm sorry, Ludo. You must forgive me. I did not mean to imply that there could be anything improper in Hester's conduct. I just thought it possible that Fachie might comport himself differently around her, if he had genuine feelings . . .'

Ludo stared at him, shook his head and walked on. 'How is it possible that you have been here the best part of two years, and you still don't understand anything about anyone?'

Elspeth cast her expert eye around Dr Fraser's drawing room, which she knew to be hardly in use from one year's end to the next. All was precisely as it should be, nothing but in the best and most modest taste. Not a thing changed in twenty years. Mrs Swanson was unassailable in her housekeeping and Miss Elspeth thought it a pity that there had not been a bigger household at the manse on which her talents might have been exercised. All chance of that, though, had gone with the young Mrs Fraser at her first and only confinement, and the baby with her. People had expected Dr Fraser to marry again, in due course, but he had not done so. Somehow, the man contained within him that family there should have been, and people had come to realise that there was no room for anyone else.

Yet here was a new parlourmaid come in to offer them refreshments, while they waited with Mr Fordyce for Dr Fraser's return from a call to a congregant's dying.

'Well, my word,' opened Mr Fordyce, 'but this is a new face, if I am not mistaken?'

'Yes, sir.' The girl made an uncertain curtsy. 'I am just this week started in Dr Fraser's service.'

'And that is an Edinburgh accent.' Miss Elspeth's observation was more in the form of an accusation than a question.

'Yes, ma'am,' said the young woman, setting down her

tray before hastily departing, having besought that they should ring the bell if they needed her.

'Well!' said Miss Elspeth before the drawing room door was rightly closed.

'An Edinburgh parlourmaid,' said Miss Anna. 'What do you think it might signify, Elspeth?'

Miss Elspeth had to confess herself stumped as to what the doctor was about, and so the sisters appealed to the greater worldly experience of Mr Fordyce. Mr Fordyce gave thought to the question as he sipped at his elder wine. 'Perhaps,' he said finally, 'there are some new fashions amongst the domestics that Dr Fraser has come upon in Edinburgh and which he wishes to introduce to the Black Isle, though I cannot think for the life of me what they can be.'

'Perhaps,' ventured an emboldened Miss Anna, 'she is the poor distant relative of some parishioner here in Resolis, whom Dr Fraser has taken into service as an act of charity.'

'There is no shortage of such poor relatives on the doctor's doorstep,' countered Miss Elspeth. 'And I cannot think that any domestic fashion Mrs Swanson is not already mistress of can require to be introduced to the Black Isle, be it of Edinburgh or not.' Thus chastised, Mr Fordyce and Miss Anna kept any further thoughts on Dr Fraser's new parlourmaid to themselves and resumed their earlier dissection of the Gardeners' procession and ball. Miss Elspeth kept her eye on the road, for signs of the gig from Cromarty House.

First to appear were Mr Mackay and Willie Hossack riding almost abreast, Hossack on his sturdy old workhorse clearly making some long point to the minister. A little further back than Elspeth thought quite proper, was the minister's wife. The girl had a disconsolate look on her face and should really have been sitting with a straighter back. The first Mrs Mackay had been a fine horsewoman, although of course there had been other deficiencies.

Next over the brae were Ludovic Cameron and the schoolmaster. There was no sign of Janet Cameron, of course, and Elspeth thought for the hundredth time what a waste it had been inviting the woman to become part of the library. When she had challenged Sir William, privately, as to what he was about in suggesting it, he had simply said, 'She heard me discussing it one day in the coffee room and asked. She likes to read.' The latter point had so disarmed Elspeth that she had been unable to make a response. Much benefit might the rest of the members accrue from Janet Cameron's reading, when she was too busy to discuss it with them. Elspeth would certainly make the point at the annual general meeting, to take place in September. There were other ladies who might more usefully be invited to join in Mrs Cameron's stead, and in her bleaker moments Elspeth almost regretted that Arabella Juniper was not a possibility.

Elspeth continued to look towards the road and Mr Fordyce rose to greet every new arrival until such time as Dr Fraser himself might appear to take over the role of host. There was no sign yet of Sir William on his favourite hunter or of the gig from Cromarty House, and then Mr Mackay explained that Sir William was called away to business in

Inverness, and that Lady Charlotte was indisposed. In her quiet disappointment, Elspeth forgot her curiosity about Dr Fraser's new housemaid.

The Reverend Dr Micah Fraser breathed deep as he strode down the fields from Donnie Manson's croft towards his own house. The peewits and redshanks and countless other birds were swooping and calling over Udale Bay, but Donnie Manson that had known the cry of every one of them was no longer of this world. 'Well done, good and faithful servant.' How often had Micah yearned to hear those words himself? But it was not his time. The Lord had made him hale and hearty and there was work in this world to be done before he could go to his rest. He could see the manse, like a sharp white stone folded in the dip of the valley beneath him, sparkling there and full of sinners. Books, was it, they thought they had come to talk of? Micah braced his shoulders and strode on. He was ready.

He went in by the back door. Bella Swanson was standing over her plates of petticoat tails and sugar teacakes and almond wafers, explaining all to the lassie. An Edinburgh lodging house was all very well, but Mrs Swanson had a reputation of forty years' standing that she was not willing to see ruined in the minister's own dining parlour! The lassie bobbed a curtsy and said, 'Yes, Mrs Swanson,' as if she was embarking on her life's work, instead of an interlude that would take her far, far away from this house and never over its door again.

'You haven't been into the drawing room now, Louisa?'

'Only to the two ladies and the old gentleman.'

'The Misses Rose and Mr Fordyce were here early,' explained Mrs Swanson. 'I sent Teenie through instead when the rest of them began to arrive.'

'Quite right, quite right,' said Dr Fraser. It was a nice touch, he thought. Elspeth and Anna Rose would be having such a good clack about his new parlourmaid, the effect would only be heightened. And poor Teenie, though still not entirely convinced she was not to be usurped by the newcomer and put out on the road, nodded, as if she knew what was going on.

'Miss Elspeth was awful keen to know what Louisa was all about, but I told her I didn't know.'

'Quite right,' said Dr Fraser again. 'You're a good girl, Teenie, and a credit to us.'

Teenie pinked and was so overwhelmed at the praise that she curtsied to minister and housekeeper both.

'And remember, Louisa,' said Dr Fraser, addressing the newest addition to their household, 'when I ring two bells, you will come and you need fear nothing, for I will be there every minute.'

The young woman nodded, a determined look in her eye. 'Yes, Dr Fraser, I'll remember.'

Then Micah Fraser strode into his drawing room, clapping his hands as he surveyed his guests. 'Well, well, a fine day for our gathering, but I do not see Sir William Mackenzie or Lady Charlotte. All is well at Cromarty House, I hope?'

What appeared to him to be a very significant glance passed between Alasdair Mackay and his wife before Alasdair spoke up. 'Sir William had some business at Inverness that would not keep and Lady Charlotte – was not disposed to come without him.'

'Well, we shall muddle along without them. They will have sent on their books?'

Rachel Mackay started to mumble something as to why they had not but was drowned out by Miss Elspeth Rose. 'This is why a suitable location for keeping the books between times must be secured. I will be proposing most strongly that Mr Gilfeather speaks to Mrs Cameron about a cabinet in the coffee room . . .'

'Quite so,' agreed Dr Fraser. 'But where is the estimable Mrs Cameron?'

Ludovic swallowed. Oh, what a fish the boy could be sometimes, thought Micah. 'She sends her apologies, but with the work of the Gardeners' ball last night, she has not the time to attend upon the library, but says you must call at the hotel when you are finished with your latest book and you and she shall have a good talk about it over a pot of coffee.'

Miss Elspeth bridled yet again. 'This is quite irregular and it is a pity Mr Gilfeather could not be here to give his view on it. This is not a private library. How is intellect to be encouraged and understanding fostered if opinions are not available for all to hear?'

'Well, no one could complain of your opinion not being

available,' commented Willie Hossack. 'But here, Dr Fraser, I have to ride onto Dingwall today, so might we get on with it? You're come late, as it is.'

'I am sure Donnie Manson would greatly regret having inconvenienced you, Mr Hossack, but as you are in such a hurry, you will no doubt be succinct in giving your opinion of your book?'

'Succinct enough,' said Willie Hossack decisively, laying the two volumes of Charles MacFarlane's *Constantinople in 1828* on the table in front of him. 'My opinion is that they'll bear a watching yet, the Turks. And now, minister, you have had my opinion and I am ready to take my tea, or is everyone to give their view of the book they have just finished with before the kettle is hung over the fire? I doubt we will all be dead of thirst before then.'

There was no denying Willie Hossack was on a short fuse that seemed to get shorter the longer his son was at home. Dr Fraser could not blame the man, but he was going too far. Miss Elspeth's fingers were twitching, as if she yearned to have her pen in them, adding another note to the already lengthy memorandum she was composing for the annual general meeting. He foresaw propositions and blackballing. 'A wee while yet,' he wanted to say to her, 'there's more to come.'

Despite Hossack's curt review, others who had read it fell to sharing their own thoughts on *Constantinople*, its literary merits, their preferred scenes and what had astonished them. Miss Anna expressed the hope that at least the author would not play the tricks upon his reader that she had encountered in her perusal of *Hajji Baba*, which she had really not found very amusing at all. Mr Fordyce gently reminded her that the Turks and the Persians were quite different people, but she could not entirely get the distinction clear in her mind, protesting that she was certain they were all Mohammedans. She hoped that Mr MacFarlane had reported what he himself had seen, and not invented ridiculous characters that he claimed had written the book. She did not like this fashion for people who wrote books pretending that they were other people.

As her sister was telling her she made a fool of herself and must surely understand there were different literary forms and that artifice in novel-writing had its place, Dr Fraser came to Miss Anna's rescue. 'But Miss Anna is right. People should not present themselves to the world in any character other than their own. Now, I think I must ring for the tea.' He rang the bell twice then bent to speak more quietly to Elspeth Rose.

'You must forgive me, Miss Rose,' he confided, 'but the book Mrs Cameron wishes to discuss with me is Captain Hall's recent account of his *Travels in North America*. Young Ludovic has spoken of taking ship for those parts, as you know, and, given the absence of a father to guide him, Mrs Cameron wishes to take my advice privately on it.'

'The best thing Duncan Cameron did for that boy was to take himself to the other side of the ocean and not come back.'

'You have it exactly, Miss Elspeth. But look now, here is young Louisa, with our tea.'

Everyone in the drawing room gradually turned in anticipation of the delights to be brought through from the manse kitchen. Everyone, that is, save for the doctor himself and the schoolmaster.

John Learmonth was at first too taken up with some gentle raillery of his friend Ludovic to pay any attention to the entrance of the housemaid. He thanked Miss Elspeth as she passed him his cup, but Ludovic's scanning of the approaching tray of cakes and confections caused him to look up too, and when he did so his face changed in a manner every bit as gratifying as Dr Fraser had hoped for. The young man forgot his wonted composure and actually stared, for a moment, his mouth a little open, and something in his eyes akin to horror.

'We have just been saying – have we not, Elspeth,' twittered Miss Anna, 'that you have got a new parlourmaid, Dr Fraser. I hope Teenie is not leaving?'

Poor Teenie, in the act of bringing the teapot in to set on the trivet, flushed and lifted her eyes to the doctor in piteous appeal.

'Indeed, Miss Anna, I would not hear of Teenie leaving and no more would Mrs Swanson. Yon pig-man of Kenny Anderson's has a deal more courting and walking home from the kirk of a Sunday before I would begin to entertain his suit for the hand of so worthy a housemaid.'

Teenie, in her relief and mortification, could not prevent

a scandalised, 'Dr Fraser!' from escaping her lips before hurrying to the kitchen to fetch the sugar, which had been forgotten.

Dr Fraser beamed after her, chuckling. 'No, Teenie shall stay, but Mrs Swanson tells me I am a most provoking man to look after so Louisa has come to share the burden of the household a while.' He would let Learmonth stew a bit longer.

'From Edinburgh, I believe?' enquired Miss Elspeth, the bit once more between her teeth.

'Indeed,' said the doctor. 'Mr Mackay and I lodged in a most respectable house while we were at the late Assembly in May, did we not, Alasdair?'

'A very well-run establishment,' agreed the other minister.

'And while there, we first met young Louisa here, who helped her mother run the house. But Louisa's good and sensible mother was worried that her daughter did not thrive in the town and thought she would be the better of a change of air and so it was arranged that she might come here a while, to restore her . . . health.'

Rachel Mackay looked somewhat quizzically at her husband as the doctor told his tale, before saying to the housemaid, 'I hope it will suit you well here, in Resolis. I am sure Dr Fraser's household is less taxing than an Edinburgh lodging house.'

'Thank you, ma'am,' said Louisa holding out the plate of almond wafers before moving on. When she arrived in front of John Learmonth she said suddenly, 'Mr Lamont, you are here!'

And Dr Fraser was glad he had reminded Mrs Swanson only to look out the second-best crockery, for the cup the schoolmaster had been holding fell from his fingers and smashed into the fireplace, in at least a dozen pieces.

TWENTY-NINE

A True History of Mr John Learmonth

It was well after eight when they left Micah's manse for the ride home. The tide was out and the seabirds made an elegant stage of the mudflats of Udale Bay. The air was almost still. 'The midges will be wild across the water tonight,' Dr Fraser had observed as he'd seen them off. There would be plenty of light yet to guide the members of the library safe back to Cromarty. The honeysuckle, tumbling around the hawthorn and hedgerows, filled the air with scents that were almost indecent. Alasdair's mood seemed to have softened a little, as it often did in Micah's company. There was only room for one great emotional force when Micah was in a room and all else must be edified or crushed by it. As they rode up the brae from the manse towards Newhall bridge and the Cromarty road, Rachel wondered which of those fates awaited John Learmonth.

'What was this great revelation you thought Micah had for us? All I saw was that he had got another housemaid, who thought she knew Mr Learmonth but didn't seem to know his name.'

'Then you saw but you did not understand.'

'Alasdair, I will turn this pony round in the road and go back and ask Micah to his face, if you do not tell me.' She would not do this. Dr Fraser had asked the schoolteacher to remain behind a while, saying he had a private matter to discuss with him, and Rachel had no wish to find herself in any way part of that conversation or, even worse, to be forced to accept John Learmonth's escort back to Cromarty. 'Are you telling me the great revelation is something to do with the housemaid?'

Rachel thought for a minute he was going to put her off again, but he screwed shut his eyes a minute then opened them. 'Yes, Rachel, that is exactly what I am telling you.'

John was conscious of no sound within Dr Fraser's study but that of the moving pendulum on the longcase clock in the corner. Ludo had wanted to wait for him, but the minister had all but bundled him out of the door and into Mr Fordyce's carriage where the Rose sisters were already seated and impatient to be gone, Miss Anna worrying that they wouldn't get past the trees at the edge of the Newhall estate before the bats came out. The last thing John heard before the door shut on the sound of the departing carriage was Dr Fraser calling that they need not worry – should his business with Mr Learmonth take too long, they would soon find him a corner in the manse where he might lay his head.

John considered his options. He might stand his ground and tell the Resolis minister to go to Hell, but truly, he knew that, were one of them destined for that place, it was unlikely to be the burly Highlander. He looked at the window of the minister's study, the sash already up, and pictured himself clambering out into the orchard beyond, like a schoolboy fleeing his classroom. But what then? It had always been going to come to this, somewhere. Where would he run to that he would not be found? He would have done better to have gone to a city, where no one is known, than to this northern place, where everyone is known, be there a hundred miles and as many mountains and firths and lochs between them. He sat on the chair Dr Fraser had indicated he should take, noting the identical empty chair next to it.

The heartiness of Dr Fraser's manner to his departing guests was put away at the door after the last of them left, and the man who presently took his seat across the solid oak desk from John had a face like a frozen rock. He said nothing, but staring without the hint of a blink, he picked up the bell on his desk and rang it. Twice.

John did not turn around when the door opened. He heard the almost-forgotten footsteps, caught something of that almost-forgotten scent as she came into the study and stopped by the chair beside him. He continued to look straight ahead.

'Louisa,' said the Doctor, 'take that seat there, if you will.'

'Yes, Dr Fraser,' she said, taking the empty chair.

'Now, I charge you to say honestly, as God is your witness and sees all our actions and the very workings of our hearts, do you know this man?'

'Yes, Dr Fraser, I do,' she said. 'It is Mr John Lamont, that lodged in my mother's house in Edinburgh in the years 1829 and 1830 and went to classes at the Divinity Hall of the university.'

Dr Fraser turned a glower on John. 'You do not deny this?'

John felt his shoulders slump. 'No,' he said, 'I do not deny it.'

'And what is this man "John Lamont" to you, Louisa?'

'He is my husband, sir.'

Again John felt the minister's eyes on him. 'And do you deny this?'

'No,' he said, hardly able to articulate the sound. 'Though I may wish to deny it, I cannot.'

'No,' said Rachel. 'This cannot be.'

'Well, Micah is convinced it is the truth, and I must own to believing the young woman myself. She seems a decent, respectable person and her mother's is a decent, respectable house. Why should either of them concoct a tale that does no good to the reputation of the daughter and could do nothing but harm the trade of the mother's boarding house?'

'And she believes John Learmonth and this "John Lamont" are one and the same?'

'The names are easily enough mixed. A divinity student

by the name of John Lamont came to them about three years ago or so. Mrs Gavin – that is the mother's name – had long provided lodgings for two or three such young men in an attic room of her house. Her daughter, naturally enough, assisted her mother in the running of the establishment. You may guess what happened – an attachment was formed, but it was understood, particularly on Mrs Gavin's advisement, that matters should proceed no further until such time as Mr Lamont was established at least in a schoolmaster's post. The young man, as young men will, became impatient and persuaded the daughter – Louisa, whom you saw today – to contract a secret marriage with him. The foolish girl went along with him, but like so many before her she found her folly outlasted her bliss, for Lamont soon repented of his hasty action and discovered he was perhaps not quite so much in love at all.'

Rachel had difficulty speaking. 'He abandoned her.'

Alasdair nodded. 'He abandoned her, but only after attempting to convince her that as their marriage had been contracted and conducted in secret, they might each walk away from it as if it had never been, and no one be any the wiser. There would be no harm done.'

'No harm! But her character! She . . .'

'Yes. But she was of stronger mettle than he. She told him that she was his wife in law and in fact, but most of all in the eyes of God, and such she would not deny and intended to remain.'

'This is why he fled to Cromarty.'

'Yes. We made enquiries about our "John Learmonth" amongst the young men of the Divinity Hall. We learned from some of the more senior students that two or three years ago there had been two friends amongst them whose names were forever being mixed up – John Learmonth and John Lamont. The *real* John Learmonth, who did indeed hail from the East Lothian village our interloper claims to be from, took ship for Quebec at about the same time as *our* schoolmaster set foot on the smack for Cromarty. Micah is certain that the two exchanged their certificates and thus their names. He suspects money also changed hands. It seems the absconding husband calculated that should his abandoned wife take it into her head to look for him, she would find herself crossing the Atlantic. And so "John Learmonth", his certificates and letters of recommendation in order, felt himself safe in answering our advertisement for a suitably qualified schoolmaster. He took the first and farthest away opportunity to come his way and it landed him here where he lied to all our faces. And Micah has found him out.'

Rachel could hardly believe it. At last, she said, 'Do you think anyone else knows – Ludovic? James Craig?'

Alasdair shook his head. 'I have heard them bait him myself, for casting up all the opportunities Edinburgh has to offer in exchange for our little schoolroom. I have never been entirely convinced by his claims that he was drawn here by the newspaper columns of the *Cromarty Correspondent* and a desire to visit the ancient graveyards of the north.'

'We were all taken in,' she said.

'Not all. Micah saw it from the first – a wariness about him, an air of obfuscation. I had the feeling Learmonth sought to avoid me as much as possible. I persuaded myself that my dislike of him was grounded in my insecurities about you. But Micah – who, let us be honest, knows from long experience what it looks like when a man is trying to avoid him – saw it. After the dinner we had at our manse, he was suspicious of Learmonth's aversion to discussing his home and any sweethearts therein, but an exchange of letters with the Presbytery at Dunbar reassured him of "John Learmonth's" *bona fides* – for a time at least. But our schoolmaster had slipped up when he'd given Micah the name of his Edinburgh landlady. It was an easy enough thing to find her. She knew nothing of a John Learmonth, only a John Lamont, and eventually the whole story of her daughter's abandonment came out.'

'So, Micah brought her here to confront him.' Rachel closed her eyes. 'I pray God that he is mistaken.'

'But surely it would be a good thing for the young woman to find resolution in her predicament and he be forced to acknowledge his obligations as a Christian and a man?'

'Yes.' Rachel's voice almost died away 'But if he is married to that housemaid, he cannot marry Charlotte when William divorces her, can he?'

'Charlotte?' Then he understood. 'John Learmonth is the father of Charlotte's child?'

'Yes,' she said, 'I believe he is.'

*

Dusk had fallen by the time they reached home, and the bats were swooping and swirling from the trees at Cromarty House over to St Regulus graveyard and then to the manse, safe in their territory regardless of what passed amongst the humans below.

Miss Juniper had returned to her girls at supper time, Mrs Cramond having promised she would send for her, should Lady Charlotte waken before Mrs Mackay arrived home. Extinguishing all but one candle, Rachel took up the vigil, and when they were alone, she took Charlotte's hand and wept. 'All will be well,' Miss Juniper had used to say to them, but all would never be well again.

After a moment she felt Charlotte's fingers move in her hand and saw her eyes open.

'You,' Charlotte said with a smile.

'Yes, my darling. Me.'

'I'm so sorry, Rachel.'

Rachel shook her head. 'I don't understand though, Charlotte. The schoolmaster – why?'

Charlotte stared at her and then closed her eyes as if it would shut out the fact of what Rachel had just said. 'How do you know?'

Rachel had hoped, even now, that Mairead had been wrong. 'Good God, Charlotte. What were you thinking of? And to think of Charles Munro and how he felt for you and how honourable he was . . .'

At this Charlotte broke down entirely. 'I know! I know! Do you not think I would kill myself this very minute were it not for the child? It was because of Charles that it happened.' There was a look of terror on her face. 'But how did you know?'

Rachel wet her lips. 'You were seen with him. In the grounds of Shandwick House.'

'Oh, God. Seen!' Charlotte put her head in her hands.

'No. Not – that. Not entirely seen. Just – you were seen being led by him, into the woods. Very late at night.'

'Who?'

'One who will not speak of it to anyone else. But you must tell me, Charlotte – did he force you?'

Charlotte was desolate. 'No.' She took in a breath and closed her eyes again, summoning her strength. 'It was the second night of our visit. Charles had appeared with Captain Ross, if you remember.'

Rachel remembered. She had thought the major must be the father of Charlotte's child.

'I had seen him – Charles – by chance in Tain that day. We had – a moment, I suppose you might call it, in the collegiate church. It was the most perfect moment of my life and I thought it would sustain me until I might one day see him again. When he appeared at Shandwick House, my hopes ran wild – I thought he had not been able to part with me after all, but then he left again. That is when my reserves abandoned me. I felt lost, destroyed almost. I could not see how I might exist without him. I got up in the night intent on walking down to the sea and ending my misery. But John Learmonth suddenly appeared in the grounds. God knows what he had in mind, but I think he was looking for you. He seemed angry somehow. But one desperate creature recognises another, and he realised what I was about. He would not let me carry on to the shore. I struggled against him and he had to hold onto me hard. Our bodies were very close and we were two lost, desperate people who by increments of madness gave vent to our desolation in each other. I lay down in the woods like a common tramp, Rachel. He begged my forgiveness afterwards, as if he could not quite believe what had occurred. I was at such a distance from my own self that I hardly believed what it had done. I told myself it had not, and for a time I believed that, until nature began to show me her proofs otherwise.' Charlotte sat back on her pillows, the confession having exhausted her.

'Does he know about the child?'

Charlotte shook her head. 'We have not spoken to one another since. I hoped I might persuade William the child was his, but . . .' She gave a small and bitter laugh. 'So now the schoolmaster is to be informed that he must move on from Cromarty and that when William has managed to divorce me, he must marry me. Oh, how he will wish he had never set foot in this town.'

'Charlotte,' Rachel said, 'John Learmonth cannot marry you.'

'But he must! You heard what Alasdair said William's terms are – I am to leave here, and be divorced, and he will maintain me and the child until that time, then the father must marry me. John Learmonth *must* marry me.'

Rachel took both of Charlotte's hands in hers. 'He cannot marry you, Charlotte. His name is not even John Learmonth, and he already has a wife.'

Alasdair was in his study. It was almost time for family worship, and he would have to compose himself, for the servants were already curious enough about why Lady Charlotte Mackenzie was ensconced in one of the manse bedchambers after arriving in the middle of the night, in a storm. He was opening his Bible to find the right passage when a terrible cry from upstairs almost made him drop the book. Telling the servants to stay in the kitchen, he ran for the stairs.

Charlotte was crumpled on the floor by the bed, like a discarded heap of linen, and Rachel was leaning over her, her face alabaster.

'What's happened? What's wrong?' he asked his wife.

'I told her. The truth about Learmonth, or Lamont or whatever his name is.'

Charlotte raised her head then to look at him. Her eyes were red hollows and her hair all dishevelled. 'I am lost, at last, Alasdair. Lost. I think you always knew it. I think you saw into my soul.'

'I told William not to marry you. I wish he had listened.'

'Alasdair!' Rachel was horrified, but what good was it to pretend any more, what good had it done keeping from his wife that every time he looked at Charlotte he saw that same detachment from her own life that he had seen in Elizabeth? God had taken Elizabeth before her disgrace had exposed itself to the world, but Charlotte had ensured that *her* disgrace would be paraded for all to see. He should have made William listen. Too late. Too late.

Then Rachel was in front of him, as if Charlotte was not there, collapsed on the floor. 'If William is determined on throwing her off and Learmonth cannot marry her, what is to happen to her?'

He looked around the disordered room. 'I don't know.'

'Put me out.' Charlotte hauled herself up and gripped the edge of the bedstead. 'Put me out on the road to take my chances. The cholera is almost at the door anyway. Have you not heard? William told me two days ago – he had seen it in the paper. It is on a Revenue cruiser out in Cromarty Bay. Put me out on the road and let me take my chances. I am finished anyway.'

PART FOUR

Late Summer/Early Autumn, 1832

THIRTY

August

The Roup of Cromarty House

In Miss Juniper's cottage, there was none of the usual activity of preparing for the morning's lessons. The excitements of the previous evening, when the packages labelled with their names – Miss Arabella Juniper, Miss Alicia Middleton, Miss Mairead Buchan – had arrived by cart down from Cromarty House, had now given way to the truths of a sombre dawn: Lady Charlotte was gone, and she was never coming back.

The gifts for Miss Juniper had been sorted and put away – the beautiful lacquered tea chest from Lady Charlotte's own parlour into the dresser, the Turkish shawl folded and laid in a drawer, a pretty carriage clock set by Miss Juniper's bed, the golden locket that opened to reveal portraits of Charlotte and Rachel that Sir William had had done as a wedding gift to his wife hung around the old lady's neck. Their teacher, usually so talkative from morning to night, had been very quiet as they had taken their bread and milk, and then said that she felt the need of a walk, by herself, and that perhaps they might look over their French lesson again, in preparation for their visit to Madame Perrin's in the afternoon.

It was just as she'd been going out of the door that Mairead had got up the courage to ask her where she was walking to, and Miss Juniper had said she really didn't know. Which was the worst thing Mairead had ever heard her say, but still she would not let the girls go with her. Off out into the morning she had gone, the locket round her neck and her old brown shawl about her shoulders, like a poor lost sparrow with a broken wing.

So Mairead and Alicia went upstairs, to practise their French. Their books, though, remained closed, as Alicia instantly began to discourse, in French, on the loveliness of the two dresses sent down for her from Cromarty House, with a handwritten card from Lady Charlotte, *Because we are the same size, and you must be properly fitted out when you make your entrance into the drawing rooms of London*. Alicia had slept with the card under her pillow and on waking her hand had found it so it was the first thing she read that morning. And now she was wondering, for the hundredth time, how long it might be before Stanislas was sufficiently established in his new position that they might marry and she make her entrance to those London drawing rooms, and whether the dresses would still be in fashion.

Mairead had sighed with Alicia over the dresses for as

long as she had been able to pretend interest. It was the half-finished tapestry, complete with the requisite threads that Lady Charlotte had also sent down for Alicia that really interested her. 'Oh, dear, if only it were that simple,' Miss Juniper had somewhat gnomically said when the tapestry had emerged from the package, 'but Charlotte always did have the most peculiar notions.'

Mairead's package had contained no dresses. Mairead and Lady Charlotte were most certainly *not* the same size and she was glad that Lady Charlotte had not attempted to pretend they were. Instead, there was a profusion of ribbons, of almost every shade, and another shawl that, as both Alicia and Miss Juniper remarked, picked out the gold and russet tints of Mairead's hair and the green of her eyes quite perfectly. There had been no half-finished embroidery for her, Mairead had been pleased to see, but instead a framed map of North America, which had its own note attached. *'I had once thought to travel here but will not do so now. I think that you had better have it.'* It was to Mairead what the dresses were to Alicia, and she resolved to study and know every inch of it.

The cottage was far enough down the lane from Church Street that they were not much bothered by the sounds of people going to the viewing up at Cromarty House or to the roup in the courthouse afterwards. The girls thought of their future, not lingering too long on the sadnesses of someone else's past.

★

It was a grey rain that came from Strathconon. Everything was grey – firth, hills, sky – as if summer had grown weary of Scotland. The horses were relentless in grinding out the miles down the west side of the Black Isle. Charlotte would not have them relent. Should they fall down dead in their traces, she would get out of the carriage and walk; supposing her feet were bare, she would walk.

But her feet were not bare, and the horses were not tiring. One checkpoint then another they passed, at every bridge, every crossroads, they were questioned by the watch ordained by the county health board to check for vagrants coming in from affected places, bringing the cholera with them. Where could they possibly come from that was *not* at the mercy of the contagion? Where could they go? Charlotte tried to put all thought of the cholera from her mind and to concentrate on the rhythm of the horses. They seemed as much imbued with their mission as she was, as, beside her, Morag Mackenzie was. The witch sat there, unmoving, in her deep black, almost the only thing Charlotte could see that was not grey. Grey would be too light and joyful a colour for Morag, but oh, how much rejoicing there must be today in that coal-black heart.

William had not returned from that visit more than two weeks ago to his lawyer in Inverness. His man had been sent back to give instructions – about the packing and sending on of Sir William's things, the marking of the furniture and paintings for sale, the closing up of the house. The estate would continue to be farmed and the household servants kept on, doing next to nothing until William was able to give up the lease. It had been given out that his affairs in the Caribbean, some unrest amongst the slaves on his plantation, had called him to Glasgow, and from there he would take ship and cross the Atlantic. Perhaps that's where he would actually go. Charlotte had not been informed.

Alasdair spoke without turning around from the mirror, where he was in the act of tying the white cravat at his neck. Rachel knew his mind was on the previous evening's meeting of the town Health Board, but eventually he managed to force himself to say something. 'Was she all right?' he asked at last.

Rachel was sitting on the bed, still almost numb. 'Better than I was.'

Alasdair made no response to this. He pulled on his black jacket, sorting his lapels, checking on his cuffs. 'And will you go up again, later?'

'What, to the house? You do know what day it is?'

'Yes, Rachel, I know what day it is. It is Friday, the seventeenth of August, and at noon precisely, in the court-house commences the roup of Cromarty House and all its appurtenances. I thought you might wish to go up to the house, for a last look round. There's no telling when it might be opened up again, or who might have it when it does.'

Rachel shook her head. 'I know they are only material things, Alasdair, but it saddens me to think of the house empty, those things that gave her joy all gone to boxes and lots, put away to be handed to the highest bidder.'

He turned around and looked down at her. 'Those things gave her joy for half an hour, half a day, if William was lucky, and any sadness I have is for him. Everything that has befallen Charlotte, she has brought upon herself.'

'You are too harsh. Charlotte hoped for happiness in her marriage, just as I did. She was not lucky, as I have been, but she did hope. It is hard to see the world around me empty itself of her, erase her.'

He reached for his hairbrush and began to pull it through his hair. 'Charlotte is not dead, Rachel. Have you thought of all who might lose their livelihoods to a higher bidder today? Men, women and children who believed themselves secure until her actions forced William to quit Cromarty and give up his lease on the property. Shops, inns, farms, houses, even the brewery – Sanders Gilfeather tells me that more than half the clients of the bank are already at the very limit of the rent they can go to and can pay no more. Should some stranger come with the money to outdo them, they will be out on the road and no option but to take their chances on one of those boats.' He flung out an arm towards the window, and beyond it the sea and the latest ships, waiting to depart for the Americas. Such was the strength of his feeling that the hairbrush flew from his hand and hit the window. They both stared at it and he went to pick it up, calming himself as he did so. 'I'm sorry. I know it is hard for you that she is gone, but for others, the days and months to come will be much harder.'

*

Miss Anna looked out of the breakfast parlour window at the people already passing on the street, whether to the courthouse where the roup of the policies and tenancies of the Cromarty estate was to take place, or in the other direction, up to the house itself. 'You know, I think it wrong that this has been permitted to go ahead. I am sure there are strangers in the town, and who is to say where they have come from and what they have brought with them?'

'No one is permitted into the parish from the infected areas, Anna. There are watches on the roads and at the harbour. The Health Board would not have allowed it to go ahead, if there was a risk.'

'But I heard yesterday that the Lammas Market at Tain has been postponed, on account of the cholera.'

'That was wise. But Tain is in the very eye of the storm. The cholera is raging all around it.'

They had prayed, that morning, for the poor people at Inver – a scrap of a village on the Dornoch firth with hardly a hundred souls, and over fifty of them taken by the contagion. Word was that in the seaboard villages now, just around the North Sutor, there was hardly a soul to bury the dead.

Mr Gilfeather had called on them last night, after the meeting of the Health Board. The cholera was at Nigg already, he'd said. Nigg, just across the water from them, so close that in other summers the young lads would swim across the narrow neck of the firth, to show off their prowess. From the upper windows of this very house they could see the cottages of Nigg straggling along the shore. A seagull might leave their roof leads and land on the pier at Nigg in the time it would take them to walk from their front door to the kirkyard gates. The Health Board would require the assistance of the Ladies of the Friendly Society in dispersing provisions amongst the families of the afflicted, when the contagion came, as it would certainly come. Drs Smith and MacDonald had ordered in a good stock of medicines, dung heaps were already being removed as soon as they were started, on pain of great fines, arrangements for the safe burial of the dead were being looked to. Cromarty would not be found wanting.

But the business of the morning was the roup of Cromarty House, and the streets outside were alive with curiosity and bustle. Carriages were already passing from Poyntzfield and Newhall and Braelangwell, the local gentry and the better sort from neighbouring towns come to buy up the Mackenzies' fine furnishings at a bargain. Elspeth rang the bell for her cape and bonnet. Mr Fordyce had offered to take her up to Cromarty House in his chaise, thus saving her a brisk walk up the hill.

Anna, usually the victim of an insatiable curiosity to look upon lovely things, had refused to go, and made one last attempt to stop Elspeth from going either. 'But you don't know who you might find yourself mixing with there, Elspeth, and how would I ever do without you, should the cholera take you? And I am sure there is a breeze getting up. Should it turn north-westerly, who knows what might be blown here from Easter Ross. Cannot Mr Fordyce choose a painting for us? His taste is exactly right, you know – dear Pap always thought so.'

Elspeth sighed as she pulled on her gloves. 'There is no breeze, Anna. The firth is as calm as a millpond. Besides, if the cholera were carried on the breeze, Cromarty would have been amongst the first places to be afflicted and not a soul on the Buchan coast would have survived at all. To the taste of Mr Fordyce I make no objection, but,' she hesitated, 'there is a painting that was once in Cromarty House and that I am curious to see, if it is still there, of course. I have not seen it for many years, and I did not like to ask Sir William about it.'

'But that was unlike you, Elspeth!'

Elspeth gave her sister, who had already clapped a hand over her mouth, a long look. 'If you are insistent you will not come, Anna, you might begin drawing up the bedding lists. All bedding of the cholera victims will have to be burned and replaced. A list will have to be drawn up of what the Ladies of the Friendly Society can supply in its place. You know the sort of thing. If you make a start on it this morning, I shall help you finish it this afternoon, and we may send copies out to the ladies tomorrow. From what Mr Gilfeather tells me, there is little time to be lost.'

Charlotte looked at Morag Mackenzie. She wondered if William would miss the old woman who had declared that she had had quite as much of the Caribbean sun as she had been meant for. She would wait out her remaining years in the turret or attic room of some family stronghold, spreading misery amongst any new young wives that might have the misfortune to fetch up there.

They travelled in silence, south-westwards, down the sleeve of the Black Isle. Charlotte wondered that she had never noticed before how many burial grounds there were lining the coast. Kirkmichael, Cullicudden, Urquhart, all looking across the water, to something better.

At last the carriage came to the Leanaig, that twisted down towards the old Scuddel Ferry, where Thomas Telford's bridge now spanned the Conon. The hills of Strathconon flanked away to the south-west, and ahead of them was the massif of Ben Wyvis, shrouded by cloud. 'The most beautiful prospect in the world,' William liked to say of it. Well, he was far enough away from it now.

The ruin of Kinkell castle was behind them now. More Mackenzies – even their dead could not be avoided here. It had been given out that Charlotte would be travelling into Ross, into Mackenzie country amongst William's relatives. It had not been specified whether she might stay with the Mackenzies of Conan, or of Ord, Fairburn, Coul, Brahan or Castle Leod. Perhaps she would even be put to his relations at Scatwell, so far up Strathconon she would hardly be seen again. It had been mooted outside the kirk of Cromarty on Sunday that poor Lady Charlotte would be passed from one to the other, like an unwanted parcel until such time as Sir William deemed his affairs in Guyana sufficiently settled that he might send for her. Having thus passed out of the world of their small town, she would soon be forgotten.

At his mother's instruction, Ludovic shifted the cabinet three inches to the left as Mr Fordyce had suggested.

'It is a fine cabinet,' repeated the old gentleman. 'And I'd go as far as to say it looks better here than it did in Cromarty House.' There was a pause. 'Or at least as well.'

Her lips slightly pursed, Janet Cameron assessed the thing again and Ludovic prepared himself for further shiftings, but at last she said, 'Well, I daresay it will do, Mr Fordyce. And if you are happy with it, no one else can have cause for complaint.'

A guffaw from the seat nearest the reading room window signalled that Dr Fraser was not quite as engrossed in the latest edition of the *Inverness Courier* as might have at first appeared.

'You have something to say, I take it, Dr Fraser?' said Mr Gilfeather, looking round his week-old copy of *The Scotsman* from the seat opposite.

The minister lowered his newspaper. 'Just that if Mrs Cameron is in hopes that no one will find fault with the new library arrangements, I fear she is likely to be disappointed. Was Miss Elspeth Rose, for instance, consulted?'

A sound not very far from derision escaped the bank manager. 'Consulted? Has the woman not been demanding this very thing for months now? The minute book of the library is half taken up with her complaints on irregularities in the passing of the books, and the need for them to be stored and discussed in the one place. Here now is a solution that has cost us not a penny, only the good grace of Mrs Cameron to allow it in the reading room.'

'I think the shutting up of Cromarty House too high and sorrowful a price to pay for our bookcase,' said Mr Fordyce. 'And we must also bear the loss of two members from amongst our number. Sir William was always genial company, and Lady Charlotte had such a sensibility. A great loss.'

'Well, I suppose it made little enough sense to keep the house open just for her and Morag Mackenzie, when he might be away years.'

Mr Fordyce accepted the cup of coffee Hester had just poured for him, thanking her with a kindly smile, then leaned towards Mr Gilfeather. 'But to go to Guyana when there is so much restiveness amongst the slaves, with all the talk of emancipation. I am surprised that he should risk it.'

Mr Gilfeather gave another 'hmmph'. 'He says he has his investments to look to, and that must be the next great question, now that the Reform is finally passed.' He pointed to the newspaper. 'An election must soon follow, and then the abolitionists will have the Commons. The question of the compensation is not settled. Sir William would do better in protecting his investment by staying at home and standing for Parliament than in running harum-scarum to his plantation.'

'Well, I am pleased he has not taken Lady Charlotte with

him,' said Mr Fordyce. 'Even if she is lost to our society. She has always been such a delicate creature, and you know, in my time in the Tropics I saw many a white woman succumb to the effect of the heat and unhealthy miasmas of the place. Poor Lady Charlotte has not been looking at all well of late. I hope the mountain air of the west might suit her better. I should very much have liked to have heard her thoughts on Bishop Heber's *Poems*, which I believe she was to have from Mrs Mackay next month.'

The bank manager was unperturbed. 'The library must stagger on as it is a while yet. We cannot be admitting new members until they have been agreed at the Annual General Meeting – it would put the whole thing wrong.' He took up his pipe and glowered over the bowl as he packed in the tobacco. 'Which I am never done having to tell people in the street, and indeed in the bank itself.'

'There are plenty who are eager to fill the vacant places,' agreed Ludo.

'Oh, but this is good news,' said Mr Fordyce. 'I wonder whether the new Mrs Learmonth will be one of them, do you think? Such a charming young woman.'

Ludo hardly knew how to answer. It had been a matter of some astonishment to the group of friends congregated in the clockmaker's parlour only last week when John had advised them of his intention to marry Dr Fraser's new housemaid. They had thought it was a joke and would not believe him, to the extent that he had got up from the table in anger and stormed out, letting the door bang behind him. They had not known what to make of it, and when Ludo and Stan had eventually caught up with him, they could get nothing out of him but that it was too late, everything was too late. The next day the news had arrived in Cromarty of Dr Fraser's reading of the banns at Resolis kirk. To Ludo's great regret, their friend had seemed to avoid them ever since.

Dr Fraser lifted his paper again. 'I do not think the young woman will have a great deal of time for reading books. In fact, I believe Mr Learmonth himself may create another vacancy in the library. There is word that he will return with his wife to his own part of the world, after their private ceremony has been conducted. A position in a school near Linlithgow has been offered to him. He tells me he intends to take it.'

Ludo could not believe what he was hearing. That John had evidently made Dr Fraser his new confidant while ignoring his friends was to him inexplicable. And everyone was looking at him now.

'You have not mentioned this, Ludovic,' said his mother.

Ludo worked his lips, trying to think what he might say. In the end he could offer nothing better than, 'I think it being so private a matter, John did not wish his business noised around.'

'Then perhaps he should have conducted it elsewhere,' said his mother, giving one final rub of her duster to the front of the glass bookcase before going back to her kitchen.

★

Charlotte could see the river Conon now, snaking to where its mouth would meet the firth. At last the road turned and Telford's bridge and the coaching inn beside it came into view. And there *he* was, standing outside it, waiting. It had seemed impossible, when Miss Juniper had finally declared it the only course of action that could be taken. Even Rachel had thought it impossible, but Miss Juniper had said no, she would write to him. Of all men, he would not fail Charlotte, he would come, the old lady had assured her. By some miracle that Charlotte had scarcely hoped to believe in, the reply had arrived within two days. Yes, he would come. He would drive to the very doors of Cromarty House and break them down, if need be. He would not abandon her.

As if reading her thoughts, Morag Mackenzie spoke. 'You have destroyed one man and now you think to destroy another. You will end in Hell, whither the bastard you carry will doubtless follow you.'

They were the first words the old woman had uttered since they had been handed up into the carriage at Cromarty House, and they broke any last thread tying Charlotte to her past. She very carefully loosened the pins of the veil she had attached to her hat and as she lifted it from her face she said,

'That being the case, Morag, I shall bid you not *adieu*, but *au revoir*.'

They watched as Morag Mackenzie, having left her own, insignificant baggage at the inn to be picked up later by the carter, started along the riverside path that would take her to

Conan House. The mist was already coming down over the water, obscuring trees and bushes and even the river itself.

'She said I would go to hell,' said Charlotte as the slowly diminishing black figure was eventually obscured from their view.

Charles Munro traced his hand down the side of her face. 'Then you must take me with you, for I will not let you leave me.'

She sank her head into his chest. 'Are you really certain? You know everything, and you still want me?'

He made her look at him. His eyes had the same power they had had that first day in the dining room of Cromarty House and now they possessed her, entirely. 'I have never been more certain of anything in my life.'

'And you really believe it will be all right?'

He signalled for the stable lad to bring round his chaise. 'Yes, it will. We are going far into my own country, where no one will think of questioning me. And by the time we are finally free to marry, no one will remember that we ever were not. From this moment, I am that child's father and I will be your husband, and any who chooses to dispute that with me will regret the day they were born.'

He handed her up into the chaise then got up himself and took hold of the reins. As the carriage rumbled away from the inn, across the bridge, past the toll-house and northwards, towards the Munro country, the mist crept ever further over the river so that when Charlotte turned to look behind her, she could see nothing at all.

THIRTY-ONE

Late August

Ribbons on the Breeze

Mrs Cameron had gone with the kitchen maid and boot boy to supervise the fetching of ice from the ice house above the links, and there was no one in the kitchen but themselves. Hester flicked Ludo's ear as she lifted his bowl from the table. 'Why so glum, brother? You cannot still be sad that Mr Gilfeather would not allow you the time off to attend the Reform celebrations in Inverness? So much speechmaking, and you would have got caught up in one of those dinners with a hundred toasts. I have read the reports, and I can assure you, there would not have been one of those fine gentlemen standing by the end of it. You know you cannot keep up with those types of fellows.'

'But I'm sure Stanislas and James Craig . . .'

'Oh, yes, Mr Craig and Stanislas will certainly have listened to the speeches, and then found their way to a cheery hotel or tavern, but *you* would have ended up amongst the clerks of the Caledonian Bank of Inverness who would have got you befuddled with their toasts.'

'But, Hester, you have never *met* an Inverness bank clerk,' Ludo protested, attempting to assert himself.

She was undaunted. 'I have no need to. I have heard Mrs Gilfeather speak of them, in this very kitchen, and it was most shocking. You must remember that you are a person of consequence now, and your behaviour will be watched and your vote courted.'

'Well,' said Ludo, getting up from the table. 'It's not that I really wanted to attend the Reform celebrations. I mean, I'm pleased the bill has finally passed, of course, but there's little point in anyone courting my vote – my mother is quite clear I must vote for the Mackenzie faction, even though Sir William is no longer here. She says he always treated us very fair, and we should know where our loyalties lie. Which particular branch of the Mackenzie faction is to have my vote is yet to be established.'

Hester kept her thoughts on loyalty and the fairness of Sir William to herself. His many relatives might be busy squabbling with the adherents of the opposing Munro faction over the coming election in the letter pages of the newspapers, but he himself would be well on his way back across the Atlantic by now. To attend to 'his affairs' in Guyana as had been given out. She wondered whether Sir William might see her mother, when he was there. She wondered whether he might even recognise her. Probably not. There was no reason why he should. One item of property amongst many others. Sold on, like an old chair after the death of Duncan Cameron – Ludo's father, Hester's father – because she was no longer needed. One less item on which he might claim compensation, when the day came.

The word 'compensation' bounced like a ball around the reading room of the hotel as the local gentlemen took their snuff, pushed tobacco into their pipes and demanded more sugar in their coffee, all the while declaiming against the abolitionists. And they thanked her most kindly, as if she had known no other existence but as parlourmaid here in the Commercial Hotel. There was no point trying to explain that even to Ludo.

'So,' she said, brushing with her cloth at some of the crumbs now decorating his waistcoat, 'what is it that has you so gloomy, if it's not having missed out on the celebrations in Inverness?'

Ludo turned his head away slightly and his eyelashes began to beat a little too quickly. Hester felt her heart go out to him as it had done the first time she had seen him, this pale, slightly chubby brother she had been presented with on entering the kitchen of this Cromarty hotel for the first time, almost ten years ago. It had not been Sir William who had brought her here, but his old nurse, Miss Mackenzie, who had travelled with him to Demerara to supervise his household, then travelled back to Scotland with him, when he had had enough of it. On that voyage back, it had been Hester who had come under her supervision, for thousands of miles and endless weeks of being catechised and told how grateful she should be for Sir William's benevolence in freeing her at her worthless father's request. Miss Mackenzie had, give her her due, taught Hester the rudiments of reading and writing, that she might read the scriptures, and make notes of sermons. She had never, though, spared a thought or a word in her prayers for Hester's mother. But Hester did, in her silent, private prayers that Morag Mackenzie could not see into. She thanked God that it was her mother's own sister, a free-coloured businesswoman, who had bought her. She did not know if Auntie would get compensation, when abolition came, but now her mother worked as a huckster, selling goods at the markets and carrying Auntie's Bible, that she was not able to read, to church on a Sunday, and Hester thanked God that no man would ever own her again.

Four and a half thousand miles to this kitchen she had travelled, where Morag Mackenzie had prodded her towards another woman, saying, 'This is the child of whom Sir William wrote to you. You understand that she being now freed, there would be difficulties in sending her back?'

The woman, Mrs Cameron, who was younger than Morag Mackenzie but older than Hester's mother, had not smiled the way some of the ladies on the ship had smiled, smiles that spoke of their own Christian goodness rather than any real interest in her. Mrs Cameron had told Morag Mackenzie that she understood that perfectly well, and that she would be responsible for the child from now on. When the old witch had left, this Mrs Cameron had looked at

Hester a while then said, 'You have his eyes, but it cannot be helped, I suppose,' then sat her down and fetched her a bowl of bread and milk and told her that the boy seated across from her was called 'Ludovic' and that he was her brother. The plump white cheeks of the boy had pinked at this, the eyelashes had started to bat, and the face had opened into a smile that was one of the best smiles anyone had given Hester in her whole life. They'd been instructed that no one outside the family was to know of their relationship, because it was no one's business but theirs. Hester was told her position would be of parlourmaid, she must be a dutiful daughter of the house and she would be raised to be a woman who would one day run a business of her own. Ludo was told that he must always look after his sister. This last to Hester had been an astonishing remark, but she couldn't have said how many days afterwards it had been – not as long as a week, anyway – that she had realised that it would be her who would have to look after him, so gentle and soft-hearted was this boy.

Now, so many years later, he was standing before her, still too soft. 'Tell me, Ludo, or I shall make you late for the bank: what is the matter?'

He bit his lip and then spoke. 'Well, you know James and Stan are not expected back until this evening, because they stayed two days in the town, because Stan required to visit tailors and stationers and outfitters of all sorts to order up the accoutrements of his new life?'

'Yes.'

'Well – that's it. Before we know it, we will be in September and he and his trunk will be boarding the London smack and be gone.'

Hester laid down her cloth. 'And you will miss your friend.'

Ludo nodded. 'I don't begrudge him this good fortune – heaven knows he deserves it, and he is far too fine a fellow to be seated behind a clockmaker's counter in Cromarty for ever, but I already feel the absence of John . . .'

Hester had little sympathy to offer in the matter of John Learmonth. As far as the rest of Cromarty and the Black Isle were concerned, the schoolmaster had very quickly fallen in love with Dr Fraser's new housemaid, married her in a private ceremony in Resolis manse as soon as he was able, and taken his new bride home to their native Lothian, where a position in the grammar school of a respectable town had fallen vacant. Hester, having heard the truth from Mrs Cameron, in whom Dr Fraser had confided, knew different. 'You are better off without the society of a man like that, Ludo.'

'Oh, I know what he did was wrong,' he assured her. 'Very wrong. And it is right that Dr Fraser made him face his responsibilities, but for all that he was my friend. I will not deny he was a bad *husband*, but his was a very youthful mistake and I'm sure he will be proving a better husband now. He really is in every other respect a very good sort of fellow and I cannot help missing his company. Once Stan is gone too, things will be . . . as they were before.'

Hester handed him his hat and touched his cheek. 'They will not, Ludovic. You move in a wider society now and are respected almost as Mr Gilfeather is respected. You are no longer a schoolboy or college student to be baited by the likes of Fachie Hossack.'

Ludovic was sceptical. 'Will I not be?'

'No. You are a man of consequence. You have the vote. Besides, Fachie will be gone soon, and for good, God willing. Both he and his father speak of little else when one or other of them is in the coffee room, to anyone who will listen. They have different views as to how that circumstance is to be brought about, but it is the intention of each that Fachie should be as far as is possible from Cromarty, as soon as is possible. It is just a question of waiting. Mrs Hossack will not hear of him being sent away anywhere until the danger of the cholera is past.'

'So that is what I am to hope for? That I might wait out both the cholera and Fachie Hossack?'

Hester now let out a humph of impatience as she started to clatter the bowls in the washing basin. Their father had been a brute, and although Mrs Cameron *did* have a heart, she kept it well covered, so how in the world was it that Ludovic could be so hopeless and soft? Thank God for Mairead, or she, Hester, would have to stick to him like glue for the rest of his life, for she could not imagine him getting through it on his own.

Softening, she put a hand on his arm. 'I know you have been lonely, Ludo, but you will have more friendships, and

Stanislas goes only to London, not the moon. What you must now concentrate on is securing Mairead.'

Her brother appeared to be taken by a sudden choking, which she ignored.

'It will not be so very long until Mairead is old enough and you established enough . . .' He was now blushing so much that the temptation to tease was very great, but she pressed on. 'She is a most sensible girl. Her visit to Easter Ross with the library seems to have wrought a great change in her – she has got over all her old foolish fancies and would make an excellent banker's wife, when the time is right. Then, when one day the young *Mrs* Cameron might wish to visit her old friend the young Mrs, or rather *Countess* Jeszewski at her fine London residence, you and Stanislas may laugh together again and remember your Cromarty days.'

Ludo beamed and bent to peck her on the cheek. 'There are many conditionals in there, Hester.'

'That's as may be,' she said, going back to her work, 'but all you have to do is continue to be Ludo; the rest, as God wills, will see to itself.'

It was a sparkling morning as Stanislas reached out a hand to help James disembark from the Kessock Ferry. Once on dry land, James stretched out his arms and shook his legs, ready for the twenty miles' walk home. He was heavier laden than he had been on their walk in the other direction, three days ago. While in the town he had fulfilled a commission from Mrs Hossack, and now a heavy wooden case sat at his feet, lifted off the boat by Stan, despite James's arguments that he could do it himself. The clock was an ugly, gaudy thing, but its mechanism was good and James would not have thought of entrusting it to the carter who was to transport the more cumbersome of Stan's purchases by road. 'I did not like the look of that fellow,' he'd said, after Stan had returned from arranging his business with the man that morning.

'You are too suspicious, James. He has just been celebrating the passing of the Reform a little hard, I think.'

'What, for two days?'

'Well, it was a much more sensible arrangement than you and I attempting to carry my new trunk and everything in it all the way across the Mulbuie and home. We may enjoy the glories of the summer day at our leisure.' Whistling, and before James could stop him, Stan set off up the road ahead of him with Mrs Hossack's cumbersome new clock tucked under his arm.

As they walked, the sun climbed ever higher in the blue sky and James was glad when they came to the inn at Allangrange, where they took an early dinner that they ate outside. They passed through the fishing village of Avoch and then the town of Fortrose before crossing the burn of Rosemarkie and taking the road up onto the moor. James, walking a little behind Stan, thought to beguile the time by telling stories of the unquiet spirits said to have been encountered high on the Mulbuie when night fell. Stan's responses were intermittent – he was wont, at times like these, to ponder too much on his own country, his own stories, and perhaps James's tales were ill-chosen for his audience. 'But we will not fear seeing such things on a day like this,' he said, 'when the sun shines and the world around can be seen clear for miles.'

'No.' Stan sounded a little breathless, his voice almost queer. 'And the colours are dancing, like ribbons and flags.'

James reflected that this was true. The moor was not bleak today, but alive with birds and butterflies and buzzing insects without number. The purple of the heather was dotted about with yellows and whites and pinks of all manner of wildflowers that put to shame all the splendours of the procession they had witnessed two days ago in Inverness. The breeze that found them on the moor, with so few trees to impede it, was as warm as if it had come direct from the Mediterranean.

As they came in sight of the Raddery Burn where they planned to stop and refresh their flasks, James noticed that Stanislas, still ahead of him, appeared to be tiring. He himself had always been robust, but he was not getting any younger. His sixtieth birthday was two summers behind him now and he was starting to feel the years a little, in his limbs and lungs. Nevertheless, he had let poor Stan carry that damned clock far enough now and was determined to take his turn for the last eight miles or so home. He was about to say this when he saw Stan stop and then double over, sick, before he got to the edge of the burn. James called to him and quickened his pace.

Stan, trying and failing to right himself before he was taken by a second bout of vomiting, half-turned to look at him and it was as if a ghost had taken hold of the young man's being. The perennially pale face was beyond white, a pallor upon it so sickly and damp that James was instantly shaken by a dreadful certainty. He threw down his own pack and began to run, catching Stan just before he hit the ground. The chimes of Marjorie Hossack's clock clanged out the new discord of their world as it tumbled into the waters of the burn.

Ludo just managed to catch himself before his forehead hit his desk, but too late to prevent the splat of ink from his pen leaving a trail across the page of the ledger he was working on. He glanced quickly round, but Mr Gilfeather's office was still empty and the clock told him there was half an hour yet before the bank manager, who kept to the older, later, dinner-hour, would be back in his place and like to catch Ludo falling asleep over his work. Ludo himself took his dinner as early as could be countenanced, which on days of hazy heat such as today meant that at least an hour of the afternoon would pass in drowsy stupor, punctuated by jolts of his head and splats of ink.

He wondered whether Stanislas and James might be too weary on their return from Inverness to put up with a visitor wishing to hear all the news of town, and to see what Stan had bought in preparation for his new life in London. He thought he might beg a dish of whatever there was for supper from the hotel kitchen, to take down with him to the clockmaker's house, for they were sure to be very hungry.

He was pulled away from his reverie by the sounds of a commotion at the front step of the bank. There being still no sign of Mr Gilfeather, Ludo got to his feet, drew back his shoulders and went to see what it was all about. He had hardly got the door open when a porter from the harbour all but fell through it.

'Daniel Stevenson!' Ludo exclaimed, 'are you drunk?'

'Not a drop have I had today,' said the grim-faced porter. 'I must see Sanders Gilfeather.'

'Mr Gilfeather is not—'

But Ludo's protestation was interrupted by the manager's voice, coming clear from the back of the small crowd now assembled at the bank door. The crowd quickly parted, but Mr Gilfeather did not move. 'Well then, Daniel, what is it?'

'You'll need to tell the magistrates, Mr Gilfeather, and call together the Health Board. The word has come off a boat at the harbour mouth: the cholera is in Inverness.'

It was five hours later, the bank long shut and the streets of the town almost bouncing with people out and about, forming themselves into groups, looking for other groups to go with them to the magistrates to demand that *something* be done. All up the coast, infected villages were cut off by the outside, the country folk wishing to keep themselves safe and their coastal neighbours might rot together. Why should not Cromarty, beset on all sides by the encroaching disease, close *itself* off? They must man the road ends, block off the harbour, let no one through. In the council chamber of the courthouse, on the other hand, through the smoke of a score of pipes, complaints were puffed loud about the disruption of trade and the loss of revenue, to say nothing of the coming political meeting, so essential to the implementation of the Reform. Were respectable gentlemen to be prevented from entering the town by restrictions that could surely only apply to contagion-ridden vagabonds? Had there not been one ship after another at the head of the firth for months now, flying their yellow flags, yet never a breath of cholera come into the town? Let workmen and labourers form themselves into associations of defence if they liked: Cromarty would not be closed to the world.

Ludo was at neither the meeting of merchants and magistrates nor the convocation of labourers and apprentices. At the very moment, not a minute sooner than its usual time, that Mr Gilfeather had turned the key in the lock of the bank door, Ludo had set out and all but run ahead of his startled manager and the junior clerks, to knock on the door of the clockmaker's shop on Church Street. The door being locked and he receiving no reply, he had then made his way around the back and after again fruitlessly knocking, peered in at the kitchen window to confirm what in his heart he already knew: they had not come home. He ran then back to his own home, eager to throw off his banking clothes and throw on something more appropriate to the journey he intended. He was met in the hallway by

Hester, carrying a tray of the best china into not the reading room but the parlour.

'Take care, Ludo! What can be your hurry?'

'I need to get out on the road.'

'Out on the road?' came a quivering voice from the other side of the opened parlour door. 'But surely, Ludovic, my dear, you cannot think of it?'

It was Miss Anna, the terror of the contagion that was now drawing its breath at the very edges of their town huge in her kind eyes.

'I must, Miss Anna,' he said. 'I must find my friends.'

'Your friends?' she said, some little comprehension dawning, as for the second time that day, Ludo heard an urgent hammering at the door.

'No,' he said.

'He says there can be no doubt.'

A farm lad from up by Navity had been given the farmer's own horse to bring the news down to the hotel. A stockman crossing the Mulbuie had seen a strange pennant flapping from the roof of a shepherd's hut above Raddery Burn. On going closer, and calling out, a man had appeared at the hut door and told him to advance no further, for there was cholera within. It was James Craig, who prayed that word might be taken to Cromarty that his apprentice had been taken ill, and that medicines must be sent. The farmer had seen to the food and blankets and water pails that had also been asked for, though the clockmaker had commanded that no one should come within a hundred yards of the hut.

'No,' repeated Ludovic, the fears that had beset him since the early afternoon now realised and depriving him almost of breath. But someone else was saying 'no', too, and very firmly.

Ludo turned around at the familiar voice, uncomprehending. It was Miss Elspeth. 'No, Anna, you will not go.'

Miss Anna, already on her feet, was not listening to her sister. 'Ludovic,' she was saying, 'you must lend me the hotel pony.'

'You will *not* go, Anna!' her sister repeated.

'Elspeth, I will.' She was gathering up her cloak and bonnet. 'Now, Mrs Cameron, you must send to Mrs Gilfeather for the medicines, for she has charge of the store, and Ludovic shall escort me up there.'

'No, Anna!' said her sister, for once in her life looking the more frightened of the two. And Miss Anna Rose, who for once in *her* life did not look frightened of her sister at all said, 'Ah, but Elspeth, I must go. You know I must.'

James leant over Stanislas, stretched out on the dirty straw pallet. Thank God for the water pail. He had lost count of the number of times he had filled it from the burn, only to return to find that Stan had vomited again, or that a thin white diarrhoea seeped into the rushes. No amount of water, scooped with a ladle and poured into Stan's throat, seemed capable of replacing what his body was losing.

He tried to make Stanislas keep quiet, to conserve his

strength, but he filled the hut with words in his increasing and desperate agitation. 'London', 'Lach-Szyrma', 'Alicia, Alicia,' and, as time wore on, words that James could not understand, running together like lines from a poem, slipping, tangling, being lost, as if even to Stanislas their sense was fraying, disappearing, leaving him.

As often as James left the hut to go to the burn, he consulted his pocket watch. How long, how long? Darkness was falling and then only the intermittent light of the moon let him see where on the mother-of-pearl face the silver hands of his watch had reached since last he had looked. Fourteen hours since Stan had made his bargain with the carter. James saw it again in his mind's eye, remembered the sickly man spitting upon his hand and offering it to Stan who, a little disgusted, had shaken it anyway. Fourteen hours. Maybe the carter was dead now. Maybe he was in Hell already. James tried to chastise himself for the thought but gave up the attempt for lack of conviction. But still the hands of his watch moved on. Fourteen hours since the carter. Twelve since they had got off the Kessock Ferry. Nine since they had taken their dinner at Allangrange, seven since Stan had fallen ill. And then, Dear God, how long, how long since someone had at last passed within shouting distance? The herdsman from Navity, how long even to make him understand, for him to promise that he would have a message sent?

How long? It didn't matter. Too long. Too long had it been only a minute since that carter had held out his infected hand, and Stan had taken it.

Stan was murmuring now, trying to speak. James lifted the ladle but Stan turned his lips away, he could take no more. '*Gwiazdy*,' he said. James shook his head. 'I'm sorry my boy, my dearest boy, but I do not understand.' A look of clarity passed briefly over Stan's face and by a tremendous effort, he spoke again, this time in English. 'Stars,' he breathed. And James knew. He remembered one night when they had stood by the seafront of Cromarty and looked up at the myriad wonders of the sky and Stan had said it gave him comfort to know those same stars sparkled over his homeland.

James passed a hand over Stan's forehead, the skin already tinged with a blue hue. He bent over to begin lifting him, but Stan suddenly retched up whatever ghastly fluid remained in his body, then retched again, with nothing, his whole frame contorted in the agony of it. James held Stan's head to his chest and kissed the sodden locks now plastered to the skin by sweat and vomit, then by a great effort, he pulled Stan up beneath the arms before hooking his arm behind the boy's knees. Finding a strength he thought had long deserted him, he staggered from the hut to collapse to his knees and release his burden as gently as he could onto the heather.

'There,' he said, when at last he could find his breath. 'There you are, dear boy. Look at them brimming in their majesty for you, Count Stanislas Jeszewski.'

Stan smiled. James was sure it was a smile, and he was certain that he heard Stan try to say something. It might have been '*Gwiazdy*', and then, it was over.

THIRTY-TWO

September

Butterflies

The books lay on the table, where they had been for over a fortnight. Never before in her life had Elspeth found herself unable to read. Even all those years ago, when the terrible news had reached them of the foundering of Captain Bain's sloop in a storm off Buchanness, taking their beloved Pap to the depths of the sea with it, Elspeth had managed to read. She had read then as if her life depended on it, while Anna had collapsed into an hysteria that had almost carried her off. But, since that night over two weeks ago on the Mulbuie, and the dreadful days that had followed, she had found her mind would not hold a line or a thought or a single exchange printed on those pages. She hardly knew which book had been hers and which Anna's. She looked at them now and forced herself to think. Yes, that was hers, the *Hajji Baba*. She ought to have passed it to Mr Hossack, by now, and Anna ought to have given the *Life of Byron* to Mr Learmonth, the schoolmaster.

But then, she thought, it was as well Anna had *not* given that book to the schoolmaster, for he was gone, and could no longer be a member of the library, but might have taken the book with him anyway. It was a pity though, perhaps he might have profited by reading it. Perhaps the noble lord might have profited from living the life of a schoolmaster. Elspeth shook her head as if to dislodge the disparate thoughts by which it was beset.

She herself ought now to be receiving MacFarlane's *Constantinople* from young Ludovic. But how, now, were they to talk of books, after what had been? It had been dark, that night, by the time they had reached the place on the Mulbuie where the shepherd's hut stood desolate in the midst of desolation. Elspeth had refused to consent that Anna should come to this place without her, to give what help and succour she could to the beleaguered clockmaker and his apprentice. Ludovic had tried to dissuade them. Everybody had tried to dissuade them, but the Rose sisters had not lived over a hundred years between them in Cromarty to be told what they might not do, when they already knew what was right. The self-appointed guards policing the way in and out of the town had soon felt the scimitar lash of Elspeth's tongue and repented of their impudence, and so Ludovic had not had to employ the horsewhip upon them, as he had threatened to do.

The farm boy who had run down to the town with James Craig's message had ridden up behind Ludovic, to guide them to the place. He had hopped off and walked ahead of them the last mile, bearing a lantern. Elspeth was not a superstitious woman, and even as a child had paid little heed to the stories that were told of things people had witnessed at night on the moor, but when the boy had stopped at last by a solitary tree that had been blasted by lightning and held up his lamp, she had almost cried out. A pennant fluttered from a blackened branch, a strip of torn cloth. Yellow, it was. Yellow as the pennants of the quarantine ships in Cromarty Bay. Cholera yellow.

Elspeth could see nothing of what was beyond it at first, but the boy had halloed and she discerned a small rubble structure some thirty or forty yards distant, patchily thatched and without light or chimney smoke. And then there was some movement near it.

'James!' she had suddenly heard Anna say, and it was only Ludo Cameron taking hold of her sister as she tried to rush past him that had stopped Anna from flinging herself into the house of contagion even then. 'No, missis, ye must no',' the farm boy had urged. 'The clockmaker wilna have it that anyone should go closer.'

Ludovic, too, had been warned to stay back, but giving Anna into the care of her sister and ignoring the urgings of both the farm boy and the clockmaker, had gone on, until the figure near the hut had called out in an exhausted voice, 'It's too late, Ludovic. Too late.'

Ludovic had nonetheless gone on, and begun to run, but not quickly enough to be able to catch hold of the clockmaker, who she could then see had been leaning on a shovel, but now fell to the ground.

When Ludo had almost reached the clockmaker, he had come to a sudden halt then let out a terrible moan, collapsing to the ground with his head in his hands. Elspeth had not been able to help herself but to go and look on what he looked on. James Craig's shovel had fallen at the edge of a hole dug into the heather and the peat. James, who was now somehow crawling back to the hut, had been shovelling soil back into it, desperately trying to fill it in, to give some decency to the beautiful, ravaged young man whose face looked up at them now, illuminated by moonlight. Ludo had let out another desolate groan and might have fallen upon his friend's body if she had not taken firm hold of him. And that was why none of them, not her, nor Ludovic, nor even the young farm boy who had crept forward with an awful fascination, had noticed Anna slip by, to reach the hut just as the clockmaker did, and bend down to try to heave him inside.

There was nothing Elspeth could do then. Perhaps she could have sent Ludovic in to forcibly drag her sister out, but in the shock and horror of the open grave and Anna's unimaginable folly, she had been frozen. In a stupor. By the time she had recovered herself, begun to think clearly, it had already been too late. Anna had been in the hut with the sick man and was calling for the blankets and clean linen they had brought, and for the boy to fetch more water. Somehow, for the first time in their lives, Elspeth had done her sister's bidding while Ludovic had completed the filling in of his friend's grave, and scoured the moorland ground for the branches of a tree that he fashioned into a cross to set over it. They had been exhausted, all of them, by the time the sun had begun to rise out of the sea and to send golden pink and purple ribbons across the moor. A curlew, first of the morning, had begun to tell Stanislas Jeszewski's litany, to be joined by the songs of other birds of all sorts, and the moor had gradually become the scene of so much life and busyness amongst the inhabitants of the natural world that it seemed to mock them.

A butterfly was fluttering now, right up outside the drawing room window, here on the first floor of the house. Had it come down from the moor? she wondered. Had it been there, that morning, over two weeks ago? How long did a butterfly live anyway? She didn't know.

She realised she was seated, now, in her favourite reading chair, above which she had hung the small portrait of a young Sir William Mackenzie that she had got at the roup of Cromarty House. Morier's book was in her hand. *Had* she read *Hajji Baba*? No, but she was almost sure there had been some controversy about it that evening when the library had been gathered in this very room and she had tried to make them discuss the books. Anna had got upset about something in it and would not allow it to be discussed. There was something about old women, but something else too, she was almost sure, to do with the means employed by the Persians to guard the virtue of their womenfolk. But could they be virtuous, that were not Christian? Elspeth was bothered that she could not remember the passage that

Anna so objected to, that she had let the thing pass without making Anna justify herself, but there had been so much to manage, that evening, and she could have heard Anna's silliness at any time, without subjecting the company to it.

Now, she began to flick back and forth indiscriminately through Morier's book. His subjects seemed to be much exercised, in their voyage from Persia to England, over the matter of hygiene and contagion. She passed swiftly over that. Then her attention was caught by the word '*murwari*' and as she repeated it, she thought she might have heard Lady Charlotte murmur it that night, trying to make sense, she supposed, of Anna's fuss. Yes, here it was – the Murwari who was to act as guardian over the seraglio was to be of 'choice deformity'. What could that mean, 'choice deformity'? Elspeth read on. '. . . the most vindictive, spiteful and inexorable of his species, as watchful as a lynx, as wary as a jackal . . .' She mouthed the words again. 'vindictive', 'inexorable', 'watchful'. Oh yes. And poor Anna had seen in this description the very picture of her own Murwari and so had wanted the book put away. The fuss she had made had all been for Elspeth's sake. Elspeth closed the book and sat a long time, wondering about the choice deformity of her own heart and glad the butterfly, who occasionally batted against the window, was on the other side of the glass.

'Is she any better today?'

Miss Juniper seemed to have aged ten years in the last two weeks, since the news had been brought to Cromarty of the death of the clockmaker's apprentice. 'Mairead has got her to sit up and to take a mouthful of tea, but she will still say nothing but that she wishes to be buried with him. And oh, I do not know but she might, soon enough . . .'

Rachel had seldom seen her old schoolmistress weep. The whooping cough that had carried off a little girl new arrived at their school, many years ago; the influenza that had taken two sisters, not long arrived from the Caribbean when their father had put them to her school because his family did not find it quite convenient that they should reside with them. Those had been blows that had dented the old lady's armour and Rachel was determined that Alicia Middleton should not be added to that litany of loss.

'She will not,' she said, setting her foot on the stair, 'she will not.'

The bedroom curtains were closed against the sunlight and there was a mustiness to the room, despite the bunches of lavender and thyme that Mairead had scattered on the floor, and the roses that had come from so many gardens in Cromarty – her own garden in the manse, from Fordyce House, from Mrs Gilfeather's. People who had guessed the lovely secret of the pretty Cromarty girl and the romantic Polish count. When the petals fell, more flowers would arrive at the door of the little cottage.

Rachel whispered to Mairead. 'Go and take some air. I will sit with her now.'

As the door closed softly behind Mairead, Rachel put her fingers to the cheek of the girl lying in the bed and swept back the hair, usually so pretty, so carefully curled and ribboned, but now dull and lank and unattended.

'Alicia,' she said, 'I want you to sit up and listen to me.'

The girl said nothing, but turned upon her eyes that Rachel wondered could have any tears left in them. Rachel squeezed her hand then said, 'I need you to sit up now, Alicia, for I must talk to you and you must listen to me. Here.' She slipped her hand beneath the girl's shoulders and softly lifted them to put another pillow behind them. Then she poured out a cup of barley water from the jug she had brought upstairs with her and lifted it to the girl's lips. To her relief, after a moment's hesitation, Alicia took a sip.

'Good,' said Rachel. 'Now, I am not come to tell you that it was God's will that Stanislas should die and you be left, for I do not pretend to know God's will, and whatever my husband, or Dr Fraser, might say, neither do they. I am not come to tell you that your grief will end, because it will not – you will carry it with you, in a place that will be its own special place, until your dying day. But you *will* be able to bear it, whatever you might think now. There will be a day when the grief is there but the pain of it does not double you up like a knife in your middle, when you will be able to breathe without weeping, speak without howling.'

Alicia gazed at her as if she were speaking in an unknown language, but then said, 'I don't want the pain to end. I don't want to live like that. I want to die and be with him.'

Rachel leaned forward and put her lips to Alicia's forehead. 'I know that. You know that I know that, that I have felt that. I too have believed I would never again be able to put one foot after the other. But here I am, in front of you, and here,' she placed a fist to her own breast, 'is my love, my pain, that I carry through this world every day. A boy called Alexander that died seventeen years ago in the Belgian mud still lives, here, and after his mother and father have died and been buried, I will be the last to carry him in this world. And you must do this, for Stanislas. His friends will grieve him, but not as you grieve him. They will remember him, but not as you remember him, and they cannot carry his spirit through this world as you can because they did not know him in his very heart as you did. You will live, and he will exist in you, and you will carry his light and see the things he could not and be to the world the good that he would have been.'

Alicia was staring at her now.

'Do you understand me, Alicia?'

The girl's eyes were huge, but there was a glimmer of something in them that had not been there before. Very slowly, she nodded. Very softly, almost inaudibly, through dry, cracked lips, she said, 'Yes, I understand.'

Hester opened the window to let out the butterfly that had somehow got trapped in the room then she snuffed out the candles in the parlour. There would be no more guests this evening. Since the cholera had begun to rage in Inverness and the outlying parishes, almost no one from outside of the town came into Cromarty. Those who wished to must contend with the association of citizens that had formed itself into a town guard, and risk being kippered in the 'smoking shed' that had been brought into play, while still the magistrates worried about trade. Mrs Cameron, out tonight nursing a cousin whose cancer would take her before the cholera ever found its way past the young men and their staffs and pitchforks, had said Hester might lock up early if there were no customers or unexpected travellers seeking accommodation.

There was no one else in the hotel. The little boot boy would be snug in his own bed in his grandmother's cottage in Fishertown, and the scullery- and housemaids had been permitted to go home to their own families, until the contagion be past. Hester tried to remember when last she had been alone. Had she ever actually been alone? No. Not when she had been little and lived with her mother and brothers and so many aunties and cousins in the slave quarters of the Mackenzie estate in Demerara. Not when she had crossed the ocean, going the opposite way from the one her grandmother had been forced to travel, and forever under the vulture eye of Morag Mackenzie. And not one single day since she had come to this town, and this hotel. But she felt alone now.

Hester listened to the building, the creaks of floorboards and the sigh of roof timbers in the silence that was not silence. And the sea – the night was still and yet the sea bore back and forth upon the shore with so persistent a rumble, it seemed to be deciding whether the town should be left alone tonight, or not. Hester thought of Mairead, lying awake beneath the beams of Miss Juniper's small cottage, so much closer to the shore. Mairead had told her once that she often lay awake, listening to the sea, imagining all the drowned souls who had been lost to the town slowly rising from the waves and coming walking up the beach, to try to find their way home.

Tonight, as she went about the hotel, covering fires, snuffing candles, turning keys and shooting bolts, Hester could not help but think of the dead of Cromarty, people she had known since she had come here and who were now gone. Usually they would hold family worship, herself, Mrs Cameron, Ludovic and the servants, but tonight, Hester knew she would have to burn her own candle late, poring over the pages of the gospel, before she might drive the visions of Mairead's imaginings from her mind.

The sky was already darkening as she crossed from the parlour to the reading room, to make her final check that all was secure. She lifted her candle on entering the room then almost dropped it. There, sitting in the shadows, in the chair usually favoured by Dr Fraser, was Fachie Hossack.

Hester had managed to keep hold of her candlestick but had not managed to stop an exclamation of shock from escaping her lips. In his chair, Fachie pouted. 'Don't tell me you are closing up now, Hester. Surely your mistress will not permit that?'

'The mistress is not here,' she said, instantly wishing she had not.

'Ah, yes. She's with the old woman Jess Patience, isn't she? I was attending Dr MacDonald when he looked in on her. She has a few hours yet before she goes to bother the boatman of the Styx. So,' now he smiled, 'how might we entertain ourselves while Mrs Cameron hovers over the deathbed?'

'I am closing up, Mr Hossack,' she said.

'*Mister* Hossack, is it? *Mister* Hossack is my father, Hester. It was "Fachie", when I was Ludovic's playmate.'

'You were never his playmate, only his tormentor.'

'Oh, now, those were youthful japes, nothing more. Let us drink, you and I, to old times. What is it that you people drink – rum, I suppose?'

Hester spoke through gritted teeth. 'I do not take strong drink, Mr Hossack.'

He looked at her, as if deciding which tactic he would move on to. Then he decided. 'Pity, it might loosen you up. But I *do* drink, and I happen to know Mrs Cameron keeps a fine drop of Ferintosh locked away in that sideboard. You can bring me a good measure of that. All this talk of the cholera has given me a raging thirst.' He laughed, as if he had made a tremendous joke.

'You think it is funny, the *cholera morbus*? What kind of physician are you?'

'Oh,' he said, as if to an audience, 'she has spirit though, the mulatto Mackenzie bastard.' Then he leaned towards her and said, 'The kind of physician *I* am is one that will not waste his time or his talents being called out to watch miserable old women die in miserable cottages, or to lost causes gushing out every last body fluid in filthy huts up on the Mulbuie.'

Hester felt a white-hot rage going through her. She wanted to take the flame of her candle and ram it into his face.

'But anyway,' he continued, 'I asked for whisky, and I'm still waiting.'

She realised now that Fachie Hossack was already drunk, and she knew of old that he was not a good drunk, not a kind or cheerful or even tearful one, but a nasty, leering, sneering one that would not get better until he fell asleep or blacked out. She fetched the whisky, poured a large measure, and made to leave but Fachie called her back. 'Oh, no, Miss Hester. I am not ready for you to go, yet. I want to have some company and there is none here but you.'

'I have to—'

'Sit down,' he said, waving a hand at the opposite chair, suddenly expansive, benevolent.

'I have work to do.'

'You have no work to do, apart from me. There are no other guests or customers here.' He pointed again towards the seat opposite him. 'Sit down. I'm bored, you can entertain me.'

'I am not a performing dog, Mr Hossack,' she said.

He gave a curt laugh. 'A performing bitch, though, maybe?'

Hester slammed the bottle down beside him and turned

on her heel for the door. Let him drink himself senseless. She would bolt the door to the attic stairs and let him rampage around the rest of the place as he liked. But he sprang forward and grabbed hold of her wrist. She tried to shake him off but he had a firm hold on her.

'All right then,' he said, 'but you can fetch me a book before you go. Out of that cabinet.'

'Those books belong to the library.'

He made a dismissive 'pftt' sound. 'The library? Who's left of the library? Besides, my father is a member, he's paid his dues and you may be sure he's never read a damned page of any of the volumes in there.' Letting go of her arm, Farquhar lifted one of the candles she had lit and himself went over to the cabinet. He crouched down and made a show of examining the small number of volumes that had been returned there, awaiting the next gathering of the library's depleted membership.

She knew she should have left then, but she had a sudden vision of Mr Fordyce, and his distress should Fachie take it into his head to do harm to the books.

'What have we here then? Heber. Ah, yes. The good Lord Bishop of Calcutta. Have you been to Calcutta, Hester?'

She said nothing.

'They are dark there too, you know.' He cocked his head, appraising her. 'A different dark, I think. I have not been there myself, but I believe there are opportunities for a man of wit and intelligence. And I do not mind dark.'

Still she said nothing, but she kept her eyes on him,

feeling now that to look elsewhere would be an admission of weakness.

This seemed to please him greatly. 'You look at me very boldly, Miss Hester. But then you always did. I like a bold woman. I have no time for simperers.' He straightened up and took a step towards her, a volume of the Heber in his hand. She tried to step back, but there was nowhere to step back to – she was already at the wall. He shook his head, affecting disappointment. 'Oh, but Hester, you must not tease! Look here what our good Lord Bishop has to say about a woman who *teases*.' He turned through the pages with some purpose, pausing briefly to glance at her. 'Oh yes, while my father certainly won't have read this, library member or not, I have. Now here we are.' He had found his place. '*The Masque of Gwendolen*. Fragments only, but suggestive enough of the whole, I think you will find.'

Hester knew the poem. She had often dipped into the book of recent days, when the reading room had been quiet and the members of the library seemingly having forgotten about the books they'd left shut away in there. 'I do not wish to hear it,' she said.

'What?' said Fachie. 'Oh, but there you go again. A tease. Now here we are.' He looked at her again. 'You see, Gwendolen has been the most terrible tease, getting Merlin to do all sorts of things on her behalf, using her wiles.' He enunciated that last word very deliberately. 'Anyway, she has driven poor Merlin half-mad with desire, and he is quite ready to do anything for her – place her on a regal throne . . . make her a "queen and goddess" . . . promising her the elements shall "Wait on thee, and the countless multitude of Genii worship thee supreme in Hell!" Oh, I do like that bit, don't you, Hester? I mean. Would Hell really be so bad if you were to reign over it, be worshipped and all that? I don't think so. Anyway, Gwendolen takes fright and off she goes, simpering away, owning her folly, telling of all her remorse, all that sort of thing. Most irksome. Merlin, as any reasonable man would be, is unimpressed, and – oh, I do like this bit – says to her, "My love or vengeance must be gratified – Wherefore, proud dame, I say to thee, Be Wise!"'

Leaning so close towards her that the whisky fumes of his breath were on her own tongue, he tossed the book aside. 'Be wise, proud dame, for I *will* be gratified.'

Hester opened her mouth to call out, as if anyone would hear, but before she could get a sound from her throat his hand was over her mouth and with the other he had encircled her waist and was pushing her downwards, towards the floor.

Dr Fraser refused Alasdair Mackay's offer of a bed for the night. The light of the evening was almost gone, but it looked set fair to be a clear night, and his old mount knew the way in the dark. They had spoken and prayed long together, searched the scriptures, but had found no new answers as to why the Lord was testing them with this fresh plague, as if war, hunger, clearance had not been enough.

How long must he tell the faithful they must suffer in this life in the hope of glory in the next? What if there was none? He had not said this to Alasdair, but he knew the younger minister had seen it in his eyes.

Dr Fraser wondered if he might call in at the hotel, for a drop of the Ferintosh that Janet Cameron kept there, to warm him on the miles home, but he remembered that Janet was at poor Jessie Patience's dying. The horse took its own way along Church Street and slowed hopefully as they approached the clockmaker's. 'Ah, no, my poor beast, your young officer is not there, any more.' The animal could sense a good horseman at a hundred paces and had been drawn to the young Polish apprentice as a bee to honey.

It struck Dr Fraser though that he had not been to see the clockmaker since he had finally been carried down in a cart off the Mulbuie, days after his apprentice's death, having somehow himself managed to survive the contagion. That neither Anna Rose nor her sister had fallen victim to the disease had almost restored Dr Fraser's belief in miracles, although few in Cromarty had been surprised that even the cholera retreated in the face of Elspeth Rose. He dismounted and led the horse up around the back of the clockmaker's house, where he could see a lamp burning in the window. He tied the animal up and knocked, quite quietly, before entering.

James was sitting in his old chair by the fire, only his terrier for company now, sheets of paper on a small table at his side.

'You are out and about late tonight, minister.'

'The Devil never rests, so neither must I,' said Dr Fraser. 'I thought I had better come and see that you had not been carried off, after all.'

The clockmaker glanced at the papers beside him. 'Would that I had been,' he said, 'instead of him.'

'I have wasted too many years on such thoughts, James. No good comes of them. The Lord must have left you to us for some good work.'

James gave a laugh. 'Or perhaps he did not want an old rogue Jacobin like me in Heaven, causing trouble.'

The minister smiled as he offered his snuff box. 'How can we tell His will? Although, there is some good come of it all, I am told.'

At James's enquiring look, he continued. 'Rachel Mackay tells me their nursing of you has wrought a great change in the Rose sisters. Miss Elspeth's heart has been discovered, and along with it, Miss Anna's courage.'

James smiled. 'They have both always been there, I think, it was just we were all too terrified of Elspeth to consider it.'

They were silent for a while, then Dr Fraser said, 'There is to be a service, too, I hear?'

The clockmaker nodded. 'The boy deserves a better funeral than that we gave him. And Ludovic thinks it will help young Alicia Middleton, if she can see his grave, although goodness knows how long it will be before it is judged safe enough to wander so far out of town again. I hear the cholera is advancing over the Black Isle and will soon be in the neighbouring parishes.'

'It is in the upper parts of mine already. I think it may be some time until I am back in Cromarty. I have given instructions for extra graves to be dug, in sight of the burial grounds. But tell me – young Ludovic, how does he fare?'

'He is distraught for the loss of his friend and has been here nearly every night, reading these translations that Stanislas was always working at.'

'Of what?'

'An epic of his homeland. He could never get it finished, and now he is not as much as a footnote in it. Perhaps it helps Ludovic, I don't know. The sisters would not allow him near to help them, up on the moor. He could do nothing but shovel the earth over his friend in his grave and begin to dig the one that I proved not to need. The poor lad feels helpless to do good or to prevent ill. You have not long missed him.' James gave a sad smile. 'Some evenings I wonder if he will ever go home.'

Ludo wished he could turn back time, twelve months, to when all had been good in his life, had he but known it. But he knew he could not, and so he resolved to make as good as he could each day that was given to him. Lines from Stan's translations flitted through his head, and he tried to think which were the best fitted to give consolation at the planned funeral. Perhaps they could bind up some of the verses, to give to Alicia. He would speak to James about it.

The town was so quiet. He wondered whether he should take a walk by his great-aunt's cottage, to see how she fared, but then remembered that his mother would hardly thank him for the disturbance so late in the evening, she having told him before she'd gone out that poor Jessie was already, 'beyond the reach of human consolation'.

As he turned down Bank Street, he was surprised to see there was a chink of light showing between the window drapes of the reading room. He had not thought there would be any patrons tonight. He would let Hester get away to her bed and he would deal with whoever was there.

He turned the doorknob but to no avail. Hester must have locked up already. He took his key from his pocket and turned it, uttering a word of relief that she had not also bolted it.

There was something not right when he got in through the vestibule. Neither parlour nor hallway were lit, only from the reading room was there a chink of light. Perhaps Hester was in there, working her way through that volume of Heber's poems that she had lately been so determined on. In fact, he thought he could hear her muffle an exclamation. She was wont to be very vocal with her opinions on her reading. He put his hand on the door and went in and was, for the most infinitesimal of moments, frozen where he stood. Hester was there, on the floor, her eyes staring at him in terror and Fachie Hossack's hand pressed over her mouth as he worked with the other at trying to pull up her skirts over legs that kicked and struggled under his weight. Fachie turned and the animal sneer on his face broke the paralysis. Ludo was across the room and hauling him off by the shoulders, a strength against the dandyish Fachie that he'd never known he had.

'Get your filthy hands off my sister!' he roared.

Fachie, lip curling and attempting to get up, let out a snort of laughter. 'Sister?' he said. 'Oh, that is too good, that is really too good. The black bitch is his sister.' Fachie, on his feet now, pulled back his arm, preparing to swipe at Ludo, but only succeeded in glancing a blow at Ludo's ear as Ludovic also stepped back to swing, connecting with Fachie's jaw and sending him spiralling back to land with a terrible crunch of his skull on the fender of the fireplace that Hester had just dragged herself away from. The look in his eyes as his head hit was one of brief astonishment, before Fachie Hossack, who really should have been gone from Cromarty long ago, was gone for good.

THIRTY-THREE

Endings

Dr Fraser could see that James Craig was far from fully recovered from his recent struggle with the cholera. How could it be otherwise? The man needed to get to his bed. Pleading fatigue on his own part, he left with the declaration that he was straight for home. But even as the night air, chillier now that August had slipped into September, touched his skin, he felt the weary ache that he so often kept at bay creep over him. He looked at his horse, in whose eyes he could discern similar sentiments to his own, and said, 'All right, Uisdean, we shall admit defeat.' A matter of minutes took him to the stable of the hotel, where Janet Cameron's pony observed them complacently from its stall. The cratur and Uisdean knew each other of old. The young lad Janet Cameron kept to tend the horses and see to the boots of her guests would be long gone to his bed, and so Dr Fraser rolled up his own sleeves and soon had the tack dealt with and the beast settled for the night. Caressing

Uisdean on the neck and giving the hotel pony a nod, he wished them good slumber, and there being no discernible light at the back of the hotel, went round to the front where he was pleased to see a thin glimmer at the edges of the reading room window. At least he would not have to waken folk to get in.

The minister was about to lift the knocker when he chanced his hand and found that the door was not locked. Janet Cameron could hardly give him a tongue-lashing for the lateness of the hour if she hadn't even closed up the house yet. He would take a dram with Ludovic and then avail himself of one of her comfortable travellers' rooms for the night, or failing of that, an armchair.

Oh, but the woman was keen on saving money – there was not a candle lit in the hall and only memory and the tiny line of light down the side of the reading room door to guide him. He would certainly have to speak to her about it – a man could break his neck in such darkness. 'House!' he called, in the general direction of the kitchen. 'House!' But there came no reply. The house was as silent as the creaking hull of an empty ship. And then Dr Fraser opened the reading room door.

In the dimness, pools of yellow candlelight brought into relief a tableau of horror, of blood and dishevelment and gaping mouths and terrified, staring eyes. The face of Ludo Cameron, a sickly alabaster, gazed in disbelief at something sprawled at his feet. The girl Hester was seated in a chair a few feet away from him, as if collapsed there in shock, her hair disordered, her cap half off, a tear in her skirts. Sprawled on his back, a surprised sneer on his face yet and a pool of darkness seeping from the back of his head onto the hearth, was Fachie Hossack.

'Holy God, what has happened here?' Dr Fraser managed at last. But he knew what had happened here – it was written out before him in the dishevelment of the girl, in the very *fact* of Fachie Hossack.

He looked to Hester. 'Are you hurt, lassie? Did he . . .'

Looking down at her lap she shook her head. 'Ludo stopped him.'

Dr Fraser nodded. 'God be thanked. And you, Ludovic?'

Ludo looked up as if he only now realised someone else had come into the room. 'Dr Fraser?'

'That's right, boy. Now tell me, what happened here? You came in and found Farquhar . . .'

'He was attacking my sister.'

Sister. Dr Fraser stored that one away to be dealt with later. 'And then?'

'I pulled him off.' Ludo looked at him properly now. 'I just wanted to get him away from Hester, but he took a swing at me and missed. And I swung back and . . .'

'And you did not miss,' said Dr Fraser.

'I did not mean to . . .'

'I know you didn't, my boy,' said Dr Fraser with a sigh. He was trying to think, but before he could get all clear in his head, the girl was on her feet. 'Ludovic must not hang for this. I will say I did it. Everyone will believe that.'

'No, Hester,' protested the young man.

Dr Fraser held up an impatient hand. 'Nobody is going to hang for this, so help me. But you must do as I say, and there must be no fuss about anything. And it must be done quickly. Do you understand?'

The girl nodded, but Ludovic was still staring at him. 'I *killed* him.'

'You did not mean to, Ludovic, and you were defending yourself and your sister. Remember that. Where is your mother?'

'She is at Aunt Jessie's.'

'Mrs Patience is dying,' supplied the girl. 'Mrs Cameron is to stay with her tonight.'

'Of course, of course,' he said, remembering. 'Jessie Patience is a good woman. May God bless her final hours. Right, lassie. You must fetch me an old blanket, big enough for a shroud. And thick twine.'

She looked from him to the body on the floor, understanding beginning to dawn. 'Now, lassie, unless you would both swing!'

That was enough. She was out the door and running up the stairs.

Dr Fraser began to take off his coat and then thought better of it. Blood would not show on the thick black fabric the way it would on the billowing white sleeves of the shirt beneath. There was already some on Ludovic's shoes and the lower legs of his light grey trousers. The minister took the whisky bottle from the side table and poured a measure which he handed to Ludovic. 'Swallow that down, then get to your room and take off those trousers and anything else with Fachie Hossack's blood on it. Put on travelling clothes and put as much as you can into a bag.'

'A bag?' said Ludo almost stupidly.

'Ludovic, what I have in mind might keep you from a trial, and I pray God it will, but it might not and then there will be nothing I can do. Pack a bag with clothes and money and whatever banking certificates and the like you might have. You will be leaving Cromarty tonight, and if all goes well, it will be a very long day till you ever come back.'

Clearly stunned almost as much by this as by the events of the previous half-hour, Ludovic went upstairs to do as Dr Fraser had told him. When Hester returned with the heavy blanket and twine demanded by the minister, it was she and not her brother who helped roll the body of Fachie Hossack into it, and to secure the ends, with two good lengths of hempen rope, made in his father's ropeworks. The job was done by the time a still half-bewildered Ludovic arrived back downstairs, a bulging travelling bag in his hand and a boat cloak over his arm.

'Good, good,' said Dr Fraser, somewhat winded from the effort of rolling up the body. 'Now, boy, you must hitch the hotel cart to my horse – poor Uisdean has carried worse burdens – and you will help me carry this outside and put it on it.'

Ludovic looked almost more horrified by the woollen

sarcophagus in which the remains of Fachie Hossack were now enclosed than he had done by the corpse of the man himself. 'But where are you taking him?'

'Never mind that for now. Just go and do it.'

Ludo once gone, the doctor turned again to Hester. 'Have you a friend, lassie – someone you truly trust?'

The girl nodded. 'Mairead,' she said. 'And Alicia.'

'Miss Juniper's girls?' he asked. 'Aye, good. But not the Middleton lassie. She has had shocks enough of late, I think. The other seems hardier. I will fetch her to help you.'

'With what?' she asked.

He nodded towards the sticky black pool on the hearth and the floor, the items knocked over and broken in the struggle. 'You should not be alone tonight. Besides, this will all take some clearing and scrubbing, and you are near enough done in. Dear God, I am half-done in myself, but the job is not half done. Where has that boy got to?'

Dr Fraser heaved himself to his feet and taking a candle went out through the back way, to see what progress Ludovic was making with the cart.

Hester was left alone with Fachie now. It came into her mind that she should really start filling buckets, warming water, look out the scrubbing brushes. Pray. But perhaps Dr Fraser would do that later, when he had finished everything else. She could not make herself move. She didn't trust Fachie, not even dead. Hester sat back down and waited for the men to come back and carry him away.

It was after that, once Fachie's body was secured on the

cart and covered up, that Dr Fraser, telling Ludo to write a letter for his mother, went to fetch Mairead.

Mairead was almost asleep, and thank goodness Alicia was sound asleep, when the knocking came at the door downstairs. She heard Miss Juniper scuttle down to answer, a small and curious mouse. It was such a still, dark night and Mairead could hear nothing but the sea. Perhaps it was to do with old Jessie Patience – she and Miss Juniper had been friends, long ago.

Mairead slipped from her bed to listen and was startled to hear the tones of Dr Fraser, and then her own name. Fear for her father instantly gripped her, and she was down the stairs without even slippers to her feet. But what Dr Fraser had come to say was nothing to do with Mairead's father. There had been a difficulty at the hotel, and Hester was in need of her help. Dr Fraser warned that not a word of this was to be spoken elsewhere. Miss Juniper, who had always been fond of the Resolis minister, gave her word and soon had Mairead on her way.

'Now, Mairead,' the minister said as they walked up the vennel, 'I think you are a sensible girl.'

'I hope so, Dr Fraser,' she said.

'Good,' he said.

Dr Fraser was probably about to say more – Mairead had never in her life met a minister content to stop at one word, such as 'Good', without a homily following. Before he could go on, she spoke again.

'I hope I am sensible, but sometimes I get frightened. Of things I cannot see. Dark things. Unquietness in the spirit world.'

Dr Fraser stopped and Mairead wished she had said nothing and had just waited for the homily, for whatever he said to her now was bound to be worse.

'You do right to be fearful,' he said.

Mairead was not sure she had heard properly, but Dr Fraser continued.

'There is evil in this world. There is evil in the life beyond. There are unquiet spirits. The only armour you have against them is *true Christian faith* and your own goodness. Do you have faith, Mairead?'

She nodded her head. She had never once questioned what she had been taught in the catechism. She had never bothered her mind with the philosophies she had occasionally heard Ludovic's friends wrangle with, things that made no sense and denied the obvious truth of what Mr Mackay preached every week.

'And I think you *are* good. Miss Juniper does not accept just any girl, regardless of what people might say. And tonight you will be asked to do something that will combat a great evil, though the world might say otherwise. But I am telling you, Mairead Buchan, that what you are being asked to do tonight *is* good, for it will save a good man from the gallows.'

The streets around them were truly dark, for everyone was in bed now and almost all lights extinguished. All those people that constituted the world and what it had to say. It was just her, and the Resolis minister, and this great truth he was revealing to her. Mairead nodded again, and they walked on, as far as the corner of Oswald Lane. Here, Dr Fraser told her she must hasten on to the hotel by herself, because he had to stop a while and talk to Mr Gilfeather, and Mairead found that not only did she know her way well enough, but that she wasn't frightened at all.

When she stopped at the back gate of the hotel stable as she had been told to, however, she felt her heart hammering and thought it must be making more noise than her knocking at the gate. And then there was the approach of feet at the other side, and Ludovic's voice asking who was there.

When he opened it and saw her there was desolation in his eyes.

'Tell me what I must to do,' she said.

And then Hester was there behind him, talking of buckets and scrubbing brushes, and Fachie Hossack.

As often as not the young men who had appointed themselves guards on the roads in and out of Cromarty had fallen asleep within an hour of darkness falling, but that luck was not with Dr Fraser tonight. As he approached the first bend in the road out of the town, a figure stepped out in front of him and, holding up a lantern, bade him stop.

'Dr Fraser. You are out and about late tonight.'

'Indeed I am,' he said to the young man, 'and what

would I not give to be in my own bed. But there is word of cholera in the upper parish, and poor souls in need of sustenance and Christian charity. Mrs Cameron has been good enough to supply me with blankets and food for any that can eat, and I have got a tonic of quinine from Mrs Gilfeather.' That last, at least, was true.

'You will not go too close, Doctor?'

'No closer than a Christian need. Good night now.'

The minister did not like the lie, but the phrase came into his head, *Needs must when the Devil drives*. 'Aye, the Devil,' he murmured as he geed Uisdean on. It was not until they were past the Shore Mill that he judged it safe to turn around and say, 'We are well clear now.'

A pulling back of the sacking over the cart and Ludo Cameron emerged from underneath to take in great gulps of the salt night air, as if it might cleanse him from having lain so long next to the bound corpse of Fachie Hossack. 'Where are we?' he asked.

'A mile or so from the track up to Grants' croft. It'll not be long till we are rid of him.'

The horse plodded on, pulling without complaint its unaccustomed burden. It might have followed its own hoofprints back up the track to Grants' croft, where Dr Fraser had called late that afternoon, as he had made his way to Cromarty. He had gone to warn the inhabitants of the advance of cholera into the parish only to find that he was already too late. No one had answered his call at the door of the cottage, and when he had pushed it open with the toe of his boot, he had found the souls of Jean Grant and her widowed son already gone to their resting place, leaving behind their foul and wasted earthly remains. He had prayed at the door and sung a psalm that Jean had liked and left the yellow rag that was tied to the door. He would make arrangements for the burial of the bodies, as soon as he got home.

Now, as Uisdean drew up once more in front of the desolate cottage, Dr Fraser repeated the words of that psalm he had sung those few hours ago. The moon at last emerged out of the clouds to cast some light on the scene. 'Right then, Ludovic,' he said, 'let us get this thing done.' He handed the young man one of the strips of heavy linen he had had Hester cut from one of Janet Cameron's bedsheets. 'Cover your nose and mouth with this, and may God forgive us.'

Dr Fraser lit his lamp and went ahead, telling Ludo to fetch Fachie's bag and leave it at the door, but not on any account to go in. He opened the door and held up his lamp to reveal a scene worse than he had remembered and to let escape odours so bad they risked turning his stomach. Somehow it was the pan of days-old sour mutton broth that was worst. Poor Ludovic only had time to rip off his own face covering before vomiting in the doorway. Dr Fraser, marvelling at the cynical workings of his own mind, counted that a blessing that they might use.

Jeannie must have died first. She was in the bed and her son, Walter, dead on the floor beside her as if in the midst of his own writhing, in a pool of his own excrescences.

Dr Fraser opened Farquhar's medical bag and took out the stethoscope and a scalpel, both of which he threw towards where Walter lay. He threw the rest of the bag in after it. 'All right,' he said, 'now let us get Fachie.'

The body felt even heavier now and the unravelling of it just as gruesome as the swaddling of it had been. The eyes were still open, staring. Hester had wanted to close them but Dr Fraser had said no, they needed to be open, and so open they remained. When they got as far as the door, Dr Fraser told Ludo to get back in the cart, then he backed into the cottage alone and dragged Fachie's body in by himself, heaving it the few feet to where that of Walter Grant lay. With one last great effort he hauled Fachie's body round so that his skull lay on the hearth, as it had done in the reading room of the hotel. Then he went outside to fetch a shovel and, with supreme distaste, lifted the vomit that Ludovic had left and dropped it around Fachie's face and the floor nearby. Back outside, he washed his boots and the shovel in the burn and cast the shovel aside. 'Enough, Micah Fraser. That is enough,' he said, before trudging back to his horse, leaving the door to the cottage open to the night.

Ludovic's mind was whirling. It was as if he had been taken to a panopticon of horror scenes from someone else's life. He wanted to turn back, just a few hours, to when he had been in James Craig's kitchen, reading over Stanislas' translations, making plans to memorialise his friend. But no, he had to go further back, and not go out tonight at all, so that he might have been in the hotel when Fachie came, and then Fachie would not have tried to hurt Hester. How was it that Fachie was dead now, in those few hours, and he, Ludo, might never see Hester, nor Mairead, nor his mother again? What about the bank, what would Mr Gilfeather do? And where was Dr Fraser taking him? They were back out on the road now, and across the Newhall bridge. On the faithful Uisdean went, past Kirkmichael and the sleeping graves of Ludo's ancestors and up the brae, leaving the jagged silhouettes of kirk and tombstones silent against the night sky. Perhaps Dr Fraser was taking him to the gaol in Dingwall – maybe the cells of Cromarty courthouse were already full. The wheels of the cart rumbled on, and Dr Fraser was speaking to him and asking if he was listening, and here now coming into sight was the ferry inn at Balblair and Ludovic did start to listen, and gradually he began to understand.

EPILOGUE

26 September 1832

Ludo had been rowed from the ferry at Balblair out to the emigration ship newly cleared to leave the next day. Whether it would be allowed to dock when it arrived in Quebec, where the cholera now raged, was another question. News of his departure, when finally people had noticed it, had not caused a great stir in the town – everyone knew he had been talking for long enough about emigrating, and James Craig confirmed that Stanislas's death had finally decided the matter. Mr Gilfeather, at the bank, allowed it to be known that he had been fully cognisant of Ludovic's plans, but that the bank's business was not a thing to be noised about the town, creating uncertainty, and that one of the junior clerks that he had had his eye on would have his chance. Hugh Miller, the stonemason, whom everyone knew to be a good deal brighter than many of the bank clerks, and possibly than Mr Gilfeather himself, was brought in to begin his training at a desk, with pen and columns of numbers rather than chisel and stone.

There had been a brief sensation at the death of Farquhar

Hossack, when the news had come that his body had been found amidst a house of contagion at the remote Grants' croft. Mrs Hossack's hysteria on receiving the news had only been ameliorated by the conviction that her son had died in the cause of his profession, while ministering to the sick. Other, darker suggestions that Fachie had himself been taken by the cholera in the act of attempting to desecrate the corpse of Walter Grant in the pursuance of his anatomical obsession had been kept from her but soon attained the status of established fact amongst the citizens of town and country, who had long predicted a bad end for the ropemaker's son.

The precautions of the town against the cholera increased. Checkpoints were watched more stringently and while eminent visitors could not be kept out – for a new, reformed Parliament was to be elected, and the enfranchised of Cromarty had as much a right to hear political argument as anyone else – even visiting politicians from Inverness had to go through the smokehouse before being permitted to go about their business.

Other aspects of life in the town went on more or less as before. Miss Juniper and her girls gradually resumed their visits to the manse and other friends in the town and, all in all, it seemed they would bear their disappointments. Mairead, in fact, appeared to spend as much time at the hotel as she did at the cottage on Little Vennel and was becoming quite proficient in the articles of household management she was learning there under the eye of Mrs

Cameron. Her reading, it seemed, had at last left behind the Gothic horrors and romances of which she had been so fond, to be replaced by the practical perusal of *Meg Dodds' Cookbook* and the copy of Mrs Fanny Trollope's *Domestic Manners of the Americans* which Mrs Cameron was insistent she should study with great attention. Mrs Cameron herself appeared unchanged, or almost. One or two patrons of the hotel had noticed her pause, occasionally, and look away at something, as if in the distance of her mind, but then she would shake herself and resume whatever she had been doing, more briskly than before. It was not long before it was understood that when Ludovic had established himself at the Boston bank to which he had carried his recommendation from Mr Gilfeather, Miss Mairead Buchan would herself be embarking on one of the emigration ships. What would become of Alicia Middleton in that case could not be certain. It was thought she spent more time than was good for a young woman poring over the papers left behind by James Craig's Polish apprentice, and it was predicted in some quarters that she would lose her bloom before she had fully possessed it, and be an old maid, like Elspeth Rose.

Miss Elspeth had recovered from the temporary shock of her experiences on the Mulbuie and was now almost quite herself again, other than in the matter of her sister. Or, rather, it was Miss Anna who was no longer quite what she had been. She seemed her own age at last and had a faded rather than a foolish prettiness which was much the more affecting for it. And she seemed not to twitter such nonsense as once she had done. It had been noticed too, and much commented upon, that when James Craig had fully recovered from his bout of the cholera and was fit enough to return to church, he sat not on his old form with the empty space for his apprentice beside him, but up in the north aisle with the Misses Rose. Word of an engagement was whispered. There was even a suggestion that he might be invited to join the library, but this last was thought too far-fetched an idea to gain much traction.

The library, in the face of the vicissitudes of the year just past, continued. Those who thought it might, in its depleted state, have been allowed to wither and die had not reckoned with the renewed vigour of Miss Elspeth Rose. In her determination, Miss Elspeth had the full support of Mr Isaac Fordyce – had they not, between them, seen a good many individuals come and go over the years, some remembered, more forgotten, and yet the town went on? New tenants were yet to take up residence at Cromarty House, but a new schoolmaster was already in place and giving satisfaction. Others in the town that had taken offence at not being invited to join the library last year were ready at a moment's notice to fill the places now vacant, and surely, in fact, they might expand? It was known, for instance, that the Hossacks' elder daughter had found a husband and would be returning home with him, that he might hastily be trained to follow in his father-in-law's footsteps. Certainly, Mrs Hossack let it be known that her husband would be proposing their daughter, or son-in-law, or both.

So stood affairs in the town on the afternoon of the twenty-sixth of September, 1832, when a sombre Mr Gilfeather stood before the remaining members of the library, ready to oversee the election of new members. Once those new members had been admitted, the books for the next year would be chosen. One or two amongst those assembled put the bank manager's even more sombre than usual demeanour down to the knowledge that, despite the town's defences and the best efforts of the young men who guarded the exit and entry points, the cholera had at last found its way in. To be electing new members and talking of ordering new books was an act of defiance in the face of encroaching mortality that everyone understood as such. Surely Mr Gilfeather was not going to deny them this, albeit temporary, respite from their troubles.

But that was not the cause of the grave expression on Mr Gilfeather's face this afternoon. Alasdair Mackay knew it, because he had been in the reading room early, having a quiet moment with his pipe, when the newspapers had arrived. The minister was taking refuge from the manse, where Rachel was in a flurry of excitement and the writing of lists. He had that very morning received a letter from Charles Munro, asking that Rachel might come to Ardross in December, to be with Charlotte over the last few weeks of her pregnancy and during her confinement. There were many sound reasons why Alasdair might not have acquiesced in this, but he understood that he would be likely to find himself divorced before William Mackenzie was, should he attempt to prevent Rachel from going. He would square it with the town and the congregation, somehow.

So, Mrs Mackay was not present, but she would, the minister assured them, be here for their next gathering. The business of the election of new members took two pots of coffee and a whole tray of sandwiches more than it should have done, but at last it was concluded and their number increased to sixteen. It was agreed that Mr Gilfeather should write to the successful candidates, each care of his or her proposer, and that the choice of new books should be made, God willing, four weeks hence.

People were beginning to make movements preparatory to leaving, and Miss Elspeth had in fact reached for her parasol when Alasdair Mackay gave Mr Gilfeather a nod and the bank manager cleared his throat.

'I would beg your indulgence a little longer,' he said, adding, 'Sit down, man, sit down,' to Willie Hossack, who was already halfway to the door. 'I have a most grave and regrettable announcement to make, which I know you will wish to hear.'

Miss Anna, not entirely cured of the foibles of her previous disposition, let out a small 'Oh, dear!' before putting her hand to her mouth.

'Please, Mr Gilfeather,' said Mr Fordyce, 'be so kind as to tell us, whatever it is. We are ready, I think.'

'Ah, weel, ah weel,' said Mr Gilfeather, slipping for a moment into the vernacular of his own kitchen. 'I doubt we are, Mr Fordyce, but it must be told, nonetheless.' He then unfolded the newspaper which he had guarded since first Mr Mackay had handed it to him and began to read to them the announcement that would soon fill the columns of newspapers the world over, of the death of Sir Walter Scott. Mr Gilfeather finished his reading with the lament of the *New Monthly Magazine*:

'"The blow is struck – the lyre is shattered – the music is hushed at length."'

As the bank manager put down his newspaper, the room breathed only silence to the ticking of the mantelpiece clock. And then, little by little, came the soft sound of weeping, the blowing of a nose, the heaving of a sorry sigh. Outside, the herring gulls still glided and swooped, calling heedlessly to one another, as the sea rolled in upon the shore.

It was a good while later, once everyone else had finally left, that Mr Gilfeather closed the door of the reading room behind him and began to prepare in his mind the letter of condolence that the members had requested he write on their behalf to poor Miss Juniper.

Hester watched after him as he walked slowly up the street until he finally disappeared from sight. Turning back into the hotel, she noticed a dandelion sprouting by the door. She would see to it later, after she had set the reading room to rights. Once she had cleared away the coffee cups and sandwich plates, and puffed the cushions on the chairs and swept the new hearth rug, she took her duster round the mantelpiece and the side tables. At last, she came to the cabinet at the far wall, away from the light so the sun would not fade the spines, and saw that all was rather higgledy-piggledy, with everything put back in the wrong order. Hester sighed and turned the cabinet key in its lock and then she put the books into their correct places, in the order that the members of the library would expect to find them, which was certainly not the way they had left them.

AUTHOR'S NOTE

The spark for this book was a brief document I came across several years ago in the Highland Archive Centre in Inverness, headed, 'List of Cromarty Citizens who formed a circulating library about 1832, when books were precious, carriage costly, and communication slow and expensive.' There followed a list of the members of the library, the books they had selected, and the order in which the books were to circulate. I had gone into the archive looking for something else, but, as has happened to me before, it was the accidentally found document that I couldn't quite shake from my head, and that led to a novel.

Though set within a framework of real national and international events in the years 1831–2 – the debate and public unrest around the Great Reform Bill to extend voting rights, the campaign for the abolition of chattel slavery throughout the British empire, Russia's invasion of Poland, political convulsions in France, a cholera epidemic sweeping Asia, Europe and North America, the Highland Clearances and mass emigration from the Highlands, the continuing hysteria caused by the murderous activities of Burke and Hare – the story told of the lives of my characters in Cromarty, is a fiction. The houses and streets in which they carry on their lives and relationships are real and still exist, but the characters themselves are works of my imagination. To read the *real* history of Cromarty in the early nineteenth century, readers should turn to the work of the one actual historical character in my book, the occasionally mentioned stonemason, Hugh Miller.

Hugh Miller was born in the town in 1802, to a relatively prosperous family who came down in the world due to the loss at sea of his father, when Hugh was very young. An exceptionally bright boy, he rebelled against the confines of academic education, preferring instead to learn from observation of his elders in the town and his own exploration of the world around him. Training first as a stonemason, he went on to become a bank clerk, newspaper editor, and writer and geologist of national and international renown. His memoir, *My Schools and Schoolmasters*, about his childhood and youth, offers an immensely readable portrait of life in Cromarty, the Highlands and elsewhere in Scotland, and his *Scenes and Legends of the North of Scotland* is equally fascinating. The picture of the town in the early nineteenth century that formed in my mind's eye, and that I have tried to communicate to the page, I owe in great part to Hugh Miller, and yet I could not make him anything other than a peripheral character in my book. To leave him out of a story set in Cromarty at a time he actually lived and worked there would have been ridiculous, but it would also have been ridiculous to try to make a fiction of such an immense individual who had already told his own story. And so, Hugh passes around the edges of the novel, no doubt smiling wryly at his neighbours, but not involving himself in their drama. Besides, as Miss Anna would certainly have worried, his name appears nowhere on the lists of the real, historical, 'Cromarty Reading Club'.

All the other characters in the novel are works of my imagination, but some were suggested and inspired by real historical individuals. The character of Dr Fraser of Resolis, for instance, owes much to the actual minister of Resolis at the time, the Reverend Donald Sage, who *was* a member of the circulating library. Sage's own memoir, *Memorabilia Domestica: or Parish Life in the North of Scotland*, while understandably heavy on church matters in places, offers wonderful depictions of life, characters and their concerns in the period. Like Dr Fraser, Mr Sage was not short of a withering opinion or two, and it is perhaps telling that his son did not sanction the publication of the memoirs, with their 'graphic sketches of prominent people', until twenty years after his father's death, when perhaps those unfortunate individuals were also dead.

Another of the characters inspired by a real, historical individual, is Miss Juniper. The idea for Miss Juniper, and at least some of her story, was sparked by Hugh Miller's reference in *My Schools and Schoolmasters* to a schoolmistress who lived in the town in his boyhood. Miss Elizabeth Bond had come to Cromarty from the nearby town of Fortrose, where she had taught in a girl's boarding school. Her *Letters of a Village Governess*, 'a curious kind of medley . . . with more heart than head about it', told stories widely understood to be thinly veiled depictions of inhabitants of that town with the result that, as Miller informs us, 'Fortrose soon became considerably too hot for her.' I searched out Miss Bond's book, which was indeed dedicated to Sir Walter Scott, and turned its pages in the reading room of the National Library of Scotland, in a state of increasing astonishment. As Miller suggests, it is beyond categorisation and, in places, an absolute hoot. I was left with the impression that Miss Bond was probably a better person than many in the society she described. This feeling was enhanced when I went again to the Highland Archive in Inverness, to read the diary of an Anne Fraser who had lived (I thought in Inverness) in the period my book was set. I had gone in the hope of finding details of the social and material life of a young woman at the time. It was with some difficulty that I stopped myself from shouting out loud when I discovered that Anne had, in fact, lived in Cromarty and been a pupil and companion of Miss Bond's. Miss Juniper is not Miss Bond, but I hope they would have recognised something in each other. I know that the life and work of Elizabeth Bond are being studied by others and I hope that a biography and a modern edition of her book might one day be published.

But what about the rest? Much of what I know about

the wider history of Cromarty I owe to the work of Dr David Alston. His *My Little Town of Cromarty: the History of a Northern Scottish Town* (Birlinn, 2006), helped me understand the development of the town over the centuries and particularly its economic background. Anyone visiting Cromarty for the first time – a small, not easy to reach town at the very tip of the Black Isle in the north of Scotland, its streets alternating with fisher cottages and fine Georgian mansions – must surely look about themselves and wonder, 'How on earth . . .?' David Alston's book will tell them.

But more recently, Dr Alston has brought out *Slaves and Highlanders: Silenced Histories of Scotland and the Caribbean* (Edinburgh University Press, 2021). To someone who grew up in the Highlands in the nineteen seventies and eighties, believing that Scotland's involvement in the transatlantic slave trade and in the enslavement of people on American and Caribbean plantations was primarily the doing of the Glasgow tobacco lords, this was quite literally a breathtaking read. Until relatively recently, the involvement of Highlanders in these plantations, and the profits made from them, particularly from compensation after the abolition of chattel slavery, was hidden in plain sight. A great deal of academic work in recent years has brought Scotland's heavy involvement in all aspects of the Caribbean trade to light, and continues to do so. An online National Library of Scotland discussion between Dr Alston and Dr Jaunita Cox on 4th November, 2021, was illuminating. Discussion has been brought beyond academia and into the public domain through the work of heritage professionals and television programmes such as the actor David Hayman's 2018 BBC 2 series, *Slavery: Scotland's Hidden Shame*.

And yet, as far as the Highlands go, it was all there – in the newspapers of the period, in the childhood memories of Hugh Miller, of Donald Sage, and in the life of Miss Bond. Hugh Miller recalls a fight at school with an unnamed black boy, recently arrived from the Caribbean; amongst Donald Sage's best friends at school in Dornoch were Fergus, John and Alexander Hay, three brothers come from the West Indies, the children of a Scots planter and a black woman. Miss Bond wrote of girl pupils from the Caribbean, and Anne Fraser's diary recalls how she mourned the death of one of them. Instances of the children of white male planters and enslaved or previously enslaved women of colour being brought to Scotland to be brought up (while their mothers were left in the Caribbean), are discussed by Lorna Steele in her September 2020 'Learn with Lorna' YouTube talk for Highland Archives. My character, Hester, was written partly to acknowledge those, often unnamed, children.

As I said at the start, the houses from which my characters emerge, the streets they emerge onto, are still there. The bank where Mr Gilfeather kept a wary eye on Ludo would have been the *Commercial*, not the *Caledonian* – I changed the name to avoid confusion with the hotel. Cromarty House – untenanted and subject to an inheritance dispute at the time my novel is set – is a family home, as are many other properties in the town, some of the names of which

I have changed slightly for that reason. You can, though, visit the old East Kirk, and sit in the 'box' I accorded the Misses Rose, and imagine, as I did. You can visit the cottage Hugh Miller was born in, and the house he lived in for a time with his wife Lydia (remember his dance partner at the Gardeners' ball?). You can have a drink and something to eat in the former Gardeners' Lodge (now the Fishertown Inn). You might, though, be curious about the domain of Mrs Hossack: the house once home to the owner of the ropeworks, still looking out to the harbour, is now the Royal Hotel. Three of the four ranges of the ropeworks have survived, to become private homes. The old graveyard of St Regulus, where Rachel found solace, and the restored aisle and kirkyard of Kirkmichael that so fascinated John Learmonth, can still be explored. You might go to an arts event in the Old Brewery, or at the Stables of Cromarty House, or even sit in the Courthouse under the disapproving eye of the magistrates. You might book yourself in for a writers' retreat in the Cromarty Arts Trust house, just along the road from the former Commercial Hotel where Mrs Cameron held sway. You might even decide to write a book . . .

Shona MacLean, Conon Bridge, March 2025

ACKNOWLEDGEMENTS

The idea for this book was born in an archive – the Highland Archive Centre in Inverness – and nurtured in a series of libraries: Inverness Library, Elgin Library, Dingwall Library, the Miller Library in Thurso, Innerpeffray Library and the National Library of Scotland. I am very grateful for the patient and knowledgeable help of all the archivists and librarians along the way, without which I would not have been able to read many of the books my characters read. My one disappointment is that I was not able to visit the historic Leighton Library in Dunblane, undergoing restoration as I wrote, but now again open to the public. A special word should go to Melanie Manwaring-Mckay of the University of the Highlands and Islands, who shared her knowledge of Highland book history at an early stage, and invited me to host a 'Meet the Books' session with Inverness Library's Special Collections, and also to the staff of that library who have very patiently, and more than once, shown me how to use the microfilm reader.

In April of 2023, I attended the two-day 'Reading and Book Circulation' conference hosted by Stirling University as part of the 'Books and Borrowing 1750-1830' project, where speakers cast expert light on a whole historical world of readers, libraries and borrowing. The ongoing work of the project can be accessed at https://borrowing.stir.ac.uk

and is a priceless and fascinating resource for anyone interested in the history of the book, and I'd like to thank all those involved.

In Easter Ross, I would like to thank the Trustees of St Duthac's Church and Tain Museum. I would also like to thank Hilary and Jens Andexer for kindly allowing me to see Old Shandwick House, and Colin Dodds for taking the time to show me around and for sharing his knowledge of the building.

Over the long period of me thinking about and eventually writing this novel, my family has been as tolerant as ever, and long ago learned it was better not to ask, 'How's the book going?' I am sorry that I won't be able to give a copy to the late Highland writer, Elizabeth Sutherland, who gave very generous advice and encouragement at an early stage and delighted to hear of Miss Bond. Writing can be a fairly solitary experience, and while I suspect many of us like it that way, I'd like to say a special thank you to two friends in particular – Jennifer Morag Henderson and Sarah Fraser. Over many cups of tea and coffee and many a woodland track, Jennifer and Sarah have listened and encouraged, and refreshed me with talk of their own writing and, always, what we're reading. They must feel they have lived with this book for as long as (possibly longer than) I have.

Lisa Highton, my agent, took up the challenge of me and my idea for the book when authorial bewilderment was at its height. She got behind me immediately, and very patiently, but firmly, pushed this book towards and over the finish line. (She also pushed several unfortunate characters over Cromarty harbour wall, but we shall not speak of that . . .) She's given friendship, advice, support and encouragement from day one, as well as *effortlessly* performing entourage duties from Achiltibuie to Toronto and points in between. Thank you, Lisa.

I'd like to thank Tricia McCarter for her patient response to my queries on reading on the experience of enslaved people. To all those at my publisher, Quercus, who've been involved in the many stages that go towards making a book, I am very grateful, especially in this year of changes and passing of batons. Special thanks in that respect go to Flo Hare, Cassie Browne and Vanessa Phan. Copy-editor Liz Hatherall saved me from a howler of which we must never speak, and Nicola Howell Hawley has again delighted me again with her map. Most of all though, I'd like to thank my exceptional editor, Jane Wood, to whom this, our twelfth book together, is dedicated.